Michael Cordy worked for ten years in marketing and advertising before giving it all up to write *The Miracle Strain* (now called the *The Messiah Code*), which has since sold in over twenty-five countries. He is the author of two other novels, *Crime Zero* and *The Lucifer Code*. He lives in London with his wife, Jenny.

NEARLY NEW BOOKSHOP
PRESQUE 9
WE BUY AND SELL PAPERBACKS
SPECIALIZING IN CURRENT
BEST SELLERS
5484 SHERBROOKE ST. W.
AT GIROUARD
MONTREAL, QC.   H4A 1V9

D0696593

www.booksattransworld.co.uk

Also by Michael Cordy

THE MESSIAH CODE
CRIME ZERO
THE LUCIFER CODE

and published by Corgi Books

THE VENUS CONSPIRACY

Michael Cordy

CORGI BOOKS

THE VENUS CONSPIRACY
A CORGI BOOK : 0552148830
9780552148832

Originally published as *TRUE* in Great Britain by Bantam Press,
a division of Transworld Publishers in 2004

PRINTING HISTORY
Bantam Press edition published 2004
Corgi edition published 2006

1 3 5 7 9 10 8 6 4 2

Copyright © Michael Cordy 2004

The right of Michael Cordy to be identified as the author of this
work has been asserted in accordance with sections 77 and 78 of
the Copyright Designs and Patents Act 1988.

All the characters in this book are fictitious, and any resemblance to
actual persons, living or dead, is purely coincidental.

Condition of Sale
This book is sold subject to the condition that it shall not,
by way of trade or otherwise, be lent, re-sold, hired out or otherwise
circulated in any form of binding or cover other than that in which it is
published and without a similar condition including this condition
being imposed on the subsequent purchaser.

Typeset in 11½/13pt Garamond by
Kestrel Data, Exeter, Devon.

Corgi Books are published by Transworld Publishers,
61–63 Uxbridge Road, London W5 5SA,
a division of The Random House Group Ltd,
in Australia by Random House Australia (Pty) Ltd,
20 Alfred Street, Milsons Point, Sydney, NSW 2061, Australia,
in New Zealand by Random House New Zealand Ltd,
18 Poland Road, Glenfield, Auckland 10, New Zealand
and in South Africa by Random House (Pty) Ltd,
Isle of Houghton, Corner of Boundary Road & Carse O'Gowrie,
Houghton 2198, South Africa.

Printed and bound in Germany by
GGP Media GmbH, Poessneck.

Papers used by Transworld Publishers are natural, recyclable products made
from wood grown in sustainable forests. The manufacturing processes
conform to the environmental regulations of the country of origin.

For Jenny

ACKNOWLEDGEMENTS

As ever, my most important thank you goes to my wife, Jenny, who not only helped me with characters and plot lines, but also in the research of the cutting-edge science that underpins this novel.

In addition to various articles in *New Scientist* magazine, the following sources proved particularly useful: 'Alteration of the platelet serotonin transporter in romantic love' in *Psychological Medicine* by D. Marazziti, H. S. Akiskal, A. Rossi and G. B. Cassano (Cambridge University Press, 1999); *The Science of Love* by Glen D. Wilson and Chris McLaughlin (Fusion Press, 2001); and *Neutral Buoyancy* by Tim Ecott (Penguin, 2001).

I am grateful to my editor, Bill Scott-Kerr, at Transworld for his patience and perceptive eye, and to Hazel Orme, whose skills as a copy-editor added more than a final polish.

Last, but not least, I thank my agent, Patrick Walsh.

Fetch me that flower, the herb I showed thee once,
The juice of it on sleeping eyelids laid
Will make man or woman madly dote
Upon the next live creature that it sees . . .
William Shakespeare (1596)

Most of our products are nature-identical, which means that their
chemical structures and properties cannot be distinguished from
the ones found in plants or animals.
Roche Pharmaceuticals (2003)

PROLOGUE

'Wake up, Max. Wake up! We've got to leave.'

Max doesn't hear his mother's urgent whispers. He is lost in his dreams, riding the gleaming red bike he hopes to get for his ninth birthday tomorrow. A few hours ago he was so excited that his mother had to soothe him to sleep, stroking his forehead with her cool hand. Now nothing stirs him. Not the full Hawaiian moon, which shines through the thin curtains, bathing his tanned skin and white-blond hair in a blue glow. Not the waves breaking on the beach behind the isolated clapperboard house. Not even the harsh voices and heavy footsteps on the sandy deck outside.

Now the same cool hand that earlier soothed him to sleep shakes him. 'Wake up, Max. Now.'

His eyes flicker open. His mother is in a white nightdress and looks anxious; her high cheekbones are etched into sharp relief by the shadows and her long fair hair shimmers in the blue light. 'They've come for us, Max. We must leave. Quickly and quietly.'

He groans. 'Not again, Mum. I'm sleepy.'

'This isn't a practice, Max. It's real. They're here.'

He hears the guttural voices outside and something cold uncoils in his stomach. He is suddenly wide awake, his birthday forgotten. 'Is *he* here?' he whispers.

Eyes wide, she nods and puts a finger to her lips.

As she leads him across the main corridor to her bedroom there's a rending crash. The front door buckles and an axe blade appears through the splintered wood. The bungalow's secluded position on the north-western shore of Kauai, the most westerly of the Hawaiian Islands, concealed them once. Now its isolation renders them defenceless.

Inside her bedroom his mother locks the door and they push the chest of drawers in front of it. She reaches under the bed and pulls out a baseball bat, two ready-packed rucksacks and a plastic bag, which contains a wad of US dollars and three passports: a United States passport in her maiden name, Collins, and two passports bearing Max's photograph – one Swiss, the other American. The Swiss passport carries his full name Max William Kappel. The American passport carries his middle name and his mother's maiden name: William Collins. She rolls back the rug, pulls a brass latch embedded in the wooden floor and opens a trap-door to the crawl-space beneath the house.

They drop on to the sand, and as they wriggle between the struts supporting the house Max hears heavy footsteps on the floorboards above. His mother pulls him towards the front, but he can see legs pacing by the porch. He shakes his head and points to the frangipani by the side of the house. It will take longer, but the trees provide cover.

The warm air is thick with the cloying scent of frangipani blossom as they crawl away from the sea to firmer ground. When the moon disappears behind the cloud they use the darkness to hurry across the dirt track by the front gate and disappear into the carport where the old jeep is parked. Max is tall for a nine-year-old, bigger than some teenagers, but he is uncoordinated and runs awkwardly. When he reaches the shelter of the carport he is panting hard. As his mother unlocks the jeep he looks back at the house, which has been their home for the last two years. The fractured front door gapes like a broken tooth and torches flash inside. He looks to the jetty beyond, and sees a large white yacht moored beside their small dinghy.

As he opens the car door he detects a distinctive odour in the air. He remembers the acrid smell from somewhere, but can't place it. She releases the handbrake, turns the ignition and presses her foot on the accelerator.

Nothing happens.

She tries again. Still nothing.

'Shit.'

For the first time he sees panic in her eyes and

his stomach somersaults. This isn't like the other drills. This isn't fun at all.

She tries again.

Nothing.

A shadowy figure steps in front of the car and throws a tangle of severed cables on to the bonnet. A cigarette tip glows in the dark and Max now recognizes the familiar tobacco smell he detected earlier. His father is here somewhere.

Max's door is yanked open and strong hands pull him from the car. For all his size, he is no match for the man pinning him down. He yells and struggles, but his attacker is too strong. The man has long, jet-black hair tied into a ponytail and smells of seawater and sweat.

'Leave my son alone,' his mother shouts, clambering out of the car. She hits the man with the baseball bat, and Max jams two fingers into his left eye as hard as he can. The eyeball feels like a hard-boiled egg and the man screams, but Max keeps gouging, desperate to break his grip. Two more men appear, knock his mother to the ground and pull Max's hands behind his back. The first man pushes his face directly into Max's: his swelling eye socket glistens with gore and his remaining eye glares with such fury that Max squeezes his own shut.

'*Achtung*, Stein!' a familiar voice warns from the shadows. 'Don't damage the boy. Take them to the boat.'

The men drag Max and his mother down the

beach to the sleek white motor yacht. The wind is stronger now and the scudding clouds clear when they reach the jetty. In the moonlight Max sees his father. He is immaculately dressed in pressed trousers, blazer and tie. His neatly combed hair is as shockingly white as Max's. A distinctive black cigarette glows in his lips. He barely glances at Max before he turns to his mother. His unblinking, pale blue eyes are cold. 'You shouldn't have reverted to your maiden name, Jean,' he says matter-of-factly. 'That's what led us to you.'

She steps closer to him, unafraid. 'Helmut, let us be. You've nothing to fear from me. If I'd wanted to tell the authorities anything I'd have gone ahead by now. I no longer care what you've done, but I can't allow you to corrupt my son.'

'*Your* son?' Helmut Kappel swells before her, as if unable to contain his rage. Yet his voice is so quiet it is barely audible above the gusting wind. 'He's *my* son. The boy's a Kappel. He has duties. A destiny.' He pauses, and when he speaks again his voice is softer. 'You shouldn't have left, Jean. I can't believe you did. No one leaves a Kappel.'

'I don't love you any more.'

His eyes darken. 'What's love got to do with it? Duty and loyalty are all I asked of you.'

She blinks as if he has slapped her face. 'But I did love you once, Helmut. More than you'll ever know. I just can't accept the crimes you committed in the name of your family.'

'It was *our* family.' He takes the black cigarette

from his lips, studies the gold filter and flicks it into the sea. 'Enough of this.' He turns to the man with the jet-black ponytail, who has wrapped a bandage over his bloody eye. 'Your men can put her on board, Stein.'

'I'll stay with the boy, Helmut,' says a stockier, bearded man, with similar pale eyes and white-blond hair. He is dressed in a formal lightweight suit, Max's Uncle Klaus, his father's younger brother. 'Until you return.'

'No, Klaus. I want him to see this.' Max's father turns away with a flourish, revealing a glimpse of scarlet lining in his sober blue blazer. 'The boy must learn.'

The yacht is over fifty feet long with cabins in the bow, but the men bundle Max and his mother into the exposed stern. A man sits on each side of Max, holding his wrists, while Stein and another man sit with his mother. The anchor is raised and the yacht casts off. His father nods to Uncle Klaus at the wheel and the idling engine roars into life, taking the craft out into the Pacific.

His father looms over him like an Old Testament prophet. 'I'm taking you back to Zurich to continue your education. You're my heir, Max. Your mother stole two years of your life but you'll catch up. You're a Kappel.'

Max strains to see past his father but the men tighten their hold on his wrists. 'What are you doing to Mutti?'

'Forget about her, Max.' The clouds again

conceal the moon, darkening his father's face. 'You must learn, my son, that love brings nothing but sorrow and chaos. The world would be a better place without it. At best it is a trivial distraction. At worst it's a dangerous sickness that softens the mind and clouds the judgement. It must be controlled.' Helmut Kappel glances over his shoulder at the woman to whom he has been married for eleven years. 'No one is immune to its poison. Duty and loyalty are all that matter in a family, but your mother never understood this.'

'Don't listen to him, Max,' his mother says. 'Duty and loyalty are meaningless without love.'

Helmut Kappel straightens, and Max sees that Stein has knotted a rope round his mother's legs. His eyes follow the wet coils, which lie on the deck like a dormant python. His heart jumps when he sees the stone block by her feet.

'How deep is it here?' his father demands.

Uncle Klaus checks the charts, then peers through the rain and intermittent moonlight to the high, serrated cliffs of the Na Pali coast. 'Drops straight to the ocean floor – over two thousand feet.'

'Stand her up, Stein.'

'No,' Max shouts. 'No, Vater, no.' He reaches for his mother but the men tighten their grip on his arms.

His mother's eyes are fierce with passion. 'Don't hate your father for this,' she says. 'Don't let him make you like he is.'

Stein stands her on the side of the boat, stares at Max with his single eye, and smiles. As the clouds part again, the moon shines like a silver sun and his mother's white nightdress glows in the ghostly light. At a signal from Kappel, Stein wrestles the block overboard and, as the slick coils slither after it, she raises her arms high above her head, as if preparing to dive. She looks so beautiful, so composed, that the men stare in awe and relax their grip.

'Be good, Max,' she says. 'I love you.'

Marshalling all his strength, Max wrenches himself from the men's grasp and lunges for her as the taut rope plucks her overboard.

'Stop him!' his father shouts, as Max grips her wrists and takes one last deep breath. When the water engulfs him he feels no fear. On land he is awkward but in water he is in his element. If he tries hard enough he will save her. His mother was once an Olympic swimmer. Together they will swim against the weight of the block.

In the submarine moonlight her eyes widen with shock and bubbles issue from her mouth. The fall has winded her, driving precious air from her lungs. It is up to him now. He must pull her to the surface. He kicks against the weight of the block, straining with all his power, but it continues its inexorable descent.

Her hands pull at his, trying to release him from their bond, but he will not let go. When the inky blackness closes in, she stares up at him, imploring him to release her. But he continues to hold her. The cold floor of the ocean seems an infinitely warmer place than that which awaits him above. 'I love you,' he declares silently, staring into her eyes.

Then his body betrays him. The build-up of carbon dioxide in his blood triggers the need to breathe before he blacks out, and in its panic his body obeys only one involuntary imperative: to survive. He releases his mother's wrists and kicks for the surface. When he breaches it he gasps for air as greedily as a newborn. Rough hands grip him and lift him on to the boat.

Shivering on deck, he retches, hating himself for letting his mother die but hating himself more for living. His father scowls down at him. 'You'll learn never to do anything like that again, boy,' he says. 'You'll feel no emotion, show no pain.'

PART 1

NATURE IDENTICAL

1

Thirty Years Later: 28 July

Buzz, buzz, buzz.

The pitch of the entrance buzzer cut through the low hum of air-conditioners, the silky purr of expensive scientific apparatus and the Eagles singing 'Hotel California' on the CD deck. The noise startled Professor Carlo Bacci, who was sitting in the office of his small private laboratory in the northern suburbs of Turin. He looked up from his computer screen and reached instinctively for the still-warm vial of white powder on the deck beside him. Its label read: 'Test Sample. NiL Version #072. Trial #2. Imprint: Self'. He checked his watch. It was almost six o'clock in the afternoon. He had sent his technician home early so he could complete this final trial undisturbed.

He opened the top drawer of the desk and retrieved a reusable second-generation vaccine gun no bigger than a lipstick holder with PowerDermic embossed into its beige polypropylene shell. He inserted the vial of white powder into its hollow base, then slipped it into the worn cotton jacket hanging over the back of his chair.

Buzz, buzz, buzz.

Despite the air-conditioning, beads of sweat formed on his high forehead and his heart beat faster. He was doing nothing wrong: how could bringing happiness to the person you love be wrong? Still, he knew that today's trial was un-ethical, and old ethics died hard. He was almost sixty and had spent all his professional life in scientific research in the United States, working for Ivy League academic institutions and the big pharmaceutical companies. Years of dealing with profit-obsessed men in Armani suits, however, had taught him that paying lip-service to ethical guide-lines didn't always mean doing the right thing.

And it never meant receiving the rewards and recognition he deserved.

Buzz, buzz, buzz.

He decided to ignore the buzzer and return to the computer screen to finish what he had started. In late July Italy was always hot, but this week the mercury hovered in the high thirties Celsius. Who-ever was standing on the baking Tarmac outside the anonymous rental unit at the rear of the Agnelli business park would return if it was important.

He smiled, and in the curved chrome of the desk lamp the olive skin around his dark eyes creased into a thousand wrinkles. He looked a little mad in the distorted reflection, but he didn't care. He glanced at the photograph of his daughter on his desk. Isabella would never approve of what he was doing, but his resolve hardened when he thought of what Leo had done to her. When eventually he revealed his work to the world he was sure she would understand: his discovery meant that no one need ever be unhappy again.

The screen showed a four-column spreadsheet entitled: 'NiL Testing Schedule. Version #069'. The first column was labelled 'Injection Date'; the second, 'Subject'; the third, 'Duration'. The fourth, 'Genetic Facial Imprint', contained computer-generated images of women's faces. Fifteen trials had been recorded, not enough for a statistically significant sample but enough for Bacci to know that his drug worked.

The 'Injection Date' column confirmed that the first twelve trials had taken place at weekly intervals over a three-month period. Each woman's full contact details were noted below the image of her face, although none had been aware of the experiment. Most had never even met Bacci. The 'Duration' column showed that each trial had lasted between forty-seven and forty-nine hours. The same entry occurred on each line under 'Subject': 'Self'. The twelfth trial had ended over a year ago, followed by a break of almost three months.

When the trials had resumed, nine months ago, the pattern changed. The last three entries still occurred at weekly intervals, recorded duration was still around forty-eight hours, and employed the same subject. However, they featured only one 'Genetic Facial Imprint': the same woman's image appeared in each experiment – she had a wide, round face, a button nose, warm hazel eyes and curly chestnut hair. Beneath it was her name, Maria Danza, her age, forty-four, an address and phone number.

He scrolled down the table and a horizontal red line appeared. Under the line was a new heading: 'NiL Testing Schedule. Version #072'. There was only one entry, dated three months after the last Version #069 trial, with the same subject, and genetic facial imprint, Maria Danza, but there was one crucial difference: 'Duration' contained the word 'Ongoing'. That was six months ago.

Bacci felt for the primed PowerDermic vaccine gun in his jacket pocket, then typed a second entry into the Version #072 table. Although he hadn't yet injected the powder he planned to do it tonight, so he entered today's date. He left the 'Duration' column blank and double-clicked on the fourth, importing an image from the database linked to the Genescope in the adjoining laboratory. The face that appeared under 'Genetic Facial Imprint' wasn't a woman's but Bacci's. Beneath it he typed, 'Self'. Finally he moved his cursor to 'Subject' and paused.

The earlier trials had been unauthorized and unorthodox, but they had only affected himself. Today's trial was different: he was stepping over an ethical line he had never crossed before. But it will be definitive, he told himself. It will prove beyond doubt that the drug works and guarantee funding. His cousin Marco Trapani had already recommended a private bank. Anyway, he thought, this is bigger than Maria and me, and if it makes us happy in the process, where's the harm? Anyone else would use the drug if they had the opportunity. He typed Maria Danza's name into the 'Subject' box of today's trial.

His shoulders tensed. His cellphone was pulsing. He picked it up and checked the display. '*Ciao*, Maria. I hope you're not calling to cancel.'

There was a smile in her voice. 'Of course not.'

'Good. It's our anniversary, after all. Three hundred and sixty-five days.' He detected a sigh. 'Don't worry,' he said quickly. 'We'll keep it light, I promise.' Maria was fiercely independent: she had her own business, had survived a poisonous divorce and couldn't have children. She had told him on at least three occasions that she didn't want their relationship to become too serious – she certainly didn't want to get married again.

'Let's just have a good time, okay? Where are you?'

'In my lab.'

'You must be busy.'

'Just finishing. I'll cycle home to get my car and pick you up at seven.' Maria owned and managed a chain of mid-price jewellery shops in Turin. She lived in an apartment above the flagship store near the Duomo. 'We can go on to the restaurant.'

'I've a better idea. I'll pick you up in my car.'

He smiled. 'Okay, meet me at my house.'

'Not at the lab?'

He looked through the glass partition dividing his office from the laboratory. Eppendorf tubes, a Petri dish containing two strands of his hair, a pipette and other debris from today's sample lay scattered on the workbench. He would need to put everything in the autoclave and clear up all trace of what he had done before the technician returned in the morning. 'I've got to change.'

'I'll drive you home.'

This wasn't what he had planned. He checked his watch and put on his jacket. 'I'd rather meet you there. I'm leaving now.'

'And I'd rather meet you at your laboratory.'

'Why?'

She laughed. 'Two reasons. One, I've never seen inside it. And, two, I'm already there.'

Panic rippled through him and his eyes leapt to the computer screen. Her face stared out at him. Calm down, he told himself, quelling a rush of nerves.

'What do you mean?'

'I've been standing outside pressing the bell for the last fifteen minutes and it's hot. Please, hurry up and let me in, Carlo.'

He took the PowerDermic vaccine gun out of his jacket pocket and held it in his trembling hand. The device was a needle-free, second-generation hypodermic designed for children and patients with needle phobias. It used compressed helium to fire micro-fine powdered drugs at three times the speed of sound through the stratum corneum. Once past this thin but tough surface layer of human skin, the drug dissolved into the bloodstream. The process was silent, painless and left no mark. She would never know what he had done.

He took a deep breath. I'm doing nothing wrong, he told himself again. Then he walked to the door, careful to conceal the gun in his right palm. 'Give me a minute, Maria. I'm coming.'

2

A Week Later: 5 August

Isabella Bacci's father had left two voicemail messages: one at the neurology department of Milan University Hospital where she worked, and one at Phoebe Davenport's Milan apartment where she had been staying since Leo ended their engagement exactly twenty-six days ago. In both he had sounded excited and had summoned her to dinner: 'Bella, there's something I want to tell you. Something I want you to be the first to know.'

When she had called back to confirm, she'd got his voicemail. As she steered the small Fiat through the northern outskirts of Turin she wondered what her father wanted to tell her. The drive from Milan took an hour and a half but in the Fiat, which strained on the *autostrada* like a souped-up lawn-mower, it seemed longer. She changed the CD for a mix she had burned on her Mac and turned up the volume. Pink belted out 'Just Like A Pill' just loud enough to compete with the whining engine. She had bought the tiny car when she first arrived in Italy, almost a year ago, because it was ideal for parking and driving around congested Milan. For longer trips, though, they had used Leo's car. But now Leo had pushed her out of his life, and everything had changed.

She flexed her stiff shoulders and looked down at the solitaire diamond engagement ring, which she had moved to her right hand. She should take it off altogether – but not yet. As long as she continued to wear it there was hope that he might return to her. She hated herself for being weak, but she could remember her joy when Leo had proposed to her back home in the States. He was Italian, studying international law in Baltimore, and when he had asked her to follow him to Milan she had agreed, giving up her life in the States without a thought, including a medical and research career at the prestigious Johns Hopkins University. It had been a romantic leap of faith, but her father was in Turin and her oldest friend Phoebe was based in Milan; Isabella had quickly found a post at Milan University Hospital. She had been so certain and full of hope.

She turned into the neglected drive that led to her father's villa. It was a modest, wisteria-clad house in a pleasant residential suburb, and in the soft golden light of early evening it looked almost beautiful. His battered old Lancia stood in the drive and his Cannondale mountain bike, which he rode every day to the Agnelli business park where he rented a laboratory, leaned against the porch.

Looking at the ramshackle scene, it was hard to believe that six or seven years ago he had inherited enough money to allow him to wash his hands of big business in the States and set up on his own here in the Old Country.

The only time he had allowed her into his laboratory, however, she had seen where the money had gone: his equipment was easily as good as what she had access to in the laboratories at the university hospital. But whenever she probed about his work, he always said: 'When I'm ready, Bella, I'll show you everything.' Perhaps that was what he wanted to share with her today.

She parked the car beside her father's and checked her face in the mirror. She brushed her shoulder-length black hair off her face – large brown eyes, full lips and a strong nose. At least her eyes weren't red from crying like the last time she had visited.

The front door was wide open and the smell of cooking mingled with that of the blossom. She went into the airy hallway, and headed for the kitchen. She stopped in the doorway. Her father stood over the stove, a blue apron tied round his generous girth, stirring a pot of his trademark pasta sauce. All around him there were discarded pans, onion skins, garlic bulbs and herbs. In the light from the window a tall bottle of translucent green olive oil and a bowl of blood-red tomatoes glowed like a still-life painting. Leonard Cohen was singing 'Suzanne' on the old Sony sound system in one corner. The scene transported Isabella back to her childhood. Ever since her mother had died, sixteen years ago, a month after Isabella's seventeenth birthday, Carlo Bacci had been both parents to her. She stepped forward and put her arms round him. 'Hello, Professor Bacci.'

He turned, and his dark eyes lit up. 'Hello, Dr Bacci.' He dipped the wooden spoon into the bubbling sauce, blew on it and passed it to her.

The taste sent saliva rushing to her mouth, but something was missing. 'More lemon, I think.'

He tasted it. 'You're right.' He squeezed half a lemon into the pan, tasted again and nodded. Then he put down the spoon and wiped his hands on his apron. He went to the fridge, poured a glass of Asti and passed it to her. 'For my daughter with the sweet tooth.' Then he helped himself to a glass of Barolo. In the alcove behind him, Isabella saw empty biscuit tins and wine bottles. Her father was an inveterate hoarder. His second bedroom was filled with stacks of yellowing, out-of-date science periodicals and newspapers. She had given up nagging him to clear them out.

She sipped the Asti. 'So what's the news, Papa?'

He took a gulp of his wine. 'Let's wait for Maria. Don't worry, it's good.'

'Is it about your project? How's it going?'

He tapped his nose and winked, as he always did. 'I'll tell you when it's finished.'

She smiled. He had let slip once that his project might help her own research into prosopagnosia, but nothing more. She put down his secrecy to his disillusionment with the pharmaceutical companies in the United States: he had never received the recognition she knew he craved, and still believed that the companies he had worked for had stolen his best ideas. Now he trusted nothing and no one with his work. Not even her.

'How's *your* work going?' he asked.

Isabella was a neurologist at the university hospital, and spent two days a week conducting research into a rare and curious disorder, prosopagnosia. Also known as face-blindness, it was a neurological condition that rendered someone incapable of recognizing human faces, even when they had perfect sight and an excellent memory.

She tapped her nose and winked. 'I'll tell you when it's finished.'

'*Touché.*' He laughed. Then he stroked her back. 'How are you feeling, Bella? You certainly seem happier than the last time I saw you. Has he come to his senses yet?'

'No.'

'He will.'

She shrugged and twisted her engagement ring self-conciously to hide the diamond. Her father had been supportive when she had come to see him after the split, which had stiffened her resolve not to run back to the States. He had hugged her, called Leo a fool and said how much he wished her mother was still alive because she had always known what to say. His support had been unconventional, too: he had used his own prodigious knowledge of neurology and genetics to explain clinically why she couldn't get Leo out of her mind and why she felt compelled to call him at every minute of every day. Even why she had spied on his apartment to watch Giovanna settling into the home from which she had been ejected. Her father's insights hadn't eased her pain – knowing why something hurt didn't stop it hurting – but the earnest way in which he had promised her it would all work out for the best had cheered her. 'I'm not sure I want him back, Papa.'

He glanced at her ring. 'If you decide you do, you'll get him.' He sipped his wine. 'Are you still living with Phoebe?'

'Just till I get a place of my own.'

'She's been a good friend to you.'

'The best. She's going to help me move the last of my stuff out of his place over the next week or so. Then we're going on holiday together.'

'Great. Where?'

'The French Riviera. Antibes. The Hôtel du Cap Eden-Roc.'

He whistled. 'Wow!'

She laughed. 'We're not paying. The hotel likes to keep its quota of A-list celebrities and the manager virtually begged Phoebe to take a couple of suites. Her sister and Kathryn Walker are in Europe so they'll be joining us.'

'Fantastic.'

The phone on the wall rang. Bacci listened for

the message. 'Carlo, it's Marco Trapani.' He picked up the handset.

'*Ciao*, Marco.' He took a pen from beside the phone and made notes on the pad. 'Really? Four days' time. August the ninth. You sure you don't mind? It would be great to meet them. Thanks, Cousin.'

When he put down the receiver, Isabella whistled. 'Was that *the* Marco Trapani – as in Uncle Marco Trapani, the Mafia guy?' Half a century ago her grandfather had fled Italy with his Sicilian bride and young son to restart his medical career in Boston and avoid becoming entangled in the Trapani 'family business'. He had told her stories about the Trapanis. 'They may be family, Isabella,' he would say, 'but, apart from your grandmother, never trust a Trapani.'

Bacci frowned and crossed his arms. 'That's ancient history, Bella. Marco's a respectable businessman now. Doing well, too. Anyway, you keep telling me how bad I am with money and he's only recommending a bank to protect my business interests.'

She couldn't argue with that.

'His bankers are having an anniversary party next week and he's invited me to meet them.'

A horn sounded twice in the driveway.

Bacci's face flushed. 'That'll be Maria.'

Isabella turned to the door, almost as excited as her father. Now, finally, she would learn why he had summoned her to dinner.

3

Maria Danza was in her forties and younger than Isabella's father, but she had a similar zest for life. Isabella liked her, which had helped bring the couple together; they had met while her father was choosing her a birthday gift in one of Maria's jewellery stores.

For a long time Isabella had thought her father would never get over her mother's death, so she was delighted when Maria had come into his life. However, it was clear from the outset that although Maria was fond of Isabella's father, she didn't want to be tied down. But today, as Maria stepped into the kitchen, Isabella noticed something different about her. As usual, her round face was lightly tanned, the hazel eyes beautifully made up, her hair smooth and shining, and she wore a smart red linen suit, which accentuated her full figure. And, also as usual, she was a walking advertisement for her business: she wore a bracelet, an enormous pair of dangling earrings and a pearl necklace. Unusually she looked radiant, and when she embraced Isabella she was glowing.

Bacci poured her a glass of Barolo and put his arm round her. He was grinning like a schoolboy. 'Bella, the reason I asked you over tonight is that I want you to be the first to know that I've asked Maria to marry me.'

Maria giggled, blushed, and displayed an ornate engagement ring. 'And I said yes.'

Isabella was stunned. She could never have guessed this. Maria wasn't the marrying kind. 'Once bitten twice shy' was how she had put it. But now she was gazing at her fiancé with dove eyes. Isabella was surprised at how emotional she felt. She was delighted for them both – but, if she was honest, a little envious too. 'That's fantastic news,' she said. She admired the proudly displayed diamond and sapphire ring. 'It's beautiful.'

'It was my great-grandmother's.' Maria smiled as if she was going to burst with happiness.

Bacci beamed. 'I've always believed that life is meaningless without love and that everyone deserves to experience it at least once in their lifetime. When your mother died, Bella, I told myself I'd had my turn.' He turned to Maria. 'But now I realize that true love should be a human right, not just an accident of chance and chemistry.'

Isabella thought of her mother, and was sure she would have agreed that he deserved another chance at happiness. 'Have you fixed a date?'

'November the twenty-second,' her father said.

'Please say you'll be a bridesmaid,' said Maria.

'I'd be honoured.' Isabella kissed them, then raised her glass. 'To the happy couple.'

As they drank, Isabella watched how her father and Maria looked at each other. She thought of Leo and felt a stab of sadness. Her father had found true love twice in his life: would she be lucky enough to find it once? She slipped off her engagement ring and put it into the pocket of her trousers.

As if reading her thoughts, Bacci hugged Isabella, and whispered, 'If an old buzzard like me can find true love, Bella, anyone can – especially someone as beautiful as you. If you want Leo back, he'll come, I promise.'

'Sure, Papa.'

'I mean it,' he said, stroking her hair. 'It's a scientific certainty, and one day I'll prove it to you.' She smiled at his optimism.

When she turned away, she didn't see him take two hairs from her head, check that the follicles were attached and place them carefully on a dish next to the notepad by the phone, which read:

Marco Trapani.
Find out more about Kappel Privatbank and Comvec.
Kappel anniversary 9 August.

4

Some hours later and six time zones away, a predator swam through the Caribbean. Its tail fins were almost four feet long and its slick black skin gleamed in the moonlight. As it neared the shore of St Martin in the French West Indies, it raised its head.

Light from the moon reflected off the crescent of sand and La Samanna, perched high on the bluff overlooking the Baie Longue. The hotel's exclusive beach cottages lined the palm-fringed bay. It was almost three o'clock in the morning in August, low season in the Caribbean, but lights still shone in a few cottages.

Reaching the shallows the creature lay still, ensuring that the coast was clear, then rose to its full height. Max Kappel was over six feet five inches tall and covered from head to toe in skin-tight black neoprene. He wore no scuba gear, just the simple equipment of a free diver: a small face-mask and outsized fins. He removed the fins and strapped them to his legs, then pushed the mask on to his forehead and counted the cottages. He headed for the fourth.

He rinsed his sandy feet in the water-filled shell on the veranda, then glanced through the locked sliding doors that led into the lounge, and crept to the bedroom window. The louvred glass slats were open but a fine mesh prevented mosquitoes entering the room. The air-conditioner was switched off and the ceiling fan whirred noisily. He peered through the slats and smelt a heavy, cloying perfume. A man lay on the bed, eyes closed, mouth open, fat sun-tanned belly rising and falling with each snore. He was naked, save for a thick gold neck chain, gold watch and two gold rings. His stubby penis was still erect. On one bedside table a torn condom wrapper lay beside a smudged white line of cocaine and two blue tablets. On the other, a bottle of Armagnac stood next to three empty glasses. The rims of two were smeared with lipstick. The man's companions had departed. The party was over.

He heard distant footsteps and eased into the shadows. The Corsican might be *en vacances*, but he would have a bodyguard in attendance. He waited until the footsteps receded, then moved to the sliding doors. The sea air had corroded the simple metal catch. He pulled out a wire from one of the waterproof pouches attached to his belt, bent it into a loop, then inserted it into the small gap between the doors and curled it round the catch.

He pulled, and heard a small click. As silent as a shadow, he stole into the sleeping cottage.

The Corsican smiled in his sleep. Since the 1970s, Antoine Chabrol had exploited France's colonial links to buy into the poppyfields and marijuana plantations of Indochina, the Middle East and North Africa. Now in his sixties, he controlled the production of almost half the heroin supplied to Europe and America.

Over the years, numerous distributors had tried unsuccessfully to muscle in on his market, and he took great pleasure in squeezing out the latest upstart: the Trapani family. The Sicilians had demanded a partnership deal because their pet scientists had developed a process that would make his product safer and more consistent in quality. But safety wasn't his or his Corsican brethren's concern so they had cut off the Sicilians' supply. Now he had heard that Marco Trapani was briefing his scientists to create a cheaper synthetic heroin. In time Chabrol would control that, too. He grinned in his sleep as he pictured Marco Trapani wearing a Corsican Smile – his throat cut from ear to ear.

One thing Chabrol no longer controlled was his prostate, and the insistent pressure on his bladder pierced his dreams. He rolled out of bed and padded across the cool terracotta tiles to the bathroom. He remembered the two *putains* who had serviced him earlier. He had asked his contact in

Marigot to supply him with two underage girls prepared to do anything, and both had exceeded his most depraved imaginings.

He stepped into a puddle and frowned. He had told the girls not to use the shower. He rubbed his eyes and glanced at the luminous dial on his gold Rolex: 3:11. Not bothering to switch on the bathroom light, he shuffled past the bath to the lavatory and groaned. That was the problem with Viagra: it got you up but it kept you up for hours. Concentrating hard, he relaxed and emptied his bladder. As happened often now, when he thought he had finished he felt a pressing need to carry on. After the third false stop, a sound snapped him fully awake. The bathroom door had closed behind him.

The lock clicked and he swivelled round. When he saw the towering black figure in the gloom his first instinct was to call out, but before he could open his mouth something cold and metallic pressed against his lips. Then a huge hand gripped his right shoulder and turned him back to the lavatory. The gun barrel moved to his neck. When he looked down his erection had gone and the sporadic flow had become an unstoppable stream.

'*Après que vous ayez finit, Monsieur*,' someone whispered in his ear.

5

As Max Kappel stood in the gloom, pressing the silencer of his Glock against Chabrol's tanned, flabby flesh, he felt nothing. No excitement, no disgust, no fear and certainly no pity. He was simply doing a job for his father and the family business. It was no different from any other job he had done in the past. When Chabrol had finished, Max passed him a towel to cover his nakedness. 'Lower the seat and sit down.'

The Corsican's tanned face was pale. 'Who are you? What do you want?'

Max watched him with detached interest. Even the toughest men find it difficult to control their fear in the early hours, particularly when an armed stranger surprises them buck-naked while taking a piss. He sighed and sat on the side of the bath. 'You've been making life difficult for one of our clients.'

'Who?'

'Marco Trapani.'

Recognition flickered in the Corsican's eyes. 'I know you. You're with Kappel Privatbank.' He recovered some of his composure. 'You came to my offices in Ajaccio.'

Max nodded. 'To negotiate an agreement on behalf of our client. I pleaded with you to be reasonable. Do you remember your parting words?'

A malevolent grin flashed across Chabrol's features. 'Trapani's going to be a dead client soon so why don't you fuck off back to Zurich?'

'You have an excellent memory, Monsieur.' Max reached into one of the waterproof pouches on his rubber belt. He retrieved a glass vial of snow-white powder and a PowerDermic vaccine gun. 'But when you threaten the life or livelihood of one of our clients you threaten the Kappels.' He inserted the vial into the base of the gun with the deft precision of a marksman.

Sweat sheened Chabrol's forehead. 'What's that?'

'Your passport to oblivion.'

'Surely we can come to an agreement,' Chabrol said. 'You're a banker.'

'It's too late. You should feel honoured, Monsieur. If you were going to have a simple accident we might have used Stein and his ex-Stasi agents. They're very good – the East Germans trained their secret police well. However, when we use one of our proprietary poisons we prefer to keep it in the family.'

Max tapped the glass vial and the white powder

flurried like snow. 'This is a genetic poison developed by my brother at our Comvec laboratory. It's a gene-therapy viral vector that targets and accelerates any inherited mutation in your DNA, bringing forward your natural death. This version focuses on the heart. Since we know you're a user, Monsieur, we've blended it with grade-A cocaine to make your heart attack more credible.' Holding the Glock in his left hand and the primed vaccine gun in his right, he moved closer. 'It's a good way to die. One of the best.'

Chabrol, white as the powder, stared first at the vaccine gun and then at Max's impassive face. When he realized he would find no mercy there, his eyes darted to the window above the lavatory.

'Don't shout for help,' Max said calmly, and levelled the Glock at Chabrol's groin.

'But—'

'Ssh. Everyone should die like this.' He placed the vaccine gun near Chabrol's shoulder. 'Don't be afraid. I'll stay with you till the end.'

Looking directly into Chabrol's terrified eyes, Max activated the gun. There was a barely audible *ssh* and the vial emptied. Otherwise there was no sign that the white powder was exploding into the Corsican's bloodstream.

For a second nothing happened. Then Chabrol's body went rigid and he began to tremble. The drug paralysed him, then stopped his heart. Max held him, supporting his bulk.

In Chabrol's eyes he saw the man's confusion,

hatred, fear laid bare. Not much affected Max any more, but it still touched him to watch someone die. It was as though their final spark jumped across his emotional void and fleetingly ignited the vestigial embers of his own humanity. The instant Chabrol's pupils dilated, Max released a deep sigh.

After he had laid Chabrol's body on the floor he left the cottage. On the beach he glanced at the global positioning system strapped to his wrist and confirmed the whereabouts of the yacht. Then he put on his fins and mask, and disappeared into the Caribbean, cutting through the water with slow, powerful strokes.

It took fifteen minutes to return to the yacht. He pulled himself up the ladder and rolled on to the deck, stripped off his wetsuit and stood naked in the warm night breeze. He stretched his muscles, taut after the swim, and checked his watch. He had been gone fifty-seven minutes. He opened the fridge in the galley, drank a small bottle of Evian and studied himself in the mirror. He remembered his first kill, staring afterwards at his reflection, searching for some change in his face. He hadn't found one then and he couldn't see one now. For an instant, though, a different pair of blue eyes stared out of the mirror. His mother's. He blinked and the image vanished.

He descended to the main cabin. Delphine lay asleep in bed, her face framed by ash-blonde hair, the sheet revealing more of her naked form than it concealed. He was still pumped with adrenaline, and the sight aroused him. He pulled up the sheet and slipped in beside her. She stirred and reached for him. 'Been up, Max?'

'Just to get a drink.'

Her hand brushed his groin and she opened her eyes. 'You *have* been up.'

He smiled. 'Must be the warm night air.'

'Really?' She was stroking him now. 'Nothing to do with me?'

'Never even crossed my mind. You're far too much of a lady.'

She straddled him. 'Oh, yeah?'

He smiled. Delphine was the daughter of Henri Chevalier, the head of one of Geneva's oldest and most respected independent banks. 'I might have misjudged you.'

As he entered her, she gasped. 'I love you, Max.'

The pleasure pulsed through him, but he frowned.

'I love you, Max,' she said again.

He rolled her on to her back and responded to the rhythm of her body. Her declaration elicited only regret. Why, when it was going so well, did they always have to fall in love with him?

6

Four Days Later: 9 August

Today should have been a proud celebration but as Helmut Kappel stared through the tinted, sound-proofed windows of his study and watched his guests on the lawn he felt only impotent rage.

Schloss Kappel was an austere stone mansion set in twenty acres of grounds south of Zurich. A large marquee stood between the crenellated towers and a band played on a floating island in the lake. Etched against the blue sky, white banners proclaimed: *Kappel Privatbank – 200 Jahre Jubiläum.*

He had invited every major client, the legitimate who brought respectability, and the criminal who brought profit – although in his experience the only real distinction between them lay in how long each had possessed their wealth. A few were famous. His third wife, Eva, was talking to the fashion designer Odin. The flamboyant Norwegian's distinctive strawberry-blond hair hung down to his shoulders and he wore the trademark furs and leathers that had made his Viking style so popular.

Helmut had once thought his wife decorative, but she no longer pleased him. She hadn't borne him an heir – both his first and second wives had managed that.

Behind them a minor member of the Monégasque royal family was deep in conversation with a Swiss investor. Don Marco Trapani, one of Kappel Privatbank's long-standing clients, was speaking with Joachim, Helmut's younger son, and a large man he didn't recognize. He remembered then that Trapani had wanted to introduce his cousin, a scientist, to the bank. Helmut looked at the man's ill-fitting suit and frowned. By the lake, his elder son, Max, was holding court. He looked tanned and confident after his productive Caribbean vacation, Delphine Chevalier at his side. They made a pleasing couple.

Helmut shifted focus to his reflection in the window and brushed back his white hair till every strand was in place. He never tired of admiring himself: he looked good for a sixty-five-year-old. He was over six feet tall and lean, with an erect Prussian bearing. He wore a dark suit, a pale blue shirt, which matched his eyes, and a bright silk cravat that covered the purple scar tissue where a tumour had been removed from his throat. The disease had reminded him that time wouldn't wait for him to fulfil his destiny. Despite the doctors' advice, though, he had made only one concession to the cancer: he occasionally substituted cigars for his beloved handmade cigarettes.

Today he took another black Sobranie cigarette from the silver box in the top drawer of his desk, placed the gold filter in his mouth and lit it.

His brother cleared his throat. 'I told you it was pointless holding such an extravagant celebration. Not only does it draw attention to us, it costs us money we can ill afford.'

Helmut didn't respond. His brother's caution had its place but Klaus had no sense of occasion. 'I can't believe that not one of them is coming,' he said. The surgery made it impossible for him to speak in anything louder than a rasping whisper.

His brother tugged at his beard. 'Hudsucker, Corbasson, Lysenko and Nadolny have all declined the invitation.'

'You think they really will close their accounts?'

Klaus shrugged. 'Apparently we're no longer respectable enough for their aspirations.'

Helmut ground his teeth.

Klaus continued, 'They are our biggest clients, Helmut. Not one is worth less than a billion dollars. This won't be like losing the others. If they all leave at the same time and withdraw their funds, it could be critical. Particularly with Comvec draining our resources.'

Comvec was Kappel Privatbank's wholly owned biotech consultancy, set up by Joachim to service the swell of small genetic-engineering and gene-therapy start-ups seeking technical, regulatory, legal and commercial advice before launching on the market.

Comvec's potential for reducing the Kappels' dependence on its banking interests was huge, but so far the venture had cost the bank money. 'How critical would it be if all four clients pulled out?'

'We should survive. Just.'

Helmut looked up at the past leaders of the Kappel dynasty, whose portraits lined the walls of his study and the hall outside. All were male and sported the family's trademark pale blue eyes and shock of white-blond hair. All had expanded the business during their leadership, leaving it stronger. 'Survival isn't good enough.'

'But we have to face facts, Helmut. In the last decade the number of independent private banks in Switzerland has fallen by forty per cent. The country's secrecy laws may still be strong, but the new anti-terrorism measures mean that the Federal Banking Commission's regulations are tighter than ever. It's become increasingly perilous for us to launder suspect money, and banks in the Caymans can provide those services cheaper. More and more clients are turning to the bigger banks. Our reserves are at an all-time low and the economy is in recession. If we lose our four biggest clients we'll be forced to liquefy investments at the bottom of the market. We'll be *fortunate* to survive.'

Helmut paced the room. 'Do you think I don't know that, Klaus? We made the bastards rich. When they came to us they had nothing. How dare they tell us they need a more respectable bank? They were grateful for our skills when we pushed them up the greasy pole. So what if Warren Hudsucker's become a US senator. I don't care if he's the Queen of England. We made him.'

'I know,' Klaus said soothingly. 'We could wind up Comvec. You know what Max thinks of Joachim's brainchild, and he's got a point. It's haemorrhaging millions of Swiss francs each year with no realistic prospect of a return for at least five years.'

Helmut shook his head. 'Now isn't the time to kill Comvec, not when Joachim's just had a break-through.' Klaus was loyal and he managed the bank's administrative affairs with meticulous care, but he had no courage or vision. 'As for our errant clients, in the old days I'd have ordered Stein and his men to punish them, but until we find a way to shore up the bank we need their business. Look at the figures, Klaus. Offer them the most favourable rates we can afford. Call it a loyalty bonus. Just make sure they understand it's more attractive to stay than to leave – at least in the short term.'

Again he looked up at the portraits lining the wall and wondered what they would have done. Inevitably his eyes settled on the painting opposite his desk of Dieter Kappel, who had saved the family two hundred years ago.

The four original Kappel brothers had been mercenaries who had taken their name from the Swiss village of Ebnat-Kappel in the German-speaking canton of Graubünden. In the mid-seventeenth century, after moving south to fight for the warring Italian states, they had settled in Florence where they embarked on a more lucrative career as paid assassins. Specializing in 'natural' kills, using discreet poisons, they passed down their skills to the only people they could trust: their family. As the Kappel family's reputation grew, so did their fees and influence. Their descendants had served popes and kings.

At the dawn of the nineteenth century, though, a powerful Florentine count had avoided paying for their services by attempting to have them arrested for the assassination he had authorized. The Kappels' poison had made him convulse so violently that his spine broke before he died – and they had to flee Italy. Dieter Kappel had led the family back to Switzerland when it was becoming the world centre for private banking.

With the family's accumulated funds, the Kappel Privatbank was established in Zurich in 1804. It found a profitable niche safeguarding the ill-gotten gains of those wary of the scrutiny of conventional banks. The bank paid them low interest rates for this privilege, then lent their money to smaller clients at much higher interest.

Dieter Kappel ensured the family never forgot its core skills: he believed it was far easier to make a financial killing if you could make a real one. The bank began to invest in clients whose businesses had only one or two key rivals. Then, without the clients' knowledge, the Kappels would ensure that the rivals met with unfortunate accidents. Some clients suspected that the Kappels were responsible for their subsequent good fortune, but Dieter Kappel made it policy never to confirm this, let alone charge for it. The Kappels' reward came from the clients' success: their wealth fed the bank's. And, with time, Kappel Privatbank grew in status and respectability. During the Second World War, when clients sought to protect their wealth in neutral Switzerland, its growth surged. It also became the bank of choice for leading Mafia families, and extended its influence to the lucrative American market. A cadre of professional employees handled a wide range of day-to-day services, including private and institutional asset management, financial analysis, securities brokerage, administration of deposits, business consultancy and accounting assistance. It remained small and secretive, controlled by the family.

But now Kappel Privatbank was in decline for the first time in its history. Helmut knew they couldn't go back to being paid assassins. There was too little money in it. Professionals from the old Eastern Europe and the Russian Mafia killed for next to nothing. Clients no longer demanded finesse, just results.

Like his ancestor Dieter, Helmut had to take the business to another level. With Comvec he hoped that the promised biotech boom would prove to be the new market within which the family could exploit its unique range of skills – an offshoot had already yielded a covert dividend by developing a new generation of undetectable poisons. But his cancer had warned him that if he wanted to secure the family's future before he died, the business had to evolve faster.

'What's the latest on Banque Chevalier of Geneva?' Klaus asked.

Helmut spotted Henri Chevalier by the lake, and Delphine was still with Max, talking to a Japanese client. 'Chevalier's keen. He still believes that the only way to keep out the American conglomerates is to merge with a small private bank like ours. But I won't merge unless I can guarantee we'll be in control.' Helmut watched Delphine Chevalier gaze adoringly at his elder son and a thin smile curled his lips. He took a long drag on his cigarette and whispered. 'Klaus, please tell Max I need to see him.'

7

Even as Max entered the study Helmut Kappel found himself glancing through the window at his younger son, who was talking with Trapani and Trapani's cousin. Joachim wore a formal suit with a bright bow-tie. He was full of ideas and enthusiasm and he was committed to realizing Helmut's vision of taking the family into new areas. Joachim was not as commercially astute as Max but he was competitive, studious and desperate for his father's approval. He had a Ph.D. in biochemistry and, as well as running the bank's offshoot, Comvec, he continued the family's proud tradition of creating new and ever subtler methods of traceless assassination. Apart from his circular rimless glasses, he looked uncannily like Kappel's younger self.

Max had inherited more of his American mother's genes. His eyes were a warmer blue, his skin more tanned than those of a typical Kappel. He was taller, athletic and more socially confident than his half-sibling. Clients loved him. Helmut took particular pride in his elder son because, despite his mother's contaminating influence, he had personally moulded him into the man he was.

'What do you want, Vater? Everyone's asking for you. We need to be out there with our clients.'

'We will be soon enough.' He pushed a copy of the French *Le Figaro* across the desk. He had ringed in red the article recounting Chabrol's apparently natural heart attack. 'I hear you made the most of your vacation in the Caribbean with Delphine. Of course, Trapani will never know it was our work but he'll be delighted. You did well.'

Max shrugged modestly. 'It was Joachim's drug.'

Helmut allowed himself a small smile. 'So Comvec has its uses?'

Max ignored the jibe. 'Trapani's one of the guests asking for you. He wants to introduce his cousin.'

'We'll join him and the others shortly. There's something I need to ask you first.' Helmut paused, considering his words, confident that although Max would argue with him he would do his duty. As a boy Max had been wild and passionate, but he had tamed his son, taught him to follow the Kappel way. Helmut could still remember the time after Max's mother's death when the boy had gone a little mad. During his first winter back in Zurich, Max had donned a wetsuit, broken the ice on

Schloss Kappel's lake and dived obsessively into its freezing depths, believing that if he went deep enough he could somehow turn back time and save his mother.

His son had hated him then, but over time Helmut had convinced Max that his mother's death was not only necessary but bonded them in some dark way. Short of suicide, or avenging her death by killing his father, Helmut knew there was only one way in which a nine-year-old boy in Max's situation could survive: by embracing his father's view of the world.

Shortly after his return from Hawaii, he sent his son to boarding-school in England. It gave Max time and space away from him, and the English boarding-school system was still the ideal environment within which he could learn to control his emotions. Max went to a preparatory school in Kent until he was thirteen and then to the King's School, Canterbury, where tradition and duty were valued. Every holiday, Max returned to Zurich, and Helmut would lead his son around the grounds and corridors of the ancestral home, impressing on him the weight of his responsibility and destiny. He never let him forget that one day he would lead the family and his portrait would adorn a wall of Schloss Kappel.

Max excelled at King's, then returned to Switzerland, where he read economics at university. He completed his obligatory national service with the Swiss Army, and a professional banking qualification, then a master's in business administration at Insead near Paris.

Eventually, Helmut had enabled Max not only to come to terms with his mother's death but also to understand why it had been unavoidable: she had threatened the Kappel dynasty. Once Helmut had conditioned his son to align himself with the family's interests, the boy's grief, rage and guilt receded to the point at which he felt no emotion at all. And, with manhood, Max had evolved into something exceptional, beyond human: a true Kappel.

Now, as he looked at his son, Helmut felt proud of his creation. 'How are things with Delphine?' he asked.

Max's eyes narrowed. 'Why?'

'I've been thinking about Henri Chevalier's merger proposal.' A pause. 'You should marry her.'

Max laughed. 'But I don't want to marry Delphine Chevalier. I don't want to get married at all.'

This was another difference between his sons: Joachim flattered and coaxed Helmut but never openly challenged him. 'Marriage has a purpose, Max.'

Max laughed again. He couldn't help it. His father collected and upgraded beautiful wives as he did the Ferraris in his garage. Max also knew that twice a month he visited Madame Lefarge's exclusive establishment in Paris's second *arrondissement*, famed for its broad range of exotic sexual services. 'With all due respect, Vater, you haven't set an encouraging example.'

'I married Joachim's mother to produce another legitimate heir, should anything happen to you. I married a third time because Eva is more outgoing and better at entertaining clients.'

'Isn't she also younger and more attractive?'

His father glared at him. 'Marriage is an ideal way to gain control of Banque Chevalier. Anyway, Delphine dotes on you. The family needs you to do this, Max. You're aware of the position with Lysenko, Nadolny, Hudsucker and Corbasson?'

'We'd be better off selling Comvec, which is losing millions, and sticking to what we know. We're bankers, Vater, not a biotech company.'

'We weren't always bankers, Max. And I'm not selling Comvec just when Joachim has made a breakthrough with his airborne Tag Vector.'

Max frowned. He was tired of arguing about this. 'Comvec wasn't set up to *create* costly breakthroughs. It was set up to enable *other people's* breakthroughs to reach the market quickly and *profitably*. It was about supplying the picks and shovels to those involved in the gold rush, not about us getting sucked into it.'

Joachim had sold the idea of Comvec to their father by appealing to his vanity: he had presented it as an opportunity to lead the family business into a revolutionary new field that would permanently secure its future. The original pitch, to which Max had reluctantly agreed, was that Comvec would use Joachim's Ph.D. in viral vectors, and the bank's legal, commercial and regulatory experience – plus, of course, its funds – to help embryonic bio-technology outfits specializing in gene therapy to bring their discoveries to market.

Gene therapy was apparently the future of medicine. Rather than treating the effects of disease, it promised to correct the instructions encoded within the DNA coiled inside the chromosomes of each rogue cell. It promised to cure genetic diseases like cancer and cystic fibrosis by rewriting the mistakes in the base software, so that cancer cells died when they should and the human body pro-duced the correct proteins in the correct amounts, ensuring it a long, healthy life.

Max was no scientist but he understood gene therapy in terms of sending a parcel. It involved two key elements: the contents to be sent and the package – including the address and deliv-ery mechanism – that was employed to despatch them.

Developing the contents involved engineering a DNA patch of healthy genes to correct a damaged sequence of faulty ones. Creating the delivery mechanism involved the use of genetically engineered viruses – the so-called viral vectors that Comvec developed. Joachim summarized Comvec's commercial and technical role as helping small biotech businesses perfect the most appropriate package for delivering their gene-therapy products to the correct cells and markets.

It was originally agreed that Comvec would develop a range of stock viral vectors and focus on getting the therapies to market as soon as possible. But Joachim had spent time and money engineering ever more complex viruses, resulting in his much vaunted breakthrough, the Tag Vector, which allowed a gene-therapy cure to be delivered to one individual, then spread, like a game of tag, to others via a secondary flu-based airborne vector. It also targeted the sex cells of the patient, which meant the cure could be passed down to subsequent generations. One proposed application was the vaccination of the Aids-ravaged third world.

'Vater, Joachim's Tag Vector might be technically brilliant, but it won't be commercially viable for years. It'll take decades to get the relevant approvals from the European authorities and the FDA.'

'That's your opinion, not Joachim's. I want the Chevalier merger to go ahead.'

Max sighed. 'I'll think about it, but merging with Banque Chevalier won't solve our problems. It'll only buy us time.'

'We need time, Max. I also need to know my legacy is secure. You must marry and produce an heir. You're almost forty, and Joachim is already married. He's only had a girl, but he's trying. Don't fight me on this, Max – I've indulged you enough. I've turned a blind eye to your addiction to diving, and the time you waste at your house on the Côte d'Azur. But this is one area on which I'll give no ground. You're my successor, Max. You have responsibilities. You must play your part in protecting the bank and securing the family line.'

'I accept that but at the rate we're losing clients we'll need a more radical solution if we're to protect all this.' He made an expansive gesture that took in the house, the portraits and the grounds. Then he pointed to Marco Trapani, who was talking to Joachim. 'And if we don't want to lose any more clients today, we'd better get out there and mingle.'

Helmut straightened his cravat and headed for the door. 'Tell me about Trapani's cousin again.'

Max followed his father into the hall. 'We need to do more research, but his name's Professor Carlo Bacci. According to Joachim, he's a respected scientist from the States who left big business a few years ago to set up on his own in Italy. He now needs financial backing and consultancy advice to get his project to market.'

Helmut grimaced as they walked down the corridor to the double doors that led to the terrace. Max could imagine what he was thinking: was this what the Kappels had sunk to, humouring their clients' downbeat relatives?

'Sounds like a waste of time,' Helmut rasped.

'If it is a waste of time you can blame Joachim,'

Max muttered, as they went out into the sunlight. Smiling, he stretched out his arm to greet the first client. 'Apparently Professor Bacci is particularly impressed by Comvec and its *long-term* commitment to speculative projects like the Tag Vector . . .'

8

A Week Later: 16 August

Kappel Privatbank stood on Bahnhofstrasse, in the heart of Zurich's financial district. The sturdy classical building, with its imposing portico and barred double-cube windows, seemed a strange blend of temple, fortress and prison. As Professor Carlo Bacci stood in the street and looked up at it he thought that in many ways it was all these things: a shrine to Mammon, a stronghold for its clients' riches, and a repository for unclaimed deposits.

He clutched his silver briefcase close to his side, reassured by its precious contents, laptop in the other hand. He had been so delighted with his daughter's reaction to his engagement that he was tempted to tell Isabella how he had won Maria's heart and made her happy. That would be a mistake, though: although Isabella was a neurologist and would appreciate the significance of his technical achievement she might not understand *why* he had done it. Not yet. Not until he could show her and the world the happiness his drug would bring. He thought of the hairs he had taken from Isabella's head, then of Leo. If he used the drug on Leo she would understand. Soon he would make everyone understand. But to realize his vision and share it with the world he needed more money and resources of the kind he'd once taken for granted in the States.

He strode through the huge embossed doors into the lobby of the bank. It was even more impressive inside. The floor was black and white marble, laid out like a huge chessboard. Marble pillars and tall green plants soared to the high ceiling and its gilt cornice. An imposing portrait of a man with white hair and pale blue eyes stared down from the wall behind the reception desk. The subject, Dieter Kappel, resembled Helmut but wore an old-fashioned collar and dark jacket. Suddenly Bacci realized how nervous he was.

It had been different when his cousin had first introduced him to the Kappels at the *Schloss*. He had enjoyed mingling with the glamorous guests and had been impressed that, although it had served its clients, including celebrities, for two hundred years, he had never heard of Kappel Privatbank: that was true discretion. He had also been impressed that it was a family bank – so different from the faceless international institutions he had dealt with in the past.

He had been particularly interested in Comvec. Two days ago, Joachim Kappel had shown him round the small but well-equipped Comvec facility south of Zurich. Their laboratory was good, rather than exceptional, but they had already made some major advances. Their viral vectors, particularly the airborne Tag Vector, were brave and revolutionary, and the Kappels' commitment to the venture was extraordinary. How many other banks would dare to invest in something as speculative and long-term?

But the tour of Comvec had been a relaxed public-relations exercise, and the meeting at Schloss Kappel had been in a social setting where the champagne was flowing and everyone was charming. Today was a business meeting and for Bacci everything was riding on its success. He wanted the Kappels to back him and his project, which made him nervous.

He approached the reception desk where he was directed to the lifts and told to go to the sixth floor. As he walked across to them the first opened and Klaus Kappel stepped out. Bacci recognized him from the party at the *Schloss*, but he was deep in conversation with a short, stocky man with a bald head and dark tan, and didn't notice Bacci. Klaus was tugging at his beard and shaking his head. As Bacci stepped into the elevator and the doors closed, he heard him mutter, 'All I'm saying, Herr Lysenko, is that you have everything to gain by staying with us.'

Bacci stepped out of the elevator on the sixth floor and an assistant directed him to the conference room. 'At the end of the corridor. Just knock.'

By the time he reached the imposing oak door his palms were sweaty. He squared his shoulders, smoothed his suit and checked his case. Then he knocked twice.

Sitting at the long table in the oak-panelled conference room, Max was surprised by how nervous Professor Bacci looked as he sipped his espresso and fiddled with his silver case. He couldn't remember the last time he had felt nervous – or, indeed, the last time he had felt anything.

He glanced at the file in front of him. It contained everything he and his brother had been able to discover about Bacci. Joachim had once heard him speak at a gene-therapy symposium in Basle. Apparently the professor was an unorthodox but highly respected scientist in his field of neurology and genetics. When they realized he might have something to offer, they had rolled out the red carpet. Joachim had showed him around Comvec, and although Klaus was busy with Feliks Lysenko the rest were here. Helmut sat in his customary seat at the head of the table, and Joachim beside Max, facing Bacci.

As was his wont, Max's half-brother was dressed in a flamboyant bow-tie and smoked the same Sobranie cigarettes as the father he worshipped. Although he was ten years younger than Max, his ambition to succeed Helmut Kappel was transparent. This didn't bother Max, because he knew it would never happen. Joachim was academically brilliant and their father indulged him more than he had ever indulged Max even, perhaps because Helmut saw more of himself reflected in his younger son's features, but Joachim wasn't a leader: he was too weak and too quick to seek approval.

'Thank you for agreeing to see me,' Bacci said.

'I hope we can help you, Professor,' Helmut said, with a relaxed smile. 'We are primarily bankers, but my son Max heads our business-consultancy section, while my other son, Joachim, heads up Comvec, which, as you know, specializes in bringing biotech ventures to market. Both may prove relevant to our discussions today.' He paused. 'Tell me, Professor, why did you leave the States?'

Bacci took a sip of his espresso and fiddled with the small silver case on the table beside his laptop. It intrigued Max. 'I became disillusioned. The big pharmaceutical companies I worked for did not give me the recognition or rewards I deserved. They say they want good science and cures for the world, but they don't. They just want profits.

'The big US banks are even worse. They don't care about investing in the future. They understand only one thing: the bottom line. If you've got money they'll lend you more. But if you need it they give you nothing. So I returned to the Old

Country and its simpler values, to realize my vision in my own way.'

'Have you found Italy any different?'

A sigh. 'Not really. But Marco Trapani speaks highly of *your* bank and its values. As for Comvec, its viral vectors are world class, and I was particularly impressed by your approach to the revolutionary airborne Tag Vector, which, although brilliant, won't yield short-term profits.'

Max suppressed a wry smile as he caught his father glancing at Joachim. It was doubtful that the authorities would ever allow Joachim's Tag Vector, based on the virulent influenza retrovirus, to reach the market. Regardless of how brilliant it was, he didn't see how Comvec could convince them it was safe.

Helmut smiled. 'Kappel Privatbank is, first and foremost, a family firm. Professional fund managers, lawyers and consultants run the day-to-day operations, but the main board is made up of the four family members and we take a personal interest in every strategic decision relating to each of our select group of clients. Client trust is everything to us and we treat the issue of confidentiality as seriously as any doctor. In a sense we are financial doctors. What you say to us will stay inside this room, whether or not we choose to work together.'

He cleared his throat. 'Having said that, we need to know as much as possible about your proposition. It is in our interests to expand each client's wealth and our policy is therefore to recommend the service he *needs*, not necessarily the service he *wants*. This will require a rigorous analysis of your proposal.' He passed a file to Bacci. 'We've signed the standard non-disclosure and confidentiality agreements so feel free to tell us everything. If we appear to pry, please understand that we're simply doing our job. If this is unacceptable to you, Professor, we'll shake hands now and wish you well with another bank.'

Bacci opened the file and checked the signed documents. 'No, that sounds acceptable.'

'Excellent. Anything you want to add, Joachim?'

Joachim shook his head.

Helmut turned to Max. 'Max?'

Max was always a little surprised by how charming and persuasive his father could be when he put his mind to it. 'No,' he said, 'I think you've covered everything.' He glanced down at the file he had compiled on Bacci. The professor had attended and worked at most of the top east-coast colleges, including MIT, Princeton, Yale and Harvard, and had several Ph.D.s. His distinguished career had been spent researching and developing gene therapies for the so-called 'big four' neural disorders: Alzheimer's, Parkinson's, schizophrenia and depression. Bacci's work on Parkinson's would have won him the Nobel Prize if a reputation for being difficult – among the powerful pharmaceutical companies who sponsored his work – hadn't counted against him.

Five years ago, a wealthy individual who had

benefited directly from his work on Parkinson's had bequeathed to Bacci a significant amount of money. This had inspired the professor to cut all ties with the pharmaceutical industry and settle in Italy.

But as Max scanned the file's contents his eyes were constantly drawn to a printout from the Milan University Hospital website. It showed a photograph of Isabella Bacci. There was something about the direct way in which the professor's daughter stared out at him . . . Her large, expressive eyes and lopsided smile made her appear simultaneously vulnerable and strong. Intriguing.

'It seems your last five years in Italy haven't been idle, Professor Bacci,' Joachim said. He gestured to the silver case. 'I'm guessing from your distinguished track record that you've discovered some exciting new therapy or cure.'

'It's not a cure,' Bacci said. 'In fact, it's the opposite.' He powered up the laptop and angled the screen towards them. 'I've discovered a way to stimulate a common sickness, a benign but extremely powerful mental illness crucial to the evolution of the human race.'

Helmut frowned, and Joachim adjusted his glasses. Max found himself leaning forward in his chair.

Bacci pressed a key on the laptop and the title 'NiL 072' appeared on top of the screen. Beneath it was a single line: 'Marazziti Study, University of Pisa 1999'.

'The mental illness I'm talking about,' Bacci said, 'is falling in love.' A gleam came into his eye and his earlier nervousness fell away. 'The first thing you must understand is that when people say they're lovesick, they're not exaggerating. A study conducted in nineteen ninety-nine by Donatella Marazziti and her colleagues at the University of Pisa indicated that there were strong similarities in brain chemistry between those who are in love and those suffering from obsessive-compulsive disorder, the condition typified by intrusive thoughts and an irresistible need to allay anxiety by continually repeating irrational rituals, such as hand-washing.

'In the early stages of love, people exhibit comparable symptoms: intrusive one-track thoughts focused on one person, which they know are irrational but can't get rid of, and a compulsion to do things they wouldn't normally do – follow the love object around, wait by the phone for them to call, constantly check they're where they're supposed to be. These are all classic symptoms of obsessive-compulsive disorder and are often accompanied by a high level of anxiety.' The screen changed. 'The study in Pisa tested students who had recently fallen in love and found that the feel-good brain chemical serotonin was forty per cent below normal in their brains.' The screen changed again. 'As you can see from this next chart these figures, relating to people diagnosed with obsessive-compulsive disorder, are comparable. Marazziti's research indicated that "love sickness" was a temporary, healthy version of OCD, instrumental in both human reproduction and evolution.'

Max saw his father nodding. The idea of any emotion, particularly love, being a sickness would chime perfectly with his view of the world.

'The second thing you must realize is that falling in love is a chemical process that happens in the brain, not the heart. It's a natural phenomenon regulated by a well-established three-stage biological process.'

Joachim's pen scratched furiously as he hunched over his pad.

Bacci pressed a key on the laptop and another title appeared: 'The Three Phases of Love'. Beneath it were three bullet points:

- Phase 1 – Attraction
- Phase 2 – Infatuation
- Phase 3 – True Love

Bacci extended a finger. 'In the first flush of love our sex hormones and pheromones take centre stage. Levels of dopamine in the body shoot up, stirring urgent sensations of anticipation and reward. This is of vital importance in securing the interest of and attracting a mate.' He extended two fingers. 'In the second phase the serotonin level drops and is overtaken by adrenaline and noradrenaline, experienced as the excitement and anxiety of infatuation, nature's way of ensuring we focus our mating energy on one person – it's when the obsessive-compulsive effect is most pronounced.'

He extended a third finger. 'But if infatuation is to evolve and develop into enduring, stable "true love" another group of hormones must predominate – endorphins and bonding chemicals, like vasopressin and oxytocin. Oxytocin is the chemical produced after orgasm and when a mother gives birth. The feeling of stabilizing calm and well-being it promotes is nature's reward for staying with our partner or our offspring. This third stage is nature's way of ensuring that any child produced by the match has two parents, at least through its early years.'

'So love's just a trick of nature?' Helmut said.

Bacci smiled. 'In a way. But it's the trick that makes life both possible and worth living.'

'So what's your discovery?' Max said, crossing his arms.

Bacci raised a hand in an apparent plea for patience. 'My last project in the States was at MIT and involved developing a genetic antidepressant. The sponsors, Drake Pharmaceuticals, were trying to create an alternative to Prozac with none of its side-effects. The new drug would work on a genetic level, so instead of a patient having to take tablets indefinitely he or she could be treated just once. It promised to be a breakthrough, a cure rather than a treatment for a whole host of anxiety diagnoses – including obsessive-compulsive disorder. Then, just as we were making progress, Brandt Tolzer, the makers of a leading Prozac clone, acquired Drake and cancelled the project. They preferred patients to keep taking the tablets. More tablets meant more profits.

'But before Brandt Tolzer came on the scene something interesting happened during the clinical trials of my genetic Prozac. Luckily the effects were short-term – all my test serums are designed to last no longer than forty-eight hours – but the episode scared Drake.'

'What happened?' Joachim asked.

'Put simply, Prozac-style drugs work by boosting the levels of the feel-good brain chemical serotonin. When patients are first taking Prozac they experience, paradoxically, increased emotional anxiety and suicidal urges while their neural connections adapt to the abrupt change in brain chemistry. For some reason the experimental serum boosted this effect. It didn't make the subjects suicidal, but it elevated their emotional responses. It acted like emotional Viagra. Subjects who had been strangers before the study formed intense relationships over the forty-eight-hour period – usually with the first person they met of the opposite sex.

'When the subjects were examined on an MRI brain scanner I noticed something strange. A firestorm of brain activity was centred on the inferotemporal cortex and the fusiform gyrus – the areas of the brain that specialize in human-face recognition. This activity was most intense when the subject was looking at the face of the person he or she had most bonded with during the forty-eight-hour research period. Even a photograph was enough to light up their brain scans like an explosion of Roman candles. Basically, the subjects were experiencing intense emotions – akin to those of falling in love – then associating them with the first face they saw when the drug began to take effect.'

'Love at first sight?' said Max. 'Like in Shakespeare?'

Bacci nodded vigorously. '*A Midsummer Night's Dream*. Exactly. Then, after forty-eight hours, the subjects returned to normal with no ill effects – except embarrassment. Anyway, Drake wanted to bury their mistake so I told them nothing, and when Brandt Tolzer came on the scene I left and continued to develop the serum myself. After numerous refinements I eventually came up with this.'

Bacci unlocked the silver case and opened it so that the lid obscured Max's view of the contents. He retrieved a thumb-size vial of micro-fine powder and handed it to Max. 'This is NiL Sixty-Nine.'

Max studied the label. The descriptor appeared to be an acronym, a lower case *i* between a capital N and L. There was a hash mark between it and the number: NiL #069. He held it up to the light and studied the off-white powder. It didn't look like a world-changing wonder drug.

Joachim took the vial from him and seemed more impressed. He handed it to Helmut.

'What is this, Professor Bacci?' Helmut asked. 'What am I holding?'

'The sixty-ninth iteration of the drug.'

'But what is it?'

Bacci frowned, as if the answer was obvious. 'Love. True love.'

9

'True love?' Helmut repeated.

'Strictly speaking, it's nature-identical love,' Bacci said. 'I call it NiL. Many of the flavours and perfumes – such as vanilla and rose – that we experience in modern products and foods are nature-identicals, chemical clones of natural ingredients, that deliver the same experience at a fraction of the cost. My NiL drug works on the same principle, synthesizing the chemicals in the brain to re-create exactly the experience of love.

'After analysing the original serum and its effects I discovered that it stimulated the intense feelings of anxiety and excitement associated with the first two stages of falling in love, attraction and infatuation, but not those of the third stage, so I improved it.'

'How?' said Joachim, eyes wide.

Helmut watched his sons, noting that Max didn't share his younger brother's enthusiasm. Where Joachim scribbled furiously on his pad, Max sat back, arms crossed, a quizzical expression on his face.

'I modified it in thousands of small ways,' Bacci said, 'but they all added up to two essential improvements. First, I deepened the effect of the drug.' He pressed a key on the laptop and the screen image divided into two. On the right there was a white mouse and on the left a brown rodent. Bacci pointed to the brown rodent. 'This is a prairie vole. It is unusual because when it finds a partner and mates, it forms a pair-bond for life. Mice are promiscuous and will mate with whatever partner is available. The difference in their behaviour is due to the presence of the gene that codes for the production of the hormone oxytocin, the same bonding chemical I mentioned as a key component of true love. It's been well documented that when the oxytocin gene is inserted in mice they immediately form faithful pair-bonds, and when the gene is removed from prairie voles they become promiscuous.'

Joachim was nodding hard. 'So you added oxytocin genes to the original drug?'

'Yes, along with the other bonding chemicals, such as vasopressin, I added control genes to boost the expression of oxytocin in the subject's brain. And, *voilà*, I had turned mere infatuation into something deeper, more enduring and meaningful.'

Helmut frowned. 'So it's an aphrodisiac?'

'No, it's much more than that, Vati,' Joachim said. 'Although sexual attraction is a significant aspect of Professor Bacci's drug, he's talking about stimulating the *whole* being – body and mind.'

'Exactly,' Bacci said. 'I'm talking about true love, not just lust.'

'What was the second major improvement you made?' Joachim asked.

Bacci's eyes glowed with excitement. 'Now, this is what I'm most proud of. I learned how to target the drug.' He pressed another key on the laptop and a man's face appeared on screen. 'You recognize him?' Helmut did: the man was a notorious killer, convicted in the States some years ago for raping and murdering eighteen women. He had made the international news not for his crimes but because of the way in which he had been identified and captured. 'This picture isn't a photograph but a digital composite based on DNA left at the scene of one of his crimes. More specifically, it was created from the five hundred and ninety-seven genes that specify his facial appearance – hair type and colour, bone structure, eye and skin colour, ear shape. Even his age was calculated from the lengths of the telomeres on the tips of his chromosomes. Apart from non-genetic variables like hairstyle, physical injury, surgery and lifestyle, this likeness was so recognizable that the FBI caught him within days. You must know the technology. DNA face recognition is now commonly used in many security systems. You probably use it in your bank.'

They did indeed, Helmut reflected.

'The same information about *your* face, Herr Kappel, is present in the DNA of every hair follicle on your head. From just one I can isolate your facial code gene and insert it into the drug. As soon as a subject is injected with the serum containing your DNA, your facial blueprint is imprinted on to her inferotemporal cortex. She no longer falls madly in love with the first face she sees. She falls in love with you, and you alone.'

There was silence. Helmut glanced at Joachim, and saw that he was dumbstruck – as he was. Max was frowning, yet to be convinced.

'Brilliant,' said Joachim. 'What viral vector did you use?'

'Just a stock RNA retrovirus engineered to pass the blood brain barrier, which protects the brain from contaminants in the blood.'

'How do you know it works?' Max said.

'Because I've tried it on myself. I must admit that not every iteration was a success. My first attempt at a targeted serum, NiL Forty-two, was a disaster. To test its ability across genders I inserted a randomly selected man's facial imprint into the serum, then injected myself.'

'Didn't it work?'

'No, it worked *too* well. Although I experienced no sexual desire for this man, a mechanic who serviced my car, I felt obsessively devoted to him. For forty-eight hours all the love I had for everyone else evaporated. I was so focused, so infatuated by this individual that even my love for my daughter was neutralized. I would have died for the man, probably killed for him, and when the drug left my system I was so shaken by the experience that I considered scrapping the project.' He sighed. 'But I persevered, eventually balancing the gene promoters that regulate the expression of relevant proteins so that love for the targeted individual didn't preclude my love for others. I tested it again, but this time I focused on women. I collected DNA from women near where I live and made up samples of NiL Sixty-nine. A swab of saliva from a coffee cup or a single hair was all I needed. I selected women I knew I'd be seeing over the next few days – the woman in the local fruit store, the woman next door, the woman who sat in the local park during her lunchbreak. I chose young women, old women, beautiful women and plain women. In total I conducted twelve separate experiments, and for forty-eight hours I fell desperately in love with each of them. But my feelings for my daughter were unaffected.'

Joachim held up the vial of powder. 'So whose genetic code's in here?'

'That was one of the last experiments, although it's gone beyond an experiment now. That vial contains the code of a woman called Maria. I liked her the moment I saw her and we became friends, but I was concerned our relationship might not mature into something more lasting. I lost my wife sixteen years ago and was worried I wouldn't experience the spark of love again. I'm not a young man and time is not on my side . . . so I used the drug to make me fall in love with her.

'Love's a great power for good. It's the greatest feeling in the world when it's reciprocated. Well, here it is. My vision is to sell NiL in pairs so we can create a world where the greatest source of happiness and goodwill is available to everyone. If a couple's relationship flags they can each take a drug targeted with the other's profile and fall in love again. No more divorces, loneliness or unhappiness. Like I said, it's emotional Viagra. And this time everyone will realize that their happiness and well-being didn't come from some soulless company but from *me*. The world will thank and reward me for bringing love into their lives.'

'How do you administer it?'

Bacci reached into his case and retrieved a beige vaccine gun, small enough to fit in the palm of a man's hand. Helmut recognized it. 'A standard PowerDermic gun is all you need to inject it into the bloodstream,' Bacci said.

Joachim scribbled in his notebook. 'How long before it works?' he said.

'You have to sleep before it takes effect, like restarting a computer after installing new software. The drug makes you drowsy, and while you sleep it alters your brain chemistry and subconsciously imprints the target's face on your inferotemporal cortex. You may even dream of it. When you awake your brain is primed. Apart from the curious side-effect of a healthy appetite you'll feel nothing until you see the target's face.' Bacci gave a delighted laugh. 'Then you experience a classic *coup de foudre*, as though Cupid's arrow has pierced your heart.'

Helmut frowned. 'How long does it last?'

'NiL Sixty-nine targets the somatic body cells, which have only a short life span. It lasts forty-eight hours.' Bacci reached into his silver case. 'But it's not the most advanced version.' He produced a second vial. 'This is NiL Seventy-two. It uses a viral vector that targets not only the temporary body cells but also the permanent stem cells. The effects of Seventy-two don't last a weekend. They last a lifetime. If Nil Sixty-nine is temporary love, then NiL Seventy-two is the Holy Grail – pure, everlasting, till-death-us-do-part love.'

Helmut reached for the vial and studied it. Apart from the label, it looked identical to the earlier version. His head was throbbing with the implications of Bacci's claims. 'How can you know *this* works?'

'I used NiL Sixty-nine three times to keep my love for Maria alive. Then, six months ago, when I was satisfied it was safe, I injected myself with Seventy-two. I haven't needed another dose.' He paused. 'A few weeks ago I widened the sample base. I injected Maria. I wanted to prove the drug's efficacy but I also wanted to help her. She had been hurt and was uncertain about commitment, frightened to trust love. I thought the drug would take away that fear.'

There was a moment of silence.

'Did you ask her permission?' asked Max.

Another pause. 'No. But I myself had already taken it, so I wasn't taking advantage of her. Anyway, I love her and now she's certain she loves me. We're happy.'

'Have you told her about the drug?'

'No.'

'But it worked?' said Helmut.

'We're getting married.'

'What exactly do you want from us?' Helmut's mind rushed ahead, working out how he could benefit from Bacci's thunderbolt. If it was genuine.

'I've run out of money,' Bacci said. 'I need funding and expertise to organize clinical trials and the eventual launch. But I won't use the big investment banks because they'll hijack the project and involve the big pharmaceutical companies to milk it for maximum profit. This is my idea, born of my hard work, and I intend to reap the rewards and recognition. I also want to keep control of the project because the technology is open to abuse. I see the drug being taken by couples, equal partners in love. I need you to help me realize this vision.'

Helmut waved his hand dismissively. 'We can provide what you need but our first concern is your technology.'

'Who else knows about it?' Joachim asked.

'No one. My lab technician knows aspects of the process but that's all. No one knows what it does.'

Max looked down at his file. 'Marco Trapani?'

'I've only told him I've discovered something. I haven't said what.'

Helmut noticed Max studying a photograph in the file. 'How about your daughter?'

'No.'

Helmut nodded. 'Tell *no one* about this yet, Professor Bacci. It's vital we have everything organized before we go public.'

'So you'll take me on?' Bacci said.

Max's frown grew more severe. 'If your technology is genuine.'

'It is. I told you. I used it on myself.'

Helmut raised his hand. 'Please don't be offended, Professor. It's just that this discovery is *so* fantastic we need proof.'

'How can I prove it to you without going public?'

'Joachim, you're the scientist. What do you think?' Helmut watched his younger son try to read his expression. Joachim rarely voiced an opinion unless he was confident it agreed with his father's.

'It depends,' Joachim said. 'I'd need to check out the detailed notes, formulae and overall process.'

Helmut rolled his eyes. 'What do you *think*?'

Joachim licked his lips. 'The science sounds convincing. It could be genuine.'

Helmut glanced at Max's research file. Bacci's reputation was unimpeachable and his explanation of the drug had been clear and cogent, but it was too incredible. Still, the possibilities it presented made his heart race. He looked at his older son, a man he had nurtured to respect duty and scorn emotion, a Kappel incapable of love. 'Max, what do you think?'

Max kept his face impassive. Although his father appeared indifferent he could sense he was interested. All his life, Helmut Kappel had stressed his contempt for love – seeing it as the product of a feeble, diseased mind – yet he apparently thought Bacci's drug might be more than a fanciful fairytale.

He turned back to Bacci. 'No offence, Professor, but I'm sceptical.'

'What can I do to make you change your mind?'

Max smiled. 'Frankly, only one thing would convince me that your drug works.'

'What's that?'

'If I took it myself.'

His father shook his head. 'That's not going to happen.'

'Why not? I'd only take the forty-eight-hour version.'

'It's too dangerous.'

His father was only concerned about losing his heir, Max thought. 'It's the only way to settle this, and I don't think it'll have any effect.'

'I said no, Max.'

'It's perfectly safe,' Bacci said.

Helmut Kappel turned to his younger son.

'Professor, your science sounds credible and very impressive,' Joachim said, 'but I'm sure you'd be the first to admit that your trials have been less than conventional. You can't be *certain* of its efficacy and its safety.'

'But I can. As I said, I've taken the drug myself.'

Max glanced again at the file in front of him and the photograph of the young woman. 'You can assure my father that it's perfectly safe for me to take your drug?'

'I repeat,' Bacci said, 'it's completely safe.'

Max smiled. 'So safe you'd let *your* child take it?'

'Yes.'

There was a silence as Bacci and the others realized what he had just said.

'You'd really let your own daughter take it?' Helmut asked.

Bacci stared down at the table. He adjusted the knot of his tie and ran his fingers through his thinning hair. 'I had other plans,' he mumbled, 'but maybe Leo doesn't deserve her. Anyway, it's as good a way as any to cure a broken heart.' He gave an almost imperceptible nod, as though he had come to a painful decision. When he looked up his face was pale. 'I know it's safe. If you let your son take the drug to prove its efficacy, I'll let my daughter take it to prove its safety.'

His father glanced at Max, checking he was still prepared to do this. Max nodded: it was the only way to end this nonsense.

Helmut studied the professor. Then he sighed and extended his hand to shake on the deal. 'Okay.

For a forty-eight-hour period, your daughter will be the Juliet to my son's Romeo.'

Bacci adjusted his tie again. Then he took Helmut's hand. 'Agreed,' he said. 'On one condition.'

'Yes?'

'Isabella must never know of this.'

10

24 August

Over the past couple of weeks Isabella Bacci had thought often about her father's surprise engagement. He and Maria would be married in less than three months. But now she had to concentrate on tying up any loose ends before she went on holiday tomorrow. As she took Signor Martini and his wife to the children's ward of Milan University Hospital, she stopped herself checking her watch. I've got plenty of time, she told herself. So long as I leave by four I can be in and out of the apartment before Leo returns. And there'll still be time to pack for Antibes.

When she reached the security door, Isabella pushed all personal concerns from her mind, placed her hand over a palm-shaped black pad and waited while the DNA scanner read the genetic material in her skin. Within seconds it had decoded the five hundred and ninety-seven genes that specified her facial features, and a computer-generated image of her face appeared on the small monitor. Immediately it was matched to the image in her personnel file and the door opened. She turned to the young couple and smiled. 'The hospital takes security very seriously, especially around the maternity and children's wards.' The procedure was standard. Many institutions had similar measures in place.

Signor Martini noted the model of the system. 'The Interface 3000 isn't foolproof,' he said. 'I work in the business. I could get the hospital an upgrade to the Interface 3500.' He began to explain the weakness of the current system but his wife rested a hand on his arm and he fell silent.

Isabella led them through the main children's ward to the private rooms and stopped at 109. Through the glass door, Isabella saw Sofia climb out of her hospital bed and walk unsteadily to the adjoining bathroom. The seven-year-old looked frail in her sky-blue nightdress and head bandage, but she was recovering well from the accident – a delivery van had backed into her bicycle. As Sofia neared the bathroom door she paused by the mirrored glass on the wall and frowned at her reflection, as though she were trying to remember something.

Isabella opened the door. 'Sofia, it's me,' Isabella said. 'Dr Bacci. Isabella.'

The little girl smiled when she recognized the voice, then pointed back to her own reflection. 'I know her,' she said triumphantly. 'She's my friend.'

Isabella crouched down until her face was level

with the child's. She observed her own reflection: olive complexion, shoulder-length black hair, strong nose, lopsided smile and large brown eyes. Then she reached out and touched the glass. 'That's my face,' she said. Then she pointed to the little girl's paler features. 'And that's yours, Sofia.' Finally she turned and beckoned to the couple waiting in the doorway. 'Sofia, you've got some special visitors.'

The child beamed at them. '*Ciao*, I'm Sofia. Who are you?'

The woman bit her lip, unable to speak. The man put his arms round his wife and smiled at Sofia, a sweet, sad smile. He bent and stroked the child's cheek. 'Darling, it's Mummy and Daddy.'

'Prosopagnosia,' Isabella Bacci repeated slowly, watching Sofia's parents mouth the word as they tried to come to terms with their daughter's condition.

Ever since she'd been only a little older than Sofia, Isabella had been torn between becoming a research scientist like her father or a doctor like her grandfather. The latter had teased her that scientists were dreamers, idealists who achieved little in their lifetime: only doctors had the power to cure people. But her father never tired of reminding her that without research scientists doctors had no power. The debate had lost its meaning when her mother died of an aneurysm and no one, scientist or doctor, had been able to help. In the end Isabella had decided to become both.

Now, sitting in her office in the neurology department, she wished she could do more for Sofia. 'Try to understand that your daughter's been very lucky. Her head injuries were severe, but apart from this isolated aberration, her brain functions are unaffected. The surgeons are convinced the physical scarring will be negligible.'

The mother, calmer now, nodded thoughtfully.

Isabella pointed to the screen showing the PET scan of Sofia's brain. 'This region on the right side of the brain is the inferotemporal cortex. It's a highly evolved area where visual and memory systems mesh. The inferotemporal cortex and the fusiform gyrus specialize in the recognition of human faces. It's their sole function. This inborn skill allows a newborn to recognize its mother at only a few weeks' old. This is the area of Sofia's brain that was damaged in the accident.

'Prosopagnosia, or face-blindness, is rare. People with autism and Asperger's sometimes have it. A few sufferers are born with the condition and some, like Sofia, acquire it from a specific head trauma.'

'How long will it last?' the father asked.

Isabella considered how she might feel if she was unable to recognize her loved ones' faces. Faces that even an inanimate security computer could identify. She thought of Leo and of how she had been able only recently to stop obsessing about his face. The irony didn't make her smile. 'I'm afraid Sofia will probably be face-blind for the rest of her life. Research is being conducted into prosopagnosia all the time, and I've been working in the area for a while, but currently there's no cure.'

'She'll *never* recognize us?' the mother said.

'Not your faces. Not until a cure is found. But she'll recognize your voices, the way you walk and all the other little things. Don't forget, Sofia has all her other faculties. There's nothing wrong with her memory or vision. She's just unable to recognize facial features – including her own. She'll adapt.'

'How do you know?' Sofia's father said bitterly.

'That's a good question.' Isabella stood up and walked across to the glass-fronted refrigerated cabinet on the other side of her office. A tray of stainless-steel canisters sat on the top shelf. She opened the door, selected one and rested it on her palm. The steel felt cool on her skin. 'Research Sample: Amigo Extract' was typed in bold on a white label. As she placed the canister on the desk in front of Sofia's parents the tablets rattled inside it.

'This drug is one of the latest research advances. It's derived from an illegal recreational drug called Amigo, an offshoot of Ecstasy. Amigo was created for the club scene on the west coast of the States and is designed to give the user a euphoric high that makes them see everyone as their friend –

hence the name. It has an interesting side-effect, though. It causes temporary face-blindness.

'Colleagues in the States isolated and extracted the relevant components to create a drug that *only* induces the side-effect.' She tapped the canister. 'Assuming our ethics committee gives us the go-ahead, we plan to use these research tablets on healthy volunteers. By monitoring their brain activity while the temporary prosopagnosia kicks in and then recedes, we hope to understand better what switches are being triggered in the brain. I've tried the drug myself and the best way of describing the experience was that individual faces became unrecognizable. I could still work out who some familiar people were by their hair colour and clothing, but the overall pattern of their faces meant nothing to me. This might help you under-stand.' She reached into a drawer in her desk, pulled out four small pebbles and stood them on the desk. 'Suppose these pebbles have names – Matthew, Mark, Luke and John.' She waited a moment then jumbled them up, and returned three to the drawer. She pointed to the remaining pebble. 'Can you tell me this one's name?'

The father shrugged. 'No. They all look the same.'

'It's Mark.' Isabella put the other pebbles back on the table. 'Mark is slightly bigger and bluer than the others, with a distinctive crack on the side. These pebbles are as different from each other as human faces are, but we're not programmed to recognize them as a cohesive whole. The problem for people with prosopagnosia is that human faces look as indistinguishable to them as pebbles do to the rest of us.

'The point is, the condition may be frustrating and embarrassing, but it's not debilitating. Many people born with mild prosopagnosia don't even realize they have it. They live perfectly good lives thinking they have a poor memory for faces – although prosopagnosia has nothing to do with memory. I can tell you with confidence that Sofia will learn to cope. And, trust me, so will you.'

Only when Isabella had answered Sofia's parents' remaining questions and walked them back to Reception did she check her watch again. Before she left for her holiday she had to complete her handovers. She would have to hurry, but she still had time to get into and out of the apartment before he returned.

11

Leo's apartment, which had been Isabella's home until a few weeks ago, was near Corso Italia on the southern side of Milan. She still had the keys. She had lived there for almost a year and, despite her efforts to remain detached, was so preoccupied with memories that she didn't notice the tall blond man watching her from the other side of the road. She stepped into the cool of the familiar lobby and took the lift to the fourth floor. When she unlocked the door to the apartment she was shocked by how completely the interior had been transformed.

The hall, which had boasted a battered leather chair, a cluttered desk, posters from the Uffizi and the San Francisco Museum of Modern Art, was now an essay in minimalism. The freshly painted walls were uniformly off-white and unadorned. The wooden floor had been polished so it gleamed and the only piece of furniture was a single stylish glass table, on which stood a telephone and a crystal vase of white lilies; their orange stamens had been cut off so that they couldn't stain anything that might brush against them. The only untidy features were Isabella's guitar and two cardboard packing cases by the door to the lounge; even the boxes had been taped shut and arranged like a work of art. A scribbled yellow Post-it note was stuck to one: 'Izzy. Giovanna kindly packed all your belongings for you. Please leave your keys on the hall table when you leave. Hope we can stay friends. Leo.'

Isabella felt hollow inside when she looked at the old guitar that had once belonged to her mother, and the two boxes, which contained the last vestiges of her life with the man she had travelled to Italy to marry. She walked past them into the lounge. Giovanna had changed everything in here, too. Like a dog marking its territory, she had stamped her identity on every square inch, using her money to eradicate all trace of Isabella – and even Leo – from the apartment. All the old furniture, including the huge sagging couch, which Isabella had disliked but Leo had loved, was gone. In its place a matching symphony of bland but unquestionably expensive neutral rugs and cream leather furniture had appeared. Isabella hated it.

Her eyes went to the smart Denon DVD player in the corner. Why hadn't Giovanna put that into a box for her to take away? Probably because it suited the new décor, she thought. Isabella had bought it to watch her beloved classic movies a month before Leo had dropped the bombshell that he was going back to his childhood sweetheart. 'I have to, Izzy. You must understand. She needs me more than you do.'

On the mantelpiece there was a picture of Leo with Giovanna. She and Giovanna were so different that Isabella felt a twinge of insecurity. While she was dark and athletic, with strong, asymmetrical features and a lopsided smile, Giovanna was fair and petite with a pretty button nose. And while Isabella was committed to her work, Giovanna wasn't afraid to express her need. Another factor, Isabella understood now, was that Giovanna's wealthy father was an influential judge who had promised to aid Leo's legal career. Isabella's father was a brilliant but eccentric scientist, who had spent all of his savings on trying to convince the world of his genius.

Thinking of her father cheered Isabella. His engagement to the independent Maria proved that, when it came to love, anything was possible.

Wandering through the lounge, she contemplated whether to take the DVD player. She was the movie buff. Leo didn't even have any DVDs. The shelves were empty, except for one or two ornaments. Even the few leather-bound books looked brand new and unread. Three glossy magazines, again untouched, lay on the coffee table, *Vogue* at the top. The face on the cover made Isabella smile, especially when she read the caption: 'The Billion Dollar Face: Is Phoebe *the* Face of the Millennium?'

In the corner was an elegant wooden filing cabinet. She opened it and was surprised to see reams of catalogues for curtain, wallpaper and upholstery fabrics, all indexed alphabetically. Everything was so organized, so perfect, that she felt a second rush of insecurity. Was this another reason why Leo had chosen Giovanna over her?

Beep, beep.

The sound of the car horn made her check her watch. Leo had said they wouldn't be back until six and the last thing she wanted was to see him or Giovanna. She moved to the large window overlooking the street and the distant spires of the Duomo. Two huge hoardings faced her from the opposite apartment block. One advertised a car, the other fashion. The tag-line, 'Pure Valkyrie by Odin', was written across the bottom of the fashion advertisement and the face on the *Vogue* cover smiled out at her.

Beep, beep.

She looked down and was relieved to see Phoebe sitting in her silver open-top Mercedes. Her long blonde hair hung loose to her shoulders and she wore dark glasses, but her cheekbones made her instantly recognizable as the model in the vast poster and on the magazine's cover.

Isabella opened the window and shouted down, 'The door's open – come on up.' Phoebe waved and stepped out of the car, oblivious to the double-takes of passers-by as she walked beneath the huge poster towards the entrance. She had been such a good friend for so long that Isabella sometimes forgot how famous Phoebe was. Today, as always, she looked stunning: six feet tall, blonde and dressed from head to toe in Odin – or whatever top designer she was currently modelling.

Isabella's sadness evaporated when Phoebe breezed in, hugged her, and shook her head in dismay. 'My God, what *has* she done to the place? I didn't know she'd had a complete personality by-pass.' She spoke with a cut-glass English accent. 'Sorry I'm late, Izzy, but the shoot went on for longer than I expected. Are those to go in the car?' She gestured to the two boxes and the guitar.

'Just one. I can get the other box and the guitar into mine.'

'Nothing else?'

'I bought the DVD player a month before we broke up but I wasn't sure whether I should—'

Phoebe tutted, grabbed her hand and led Isabella into the lounge. 'Unplug it and put it on the boxes. Then let's check for anything else of yours the poor girl may have *forgotten* to pack.' She looked around the room. 'Christ, talk about being colour bland. Poor old Leo – it almost makes me feel sorry for him. Izzy, you're so lucky to be out of this. He's far too weak for someone as vibrant as you.' She pulled Isabella along to the bedroom. 'Come on, let's have a snoop.'

Isabella started to protest but Phoebe just wrinkled her nose and put a finger to her lips. When they had first met back in the States, Phoebe

Davenport had been a skinny, gangly schoolgirl fresh from England, but even then she had been irresistible, and had soon become so famous that the world knew her now by her first name. Phoebe was one of those charismatic people with boundless energy who seemed to revitalize everyone in their orbit. Her late father, Sir Peter Davenport, had owned vast swathes of property in London, and her mother belonged to one of Boston's wealthiest and oldest families. The *New Yorker* had once dedicated a whole article to how Phoebe had politely declined proposals from at least seven of the world's most eligible bachelors. And yet, despite her privileged background and lifestyle, she had been a kind and true friend to Isabella: she had let Isabella use her Milan apartment when Leo had called off the engagement and forced her to move out.

Phoebe headed straight for the wardrobe. She opened the doors to reveal rows of beautiful designer gowns, skirts and jackets hanging in plastic covers, organized by colour. Isabella was impressed but Phoebe snorted. 'God, what a waste. It's all so last year, darling. More money than taste.'

Isabella laughed. 'Unlike you, of course.'

Phoebe smiled. 'A girl with money and taste is a rare and wonderful thing. We're thin on the ground.' She turned to three black-and-white photographs above the bed, each showing Giovanna in a state of undress, pouting self-consciously for the camera. Even Isabella could tell that they were amateur, but Phoebe, the model who had stayed at the top of her profession for over a decade, raised an eyebrow and said, 'How brave.'

Her confidence returning, Isabella headed for the kitchen. 'There's one thing of mine I'm definitely going to take.' She looked inside the fridge, which was virtually empty except for some anonymous glass jars, a slab of moulding cheese and a wilting lettuce leaf. Evidently the otherwise perfect Giovanna didn't cook. Phoebe was right: maybe Leo did deserve her. She opened the freezer compartment and rooted about until she came to the tub of her homemade double-choc-chip ice-cream, which Leo loved.

'Good girl,' Phoebe said, over her shoulder. 'Haven't had a choccy fix for ages.' She checked her watch. 'Speaking of treats, we'd better hurry back to the apartment and unload all this. We haven't much time to pack for Antibes.'

Isabella felt a surge of excitement. Tomorrow she would be in the South of France and a holiday was just what she needed: it was a chance to wipe the slate clean, make a fresh start.

They wrestled the guitar, the boxes, the DVD player and the ice-cream out of the front door and on to the landing. Then Isabella went back into the apartment and placed the keys on the hall table. She paused, then took a small box out of her pocket. She opened it and looked at the exquisite diamond ring. She had always understood that if a man broke off an engagement, the woman could keep the ring. But Isabella no longer wanted anything of Leo's. She closed the box and placed it on the table by the keys. The white mark on her lightly tanned finger was already fading.

She looked around the apartment one last time and was glad suddenly that it had been transformed. It was in her past now. She no longer belonged here. She had to move on.

12

28 August

Antibes's moonlit marina was calm and rows of tethered yachts lay on the still water. Isabella spotted him as she raised the Kir Royale to her lips. She nudged Phoebe. 'Look, it's Bondi.'

'Where?' Phoebe swivelled in her chair just in time to see him walk past the bar and along the marina. The man they had christened Bondi was tall with a deep tan, dark eyes and blond highlights. For the last three days he had been giving Phoebe windsurfing lessons. Tonight he was with another equally beautiful man.

Kathryn Walker flicked her auburn hair out of her green eyes. 'He's gay, Phoebe,' she said, in a tone drier than her martini. 'You might be a super-model, but however many windsurfing lessons you take with him, and whatever bikini you wear, he's not going to jump you.' Kathryn was an old schoolfriend from the States. One of the famously wealthy Walker family of New York, she had a willowy figure and skin so fair that, although she had covered herself in sunblock for the last three days, her nose was peppered with freckles.

'I don't know what you see in him,' Isabella said. 'He's a windsurf instructor and spends all his time in the sun yet he highlights his hair. How vain is that?'

'I'm telling you, he's definitely gay,' Kathryn said.

'Come on, he's gorgeous.' Phoebe turned to the fourth person in the party for support. 'Surely *you* can see that, Claire?'

Claire Davenport sipped her Bacardi Breezer. 'I'd need to meet him first.' She was just over a year younger than Phoebe and worked in publishing. She was as blonde as her sister, but not as tall.

'You'd need to meet him?'

'Yeah, to see if I liked him.'

Isabella laughed. 'I agree. I never go for a guy just because of the way he looks.' After Leo she had no intention of going out with anyone just yet, however much she liked him. But this was only talk. 'Handsome is as handsome does.'

'You're saying that first impressions mean nothing?' Phoebe pointed at another beautiful man as he passed. 'What about him? He looks like Brad Pitt.'

'So what?' said Isabella.

'Come on, you're the movie nut. Which movie star do you like?'

Isabella thought for a moment and stifled a

yawn. It was almost eleven and she was suddenly drowsy. 'John Corbett.'

'Who?'

'The guy in *My Big Fat Greek Wedding*. I liked the character he played.'

'Yeah,' said Claire. 'He played a cool guy in *Sex and the City* too.'

Isabella stifled another yawn. 'He seems kind, a man you could trust.' She looked up at the stars and listened to the others continue the conversation, the breeze cool on her skin. For the first few days of the holiday she had been preoccupied with work, but the mix of friends, sun, sea air and exercise had soon worked its magic. She had barely thought of Leo. Now, after a few drinks, she was so relaxed that although Phoebe and the others were talking about going on to a club she might have to go back to her suite.

Three tables away, Max Kappel sipped his cold *bière blonde* and leaned back into the shadows. He couldn't stop staring at her. He had breezily agreed to test the NiL drug on himself and Professor Bacci's daughter because he was so convinced it wouldn't work. But now he felt less cavalier. In the flesh Isabella was even more intriguing than her photograph had suggested, and more interesting than her classically beautiful friends, including the exquisite Phoebe. Even when Isabella sat back she appeared animated and expressive. Her huge brown eyes seemed to convey her emotions, raw and unfiltered.

After Professor Bacci had made up the serums and told him Isabella's holiday plans, Max had decided to conduct the experiment in Antibes. It was a neutral place and if the experiment worked it might pass as a holiday romance – and he knew the area because it was just down the coast from his house in St Laurent-du-Var. He still hadn't decided how he would get close enough to her to inject the drug without arousing her suspicion.

He watched her for another half-hour until she stood up to leave. Above the hubbub he heard apologies: '. . . tired . . . too much sun . . . walk in the fresh air . . .' Phoebe and the others rose to go with her, but Isabella said, 'You stay and go clubbing. I'm fine. The hotel's just up the road. See you later.' They all hugged each other, and then she was on the street. Alone.

Max waited a minute then followed her. A few paparazzi were waiting by the exit, presumably for Phoebe. When they realized Isabella wasn't a 'face' they lowered their lenses. As he followed her through the narrow streets he was as conscious of the small PowerDermic vaccine gun in his pocket as if it were a stone in his shoe. He had to stop himself touching it. Usually he felt icily confident before he hit a target, but not tonight. Killing someone was different, cleaner. Dead men told no tales so it didn't matter if they saw who killed them.

But tonight he had to inject his prey, then walk away without revealing what he had done.

Isabella Bacci had disconcerted him too. So far his targets had been hard men from whom he had no difficulty in remaining detached. She was different: so unguarded that she made him curious.

As he followed Isabella's athletic frame, he watched the other people wending their way home through the lit streets, laughing, holding hands. 'I was like you once,' he whispered into the night air. 'I felt what you feel.' He fingered the vaccine gun again. What if Bacci's claim was genuine? Would this make him feel what normal humans felt?

Suddenly Isabella stopped walking and looked down a narrow side-street. Ahead, a couple and a group of men glanced down the same alley, then averted their eyes and carried on walking. An angry cry made Max step instinctively into the shadows. Edging closer, he looked down the alley and saw three men knock a fourth to the ground. Two young men in suits passed him and walked into the narrow street, then turned back. All avoided eye-contact with the attackers and walked on as if they had seen nothing.

Only Isabella didn't move or look away. Hanging back, Max could tell that she was tempted to walk on by – she was powerless, after all, to do anything. He could almost see the indecision and fear in her eyes.

Then the man on the ground cried out as one of the muggers kicked him in the head, then again.

Isabella looked about her frantically for support, evidently hoping someone would intervene. Max stepped back further into the shadows. The few passers-by continued talking among themselves, as if to block out what was happening.

Another kick made contact and blood glistened on the cobbles, the dark pool spreading from the prone man's head like wine from a broken bottle. This galvanized her to run down the side-street towards them, shouting at the top of her voice, 'Stop it! You're killing him! I'm a doctor! Leave him alone!'

At first nothing happened. Then the man doing the kicking paused and looked at her, his face blank. The others were staring, incredulous. She halted four feet from them and Max saw her shoulders slump as the impetuous fury that had propelled her there evaporated, leaving her stranded. Her left knee was shaking and it must have taken all her courage to stand firm.

The kicker stepped towards her. He was young, with long dark hair and a round, cherubic face. A gash on his left cheek was bleeding and the toes of his pale Timberland boots were dark with blood. Then the other two stepped over their victim towards her. Together they formed a line. 'This is your business, Mademoiselle?' demanded the shortest one.

'You're killing him,' Max heard her say, voice quivering with outrage as she looked down at the victim, his head covered in blood.

The man with the stained Timberlands reached into his jeans, pulled out an ivory-handled knife and stepped towards her. She didn't move. He stepped closer.

'You have pretty eyes, Mademoiselle, but they see too much.' He pulled the blade back, poised to strike. 'Perhaps I should cut them out.'

13

Isabella didn't remain still because she was brave: she froze because she had lost all power over her limbs. She went to the gym regularly and was fit, but she was no fighter. A rush of nausea brought her out in a cold, prickly sweat. She wished she'd stayed in the bar now and walked back to the hotel with the others. She tried to shout, but her mouth was dry, her throat tight.

The man smiled and the knife glinted in the flickering light of the street-lamp. He moved closer and when she stepped back, her heel caught the kerb. She stumbled, hit her head on the lamp-post and fell to the ground, dazed.

What a pathetic way to die, she thought, looking up at the thug's half-lit face. As he thrust the knife towards her, a shadow fell across his features, and she saw movement in her peripheral vision. Time seemed to slow and her visual acuity sharpened as the blade rushed towards her in a quicksilver flash. Then, it was obscured by a dark mass inches from her eyes. A huge figure had appeared above her, the light from the street-lamp illuminating his white-blond hair like a halo. Only now did she realize that he had shielded her face by thrusting his arm in the knife's path. He had wrapped his forearm in his linen jacket but the blade had still cut him: a bloodstain bloomed on the pale fabric. He made no sound, and his clear blue eyes betrayed no pain.

Her attacker, dwarfed by the man, looked suddenly uncertain as her protector locked his massive left hand on the attacker's wrist and twisted the knife from his grip. The other two moved forward, knives drawn, but her rescuer didn't retreat: he dropped his jacket and stepped protectively over her prone body.

For a second, the attackers didn't move, then all three lunged at once. From where she lay they looked like three snarling dogs attacking a lion. But they stood no chance. He moved with unhurried, deliberate precision, landing blows with such power that they were soon limping off into the night. Then he moved to the fallen man, who was groaning and struggling to his feet. Before he could reach him, though, the man clutched his battered head and stumbled off down the dark alley. The blond man shook his head and returned to her. Before she could scramble to her feet, he knelt over her, and gently felt the back of her head where it had struck the lamp-post. His face was so close to her that she could smell his aftershave. For a fleeting instant his blue eyes stared into hers and she thought he was going to kiss her. And she wanted him to.

Then she felt something at the back of her neck, a brush of air, and the spell was broken. 'Thanks, I'm fine,' she said, suddenly self-conscious.

He smiled and helped her to her feet. She was tall for a woman, five feet eight, but he towered above her. 'You've got an impressive bump, but you'll live.'

She was still trembling, but now that she was safe she felt something else: excitement. She returned his smile. 'I don't know how to thank you. Shouldn't we call the gendarmes?'

He put on his bloodied jacket. 'I wouldn't bother. Did you see how quickly the injured guy ran off?'

She reached for his hand and pulled back the sleeve. An ugly red gash sliced across his forearm. 'Let me look at that.' She felt the pulse on his wrist. It was slow, even for someone in repose, and she contrasted it with her own racing heartbeat. 'Takes a lot to get you going, doesn't it?' She probed the wound but he didn't flinch. 'It's okay to feel pain, you know? It shows you're alive.' The cut was ugly but clean. 'You had an anti-tetanus jab recently?'

'I'll be fine.'

She retrieved a clean white handkerchief from her handbag. 'I'll bind the cut for now but you must get it seen to as soon as possible.'

'If you say so.'

'I say so.' She smiled at his calm self-assurance. 'You live around here?'

'I have a house just up the coast. You?'

'I'm staying at the Eden Rock.'

He nodded. 'I'll see you back there.'

As they walked to the hotel she studied his clothes. 'Let me pay for your jacket.'

He glanced down at the bloodstain. 'Don't worry about it.'

'At least let me buy you a drink to say thank you,' she said, when they arrived outside the hotel entrance.

Something flickered in his blue eyes. 'Thanks, but not tonight.' She was disappointed. There was something mysterious and dangerous about him that made Leo seem like a foolish boy. Suddenly he smiled. 'Be warned, though. I will see you again and when I do I'll take you up on that drink.' He turned away. 'Goodnight.'

'Goodnight. And thanks again,' she said, as she watched him disappear into the night. When she turned into the hotel lobby she realized she didn't even know his name. In the lift she rubbed the back of her neck, remembering his gentle touch.

14

Max's retreat was three miles up the coast in St Laurent-du-Var. The stucco-covered stone villa nestled in an acre of pine trees overlooking the Mediterranean. He invited few people through its high gates and never his family. Pictures of his mother adorned the walls, and locked in his desk was the US passport in the name of William Collins that she had given him in Hawaii. The house was a private place, where he dived, swam and thought, insulated from every other aspect of his life.

Max turned the hot dial on his shower until the water scalded his skin. He examined his wound, watching the blood flow down his muscled arm and drip on to the floor of the cubicle.

As the water flowed over his body, he processed what had happened, satisfied that his intervention had been quick and professional. If Isabella had been injured by the attackers, or worse, the experiment would have been compromised. It had also provided the perfect opportunity, while he examined her injuries, to inject her with the drug. It did not occur to him that the speed with which he had acted might have been due to instinct and emotion rather than cool professionalism.

He stepped out of the shower, dried himself and got out a bandage, surgical spirit and tape from the locked medicine cabinet by the bathroom door. The spirit stung, but the pain focused his mind. After he had dressed the cut, he wandered over the cool stone tiles and sea-grass mats to the open-plan lounge and a small bar where he poured himself a Glenmorangie on the rocks. When he returned to his bedroom, he reached for the PowerDermic vaccine gun in the pocket of his bloody linen jacket and ejected the spent vial. Traces of the drug he had injected into the back of Isabella's neck dusted its interior and the white label bore the legend NiL #069 (Romeo) in neat black type. Romeo contained the DNA code of his facial imprint. He had completed half of his mission.

He gazed out of the sliding glass doors to the bedroom's private terrace and could see the distant lights of Cap d'Antibes down the coast. Perhaps one lit her hotel suite. He wondered whether she was yet feeling, unwittingly, the drug's effect. He imagined her lying in bed, the powder entering her bloodstream. Perhaps it had put her to sleep. Even now his face might be intruding on her dreams as it reprogrammed her brain chemistry.

Assuming, of course, that it worked.

He opened a small black box on the oak bedside

table. Inside were two foam-lined slots. The empty one had housed Romeo. The other held a full vial of powder labelled 'NiL #069 (Juliet)'. It contained Isabella Bacci's genetic facial imprint. Max removed it, placed it in the vaccine gun and laid it on the bed.

He took another slug of whisky and walked naked to the bedroom terrace. After Professor Bacci's presentation, Max had had no qualms about offering himself as a guinea-pig. No matter how convincing Bacci's scientific explanations were, his notion of nature-identical love was preposterous. And the idea that Max, of all people, could be made to feel love was inconceivable. He hadn't felt or needed love since he was a child – and was glad of it. Love only made you sad. He got all the emotional release he needed from diving. He thought of the proposed merger with Banque Chevalier and smiled. At one moment his father had wanted to play Cupid between Max and Delphine Chevalier, and now he was to play Romeo to Isabella Bacci's Juliet. In his father's eyes, love was a commodity, a means to an end, and Max had no problems with that.

But what if the drug worked? He thought again of Isabella's face and those expressive eyes. How would it make him feel?

Despite the warm night, he shivered, sipped his whisky and looked out across the Mediterranean. He had a sudden urge to swim out, dive beneath its silver-tipped waves and seek the euphoric release of the deep. He glanced at the wardrobe where his diving equipment was stored and then at the primed vaccine gun on the bed. One offered safety, the other danger. He took a deep breath and leaned over the balcony, enjoying the breeze on his naked body. As he looked down on the gardens, shrouded in darkness, he thought he saw a solitary figure standing outside the main gates. What was he or she doing? He peered into the darkness, but realized he must have been mistaken.

His cellphone rang. He moved to the bed and picked it up.

His father's rasp cut through his thoughts like a cold wind: 'Max, is it done?'

'I've injected her but not myself.'

'Why not?'

'Don't check up on me, Vater. I'll do it in my own time.' He hung up.

He drained his whisky, then padded to the bathroom and cleaned his teeth. He returned to the bedroom, picked up the vaccine gun, placed it against his arm and pulled the trigger. He watched the powder disappear from the glass vial as the drug exploded silently through his skin.

Then he turned out the light, lay back on the bed and waited for sleep, wondering what tomorrow would bring.

NiL #069 (Juliet) exploded painlessly through the stratum corneum of Max's left arm at three times the speed of sound. The microscopic powder dissolved into his bloodstream and sped to his heart. The drug was a bullet within a bullet: each fine grain of powder contained a micro-encapsulated retroviral vector, which in turn carried a bundle of genetic instructions. After the powder reached his heart and was pumped out into the arteries, the outer structure of each micro-fine granule broke down, releasing a retrovirus programmed to deliver its payload to a precisely targeted location in Max's body.

From his heart, each retroviral bullet raced north until it reached the blood brain barrier, the border patrol at the base of the brainstem. Here, it released a string of peptides, which acted as a passport, allowing it to continue unhindered to the protected brain cells. In Max's brain, it searched through the specialized regions until its RNA messenger material detected a match with cells in the inferotemporal cortex. Finally it entered the nucleus of the first receptive cell and delivered its DNA, overwriting the cell's natural genetic code with its own instructions.

The face genetically imprinted on the infero-temporal cortex appeared in Max's dreams, but the reprogrammed DNA lay dormant in his genome, and would cause no symptoms until he next saw Isabella Bacci's face.

15

The Next Morning

Isabella wasn't a morning person. Usually she needed at least two cups of coffee before she regarded herself as fully awake. Today was different. She woke early, alert and refreshed, and when she checked her watch and saw that it was only six o'clock she didn't groan and roll over. She sprang out of bed, showered and stole out of the suite, careful not to wake Phoebe.

Isabella always felt better by the sea, but as she walked through the dew-damp gardens to the beach, she couldn't remember ever feeling so alive. She seemed to experience everything more intensely: the morning sun on her skin; the smell of the sea; the turquoise of the water; the sound of the waves lapping the shore. She put it down to the excitement of last night. The attack had been terrifying but also exhilarating, especially when she relived how her guardian angel had come to her rescue. She had tried to stay awake to tell Phoebe all about it but had fallen asleep before her friend returned.

On the deserted beach, she breathed in the salty air, took off her sandals and walked across the sand to the jetty that jutted out into the millpond-calm Mediterranean. On the water, a few yards beyond the end of the jetty, a small buoy with a brilliant scarlet flag stood proud against the seamless blue of sea and sky. When she looked back at the cape and the hotel, she couldn't see another soul. She searched the beach and an irrational sense of anticipation prickled the back of her neck, as though something was about to happen. A memory from a dream surfaced, then slipped away.

Suddenly she was starving. She glanced at her watch and was relieved that breakfast would soon be served on the terrace. She turned back, wanting to wake Phoebe and tell her about last night, when a movement in the water caught her eye. By the red flag a black shape broke the surface of the water. It looked like a seal or a shark, but disappeared before she could get a closer look. When the shape reappeared she saw it was a diver dressed from head to toe in black neoprene. A mask obscured his face but he wore no oxygen cylinders. He was oblivious to her as he swam, taking quick breaths and preparing to dive. He moved with such grace in the water that she sat down on the jetty to watch him.

His first dive was short, the second longer. She timed the third at over three minutes. When he dived for the fourth time she held her own breath. She managed less than two minutes before she had to gulp air, but he stayed under for twice that long. It was his fifth dive that really impressed her, though – and worried her. After five minutes she stood and paced the jetty, searching the water to see if he had surfaced elsewhere. After six minutes she perched on the end and peered down into the clear blue water. When she saw how deep it was, far too deep to see the bottom, she began to panic.

Max was far from panic. He was at home, falling through a liquid world to a place in which he could find total peace. He had awoken early, unusually refreshed, with a huge appetite and dim memories of a dream that featured Isabella Bacci. He was excited by the prospect of seeing her again and curious to know how, or if, the drug would affect him when he did. It was a flawless morning, so he had changed into his diving gear and hurried to the beach by her hotel.

In the water he began with rapid breathing exercises, loading his bloodstream with oxygen and reducing the amount of carbon dioxide, then undertook a series of short dives. Eventually he took a deep breath and made his final descent. Wearing a weight belt and using the buoy rope for guidance he headed down into the deep blue. He moved fluidly, making so little apparent effort he seemed to fall through the water. After dropping thirty-three feet, the pressure on his body doubled, after sixty-six it trebled, and by the time he was a hundred feet down the weight of water above him exerted four times the pressure humans usually experience on dry land.

The physical consequences on those parts of Max's body that contained no air were minimal since the tissues and bones were being squeezed by an equal amount of pressure on all sides. His lungs, however, had shrivelled to a fraction of their normal size.

As he descended he equalized the pressure on his sinuses and eardrums, and lowered his heartrate to eight beats a minute, preserving the oxygen stored in his abdomen. After less than a minute, most humans feel an almost irresistible urge to breathe, but Max had trained himself to ignore this impulse. Where his body had once betrayed him, he now had control over it. He cleared his mind and focused on an image that always calmed him: his mother's hand stroking his forehead as he fell asleep. After almost three minutes in the deep blue, where the sun's rays barely reached, she appeared before him, dressed in her glowing white night-dress, beckoning him deeper. He reached out with his right hand, as if to touch her, and smiled as the euphoria of oxygen starvation came to him like an old friend. In the blue silence, aware only of his slow heartbeat, an overwhelming sense of peace washed over him.

He knew of experienced scuba divers who used compressed air to dive to great depths in order to experience the early euphoric effects of nitrogen narcosis, ensuring that they headed for the surface before the 'rapture of the deep' made them remove their mouthpieces and drown. Max distrusted narcotics and preferred the purity of free diving. Ever since his mother died, however, he had been addicted to the light-headed hypoxia and emotional release he experienced when diving at depth. Free diving to the euphoric brink of death had become his drug of choice.

On land he felt no emotion for his father, or from him. He had no need of it. It was irrelevant. But this was his mother's realm and he could vent the feelings he supressed on land. It was better than any trip to a psychiatrist: it was as though, for a few fleeting moments, he had returned to the womb. This was where he could connect with his mother, admit his love for her and acknowledge her love for him.

He noticed the time on his wrist. He would have to kick for the surface now or risk drowning. The upward ascent against gravity and under pressure required eighty per cent of a diver's effort and was therefore most dangerous. He checked the illuminated pressure gauge beside his watch. He had descended almost two hundred feet. It seemed that he was increasingly forced to go deeper to achieve his secret pleasure. For a moment he thought he saw his mother again and felt such joy that he was tempted to continue his descent.

Then an image of his father's face cut in, reminding him of his duty and his place in the world. Suddenly he felt cold and weary. Holding on to the buoy's anchor rope, he kicked his fins and headed for the surface.

The diver had been submerged for seven minutes before Isabella saw him surface and gasp for air. When he headed for the shore, with long, powerful strokes, she walked down the jetty after him, but he swam so fast she had to run to keep up.

When he reached the shallows and stood to his full height his size made her stop and stare. His broad back was turned to her as he pulled off his mask, then removed the neoprene balaclava that covered his head to reveal a mop of white-blond hair. When he faced her, her heart began to pound and her palms felt damp. He was too far away for her to see his features clearly but she knew he was her saviour from last night.

She found herself walking towards him, pace quickening with each step. He had seen her now and was slowly approaching. She had never felt like this before: mouth dry, chest so tight she could barely breathe, heart thudding so hard that she could hear the blood rushing in her ears. Even before his face came into focus she could see him perfectly, every feature etched into her consciousness, as familiar as her own.

Her entire body tingled, on full alert, as though electricity ran through her veins. Isabella exerted all her self-control to stop herself running to him.

* * *

The morning sun was behind her, obscuring his vision as she walked towards him, but Max recognized her immediately. His chest felt tight as his pulse accelerated to sixty beats per minute, almost the average resting rate for a normal human heart, but the novel sensation was both disorienting and exhilarating. Then she was closer, and in the sunlight he saw every detail of her face. It was as though until this moment he had lived his entire life in muted black and white: suddenly it was in blinding Technicolor. His senses fizzed. Despite the neoprene suit he felt naked and raw, as though every nerve ending was exposed.

How could he not have noticed just how perfect her face was? He had seen her last night – but he hadn't really *seen* her. Not like he was seeing her now. As he stared at her, a host of intense, unfamiliar emotions swirled in his breast. She was now only inches away, as mesmerized by him as he was by her. She touched his cheek and the sensation was almost too much to bear. Panic welled in his chest, nausea churned in his belly. He was falling over a cliff, losing all control. He closed his eyes, reached out and stroked the contours of her face with his fingertips.

He lost track of how long they stood there on the deserted beach, eyes closed, lost in themselves, tracing each other's features.

'What's your name?'

He opened his eyes. 'Max.'

'I'm Isabella.' She smiled and took his hand.

'Last night you wouldn't let me buy you a drink. Perhaps I can tempt you with breakfast?'

'Good idea. I'm starving.'

As they walked back to the hotel, neither saw the man crouching at the far end of the beach, one eye peering into the monitor of a digital video camera, the other covered with a black patch.

16

'Zoom in, Stein.' Helmut Kappel gazed at the computer screen on his desk at Kappel Privatbank in Zurich. He had never regretted recruiting the man almost three decades ago. When Stein had first come to Zurich he had been a young agent working for the Stasi, escorting a corrupt senior Communist Party official who was in Switzerland to open a secret account with Kappel Privatbank; Kappel had been impressed with the young Stein's loyalty and discretion. Later the official fell foul of the political machine and was executed, but Stein escaped to the West. Since then he had handled all of Helmut's and Kappel Privatbank's security needs with unquestioning loyalty. And with the fall of the Berlin wall Stein had recruited more highly trained and grateful ex-Stasi.

'Closer. Stop. Hold it.'

The mobile phone link between Stein's digital video camera in Antibes and the computer screen on Helmut Kappel's desk in Zurich was sharp enough for Helmut to see the expression on Max's face. It was a revelation to watch him caress Isabella's cheek.

'Follow them. I want you to be my eyes, Stein. But don't let Max or the girl see you.'

Max and Isabella held hands and walked across the sand to the hotel. It was too early to judge Bacci's drug, but the expression on Max's face sent a surge of fire through Helmut's veins. If the drug could turn his son, a man inured to emotion, into a lovesick fool, it was powerful indeed. He reached for the silver cigarette box on his desk, then changed his mind and took a cigar from the wooden box beside it. He extracted a razor-sharp curved knife from a sheath strapped to his right ankle and cut off the tip. An Arab assassin had presented the mother-of-pearl-handled knife to his great-great-grandfather as a mark of respect. Helmut carried it with him always.

He puffed at the cigar and watched the computer screen avidly. There was a lull while his son changed out of his diving gear. Then he saw Max join Isabella on the hotel terrace for breakfast. The way she glanced adoringly at him made Helmut almost envious.

He regarded the picture on his desk of his third wife, Eva. She was in her thirties – three decades his junior – and blonde. He had once thought her beautiful, but she had never looked at him as Isabella was now looking at Max. Eva had married him for money and status, and Helmut

132

understood that: emotions only complicated matters. Since the trouble with Max's mother, he had avoided becoming involved with his second and third wives, insisting on cast-iron prenuptial agreements and forbidding them any contact with the family business.

However, as he watched Isabella and Max, Helmut remembered how Max's mother had once looked at him, and the way he had felt about her. He turned to the mirror on the wall by his desk and frowned at his reflection. He despised love. He recalled the bitter impotence of rejection he had felt when Max's mother had taken Max and fled. But although he had tried to eradicate love from his world, part of him yearned occasionally for its giddy, poisonous rush. He associated it with the recklessness of youth and he wanted to be young again. He thought of Bacci's drug. If he couldn't eradicate love, perhaps he could control its debilitating influence. A smile curved his lips. If he could tame the power of love, could he not tame the world?

When Isabella's friends arrived for breakfast, Helmut watched her introduce Max with pride and delight. But as Stein's camera focused on the tall, strangely familiar blonde kissing Isabella, Helmut leaned forward. He had always appreciated beautiful things, and the blonde was exquisite. He glanced again at the photograph of his wife. Eva looked plain, even ugly, beside the ethereal creature on the screen. He remembered the momentary excitement when he had bought his most precious Ferrari, the last car ever produced by the late, great Enzo himself. A similar flutter occurred in his belly now as he watched the tall woman introduce herself to Max as Phoebe.

The phone light blinked. He ignored it, engrossed in the images on the screen. Then it rang. He scowled, muted the computer link to Stein and picked up the handset. 'Elke, I told you, I don't want to be disturbed. I know Marco Trapani's been calling and I'll get back to him when I'm ready.'

'It's not Don Marco, Herr Kappel. It's Professor Carlo Bacci. He says he needs to speak with you.'

Helmut raised his eyebrows. 'Put him through.' There was a click. 'Professor Bacci, what can I do for you? You realize that the forty-eight hours aren't up yet? Our children are still in Antibes.'

He heard Bacci sigh. 'No, it's not about that, Herr Kappel.' A pause. 'You know you said I shouldn't tell anyone about my project? Well, I may have told my cousin Marco Trapani more than I ought.'

'What did you say to him?'

'Nothing specific, but he pressed me about our meeting and I was excited. I let slip about the drug, its nature-identical properties. I can't remember exactly what I said, but I may have mentioned some of its benefits. I didn't tell him any technical details, of course, but I thought you should know.'

So that was why Trapani had been trying to contact him. 'Don't worry, Professor. He's your

134

cousin, after all. But, I suggest you tell him nothing else. When we apply for patent protection it's important that no one, except you and your professional advisers, knows about your technology, or the legal standing of your patent might be compromised.'

'I understand.'

'Thank you for telling me. I'll call you when my son returns from Antibes.'

He put down the phone, and as he watched the silent screen he decided what needed to be done. He restored the audio link to the video. 'Stein, continue recording and making notes of my son's movements until tomorrow noon. Then I want you back in Zurich. Something has come up that requires your attention.'

He fingered the assassin's blade and picked up the phone again. 'Elke, get me Marco Trapani.'

17

Thirty-six hours later: 30 August

The night sky above the *al fresco* cinema was aglow with stars, images flickered on the wide, makeshift screen hanging from the north side of the old market square, and giant speakers wafted sound through the warm night air. Isabella barely looked at the screen: she had eyes only for Max.

The last two days in Antibes had been a dream. She and Max had been inseparable since they had met on the beach yesterday morning, sunbathing and swimming. When she had introduced Max to Phoebe, Kathryn and Claire, she could tell that they were impressed. Over lunch yesterday Phoebe had taken her aside to say, 'With that physique and colouring he should be modelling for Odin, not me. Where the hell did you find him?'

'I didn't.' She had sighed happily. 'He found me.' When she explained how Max had saved her life, Phoebe had laughed with amazement and hugged her.

What she found most intoxicating about Max

was that even when he was sitting at a table with Phoebe, one of the most celebrated and desirable women on the planet, he had eyes only for her. She loved sharing him with her friends and basking in their approval, but when Max was out of her sight for more than a few seconds she was consumed by an overwhelming anxiety. It was only when she saw his face again that the churning excitement in her belly was stilled. It was as if she was a teenager again, only worse. She had never felt like this before – not even with Leo.

Last night, they had dined on the seafront with the others, then gone dancing. Afterwards, she had said a hurried goodnight to Max and almost run to her room, fighting her desire to be with him. She had hardly slept.

Tonight they had dined alone. Then Max had led her quietly to the old town, where a late-night open-air cinema was showing Wim Wenders' *Wings of Desire*. 'You said you liked classic movies, Isabella.'

She had seen the film many times but was happy to sit in the flickering dark, holding his hand. It was as if nothing and no one else existed. Again she glanced at his face.

Usually he met her eyes but now he stared at the screen. It was the moment in the film when the immortal, invulnerable angel yearns to be human and falls to earth: the black and white picture turns to colour, and the angel sees, for the first time, all the vivid hues absent from his world, including the

137

red of his own blood. Max seemed momentarily transfixed by it, but Isabella didn't mind. She was happy just to be looking at him.

The film ended after midnight and they walked back to the hotel together.

'You enjoyed the movie?'

He nodded but said nothing.

'I remember watching it when it first came out. It was a week or so before my mother died.' Isabella paused. She felt as if she had known him for ever. 'I was just seventeen. She had a brain aneurysm. One minute she was there, and the next she wasn't. She knew I loved her but I never said goodbye.'

Max's face darkened. 'My mother died suddenly, too, when I was young. We spoke before the end, though.' He started to say more, then stopped himself. He shook his head, as if to dislodge an unwanted thought, and flashed a self-conscious smile. 'I could do with a drink. Fancy a nightcap?'

She hardly touched her Amaretto as they stood on the balcony of her hotel room, overlooking the sea. She was too conscious of his warm body touching hers. When he bent down and kissed her, his lips seemed to fuse with hers, and when he led her to the bed she did not resist. The rational part of her wanted to slow down – it was too soon – but another part wanted him more than she had ever wanted anything.

As he undid her dress, his hands were warm against her skin. He cupped her breasts and caressed her with such tenderness that she trembled. She unbuttoned his shirt and kissed his chest, tasting salt on his smooth golden skin.

When he laid her on the bed a rush of passion surged through her, so overwhelming it almost frightened her. She was so ready that when he entered her she felt no discomfort, only a searing, instant charge that pulsed through her.

As they moved together she tried to understand what was happening to her, but all she knew with any certainty was that at that moment she loved Max Kappel more than she had loved anyone. When she climaxed she cried out, 'Max! I love you, Max! I love you.'

And he put his mouth to her ear and whispered, 'I love you too.'

Max had enjoyed sex many times in his life but he had never made love before. Now, he felt a bliss even greater than he experienced when he was diving. It seemed that, for a few fleeting seconds, the universe had revealed a glimpse of what made life worth living.

However, as soon as he had whispered those three words, which he hadn't uttered since his mother died, the curtain closed and he regretted what he had said. He was no longer lost in the moment and it was as though a third eye had opened, allowing him to step out of himself and see his emotional euphoria for what it was. Their love wasn't real. Tomorrow morning it would have gone from their systems and they would feel nothing for each other. As she stroked his face, he told himself that all love was temporary and he should move on and forget her. There was, however, a problem. A problem Max had never encountered before.

He felt guilty. He cared for her.

Rationally he knew that this was a reaction to the drug, but that didn't change the way he felt. He had been unprepared for its impact on him. Over the years he had exerted ruthless control over his mind and body, and prided himself on his immunity to debilitating emotions. But now he was flooded with them. For the last two days he had been in a state of turmoil, riding a roller-coaster of euphoria and anxiety. A short while ago he had been on the verge of sharing the details of his mother's death with Isabella, a stranger, and attempting to explain how he felt about it. Why would any sane man choose to open that dark place and stir up memories he couldn't begin to resolve or act on? He wasn't even sure what, if anything, he felt about it.

The most difficult aspect of the nature-identical drug was that it had shifted his priorities. He had always put his interests and the Kappels' first. The drug, however, had made Isabella the most important person in his world, far more important than his family or himself. He had to remind himself constantly that the drug was unbalancing him, and that once it left his system he would return to normal. Still, it took all his will-power not to tell Isabella everything and beg her forgiveness for having deceived her. He had to be ruthless. There was no other way.

'It's all happening so fast,' she said, laying her head on his chest.

He said nothing, just stared into the dark, willing the morning to come so that everything would return to how it was.

'It's okay,' she said sleepily, her breathing regular now. 'There's no rush. We've got all the time in the world.'

18

The next morning: 31 August

The forest clearing was high in the Glarner Alps, south-west of Zurich. Away from hiker trails and main roads, it was ideal for a discreet rendezvous. Drumming his fingers on the black folder, Helmut glanced at his watch and looked down on the distant Zurichsee shimmering in the early-morning sun. Marco Trapani should be here soon and he wanted the distraction over with. He rubbed his hands together. It was the last day of August but the air was cool beneath the alpine firs.

As he opened the folder and flicked through Stein's notes and video stills, he tried to remember when he had last felt so exhilarated. Assuming that Max confirmed what Helmut had seen on Stein's video footage, Bacci's drug should enable him to stamp his name indelibly on the history of the Kappel dynasty. The opportunities were limitless.

He heard a car's engine on the isolated road that snaked up the forested mountain and walked to the edge of the clearing. A black Mercedes limousine drove off the Tarmac and parked among the trees, concealed from passing traffic. A short, slight man with smooth olive skin and thinning black hair got out of the rear door. He wore an immaculate Italian suit with a red silk handkerchief and matching tie. His eyes were as black as his gleaming patent-leather shoes. Two large men in tight suits flanked him.

Helmut opened his arms and smiled. 'Marco, good to see you.'

Marco Trapani returned the smile and embraced him. 'Thank you for agreeing to meet. But did it have to be so early and so private?'

'This is a sensitive matter.' Helmut glanced meaningfully at Trapani's two bodyguards and the driver. 'For *your* ears only.'

The Mafia don turned to the men. 'Wait by the car.' He turned back to Helmut. 'Usually I bring only one guy with me, but I've heard that Chabrol's people want blood. They don't care that he died of natural causes. They think that because I benefited from his death I must be responsible. You know the Corsicans.' He made a throat-slitting motion with his hand. 'First they give you the Corsican smile, and then, as you bleed to death, they ask if you're innocent.'

Helmut laughed. 'You're safe here. Let's take a walk in the forest.' When they were out of earshot of the guards he said, 'So, how much did Professor Bacci tell you about his drug?'

'Not a lot.' Trapani's eyes narrowed. 'You told him not to tell me anything.'

'I *advised* him not to tell *anyone* anything until we'd checked it out.'

'I'm not *anyone*. I'm his cousin, and I recommended him to you. He owes me. *You* owe me. After I asked how your meeting went he wouldn't say much, but when I pressed him he let slip that he'd created a drug that can make people fall in love.' Trapani looked hard at him. 'That sounds more valuable than the nature-identical heroin my people are developing. I could use it to make the transition from the drug trade to the legit drug industry. If my cousin's discovery is genuine.'

'It's genuine,' Helmut said, without hesitation. He told Trapani about Bacci's presentation and the trial he had arranged in Antibes. Then he tapped the folder. 'I had Max followed.'

There was admiration in Trapani's dark eyes. 'You had your own son followed?'

'I didn't know what the drug would make him do or say.' He opened the folder and showed the contents to Trapani. A video still showed Max and Isabella standing on a beach, eyes closed, caressing each other's faces. Isabella was tall and athletic, but she looked tiny beside Max in his black wetsuit. Another showed them dressed in jeans and T-shirts kissing passionately on the street. In another they were in a club, Max sitting in the corner, watching Isabella dancing in a group. The anxious expression on his face was so alien to Helmut he found it hard to recognize his son.

'If you knew my son as I do you'd understand that these pictures speak volumes. Max never shows emotion – let alone in public – and he'd never even met the girl before.' He pointed to Stein's neat diary notes, which detailed Max's every moment from when he had arrived in Antibes. 'They were virtually inseparable.'

'What does Max say about this?' said Trapani.

Helmut remembered the curt message his son had left a few hours ago: 'It works. Have returned to my house in St Laurent-du-Var to get my head straight. Contact you in a few days.' He chuckled. 'He's convinced. So am I.'

Trapani nodded slowly. 'How do you plan to exploit the drug?'

'Your cousin wants to get it approved for use as a mainstream drug, like an emotional Viagra. He sees it as a cure for divorce, broken homes and unhappiness. He wants to spread love, banish loneliness, and be recognized for it.'

Trapani smiled incredulously. 'And *you*? What do Kappel Privatbank want to do with it?'

Helmut lit a cigarette and took a long drag. He kept his face impassive. 'We always follow our clients' wishes.'

Trapani stepped close to him and his mask of suave charm dissolved. 'Cut the crap, Helmut. My cousin might be a genius but he's also a fool. I'm not. I don't know what you're planning to do with his drug but I want a share of the profits. Don't forget, you're just a banker, Helmut. A little man who looks after big men's money. You're a *servant* to your clients' needs.' Trapani jabbed him in the chest with a forefinger. 'And the Trapanis are among your oldest, most important clients. You serve me.'

As he returned the Sicilian's black stare, Helmut remained silent, his cold blue eyes absorbing the heat of Trapani's anger.

Trapani lowered his gaze first. 'So,' he said, 'what's my share?'

Helmut didn't blink.

'I demand forty per cent,' Trapani said.

Silence.

Trapani frowned and waited, raking his fingers through his hair. 'I'll accept a third. But that's final. Any less and I'll advise my cousin to pull out. I'll fund this project myself. You'll get nothing. I'll close my account and take my business elsewhere.'

Helmut's smile did not reach his eyes.

'So what do you say, Helmut? Do we have a deal?'

Slowly Helmut shook his head.

Trapani's jaw muscles clenched. 'What's your offer, then? What do I get from this?'

'Nothing.' Helmut paused. 'Not even your life.'

Trapani stepped back. 'What the fuck are you talking about?' He glanced over his shoulder and called to his bodyguards. When there was no reply he hurried back to the clearing. The car doors were open and both bodyguards lay sprawled on the blood-soaked earth, heads pushed back, eyes staring. Their throats had been slit from ear to ear. The driver sat in his seat, hands still on the wheel. He had been virtually decapitated. The windscreen was smeared with a translucent red glaze. Trapani stood rooted to the ground as though unable to process what he was seeing.

Then Stein appeared from behind the trees, flanked by two of his silver-haired henchmen. Each looked as if he'd stepped out of a slaughter-house. Stein's eyepatch, greying hair and business suit were slick with blood. In his right hand he held a Kukri: the razor-sharp curve of its gleaming steel was dull with blood. Stein smiled at Helmut: the satisfied smile of a job well done. Helmut nodded in acknowledgement. The bodies wouldn't be found for days. The Corsicans would deny the killings, but the corpses bore their signature.

Stein stepped towards Trapani but Helmut stopped him. 'Stein, you and your men have excelled yourselves. Leave Marco to me.'

As Helmut pulled the blade from the sheath on his ankle, Trapani's face grew deathly pale. He reached frantically for his gun but he was too slow. Helmut stepped forward and sliced the razor-sharp blade across his jugular. Trapani fell to his knees, clutching at his throat, trying to stem the blood spurting from the artery. A gurgling sound issued from his wound as if he was trying to speak – or scream.

Given the bank's precarious finances, Helmut was taking a gamble in eradicating a major client, but he calculated that control of the NiL drug would more than compensate for any loss of revenue caused by Trapani's departure. If he was to move the business to a new level he had to take risks, as Dieter Kappel had done before him.

He knelt beside Trapani, oblivious of the blood, forcing the Sicilian to look into his eyes and register his face as the last he would see before oblivion claimed him. 'We weren't just bankers in the past, Marco,' he whispered, prodding the man's chest until Trapani toppled on to his back, twitching in his final death throes. Helmut tapped the black folder under his arm. 'And we won't just be bankers in the future.'

19

The same morning

There was a knock at the door of Isabella's hotel bedroom. 'You awake in there?'

Isabella opened her eyes. There was a brief pause, then she heard Phoebe's voice again. 'Wakey, wakey. I know it's early, you two, but the yacht leaves at eight, and if you're late we'll sail to Monaco without you.'

Isabella got out of the bed, put on a robe and opened the door.

Phoebe looked at the crumpled bed. 'Where's Max? I thought—'

'He's gone.'

'Where?'

'Said he had to get back to Zurich. Something urgent at work, apparently.'

'When?'

'About five this morning.'

Phoebe frowned. 'Are you seeing him again?'

'Don't know. Probably not.'

Phoebe sat beside her on the bed. 'What did the bastard do?'

'Nothing.'

'I don't understand. You both looked so smitten. Hit-by-a-thunderbolt stuff. What happened?'

'I honestly don't know. It just changed.'

Phoebe frowned again and put her arm around her friend. 'You okay, Izzy? How do you feel?'

'I'm not sure.' And she wasn't. All she knew was that something strange and outside her control had happened, a subtle but irrevocable shift in the fabric of her life. For the last two days, right up to when she had fallen asleep last night, Max had become a part of her, like another limb. But this morning the intensity had evaporated. They had gone to bed as lovers and woken as strangers.

She had even pretended to be asleep when he had crept out of her room. He had left a brief note, explaining that he had to return to Zurich, but made no mention of meeting again. She felt so different this morning from how she had felt last night that she was unsure whether to be upset or relieved. Mostly she felt foolish: in the cold light of day, the whole episode smacked of one of those ghastly holiday flings people had when they were on the rebound. Along with her passion for Max, her holiday mood had gone. She felt a sudden urge to return to Milan and throw herself into her work.

'Want to talk about it?' Phoebe asked.

Isabella walked to the bathroom and took off her robe. 'No, I'm fine. It was just a holiday romance. No one was hurt.' But when she stepped into the shower and closed her eyes, she saw only his face.

20

3 September

The Kappel cemetery was at the northern end of
the Schloss Kappel estate on a raised plateau overlooking the large house and the glittering lake. In
the distance Zurich stretched out like a toy town.
As a child Max had always wondered why the dead
needed such a prime location with such sweeping
views.

Three days had passed since Antibes, and it was
late afternoon when he returned to the *Schloss*. The
air was cool, and the leaves were turning brown. As
he walked up the path to the northern plateau he
saw the first mausoleum's brass dome gleaming in
the weak sunlight. Each housed a past leader of the
Kappel dynasty. Some were constructed in marble
and stone, others in granite, copper and brass. But
all had been built with one objective in mind: to
outlast the remains they contained.

As a boy, whenever he came home from
boarding-school in England, his father would take
him round the mausoleums, making him memorize

where each of his ancestors was buried. Then he had to walk the dark corridors of the *Schloss*, matching a portrait to its mausoleum, giving names and dates. The focal point of this exercise was always Dieter Kappel. Whenever Max had passed his portrait, his father had made him retell the story of how Dieter had led the family back from Italy and saved it from extinction. At times it seemed that his entire childhood had been one long lesson. At school he was taught the dates of each king and queen of England, tracing the royal family back a thousand years, and during his holidays he had to learn the dates and lineage of his own family, going back almost half as long.

Max breathed in the mild air, automatically listing names and dates as he scanned the mausoleums. In the far corner, workmen in yellow hard hats toiled on the latest. His father had begun work on it as soon as he was diagnosed with cancer, and Max knew he was determined that it should outshine every other memorial to the dead – past, present and future.

Although it was incomplete, the twenty-foot cone of photosensitive glass was already a spectacular sight. In the sunlight it dazzled like a vast, brilliant gemstone, and for a moment Max forgot about Antibes and his raw, jumbled thoughts. Through the translucent glass shell he could see a large plinth. Like a modern pharaoh his father had arranged for his body to be preserved permanently for posterity. He had hired the German anatomist Gerhard Heyne to plastinate his body when he died, replacing all its bloods and fluids with resin. It would then stand fully clothed on the plinth, looking down for ever on his estate. It was Helmut's attempt to achieve his own immortality.

Max glanced behind him to a low, wide, modern building beside the *Schloss*. His father's temperature-controlled garage housed at least six cars. On the drive outside, a servant polished one of the racing-red Ferraris. He turned back to the glass mausoleum. For all the Kappel family's adherence to discretion, discipline and control, Max suspected that an exhibitionist streak ran through his father's veins: at heart Helmut was a frustrated showman.

'Max, you're back,' his father called to him, from the grass verge below the crystal cone.

Max noticed his father appeared different, younger: his haircut was shorter than usual and his light blue eyes were electric with excitement. He scrutinized Max and laid a hand on his shoulder. 'You look like you've been to hell and back. What was it like?'

Max didn't know what to say. How could he explain to his father, who didn't believe in love, what it was like to be in its thrall? He couldn't explain it to himself. There had been sublime moments with Isabella Bacci, but his memory of them was overwhelmed by the sensory overload and raw vulnerability he still felt. His forty-eight hours with her had been the most intense of his life – certainly since his mother's death.

It was one thing to dive and surrender to the euphoria of the deep. It was something else to take a drug that stirred feelings he hadn't previously been aware of into turmoil. The experience had threatened every certainty he relied on and he could feel panic welling inside him. He was afraid of nothing in the world but this had come from within himself, which unnerved him.

The drug had made him feel. It had made him care. It had made him weak. He was glad to have returned to his normal self.

His father gave the delighted smile of a teacher who has seen his pupil grasp a valuable lesson. 'I've always warned you about love, Max. Like Professor Bacci himself said, it's a genuine sickness, a plague. Even Plato called love a serious disease of the mind.'

'Well, I'm cured now and I won't go through that again.'

Helmut patted him on the back. 'That's why you should marry Delphine Chevalier.'

'I guess.'

His father's pale eyes lit up. 'So, this nature-identical love really works.'

Helmut's excitement was infectious. 'Yes, Vater. All we have to do now is decide what we want to do with it.'

'Excellent.'

The warm glow of limitless possibility burned within Helmut Kappel. His heir had returned unscathed by the drug, but living proof of its power. Trapani had been silenced. And Joachim, with Comvec, would master Bacci's technology.

'Do you know what this means, Max? The future of Kappel Privatbank is secure. It is exactly what we needed. Professor Bacci's preposterous love drug will save us.' He led Max down to the terrace and poured him a drink. 'The drug allows an individual to possess any person they desire. With it we can make anyone we choose fall helplessly, obsessively in love with anyone else. Our family may have risen above the need for love, but it's still the most powerful, insidious emotion. Think about it, Max! We have the power to grant a client the undying infatuation and devotion of whomever he desires. Not just sex but so-called true love – *for ever*. So long as the client is willing to pay, he can possess anyone his heart desires. Anyone in the world.' He thought through the implications. 'But that's not all. We can even decide *who* he desires. We can control the entire market – demand *and* supply.'

'It's important that we keep the drug's existence secret,' said Max, '*especially* from our clients. We can sell them its effects and benefits but never the drug itself. We must always administer it ourselves, covertly, without their knowledge.'

Helmut nodded. 'As we've done consistently with poisons.'

'Exactly. This plays to our strengths and also means we maintain complete control over the drug and its effects, allowing us to use it again and again.'

Helmut scratched his chin. 'How do we convince clients that the drug works without telling them about it?'

'By using emotional blackmail. We give each client a free trial – an irresistible, addictive taste of the drug's benefits – and once they're hooked we threaten to take it away. Unless they pay. A lot.'

Helmut smiled. 'We could hold a blind auction. Make each client bid against himself.'

'Yes,' agreed Max. 'We could invite them to a secluded controlled location, perhaps an exclusive alpine hotel like the one in Zermatt we booked a couple of years ago. You remember when we held a skiing weekend for select clients?'

Helmut stood up and paced the terrace as Max reached for his laptop. 'We tell our target clients it's a loyalty weekend, a thank-you,' he said, 'and we inject each of them with the genetic profile of a pre-selected woman. We let their desire grow, then introduce the women. For two whole days their hearts' desires are sated and they gain a glimpse of heaven. Finally, when the trial period ends we explain that an auction is in play.' He was warming to the scheme. 'They won't know they haven't any competition. Our lovesick clients will bid whatever we demand to secure the love of their lives. The fear of losing the greatest happiness they've ever known will be too much to resist. And since they'll know nothing of our drug we can use it on other clients, again and again. We both know who the first clients should be.'

As Max bent over the laptop and accessed the bank's client database, Helmut listed the names, 'Hudsucker, Corbasson, Lysenko, Nadolny. The bastards who snubbed our bicentennial celebrations and threaten to close their accounts. How much is each of them worth? In total – not just the accounts they have with us.'

Max checked their records. 'Each has assets in excess of one billon US dollars,' he said. 'Two in excess of three billion.'

'Excellent. We'll punish them *and* take their money.'

For the rest of the evening, and throughout the long cool night, Helmut sat on the terrace with his firstborn, drinking malt whisky and plotting how best to exploit the drug. They made notes, researched the target clients, and argued over what had to be done. By the time the sun rose over the lake they had arrived at a strategy with which he was satisfied.

At six thirty in the morning Helmut wiped his eyes. 'So we know what *we* want to do with Professor Bacci's drug, but what do we tell him?'

'Whatever he wants to hear,' said Max. 'I'll develop a dummy business plan that reflects his vision. He need never know what we're really going to do with the drug.'

Helmut sipped his whisky. 'In that case I suggest we call a family meeting next week.'

'That'll allow me time to go to Bacci's laboratory in Turin and check out what he's got,' Max said. 'I'll take Joachim with me – I'll brief him tomorrow.'

Helmut put down his glass. He had remembered something Bacci had said at their first meeting, which had seeded an idea of such preposterous, towering ambition that he had to check with Joachim whether it was even feasible. He certainly didn't want to tell Max about it yet. 'Let me brief Joachim. I'll explain how our plan depends on controlling the technology behind the drug, and reducing our dependence on the professor. Just make sure when you see Bacci that you reassure him we want him as a client.'

Helmut reached for a copy of *Vogue*, which was lying on the table. He opened it at a page he had marked earlier with a yellow Post-it. He studied it avidly and smiled. Although he had been up all night he felt younger than he had in years. He poured the remnants of the Glenmorangie into Max's glass, then raised his own in a toast.

At that moment Eva walked out on to the terrace in a silk kimono and sandals. Her hair was brushed back off her face and she wore full makeup even though she had just got out of bed. At the sight of the empty whisky bottle and the papers strewn over the teak table, her face screwed up in disgust. 'Have you two been out here all night?'

Helmut nodded and cast his eyes down at *Vogue*.

She picked up the empty whisky bottle between finger and thumb and held it away from her as if it was a dead rat. She glared at Helmut. 'Can I get you anything? Or have you had enough?'

Helmut's shoulders tensed. 'There is only one thing I need from you, Eva,' he rasped.

'Yes?'

'An immediate divorce.'

21

8 September

The Agnelli Business Park was in the northern suburbs of Turin, next to a dense wood of tall cypresses etched against a flawless blue sky. As Max drove up to the entrance and checked in with the gatehouse he scanned the nondescript boxlike buildings. A white sign showed a map of the park with a unit number beside each building. Bacci Projects was at unit twelve.

The site was quiet, although the car parks were full. Most of the businesses appeared to be software start-ups with gimmicky logos and American-sounding names: RiverSoft, Mountain View Solutions, Net Ark. He drove past a building with the logo VirtualX emblazoned down one side in black and gold letters, to a plain warehouse at the end of the site. There were no signs outside it, just a small white peg with '12' painted in red, protruding from the sun-browned grass. It hardly seemed the most fertile seedbed for a cutting-edge, world-changing technology. There was a lone car outside and a Cannondale mountain bike locked to a rack by the main door. He recognized the BMW convertible as Joachim's. His half-brother was in the driver's seat, waiting. Beneath his dark suit he wore a scarlet and cobalt blue Liberty print bow-tie with matching waistcoat. Max hadn't seen him since his trip to Antibes.

As they walked together to the main door, Joachim lit a black cigarette and flashed a knowing smile. 'So, Romeo, I wonder how Professor Bacci feels about what you and his only daughter got up to in Antibes?'

Max frowned. 'Let me deal with Bacci. You concentrate on checking out the equipment and the technical side.'

Joachim adjusted his glasses, but his smile didn't fade. 'Whatever.'

Bacci was waiting for them in the foyer. He wore a suit under his white lab coat and beamed at Max. Helmut had already notified him of the experiment's success but Max guessed he would have asked Isabella about her holiday.

Bacci waited for Joachim to extinguish his cigarette, then led them along a white, featureless corridor to a set of metal security doors. Max was surprised that the only security was a coded electronic lock, activated by a simple keypad. He had half expected a DNA or retinal scanner. 'I've sent my technician home so we can talk freely,' Bacci said, punching in a code and opening the door.

The immaculate white laboratory and gleaming apparatus were in total contrast to the bland, rundown exterior. The building and security might be unimpressive, but the contents were evidently world class. Beside him, Joachim nodded appreciatively; even Max could see that it easily matched what Joachim had at Comvec. The laboratory space seemed to be divided into two sections, on the right there were two doors and a host of stand-alone apparatus. The glass door at the far end of the right wall bore a yellow biohazard symbol and a notice: 'Warning! Level 2 Viral Agents'. The red door half-way down had 'Samples' etched into its glass windowpane. The left side of the laboratory contained what looked like a small production line.

'All our working practices have been officially sanctioned.' Bacci pointed to the glass door on the right. 'The small biocontainment lab isn't approved for level three or four hot agents, but it's okay up to level two, which is all we need for developing basic viral vectors.'

'You're welcome to use one of Comvec's smart vectors,' Joachim said.

Bacci smiled. 'I'm more than happy for you to suggest improvements but the two genetically engineered viruses I've been using are fine. Both get the genes into the host cells' DNA, and that's all they need to do. The Sixty-nine vector targets the short-living somatic cells and the Seventy-two targets the lifetime stem cells. Where I need help from Kappel Privatbank and Comvec is in funding, organizing clinical trials to satisfy the various regulatory bodies, and commercial advice on how best to launch the product.'

'We can do that,' Max said.

Bacci walked down the middle of the room. 'In simple terms three processes are required to make the drug. First we isolate and recombine the genes we want to insert into the target cell's DNA. This is the active ingredient of the NiL drug, the engineered DNA patch that overwrites the genetic code currently in the target cell, instructing new levels of hormone and brain chemical production and inserting the genetic facial blueprint of the love object.

'Second, we need to create an appropriate viral vector, which as you know is essentially an attenuated virus.'

'Attenuated?' Max asked.

'Tamed. Made harmless,' explained Joachim. 'Basically a virus is a non-thinking parcel of genetic material wrapped in protein, which exists to seek out hosts to reproduce itself. When it finds a host with receptive cells it enters one and usurps its genetic code, replacing it with its own. Then, when the cell containing the new viral DNA divides and replicates, the virus copies itself and spreads throughout the body.

'An attenuated virus has had its harmful DNA removed, leaving just the empty protein envelope, which can then be filled with therapeutic human genes and chemically addressed to specific cells in the human body. Therefore the properties that make a virus so dangerous also make it ideal for delivering new genes, namely its accurate targeting mechanism and its ability to replace the DNA in a host's cell with its own.'

'Exactly,' said Bacci. 'And the third process required to produce the NiL drug entails what Joachim has just said. We take the recombined genetic material from the first process – the NiL genes – and insert them into the attenuated viral vector from the second process and, hey presto, we have our magic bullet.' He pointed to the equipment on the right of the laboratory. 'The apparatus on this side is used to isolate and recombine the NiL genes, and the biocontainment lab is where we create the viral vectors.' He pointed to the left. 'The small pilot production plant on this side of the lab brings everything together and produces the drug in powder form.'

'Very impressive,' Joachim said. 'Everything from the Gallencamp incubators to the Genescope are top quality. No wonder you need more funding.' He pointed to a matt black swan-like machine on the right side of the laboratory. 'Is that Genescope a version eight?'

Bacci nodded. 'I need at least an eight for the speed and accuracy. It's been modified too. Come.' He walked over to the machine, which looked like a cross between a computer and a large microscope. Attached to it was a smaller, scanner-like device, with a white horizontal area that reminded

Max of a photocopier, and a monitor. 'Embedded in the DNA of every cell in our bodies is a copy of our entire genome, the unique genetic code that specifies every physiological aspect of our individual makeup. This code has an alphabet of four letters, A, G, T and C, which stand for the four base chemicals adenine, guanine, thymine and cytosine. These letters spell out words – genes – which in turn spell out our entire sentence of life, our genome.'

He smiled at Max. 'A human genome is about three billion letters long. These letters contain almost a hundred thousand genes. Genes don't actually *do* anything themselves. They're just code. But this code instructs every aspect of our physiological development – how our hair grows, how we age, how our cells divide, how we digest our food. We are born with this software, inherited from our parents, but with gene therapy we are learning how to overwrite and correct the programming when it goes wrong.'

He tapped the black Genescope. 'This can read a biological sample and translate the entire genome contained within it. A hair follicle is all it needs.' He pointed to the scanner device. 'This attachment focuses only on the part of the genome that codes for the human face. This allows the Genescope readings to be faster and more precise.' He pulled a hair from his head and placed it on the flat scanning surface, a shallow white tray filled with clear liquid gel. 'The gel isolates all contaminants and helps break down the sample for analysis.' He pressed a button on the swan's neck and a humming filled the air. The tray glowed with a blue, almost ultraviolet light, and less than a minute later the monitor on the side of the device flickered. Then Carlo Bacci's face appeared.

'The technology's similar to that found on most security scanners, except it's far more precise. Also, it doesn't just read the code, it extracts the relevant genetic material and splices it with the NiL genes.'

Joachim nodded, then glanced at the red door marked 'Samples'. 'Have you kept all your past versions of the drug?'

'Oh, yes. All versions, including my mistakes, are in the refrigerated sample room. There's a rogue's gallery of weird and wonderful cocktails in there. I never throw anything away.'

'I'd love to see them some time. Can I look inside?'

Bacci laughed again. 'Sure. If you really want to.'

For the next forty-five minutes Bacci went through every detailed step of the development and production process. Afterwards, Max followed him to his office and left Joachim to explore the rest of the laboratory and the sample room.

As Bacci sat down at his desk and directed Max to a chair, he was torn between relief and excitement. He had aborted his plan to give Leo the drug. Isabella had said she didn't want him back. But giving Max *and* her the drug had been a different matter. In agreeing to her involvement, he had used her as an unwitting guinea pig. He had been wrestling with his conscience ever since.

He was convinced that a holiday romance would do her no harm and from her own account he had been right. But he had been on tenterhooks until her return from Antibes. Since her mother's death they had shared most things, and as soon as she had mentioned a brief romance with a man who had saved her from vicious thugs, he had felt better. If he hadn't involved her, Max wouldn't have been there to help her. And, of course, the episode had secured the Kappels' support for his drug.

'What now, Max?'

'The Kappel board meet next week to finalize our proposal. After that I'll report back to you with a full business plan – and funding. You'll have to sign some forms and Joachim will work alongside you for a few months. He understands your area and will prove invaluable when we seek the necessary approvals. The EU and the FDA are going to be all over this so we've got to make sure our application's unimpeachable. With Joachim liaising on the technical side and myself handling the commercial aspects, we can ensure that nothing slips through the cracks. Even so, it'll still take time. You'll have to be patient – you also have to get rid of your lab technician. Joachim will be here to help and we can't allow the chance of a leak. Only employ technicians as and when you need them. And never the same one twice. Okay?'

'Okay.' Bacci smiled. 'How did it go in Antibes?'

Max pursed his lips and flushed. 'You were right. I fell in love with your daughter. And forty-eight hours later I fell out of love.' He spoke matter-of-factly as if he were discussing a profit-and-loss statement.

His obvious discomfort amused Bacci. 'How's your arm?'

'Fine.'

'She told me you saved her life. Thank you for that. It makes me feel better about involving her.' Max said nothing. For all the man's reserve and control, Bacci sensed deep, repressed passion in him. 'As a matter of interest, did you save my daughter's life before or after you took NiL Sixty-nine.'

'Does it matter?'

'You tell me.'

Max changed the subject. 'I need to ask you a favour, Professor Bacci. It's a delicate matter.'

'Yes?'

'My father and his wife are unhappy. They're contemplating divorce and wondered if you could help.' He reached into his jacket pocket and pulled out two small plastic bags. Each contained a single human hair. 'The follicles are intact. They would have come themselves, but they are proud and this is a difficult—'

Bacci raised his hand. 'Do they *both* want this? Your father and his wife?'

Max handed over an envelope. 'In here you will find a signed letter.'

He opened the envelope. The letter was a formal request for 'treatment' signed by both parties. 'Tell them it will be my pleasure. This is exactly what I developed NiL for.'

'Thank you.' Max paused. 'One more thing. On this occasion they request that you use NiL Seventy-two – the permanent version.'

22

10 September

The still night air was heavy with the acrid perfume of cigar smoke. After the monthly meeting with the non-family senior directors at Kappel Privatbank's offices, the family had retired to the *Schloss* to discuss the non-legitimate side of the business. Dinner was over and the men had withdrawn to the terrace where a white-jacketed manservant walked among them with a silver tray and four glasses: brandy for Helmut, Joachim and Klaus; malt whisky for Max. The Kappel women had withdrawn to the drawing room with Delphine Chevalier.

Helmut used the assassin's blade to cut off the tip of his cigar, then offered it to Max. He rarely offered anyone his cigarettes or cigars so this was an honour.

'Smoke with me, Max. You don't inhale cigars so it won't damage your diver's lungs.' Max hesitated, then accepted the cigar in the spirit in which it was given. As his father flicked his lighter and lit it for him, he could feel Joachim's eyes burn into him.

Once the servant had left and Helmut had closed the terrace doors, Klaus asked the question everyone had been avoiding throughout dinner. 'Where's Eva?'

Helmut sucked on his cigar. 'I'm divorcing her. The papers are prepared. You'll understand why in a moment. But, first, I need to tell you something.'

'What?'

Helmut gestured for Klaus to sit down. Max and Joachim joined him. Helmut remained standing. 'This family made its fortune and won its place in the world by understanding and exploiting two of man's most primal fears and desires – death and greed.' He looked at each of them in turn. 'As assassins in Italy we were successful, but we were still servants meting out death for our masters. Fortunately, our ancestor Dieter Kappel understood that any organism must evolve or die. So we evolved beyond servants and became business partners, bankers. For two hundred years we have enjoyed unprecedented wealth, status and success, making our clients and ourselves rich.

'Now we stand at another crossroads. Some of our clients, men whose wealth we created, threaten to close their accounts and withdraw their funds. Again we face extinction, and again we must evolve or die. Comvec was initiated to take us to the next level, but Comvec alone won't save us in time. It is no longer enough to be our clients' partners. We must now become their masters. We must use our expertise, in death and money, to exploit man's greatest weakness, his heart's desire, which we have the power not only to satisfy but to control. Love.'

'Love?' said Klaus, scratching his white beard. 'I don't understand.'

When Helmut had summarized Professor Bacci's project, Klaus frowned and crossed his arms, as sceptical as Max had been.

'Think about it, Klaus,' Helmut said. 'Imagine the chance to possess *any* woman or man in the world. Not just sexually, but their heart, their undying devotion. Who could resist that?'

'But does it work?'

'The science does,' said Joachim, from his seat on Helmut's left. He began to explain how the drug worked technically, but Klaus ignored him. 'Max, what do you think?'

Max shrugged. 'I thought it was bullshit too.' He gave a rueful smile. 'Until I tried it.'

Klaus shifted his heavy frame and uncrossed his arms. 'What happened?'

'Trust me, Klaus, it works . . .' he said, and told him about Antibes. His uncle's eyes gleamed.

'Joachim is checking out the technology,' Helmut said, 'and Max has devised two business plans. We will present one to Bacci and the other we will develop for ourselves. The Bacci plan will be a typical development schedule, including clinical trials and launch proposals. Naturally the timetable will stretch across many years, as it does with all drug-development programmes, and of course it will never happen. Our own covert proposal for using the drug will ensure that its existence is kept secret and we retain its powers.'

'But what do we do with it?' Klaus asked. 'Put an ad in the paper – "Love for Sale"?'

Helmut smiled. 'Not exactly.' He reached into a briefcase, pulled out four pale blue folders and passed them round. 'This is an outline of the project.'

Max opened his copy of the document he had helped to prepare. The project name, written on the cover in bold black type, was his choice, but he didn't recognize some of the later sections.

'From now on we only refer to the project by its name,' Helmut said.

'Ilium?' queried Klaus.

'It's the original Greek name for Troy,' Max said, 'as in Helen, the most desired woman in the classical world. When Paris of Troy stole her from her husband, the Greeks waged the Trojan war to win her back. The passion she aroused epitomizes the potential power of this drug.'

Helmut continued: 'We involve no Kappel Privatbank employees in the details of Ilium, only we four. No one else must know about the drug, especially the clients to whom we sell its benefits.'

Max listened as his father outlined the plan they had developed on the night he returned from France. The four major clients who had threatened to leave the bank – Corbasson, Lysenko, Hudsucker and Nadolny – would be the first guinea pigs. They would unwittingly receive the permanent NiL #072 drug, primed with the facial imprints of four unsuspecting women, and would then be invited to a discreet weekend retreat to meet the objects of their obsessive desire. The women would be injected secretly with the temporary NiL #069 drug, imprinted with the faces of their matching suitors, and for two days their obsessive passions would be sated. Finally, on the eve of departure, when the temporary drug was fading from the women's systems, each permanently affected client would be informed that an auction was in play and to secure his partner's lifelong love he must match a particular bid. In fact he would have no rivals and would be bidding against himself.

Max and his father had agreed on a small, controlled low-profile trial. But as Helmut described the scheme, Max realized that his father had embellished it.

'To attract our target clients, we must hold a high-profile event that symbolizes the drug's potency,' Helmut said. 'An event that pre-selects the women we wish to partner with our targets. It must be held in a venue that is both glamorous and self-contained, ensuring that everyone accepts their invitation and we maintain control of the environment.'

'Why does it have to be so high-profile?' Max said. 'I thought the idea was to keep this quiet. Extract payment discreetly from the first four clients, learn from any mistakes, then move on to others.'

Klaus was looking appalled. 'I agree with Max. Surely we need to use stealth with this, not draw attention to ourselves.'

Helmut raised his hands. 'Stealth with the drug, yes, but not the stage upon which we sell it. Our targets are busy, self-important men. We have to lure them to the auction, and once there we have to convince them that *we alone* have the power to grant them the love they crave. We must show our hand a little. Otherwise why should they believe us? Or pay us?'

'But it was supposed to be a trial.'

'Where's your courage, Max?' Joachim said suddenly.

Max turned to his effete brother. He took in the bright bowtie and the light in his eyes. Joachim had already discussed this with their father, he thought, perhaps even encouraged the more flamboyant developments. 'This isn't about courage.'

'No, it's about common sense,' Klaus agreed.

'Relax, Klaus,' Helmut said. 'Sometimes you have to risk a little to gain a lot.'

'What is the high-profile event that will symbolize the drug's potency?'

Helmut smiled. 'A wedding,' he said. 'A Kappel wedding.'

Max understood. He remembered the suggestion his father had made while they were discussing their plans for the NiL drug.

Klaus was bemused. 'Max is finally marrying Delphine Chevalier? How high-profile is that going to be?'

Helmut groaned. 'No, Klaus, Max isn't marrying Delphine Chevalier.' He took a copy of *Vogue* out of his briefcase, opened it at the page marked with a yellow Post-it and placed it on the table.

Max watched Klaus study the magazine. He looked up at his brother in evident incredulity. 'Her, Helmut?'

'Now do you understand?'

PART 2

ILIUM

23

1 October

Isabella Bacci stood outside the children's ward at Milan University Hospital and said goodbye to Sofia. She was happy the child was going home and that she had helped her parents come to terms with her prosopagnosia, although she wished she could have done more.

'Sofia, thank the doctor for all her help.'

Sofia shyly gave Isabella a folded card. On the front she had drawn a woman in a white doctor's coat. Isabella opened it and read: 'I won't forget you, Dr Isabella. Thank you. Love Sofia.'

She hugged the little girl. 'And I won't forget you, Sofia.'

Sofia's father shook Isabella's hand. 'Thank you so much, Dr Bacci.' He pointed to the Amigo extract in the refrigerated cabinet. 'When you need volunteers for trials, please call me. I want to help you find a cure, and I'd like to understand Sofia's condition better.'

'Thanks. When I get clearance from the ethical committee I'll do that.'

As they walked through the security doors Sofia's father stopped again and tapped the DNA palm pad. 'And don't forget what I told you. If the hospital wants to upgrade its security system I can do a deal on the InterFace 3500.'

'I won't forget.' She watched them walk hand in hand with their daughter down the long hospital corridor to the outside world. She stood still for a few moments after they had gone, looking at Sofia's card. Finally, she slipped it into her breast pocket and checked her watch.

Tonight she had front-row seats to watch Phoebe on the catwalk at one of the premier shows of Milan's autumn fashion week. Afterwards she was joining her and some other friends for dinner, including Kathryn Walker and Gisele Steele, the A-list movie star who had become a firm friend of Phoebe's after they had worked together on a charity project. The evening promised to be glamorous and trivial, a perfect antidote to her daily work.

As she walked through Accident and Emergency, an oncologist who had flirted with her since she arrived at the hospital smiled at her, but after Leo and Max she wanted a break from men. For the time being she would concentrate on her work. After Antibes, the only thing she was sure about was that she was definitely over Leo. But she was at a loss as to how Max could have been so passionate at one moment and so detached the next. That she had felt the same didn't make it any easier to understand.

She was annoyed with herself for thinking about Max. Phoebe had seen him at Odin's offices last week – apparently the designer was one of his clients. Until Phoebe had mentioned this she had almost managed to put him out of her mind.

In the locker room she collected her personal items. She had just enough time to go home and change. A nurse popped her head round the door. 'Dr Bacci, a man rang for you. He said it was personal.' She handed Isabella a folded piece of paper.

Max?

Isabella's heart pounded when she read the last line of the note. 'Please call him back on his cellphone.' Cellphone was underlined twice. Then she opened the paper. Her heart sank. 'Leo called.'

She screwed up the note and threw it into the bin.

24

Isabella changed into a simple midnight-blue Nicole Farhi dress, the one piece of genuine designer clothing she owned, and arrived at the imposing gates of the Palazzo Farnese just before the Odin show was due to start.

The Norwegian designer's show was one of the hottest tickets in Milan fashion week. The press delighted in portraying him as a mad, extravagant genius and from what his favourite Valkyrie, Phoebe, had told Isabella, they weren't wrong. His latest folly had been to buy an entire fjord near the Arctic Circle in his native Norway, complete with an island, upon which he had built a fairy-tale crystal palace called Valhalla.

Through the iron gates she could see that a crowd had already gathered in the courtyard, eating canapés and drinking champagne. As she scoured the faces for anyone she recognized she experienced a rush of panic. Many looked familiar, but only because they were famous. She felt like a child on her first day at a new school.

She handed her invitation to a hard-faced, stick-thin PR woman, who looked her up and down. 'Who are you? Which magazine are you with? Are you with the sponsors?'

'I'm just a friend,' Isabella said.

'A friend?' the woman repeated slowly, as though struggling to understand the concept.

'I wouldn't let her in if I was you,' said a soft American voice. 'Unlike you and me, she's just a doctor who saves lives.' It was Kathryn and she was with Gisele. They took her hands and pulled her to join them. Isabella took pleasure in the now fawning, flustered expression on the PR woman's face.

Gisele Steele was blessed with a figure that looked voluptuous on screen but model-thin in real life. She had beautiful coffee-coloured skin, large dark eyes and a short bob. 'Nice to meet you, Isabella. I'm Gisele. Sorry I missed out on Antibes – I heard you all had a blast.' Isabella liked her smile and that, despite her fame, she had introduced herself.

There was just time for a glass of champagne before they were herded into the great hall of the palazzo where the show was to take place. They had front-row seats and Isabella tried not to stare at Madonna and Jennifer Lopez.

'Look!' Kathryn whispered in her ear, and pointed.

She glanced at the far end of the front row

and saw two men taking their seats. She recognized the taller, younger man instantly and her heart somersaulted. What was Max Kappel doing here? Unconsciously she flicked back her hair and smoothed her dress. He looked even more handsome than she remembered, and she felt both relief and disappointment when he didn't meet her eyes. The lights dimmed, Wagner's 'Flight of the Valkyrie' faded in, and a murmur of anticipation rose from the audience.

When Phoebe appeared Isabella had to quell the impulse to cheer. Her friend wore a gilt band around her forehead and her gold-blonde hair hung loose to her shoulders. Exquisite frosted mascara, eyeliner and blood-red lipstick transformed her beautiful face into that of a warrior queen. A fur cape was draped round her shoulders, fastened with a huge gold clasp, over a tight bodice of gold fabric that resembled a breastplate and accentuated every curve. A short, reindeer-fur skirt showed off her long legs, and on her feet she wore open gilt sandals, with tendril-like straps that snaked up her calves and heels that added at least three inches to her six-foot frame.

Isabella had once read that Phoebe was not only the most beautiful of models but also the most graceful, which was why she was so highly prized by designers. When she passed Isabella she kept her eyes straight ahead. At the end of the catwalk she performed two complete turns, then walked back.

On her return, Phoebe moved her head slowly from side to side. She looked imperious and untouchable. As she passed Isabella again something, or someone, in the audience made her lose her legendary poise. Like a startled thoroughbred, she stumbled and fell to her knees. There was a collective gasp, then spontaneous applause as she rose to her feet and regained her composure. For a moment, though, Isabella saw an expression of shock on her friend's face. When she followed Phoebe's gaze, she saw that her eyes were on Max Kappel. But as she continued along the catwalk, Isabella realized her friend wasn't looking at Max but at the older man beside him. From his colouring and appearance, he could only be Max's father.

25

Two hours later

What the hell was going on? The question looped in Isabella's mind as she was ushered to her seat in the small, exclusive Aimo e Nadia restaurant on Via Montecuccoli.

After the show, Isabella, Gisele and Kathryn had gone backstage but Phoebe had been surrounded by admirers. The show had been a great success and, after heaping profuse praise on his brave muse for soldiering on even though she had sprained her ankle in the fall, Odin had invited his circle to his favourite Milanese restaurant to celebrate.

When Odin directed everyone to the table, he sat Phoebe between himself and Max Kappel's father. Helmut Kappel's unblinking eyes were of the palest blue and his facial expression as impassive as granite. For some unfathomable reason the level-headed Phoebe, who had fended off advances from the most desirable suitors in the world, was flirting with him – a man old enough to be her father. As if that wasn't bad enough, Isabella had been separated from Gisele and Kathryn and stranded at the far end of the table, opposite Max.

She took a long sip of wine – getting drunk seemed like a good idea. 'Max, what a surprise – I wouldn't have thought this was your scene.'

He smiled. 'Odin's our client.' He glanced at his father, who was laughing with Phoebe and Odin. 'We've supported him since he was a struggling unknown, so it's good to share in his success.' At that moment Phoebe leaned across and whispered something in Helmut Kappel's ear. The act was as intimate as a kiss and Isabella had to look away. Why was Phoebe behaving like this? She was constantly aware of being in the public gaze and was famously discreet with her boyfriends. Isabella caught Kathryn's eye. She, too, had noticed Phoebe's behaviour.

'How old is your father?' she asked Max.

'Old enough.'

'In Antibes you said he was married.'

He nodded. 'He was. Three times. His divorce from number three is due to come through any day now.' He looked over her shoulder to the far corner of the restaurant. 'A man over there keeps looking at us. He's trying to be discreet, but the woman he's with has noticed and now she's looking at us too. At first I thought they were celebrity-spotting, but I think they're checking you out.'

'Me?' She glanced round and saw Leo with Giovanna. She almost choked on her wine. Could

189

the evening get any worse? She stood up and wiped the wine off her dress.

Max stood. 'You okay? Can I get you anything?'

'No, thanks,' she said, trying not to look as flustered as she felt. 'Excuse me.'

She had to stop herself running to the Ladies', where she stood by the basin and dabbed at her dress with cold water, then stood by the hand-dryer until the dark stain faded. She wanted to go home, but this was Phoebe's evening. She braced herself, opened the door and stepped out.

Leo stood in front of her. She had always thought him handsome, but not tonight. Where his face had once seemed sensitive it now looked weak. His aura appeared diminished. She couldn't help comparing his boyishness unfavourably with Max's brooding charisma.

'Did you get my message?' he said. He glanced furtively over his shoulder. 'I've missed you – I should never have let you go.'

'You didn't let me go, Leo. You dumped me.'

'I made a mistake.'

A few weeks ago Isabella would have given anything to hear Leo say those words, but now they angered her. She looked across the restaurant and saw Giovanna rise from their table. 'Does *she* know she's a mistake?'

'It's her birthday. That's why we're here. She wanted to go to the best restaurant in Milan. I can't tell her yet. I don't want to hurt her.'

'You didn't have a problem hurting *me*, Leo, but

I was only the fiancée who'd travelled half-way across the world to marry you.'

He gestured towards Odin's table and Max. 'Is he your new . . . ?'

Isabella almost laughed. 'For Christ's sake, Leo, leave me alone.' She tried to walk past him, but now Giovanna was in her path. She had been drinking.

'Leave him alone, you bitch,' Giovanna hissed. 'Why can't you accept that Leo doesn't want you any more?'

Isabella groaned. 'Don't do this, Giovanna. If you want to shout at someone, shout at him. He's the one doing the harassing.'

Giovanna's eyes went to Leo, then back to her, and Isabella almost felt sorry for her. Then Giovanna raised a hand – but a larger one gripped her wrist.

'Is everything okay, Isabella?' Max said.

'Fine,' she said, through gritted teeth.

Max offered Leo Giovanna's hand. 'I think you should take her home.'

Leo glared at him but something in Max's tone made him lead Giovanna away.

When Isabella was back in her seat, Kathryn leaned across the table to her. 'How many more of your exes are you planning on seeing tonight?'

Isabella rolled her eyes. 'Two's enough.'

'You okay?'

Isabella raised her glass. 'I'll survive. But if Billy Bohannon from school turns up I'm outta here.'

By the time Max returned to his seat the wine had loosened her tongue. Her pride told her to say nothing, but another part of her knew that if she didn't resolve this now it would haunt her. 'What happened between us in Antibes, Max?'

Max blinked. Then he sat forward, palms together, fingers forming a steeple: he had become the banker about to tell a client why he couldn't advance them a loan. 'I'm not sure.' He gave a controlled smile. 'All I know is that it was a wonderful moment of madness.'

She was surprised by how much his clinical dismissal of the episode hurt her. Every last shred of her remaining pride demanded that she change the subject. But she couldn't. She glanced down the table to where the others were immersed in their own conversations. 'I've had crushes and holiday romances before, Max, but this was different. More intense and consuming than anything I ever felt. And I thought you felt it too.' She lowered her voice. 'We said we loved each other, Max. I don't know about you, but I've never said that to anyone before and not meant it.'

'I've *never* said it before,' he said. 'But it was a mistake.'

'A *mistake*?'

Something flashed in his eyes. Then it was gone. 'I don't do love.'

'You don't "do love"?' She felt her cheeks colouring: he viewed their two days together as something he had endured rather than enjoyed.

'You talk as though it's a choice – a weakness, like cigarettes.'

'Isn't it?' Then his voice softened. 'Can I ask you a personal question, Isabella?'

She almost laughed at his formality. 'Of course.'

'You live your life so passionately – so head on. How do you survive? How do you protect yourself?'

'From what? Love?'

He shrugged.

'No one can protect themselves from that, Max. Not even you.' The expression on his face changed and suddenly he looked like a boy. 'You can't control love, Max.'

'I can try.'

'Why?'

He frowned. 'Because it makes us weak and vulnerable,' he said.

She looked into his blue eyes until he lowered his gaze. Now she thought she understood. Someone had broken his heart. But, then, whose heart hadn't been broken at least once? 'I disagree. Love doesn't necessarily make you weak. It can make you strong – make you want to be a better person.' She stood up to leave. 'You wonder how I survive "doing love"? Well, I'm not unusual. People "do love" all the time.'

As Max watched Isabella move down the table to say goodbye to her friends, he felt an unsettling blend of frustration and admiration. How could someone so smart, passionate and brave be naïve enough to believe love made you stronger?

He admired her, though. She might be an idealist but she had steel too. She didn't flinch from living her beliefs, however flawed. He wondered how Leo could have chosen the wealthy, bland Giovanna over her, then saw that he was about to do the same thing. His safe choice was Delphine Chevalier: she would further the Kappel interests and didn't threaten his emotional status quo. Yet Leo apparently regretted his choice and wanted Isabella back – it seemed that playing it safe carried its own risks.

Max felt an uncharacteristic stab of sadness that Isabella, with all her intelligence, should be so deluded as to think you couldn't control love. Her father's drug had destroyed that myth. He glanced at Phoebe and almost sighed. Controlling love was depressingly easy.

It had been child's play to inject Phoebe covertly with the permanent version of the NiL drug. Odin was a loyal client who had never forgotten how Kappel Privatbank's funding and business consultancy had helped him succeed in the cut-throat fashion world. Max's regular financial update with him had been in the diary for months, and when he had voiced an interest in meeting Phoebe, the Norwegian designer had been delighted to schedule his star model's fitting session so that it followed their meeting. He had shaken her hand, held it a fraction longer than usual – and that was all the opportunity he needed to deliver it. Arranging the encounter between Phoebe and his father at the fashion show had been simpler still. As for love making you stronger, he had only to look at the devotion in Phoebe's eyes now to see how false that was. Even he had been surprised by the dramatic way in which she had fallen in love at first sight. Love had enslaved Phoebe Davenport, but in his father's eyes he had seen only triumph and lust. As Ilium progressed, Isabella would learn for herself how ruthlessly love could be controlled.

He had once heard someone say that the more love you gave the more you got back. But that wasn't true. His mother had given more than anyone and received little in return. Love was a tryanny that benefited the loved, never the lover.

He watched Isabella say goodbye to Kathryn Walker and Gisele Steele, then approach Phoebe. Something in her friend's tone must have reached Phoebe and broken the drug's spell, because she tore her eyes away from his father and followed Isabella into the night.

He watched his father frown, and smiled.

26

One hour later

'What is it with me? Just when I get over Leo, and never want to see him again, he comes crawling back. And then the man I think I do want says he doesn't want me because he doesn't "do love".'

Phoebe poured Isabella another glass of Amaretto. 'There's no logic with love.'

Isabella sipped her drink, willing it to calm her. Being in Phoebe's kitchen helped. Like the rest of her open-plan penthouse, it was warm and welcoming: natural wood and Italian tiles complemented by pale terracotta walls. Beyond the kitchen and the spacious living area, a large window opened on to a roof terrace and presented a spectacular view of Milan's Duomo, lit up against the night sky. Inside, the apartment was surprisingly homely for one whose lifestyle was as glamorous and nomadic as Phoebe's. She collected small penguin sculptures and didn't seem to care if they had come out of a Christmas cracker or were exquisite crystal figurines for which she had paid a fortune. There were, however, few pictures of her – except in the bathroom, whose walls were adorned with framed *Vogue* covers. As she liked to say, 'It's hard to take yourself too seriously when you're on the loo.'

Calmer now, Isabella said, 'Thanks for coming back with me. You didn't have to.'

'You're my friend.'

'I know, but I'm sorry if I ruined your night.'

'Don't be stupid. I had a great time.'

Isabella smiled. 'I noticed. What exactly was going on with old man Kappel?'

'He's not that old.'

Isabella couldn't believe it: Phoebe Davenport, the coolest, most desirable model on the planet, was blushing over an encounter with a geriatric. 'C'mon, Phoebe, you can't be serious. This is too weird. He's Max's father, for Christ's sake.'

But Phoebe wasn't laughing. 'So what? I know it's weird, and I can't explain it, but I've never felt like this before. When I saw his face, it was like I'd always known him. It was electric. I felt this rush – this need to be with him.'

'So what happened to your promise never to let anyone get under your skin until you were good and ready? Remember the Italian count? He was gorgeous, courted you for months and promised you the world, but you said you weren't ready for commitment. Now, after one night, an old guy who smokes like a chimney, speaks like he's chewing sandpaper and has had half as many wives as Henry the Eighth claims your heart. What's going on, Phoebe?'

Phoebe shrugged. 'All I know is that even now I need to see him again. Perhaps he reminds me of my father – maybe I'm looking for a father figure.'

Isabella clinked her glass against Phoebe's. 'Well, good luck, girl.' This was beyond weird, but love didn't obey the rules of logic, and who was she to tell her friend how or who to love? 'Let's just hope Max isn't a chip off the old block and your relationship with a Kappel pans out better than mine did.' She would never forget the thunderbolt when she had seen Max on the beach. Or, even more so, when she had been inches away from death and he had stepped out of the shadows to rescue her. She still marvelled at the contrast between his cold courage against her attackers and his later gentleness. That was why it was so hard to forget or hate him: she had fallen in love with his deeds as much as his looks.

Perhaps that was how it was with Max's father and Phoebe. Because the beautiful Phoebe couldn't possibly have fallen for the old man's face.

27

Three days later

Helmut Kappel stepped out of his chauffeur-driven Mercedes and strode across the car park towards Carlo Bacci's laboratory. He couldn't recall ever having felt so alive. He remembered the look on Phoebe Davenport's face when she had first set eyes on him. The sexual power had surged through him and he had felt like a young buck, the envy of every man. But that wasn't why he was so excited. Phoebe was just an exhilarating stage in the Ilium project, which itself was only the starting point in fulfilling his greater destiny. He was excited because of Joachim's phone call.

From the start of Ilium, Helmut had briefed Joachim discreetly on a related but separate project, and over the last month Joachim had not only worked with Bacci to master his NiL technology but had trawled through the professor's records and samples to find what Helmut sought. Two days ago he had called to say that today he would have something to show him. The prospect was so thrilling that Helmut had arrived early for his up-date meeting with Bacci and Max.

His younger son was waiting for him at the doors to the laboratory, hair neatly brushed, rimless glasses level on his nose, bright bow-tie showing above a white lab coat. 'Professor Bacci's out for lunch, Vati. He'll be back for our meeting at two so we've got at least an hour.' A pause. 'Do you want to wait for Max?'

'No. We'll keep this to ourselves for the time being.'

'As you wish.'

It was the first time Helmut had been into Bacci's laboratory, but he had no interest in the gleaming apparatus as he followed Joachim to the red door.

'This is the sample room. It's an Aladdin's cave.' Joachim opened the door and Helmut felt a blast of cooler air. The storeroom was lined with refrigerated, glass-fronted cabinets filled with vials. Each was clearly labelled 'NiL' with a hash sign, then a number. Below this was a small barcode. 'This room contains every iteration of the NiL drug.'

Helmut ran his fingers over the refrigerated glass cabinets, reading the labels. He tried to remember what number Bacci had said it was. Then his finger settled on NiL #042 and he turned to Joachim. 'Is this it?'

Joachim took a palmtop computer and an electronic wand from a ledge by the door, then extracted a vial from the cabinet. The palmtop beeped as he ran the wand over the barcode at the bottom of the label, and the screen changed. Joachim scanned the text and passed Helmut the palmtop.

Helmut scrolled down the screen, ignoring the scientific jargon, and read the summary notes. Its effects were as Bacci had described, and the hairs stood up on the back of his neck. 'This works? This is the one Bacci tried on himself?'

Joachim nodded, and gestured to the vials around the room. 'He's tried most of them.' He raised the NiL #042 vial in his hand. 'With this one, his exact words were, "It works *too* well." Basically, it's more intense and less discriminating than NiL Sixty-nine or NiL Seventy-two. It features the same obsessive-love aspects, but none of the sexual chemistry. NiL Forty-two has no gender bias.' Joachim smiled at Helmut, then reached into his coat pocket and extracted a PowerDermic vaccine gun. 'As you requested, Vati, I made this up at Comvec. It's NiL Forty-two imprinted with your genetic facial code.'

Helmut took the primed vaccine gun and rested it in his palm. It felt warm on his cold skin.

'As you asked, I used the same stock vector that Bacci uses for the permanent NiL Seventy-two. It'll insert the genes into the subject's stem cells and last for his or her lifetime.'

'But you could use a different vector? One you've developed at Comvec?'

Joachim narrowed his eyes. 'Given time, I could use any vector to deliver the genes. But why—'

Before he could say more, Helmut embraced his son, clasped the back of his neck with his right hand, and pulled his head close to his own. 'You've done well, Joachim, very well,' he whispered. 'I won't forget this.'

At first Joachim looked shocked. Then he flushed with pride. Helmut couldn't remember when, if ever, he had embraced either of his sons. When he stepped back, he kept his left hand on Joachim's shoulder. With the other he slipped the now spent vaccine gun into his jacket pocket. If he was to fulfil his dream, he needed Joachim's unquestioning loyalty. And by tomorrow morning he would have it. 'Say nothing of this to anyone.'

'Not even to Max?'

He squeezed his son's shoulder. 'Not even to Max. This is *our* secret.'

Joachim beamed, and Helmut could almost see his son grow in stature. 'Is this a new project, Vati? Separate from Ilium?'

Kappel paused. 'I see it more as a sub-project.' He thought of the possibilities and a frisson ran through him. He would not only match Dieter Kappel's achievements in furthering the Kappel dynasty, he would eclipse them.

'What do we call it?'

Helmut shrugged. 'Keep it simple. Name it after the goddess of love, Venus.'

Joachim grinned. 'What's it about? Who are you going to use the drug on?'

'I'll tell you everything tomorrow, including the refinements I need you to make. And don't forget – we keep this to ourselves.'

His younger son rubbed the back of his neck absently as he nodded. Then the door to the main laboratory opened and he ushered Helmut out of the sample room.

When Max entered the laboratory and saw his father's hand laid casually on his half-brother's shoulder, he sensed that something significant had occurred between them, from which he had been excluded. The trademark cravat his father used to hide the cancer scar on his throat was a brighter silk than usual, and its pattern was similar to Joachim's bow-tie. And Helmut's new, more youthful haircut made him look uncannily like his younger son. It was as if they were wearing a matching uniform and the effect increased Max's irrational but growing feeling of isolation.

Since the night of the fashion show he and his father hadn't discussed Phoebe or what had happened. Helmut hadn't even acknowledged Max's role in bringing them together – and now he seemed to be favouring Joachim, as though his half-brother were leading the project.

'Have I missed anything?' he asked.

His father shook his head. 'No, you're just in time.'

Max kept his face impassive. 'Bacci here?'

'Having lunch with his fiancée,' Joachim told him. 'Said he was making some last-minute arrangements for his wedding.' He grinned at his father. 'Everyone seems to be getting married these days.'

Max heard the door open behind him and Professor Bacci appeared, wearing the same ill-fitting suit he had worn on his first visit to Kappel Privatbank. He smiled broadly at Max, and as he shook Bacci's hand Max felt a sudden fondness for him. Something about the man's smile reminded him of his school swimming master – he'd been one of the few people who had helped him after his mother's death by teaching him to control his pain and exorcize his guilt through exercise and self-discipline.

'I hurried back,' Bacci said. 'Have you been here long?'

'Just got here,' said Max.

'Likewise,' said Helmut.

Bacci turned to Joachim. 'Everything okay?'

Joachim took his seat at the computer. 'Of course.'

Helmut reached into his jacket, pulled out an envelope and handed it to Bacci. 'Why don't we let Joachim get back to work while we go into your office to discuss business?'

In his office Bacci sat behind his desk and opened the envelope. His eyes widened. 'This is a cheque for three million euros.'

'Look at the money as a down-payment, a show

of our faith in you and proof of our intentions,' said Helmut.

Max opened his briefcase, took out a bound document and laid it, with three copies of a contract, on the desk. He tapped the bound document. 'This is our business proposal for getting your discovery to market. It's basically a hard copy of what I've already presented to you, and details all timescales and budget breakdowns. Check it and tell me if you have any questions.' He tapped the contracts. 'These are our terms of engagement, which we need you to sign.'

Bacci picked up the top copy and glanced through the text.

'We believe in your venture and are willing to take all the risk,' Max said. 'We'll provide full funding and consultancy services till the first sales kick in, including all regulatory and technical support via Joachim and Comvec. In effect, we'll be buying a majority shareholding in the venture without the control. It's your vision and you'll retain control of the project's direction. Once we reach the market you'll be encouraged to use your share of the profits to buy us out at the revised market value.' Max smiled. 'Kappel Privatbank is a bank and our offshoot Comvec was created to launch set-ups like yours successfully on to the market. We're *not* a pharmaceutical company. We want to get you up and running, then walk away with a good return on our investment. A *very* good return.

'Make no mistake, though. This is a serious commitment on our part because, as I explained in our proposal, it could take some time to reach the market. Your technology is potentially controversial so we need to ensure we're seen to be ethically sound before we approach the European and American drug regulatory bodies. Both safety and efficacy clinical trials will need to be conducted with painstaking care, and that'll require patience from both of us. In return for this commitment and long-term view, we need an assurance that if anything happens to you, all your hardware, laboratory equipment and records come to us. That way we'll be able to claw back at least some of our investment. Does that sound reasonable?'

Bacci nodded. 'I think so.'

'Good. The contracts must be signed and returned to us by the weekend.'

There was a knock at the door and Joachim poked his head into the room. 'Carlo, I've been checking your computer records for future clinical trials, and there are a couple of folders I don't understand. One's called "Prosopagnosia".'

'That's for my daughter. It's got nothing to do with NiL. Some of my work overlaps with her research and throughout the NiL project I've been saving relevant findings to share with her when we go public. What's the other folder?'

'It's an empty sub-folder in the "NiL Side Effects and Safeguards" folder. You've labelled it: "Zero Substitution Effect".'

'It's just an early safeguard I put in place. You can delete it.'

Before Joachim could say more, the phone rang on Bacci's desk. Max watched him glance down at the display and pick up the receiver as soon as he recognized the caller's number. 'Maria.' He put his hand over the mouthpiece. 'My fiancée. Sorry.'

Max, Joachim and their father moved to leave, but Bacci gestured to them to stay. As he listened, his expression darkened and his face drained of colour. When he hung up he was pale and his hands were shaking. He stood up, went over to a television set in the corner and switched it on.

On the screen a journalist stood in an alpine setting. Behind him a police cordon encircled what looked like a large white tent screening off part of the woods. The journalist spoke in a calm, clear voice: 'The decomposed bodies found in these remote woods are believed to be those of Marco Trapani and three employees. The manner of their deaths has led police to suspect the involvement of a rival Corsican Mafia.'

They watched the report in silence. Then Bacci switched off the television and returned to his desk, head in hands. 'It's unbelievable,' he said. 'My cousin's family wasn't involved in the Mafia. Not now.'

'I'm sorry,' Max said. He hadn't thought of the Sicilian since he had disposed of the man's

Corsican rival in St Martin, and had vetted Professor Bacci's background.

'It's a shock to us all,' said Helmut. 'There's no proof he was linked to organized crime, and we certainly had no reason to suspect his dealings. He might just have been in the wrong place at the wrong time.'

'I can't believe it,' Bacci said again. 'He was such a good cousin. He introduced me to you.' He pointed to the cheque and the contracts. 'He made all this possible.'

Max saw his father glance away from Bacci with the ghost of a smile on his face. It told Max all he needed to know. 'I think we should close now,' he said. 'We'll meet again to discuss any other matters.'

He waited until his father was outside in the car park before he challenged him. 'Why didn't you tell me you'd killed Trapani?'

Helmut Kappel lit one of his black cigarettes and took a long drag. For a second, Max thought he was going to deny it. 'Max, Bacci told Trapani something about the drug, not much, but enough to make him curious. He was pressuring us. He had to be stopped.'

'That's not the point. Why didn't you tell me?'

His father stopped walking. 'Max, I run this family. I decide who knows what. And I decided you didn't need to know.'

'What else have you decided not to tell me?'

Helmut looked at him hard, then slapped Max on the back. 'C'mon, Max, it's no big deal.'

'What else haven't you told me?'

'About Ilium? Nothing. You know everything now. Satisfied?' His father didn't wait for a reply, just walked to his limousine.

28

25 October

As the grand gates of Schloss Kappel opened, Isabella lowered the limousine window and showed her invitation to the elegantly dressed man with the eyepatch by the gatehouse. He waved the car on, and she glanced again at the gilt-edged card. The handwritten Gothic script informed her that Helmut Kappel requested her presence at a surprise party to be held at Schloss Kappel. All her travel had been arranged and paid for, including her plane ticket to Zurich and the limousine from the airport. No other information was given about the party, but the date, 25 October, coincided with Phoebe Davenport's birthday.

She had hardly seen Phoebe since their talk on the night of Odin's fashion show. Isabella had thrown herself into her work and Phoebe had rarely come back to the apartment: she was spending more and more time with Helmut Kappel – she had even cancelled a number of high-profile assignments to be with him. And now it appeared he was throwing her a surprise birthday party. Max would undoubtedly be there, but if Phoebe and Helmut remained together, Isabella knew she would have to get used to bumping into him.

As the intimidating grey mansion appeared in the dusk Isabella wondered what sort of party it would be. When she had called Kathryn and Gisele, they had confirmed they were coming but hadn't been able to tell her any more than she already knew. There were few lights in the windows, and the round corner towers and heavy façade brought to mind a grim but worthy institution, a psychiatric hospital or orphanage. She shivered when she thought of her vibrant young friend walking its dark corridors with her ancient lover.

There were no other cars on the driveway when hers pulled up outside the main entrance, but as soon as she got out, the front door opened and a short man in a tailcoat took her case. '*Guten abend*, Dr Bacci.'

'Good evening.'

The hall contained some exquisite pieces of furniture, but the dark wood, ancient rugs and staring oil portraits of the Kappels' white-haired ancestors made it too gloomy to be welcoming. Isabella felt as if she had stepped into another world.

'Herr Kappel and Fräulein Davenport are currently in Zurich. They will return within the hour. I've been asked to show you to your room so you can settle in.'

'Have any other guests arrived yet?'

'You are the first, Fräulein.'

'How many are coming to the party?'

'A few,' the man said vaguely, as he led her up the wide staircase and down the seemingly endless first-floor landing. Stags' heads with full antlers adorned the dark-panelled walls. 'You're in the east wing.' Eventually he stopped outside a door and turned its large brass handle. 'This is your room.' It was a large chamber with a towering ceiling, tall windows dressed with thick dark curtains and a huge bed. There was an adjoining bathroom. She quelled a nervous urge to laugh. It was like the surreal set of an Addams Family film. Even the butler, or whatever he was, looked straight out of Central Casting. She couldn't imagine living in this house.

'I hope you find the room comfortable,' the man said. 'There's a phone by the bed. If you need anything dial zero. You're requested to come down to the library at seven thirty for drinks.'

After she had unpacked, Isabella lay on the bed, but she couldn't settle. She got up, went out of her room and began to explore the old house.

A light at the far end of the landing drew her and, walking towards it, she was struck by the silence. Apart from the smell of cooking wafting up from the kitchens and the occasional sounds of servants preparing for the evening ahead, the place seemed deserted. A few paces down the corridor she came to a recess, which featured a small collection of curios. Each item was individually lit and when she read the explanatory cards she discovered they were tools of assassination.

The card next to a needle-thin lance explained how it could impale a target's internal organs and be withdrawn without leaving an external mark. Three beautiful fabrics in a glass box were silk garrottes, designed to strangle a victim with minimal bruising. A refrigerated case displayed needle-sharp ice darts of frozen poison, designed to enter a victim's warm body and dissolve. She could tell from the worn handle on the lance and the soiled garrottes that they had been well used. The macabre exhibits were in keeping with the dark house, and she wondered which member of the Kappel clan had collected them. It did not occur to her that they had once been tools of the family's ancient trade, and that its past members had designed each one.

She walked on past mullioned windows. Through the gloom she could see a lake and, on a raised plateau above the house, some small domed buildings. Eventually she came to an open door, which led to a spiral staircase. She realized this must be the eastern corner tower.

'Hello?' she called. When there was no answer she stepped through the doorway. This area felt different. The stairs were of light oak, with gleaming brass stair rods and a bright aquamarine carpet. The walls were decorated with brilliant contemporary prints. Her spirits rose. When she looked down the spiral staircase to the ground floor, she saw that it serviced a side entrance. She began to climb the stairs.

At the top she stepped through an open doorway and found herself in a circular loft space with a beamed ceiling and a wooden floor covered with Oriental rugs. Photographs of coastal views and undersea scenes dominated the pale walls. The pictures were beautiful, but strangely desolate and devoid of people. In one section of the room a desk and a dining-table stood alongside a sofa, two chairs and a television. In another area, steps led to a mezzanine level, and through the balcony rail she could see a huge bed.

Then she noticed the driftwood-framed photograph on the sideboard by one of the circular windows. Unlike the pictures on the wall, it featured people: a tanned boy with white hair and the bluest eyes stood on a tropical beach with a tall, beautiful woman holding him close.

'Can I help you?'

Startled, she swivelled round. He stood in a doorway to her left, expertly manipulating a black bow-tie. A dressing room and bathrobe were visible behind him. 'I'm sorry, I didn't mean to intrude. I was just looking around and the door was open. I called up to see if anyone was in,' she said lamely.

Max wore an immaculate black dinner suit, which accentuated his broad shoulders and set off his lightly tanned skin. He knotted the bow-tie, checked his collar and smiled. 'Don't worry about it,' he said. 'This is just the apartment I use when I'm working in Zurich. My real home's in the South of France, not far from where we met.'

'It's beautiful. Very different from the rest of the house.' She winced. 'Not that the rest of the house is—'

'Grim?' He laughed. 'If you think it's creepy, imagine spending your childhood here. But it's convenient.'

She indicated the photograph of the boy and the beautiful woman. 'Your mother?' She remembered Max telling her in Antibes that she had died when he was young.

He glanced at it. 'Yes.'

There was a knock on the open door behind her. Another man appeared in a black dinner suit, with a garish bow-tie and matching waistcoat. He looked similar to Max, but was slighter and paler, a younger version of Max's father. Watery blue eyes stared at her through rimless glasses. He didn't step across the threshold.

'Isabella, this is Joachim, my half-brother.'

Joachim was staring at her. 'You're honoured, Isabella.' His eyes moved to Max, and a humourless smile curved his lips. 'Max never lets anyone into his eyrie, not his family or even Delphine, his fiancée.'

Isabella's heart jolted. How could Max be engaged? He'd said he didn't 'do love'. She was surprised by how much the news had shocked her.

'I'll see you downstairs, Joachim.'

215

After Joachim had left Isabella turned to Max. 'Fiancée?'

'Not yet. My father might want her to be, but she isn't.'

'But she is your girlfriend?'

He shrugged. 'I suppose so.'

She headed for the door. 'I'm sorry I intruded.'

'You didn't,' Max said softly. 'I'll see you at seven thirty.'

In the doorway she turned back to him. She had to ask. 'How long has she been your girlfriend?'

He looked directly at her, blue eyes clear and cool. 'Before Antibes.'

29

At least now she understood. Or thought she did. To Max she had been no more than a passionate holiday fling, the other woman, a break from his girlfriend, a moment of madness. As Isabella showered, it felt like she was washing away any vestigial feelings for him, and by the time she had changed into her gown and left the room she felt herself wishing Delphine luck, convinced she would need it. When she met Kathryn and Gisele on the stairs she focused her thoughts on Phoebe.

Kathryn kissed her cheek. 'Do you have any idea what tonight's about, Izzy?'

Isabella brandished the gift-wrapped Swarovski crystal penguin she was carrying. 'I thought it must be a surprise birthday party.'

'Same here,' said Gisele, as they reached the hall.

Kathryn frowned. 'But it's not like she's twenty-one or anything,' she said, and pointed at two women ahead of them. 'So why has her mother flown all the way from the States? She hates flying.'

Phoebe's mother stood outside the library with her younger daughter, Claire, who waved at them. Isabella had last seen Phoebe's sister in Antibes but she hadn't seen their mother since she had left the States over a year ago, and she shared Kathryn's surprise that she had flown over for Phoebe's birthday. Mrs Davenport looked pale and appeared distant as she kissed Isabella and the others before accompanying them into the library.

The library was a grand room with crystal chandeliers and a shoulder-high mantelpiece. Servants in white jackets carried silver trays of canapés and champagne, while the four Kappel men and their partners stood in a line to greet their guests. The overall effect was striking. Not only did all the men look similar but so did their partners. All the women were different shades of blonde. Phoebe was easily the most beautiful, but the others were of a similar type. Delphine was fair and willowy, and even the older woman with the bearded Kappel was attractive. Isabella shuddered to think of her friend becoming one of them.

'Where are all the guests?' Gisele hissed under her breath.

'I think we're it,' Kathryn whispered.

Isabella took a glass of champagne and smiled politely as Max introduced her to Delphine. The way Delphine scrutinized her and gripped his arm possessively made her feel uncomfortable. She moved on to Joachim, then to the bearded man who introduced himself as Klaus, and their wives.

The introductions had been formal and vaguely surreal, but not as surreal as the sight of Phoebe standing with Helmut Kappel by the fireplace. He looked different from how she remembered him, younger and more flamboyant. His white hair was cut shorter in a fashionable, spiky style, and he wore a red cravat and cummerbund. Phoebe was rubbing her wrists and Isabella could see faint marks on her skin. As the couple greeted Kathryn and Gisele, Phoebe glanced anxiously at Helmut, as though to check he was still there. She seemed excited but not surprised by the gathering, except when Isabella presented her birthday gift.

'Oh, you remembered, Izzy. Thanks.'

'Of course I remembered. It's your birthday party.' She paused. 'Isn't it?'

Phoebe flashed a knowing smile and Isabella suddenly realized that it was the guests who were in for the surprise.

'What's going on, Phoebe?' Isabella whispered.

Phoebe squeezed her hand. 'You'll see, Izzy. You'll see.'

Isabella wanted to shake her and insist she told her what was going on, but before she could think of acting on that impulse, they were summoned into a cavernous dining room where she found herself sitting between Max and Klaus at a long table laden with crystal glasses, silver cutlery and gilt-edged china. Klaus was polite but cold. He hardly spoke or drank, and kept looking around the table as if he were watching over the proceedings.

As the first course of scallops were served, Helmut rose from his seat at the head of the table. 'Thank you all for coming tonight. I'm sorry for keeping you in the dark about the reason for the party, but because of the media we had to be discreet.' He looked down at Phoebe, on his right. She gazed up at him adoringly. Then he turned to Phoebe's mother, on his left. She looked down at her plate, pale and unsmiling. 'I have an announcement to make. It may come as a shock to some of you, but at my time of life I need to act fast. I've asked Phoebe to marry me and I'm honoured and delighted to say that she has accepted.'

A gasp echoed round the table. Isabella couldn't believe Phoebe hadn't told her what she was planning. She and Helmut Kappel had met only a month ago – if that. And she couldn't believe Phoebe was being so quiet now. It wasn't like her to defer so completely to someone else. Kathryn had almost spilt her wine and Gisele looked equally stunned. Phoebe's sister was frowning in evident disbelief. The only people to look on impassively were the Kappels and Phoebe's mother. No wonder she had been so tense: she must have known.

Apparently oblivious to the reaction, Helmut continued, 'We plan to get married on New Year's Day and we'd like you all to be there. Naturally Phoebe's mother will be the guest of honour. My best man will be my elder son, Max.' Isabella turned to Max, but he was looking straight ahead.

How long had he known? Then Helmut looked in turn at Gisele, Kathryn, Claire and Isabella. 'You four are Phoebe's dearest friends, and she'd like you to be her bridesmaids.'

Isabella checked the others' reaction before she could trust herself to look at Phoebe. She knew their thoughts were the same as hers. On the one hand she wanted to shout at Phoebe to come to her senses – why, when she could have had any man in the world, was she marrying Helmut Kappel? On the other she wanted desperately to support her friend. The last thing she wanted to do was hurt her. When she caught Phoebe looking at her, eyes bright and pleading, she smiled and nodded.

She saw Gisele and Kathryn do the same. Phoebe's sister was still frowning, but eventually even she put on a brave smile. There was a pause, which went on for some seconds, then Isabella stood and did the only thing she could think of doing in the circumstances. She raised her glass, graciously accepted the honour, and toasted the happy couple.

Later that night, after the others had retired to their rooms, Isabella, Kathryn and Gisele huddled by the fire in the drawing room, trying in vain to work out why Phoebe was marrying Helmut Kappel. Eventually they agreed that although they couldn't fathom their friend's reasons they would stop questioning her motives and give her their full, unconditional support.

Nevertheless, after Kathryn and Gisele had retired to their rooms, and Isabella to hers, Isabella couldn't stop worrying about her friend. She was thinking of Phoebe as she reached the top of the stairs, stepped on to the landing and turned left towards her room. She found herself tiptoeing, lest she disturb anyone asleep behind the doors that flanked the long corridor. She had taken four steps when a sound behind her made her stop.

Someone was groaning in pain.

It sounded like Phoebe.

Goosebumps prickled on her forearms. She turned and looked past the stairs to the centre of the house. A door was ajar, spilling a triangle of light on to the faded red and black runner that ran down the landing. She froze. Then she heard the sound again: a low, rasping whisper, followed by a breathless, pleading 'No. No.'

Isabella's mouth was dry. It *was* Phoebe. She looked around her at the silent shadows. A clock ticked somewhere downstairs. *This is none of your business*, said a small voice in her head. *Go to bed. Forget about it.*

Then she heard the whimper again and found herself walking towards the triangle of light. As she got closer she recognized the rasping whisper as Helmut Kappel's voice. 'Go on,' he was urging. 'Cry out if you want to.'

'No.' The other voice was muffled but it was definitely Phoebe's.

Isabella's heart was thumping and her palms felt

222

damp. When she reached the door a full-length mirror was visible through the angled opening. The room was obviously a bedroom but at first she didn't grasp what she was seeing reflected in the mirror. Then her jaw dropped.

Phoebe was kneeling face down on the bed, wrists handcuffed to the headboard, evening dress bunched up around her lower back. She was naked below the waist and Helmut Kappel, still in his dinner jacket, was mounting her from behind. With each thrust, he gripped her hair and pushed her head harder into the pillows. His usually pale face was red with exertion and excitement. He stared down at Phoebe with the glassy, intense gaze of an owner savouring a beautiful possession.

Then he looked up and his eyes met Isabella's. She froze, her heart in her mouth, but he didn't flinch or change his rhythm. Instead he smiled at her and thrust harder, all the time keeping eye-contact. She would never forget the look on his face – not only the mask of lust and power that contorted his features but the challenging, shame-less gleam in his eyes. It was as though he had wanted her to see him abusing Phoebe. She half expected him to raise a hand and beckon her closer. Then Phoebe moaned again and moved her head. The thought that her friend might see her witnessing this humiliating scene broke the spell. Isabella ran to her room.

*   *   *

A short while earlier, Joachim and Stein returned to the dining-table and collected the bridesmaids' empty glasses, taking care to identify which glass came from which place setting. Joachim wiped a cotton bud near the lipstick-smeared rim of each glass, then put the swab into an individual glass tube labelled with a name. After he had sealed the fourth he paused at a fifth place setting. 'You said you wanted the four bridesmaids' glasses,' Stein said. 'That place was Delphine Chevalier's.'

Joachim hesitated, then picked up the glass and took a swab sample. 'It can do no harm.'

'During dinner two of my men went through each of their rooms and combed their hairbrushes for samples. You want them too?' Stein asked.

Joachim put the five glass tubes into an envelope. 'Give me everything,' he said. 'My father doesn't want to leave anything to chance.'

30

1 November

The meeting was held at Comvec, south of Zurich. A wall of glass, engraved with the Comvec logo – an arrow entwined with the DNA spiral of the double helix – divided the soundproofed conference room from the main laboratory. It was eight o'clock in the evening and the place was empty, except for the four Kappels.

Max laid the first newspaper on the conference table and opened it at an unflattering colour photograph of his father. As Helmut leaned forward to study it, Joachim and Klaus rose from their seats for a better view.

Max laid out the other papers and magazines before his father. They all displayed variations on the same story: 'Phoebe Davenport, aged 28, the most beautiful supermodel in the world, to marry reclusive Swiss banker Helmut Kappel, 65.'

Since his father had leaked the news to the media, the world press had had a field day. Even the respectable broadsheets had covered the unlikely pairing. With varying degrees of subtlety every publication had featured the least attractive picture of Helmut that they could find and focused on one key question: how had a sick elderly man won the heart of one of the most desirable young women in the world? More than one tabloid bore the headline: 'Beauty and the Beast'.

Max was surprised that, far from upsetting his father, the pictures had delighted him. He sat smoking a Sobranie, shoulders shaking with silent mirth, as if he was enjoying some private joke. 'Excellent,' he said. 'Excellent.'

Joachim smiled with his father, but Klaus frowned. 'Is it wise to draw so much attention to ourselves? We could still revert to Max's original plan. A low-profile weekend retreat with—'

'No,' Helmut said. 'The publicity was necessary for Project Ilium. When we send out the invitations over the next few days, not one of our targeted clients will be able to resist. Anyway, we're dull bankers and this is Switzerland, the land of secrecy. The media won't discover anything damaging about us.'

Klaus seemed unconvinced – and Max agreed with him, but once his father had decided on something there was little point in arguing.

'Speaking of secrecy, Klaus,' Helmut asked, 'how are the arrangements for the wedding going?'

'Everything's in place. Odin's delighted to host it, especially as he intends to launch Valhalla as an exclusive designer hotel next year and he'll benefit from the publicity. Valhalla is spectacular, exclusive and remote enough to contain the target clients and keep out the media. It's ideal for what you want.'

Helmut laughed. 'For what *we* want, Klaus. Come on, relax! This is going to be great!'

Klaus sighed, then smiled reluctantly. 'Perhaps you're right. Anyway, the construction of the ice chapel on the lake is almost complete. Norway's having an unusually mild winter and we had to wait for the lake to freeze sufficiently to hold the construction vehicles' weight, but everything's now on track.' He clicked the remote control at his side and the plasma screen on the far wall fizzed into life. 'This was taken two days ago.'

Max let out a low whistle. The image of Valhalla's crystal spire rising from the iced lake surrounded by snow-clad peaks was straight out of a fairy-tale.

'How romantic,' Helmut said drily. He turned to his younger son. 'And the samples?'

Joachim left the conference room and entered the main laboratory. Through the glass wall, Max watched him unlock a refrigerated stainless-steel safe and take out a moulded Perspex tray. He returned and placed it on the table. It contained four plain chrome rings in individual recessed wells. A tag was attached to each ring by a thin thread. Joachim removed one and held it up. It looked solid but when Joachim turned it, Max saw that the inner edge contained a glass indicator window, through which a white powder was visible. 'Each ring has been specially designed with two chambers. One contains the NiL powder and a small explosive PowerDermic nozzle.' He pointed to a barely discernible bump on the underside of the ring. 'The other, smaller chamber is linked to a retractable micro-fine needle.' He pointed at the side of the ring. 'Apply pressure by squeezing your fingers together for five seconds, shake your target's hand and, *voilà*, you inject them with the drug and take a blood sample simultaneously.'

'Joachim, did you need Professor Bacci's help to make the powder?' Helmut asked.

Joachim shook his head emphatically. 'We don't need Bacci any more. He's been preoccupied with his wedding, anyway. We can get rid of him whenever we like.'

'But what if you discover problems further down the line?' Max heard himself say. 'We may need his expertise. He's not yet a threat, and if we eliminate him now we risk drawing attention to the project.'

'Not getting too involved, are we, Max?'

'Far from it, Joachim. I just don't want you to endanger the project.' Max could feel his father's eyes boring into him.

'Whatever you say.' Joachim reached across the table to take the remote control from his uncle. 'This ring contains NiL Seventy-two with Gisele Steele's facial imprint.' He pressed the remote and Gisele's face appeared in one quarter of the plasma screen. He replaced the ring, lifted two others from the tray and checked their tags. 'These contain

Claire Davenport and Kathryn Walker's facial imprints.' There was another click of the remote and the faces of Phoebe's sister and Kathryn joined Gisele's on the screen. Joachim checked the label on the fourth ring, then turned to Max and smiled maliciously. 'This is Isabella Bacci's.'

Max focused on the final quadrant of the screen. As Isabella's face appeared, her remarkable eyes seemed to stare at him. He felt an unfamiliar tightness in his chest, his mouth dried, and when he clasped his hands together his palms were clammy. The sensation unnerved him.

His father turned to Klaus. 'Let's play Cupid.'

Seconds later the plasma screen showed four men.

The first was Giscard Corbasson, a French media tycoon, who dominated the pornography market in Europe and the United States. His empire encompassed movie production, distribution and the Internet. Desperate for mainstream respectability, he had recently tried unsuccessfully to buy into a major American film studio.

The second was Feliks Lysenko, a Russian arms dealer, who spent most of his time in Europe and the States. Snubbed by New York and London society, he made large donations to worthy charitable causes in an attempt to buy acceptance.

The third was Christophe Nadolny, a Swiss industrialist, whose Italian design partner had independently invented a revolutionary stay-fresh food-packaging format that was both cheap and environmentally friendly. The Italian had been about to dissolve their partnership when he had died mysteriously in a factory accident; the patents and subsequent fortune had gone to Nadolny.

The fourth was Warren Hudsucker, an American real-estate magnate, who had made his fortune back in the 1980s using mob money facilitated by Kappel Privatbank. He had recently been elected a US senator and was keen to distance himself from his past in a bid for even higher office.

All four men had been struggling to make their mark before the Kappels took them on. And each had happily broken any law to slither up the greasy pole. Except for the still-handsome Hudsucker, who resembled a white-haired Gregory Peck, they looked old and bloated. Not one was less than fifty, and not one was worth less than a billion US dollars.

'According to my client database,' Klaus said, 'all are divorced, single or in sham marriages. All are basically heterosexual and open to offers, if you understand my meaning.' He glanced at Helmut and a cunning smile played on his lips. 'And, of course, each has recently threatened to move their remaining personal accounts from Kappel Privatbank, although we were instrumental in building their fortunes.'

Helmut glared at the faces on the screen. 'Regardless of everything we've done for them, they'd happily ruin us. I say, bleed them dry. But first we need face-to-face access to them to deliver the drug and to get a blood sample.'

Max checked the laptop in front of him. 'Over the next few weeks we've arranged annual status meetings with two, and I'm sure we can do the same with the others.'

Helmut nodded. 'How do we match them up?'

Joachim laughed. 'It doesn't really matter because we can make any of the clients fall for any of the women and vice versa. However, I like the symmetry of Corbasson, the French porn producer, falling madly in love with Gisele Steele, the Hollywood actress.'

Helmut smiled. 'Excellent. And we can pair Lysenko, the arms-dealing social pariah, with the wealthy New York socialite Kathryn Walker.'

'Let's give the youngest, Phoebe's sister, to the oldest, Nadolny.' Klaus was enjoying the game now.

All eyes turned to Max, who was still staring at the screen. Only Isabella Bacci and Senator Hudsucker were left. Officially he was happily married, and Christian family values had formed the cornerstone of his election campaign. But the Kappels knew it was a marriage of convenience. On Hudsucker's frequent business trips to Europe, he invariably took advantage of his relative anonymity to indulge his appetites. 'Looks like it's all arranged,' he said eventually.

'So, Max,' Joachim said, 'are you happy to play Cupid to your pretty friend and the handsome Hudsucker?'

Max saw that his father was scrutinizing his

reaction. He gave a weary sigh, stood up, and walked slowly round the table. Joachim waited nervously until Max was looming over him. 'You don't intimidate me, Max.'

Max looked down at him, impassive and silent.

'What are you playing at? What do you want?'

Max rested a hand on Joachim's right shoulder. His touch was light, but it broke his half-brother's nerve. Joachim squirmed out of his chair and stepped away like a scalded cat.

Max reached down and picked up the tray containing the rings. 'Stay in your nice safe lab, Joachim, and make your little bullets. Let me worry about going out into the real world and firing them.'

Their father laughed, and Joachim's pale face turned scarlet. But as Max held the tray he still couldn't understand why his palms were clammy.

31

22 November

As Isabella Bacci played her mother's old guitar and watched her father dance with his bride, she returned his smile. But her thoughts kept straying to another wedding at which she would also be a bridesmaid. Part of her concern for Phoebe was selfish: she missed her and had only seen her a few times since the engagement party at Schloss Kappel. It was more than that, though: she still couldn't forget the cool way that Helmut Kappel had stared at her while he abused her friend. However much she tried to convince herself that what Phoebe and her fiancé did in their bedroom was none of her business, his cruelty had unsettled her. Regardless of the age difference, she found it hard to accept that her friend was happy with him. The wedding venue was still secret, and Isabella couldn't believe that Phoebe's big day was only a few weeks away.

Today, however, it was her father's wedding and as Isabella played with the band she knew he hadn't been so happy since her mother had died. The usually unkempt professor looked splendid in a new suit, while Maria wore a beautiful, flamboyant gown and even more jewellery than usual: a pearl necklace, earrings encrusted with diamonds, two silver bracelets and at least four rings.

The wedding was a family affair and Maria's had filled most of the small church; a couple of Isabella's aunts had flown over from the States and some of the late Marco Trapani's family had come up from Sicily to wish their long-lost relative well.

After the service, the hundred or so guests moved on to a restaurant owned by one of Maria's brothers. The entire upper floor was reserved for the reception and one end had been cleared for the band and dancing. The tables at the other end still bore the evidence of the wedding feast. Another of Maria's relatives was a florist and the room was filled with white flowers; each table had an arrangement of white orchids and elsewhere there were exquisite bouquets of roses and stephanotis.

When her father's new bride beckoned to her from the dance floor Isabella put down her guitar. Maria was gasping. 'Please dance with your father, Izzy. He's exhausting me. If I'm to survive this marriage I'll have to pace myself.' As Bacci took his daughter into his arms, Maria tapped her shoulder. 'Izzy, before I forget, do you still want the flowers for the children at your hospital?'

'Yes, please. They'd love them.'

'We're taking most of them home with us and

we're leaving for Locarno in the morning. Come round before ten to pick them up.'

Isabella's father held her close when they danced, and she found his warmth and his familar smell comforting.

'Penny for your thoughts, Bella?'

'It's been a lovely day, Papa. I'm so happy for you and Maria. And I know Mama would be too.'

He smiled. 'You seem quiet.'

'I'm fine. It's nothing, Papa.'

He held her closer and guided her steps to the music. 'Then tell me about it.'

'You know I'm going to be a bridesmaid again in a few weeks?'

'No.'

'Phoebe's getting married.'

He raised his eyebrows. 'Is she?'

'It's been all over the press.'

He laughed gently. 'Sorry – you know I don't read papers or watch much TV, and over the last few weeks I've been concentrating on my own wedding. Who's she marrying?'

'Helmut Kappel, a Swiss banker old enough to be her father.'

He stopped dancing. 'Come outside and tell me all about it.'

Outside, in the gardens behind the restaurant, Carlo Bacci listened with a heavy heart.

'After losing her father I can understand Phoebe being attracted to a kind older man. But Helmut

Kappel's not that type, and she didn't get to know him, then learn to love him. You should have seen her when she first met him – it was weird. She fell for him as soon as she set eyes on him – like he was a young, good-looking guy. When they're together she can't stop staring at him. I've tried to speak to her, but she just smiles and says I should be happy for her. But she doesn't *seem* happy. It's like Helmut's cast a spell on her or something. I'm worried he's just using her.'

She waited for him to respond, and when he said nothing she laughed self-consciously. 'God, I sound so petty and jealous, but I do feel better to have got it off my chest.' She looked at him and grimaced, as if she expected him to laugh at her or to tell her to mind her own business.

He did neither. He just stood there, forehead creased in thought. All he could think about was the drug he had made up for Helmut Kappel and his wife. What had Max said? 'It's a delicate matter. My father and his wife are unhappy. They're contemplating divorce and wondered if you could help.' Bacci still had the request form signed by both Helmut and his wife, but how did he know it was her signature? He had only met her once, briefly, at the Kappel bicentennial celebration. Surely Helmut Kappel wouldn't have abused the drug. There was too much at stake.

A heavy feeling of dread formed in his stomach – and must have shown on his face because Isabella was frowning now with concern. 'I'm sorry, Papa. I didn't mean to worry you with my troubles on your wedding day. I'm just being selfish and jealous – worried about losing my best friend.'

He wanted to tell her his fears, but he couldn't – if he began, he'd have to tell her everything, including his use of her as a guinea pig with Max in Antibes. He had got himself into this and he would get himself out. 'I'm sorry, Bella. I don't know what to say,' he said.

She led him back to his party. 'Just tell me not to worry – and that if her wedding day is as happy as yours then everything will be fine.'

He smiled. 'Okay, Bella,' he said. 'Don't worry about it. Everything will be fine.' Then he turned away and the frown returned.

32

The same night

The breeze blowing into Monte Carlo from North Africa was unseasonably mild, but Helmut was glad of his woollen suit and silk waistcoat as he and Max sat on the deck of Warren Hudsucker's fifty-foot yacht. The American kept the boat moored in Monaco to use as a private bolt-hole whenever he came to Europe.

For the last hour Helmut and Max had gone through Hudsucker's personal accounts, presenting various tax-saving and investment opportunities. But, like the natural politician he was, Hudsucker had avoided committing to anything, including keeping his account with Kappel Privatbank. 'It's nothing personal,' he said, patting his thick silver-white hair, 'and I'm flattered you both came to see me. But you must appreciate my position. I'm scaling down all my investments outside the US and I need to be seen to be transparent. Maintaining a secret Swiss bank account doesn't fit.'

'It never bothered you before, Warren,' Helmut

said pleasantly. 'In the past you were grateful for our help, whether it was financial, influence with the Mafia or in eliminating rivals.'

Hudsucker adopted his best Gregory Peck smile. 'But I'm on the US Senate now. And . . .'

'And you no longer trust our discretion when it comes to handling your personal finances?'

'No, no. It's not like that. Of course I trust you.'

'Without us you wouldn't be in the Senate,' Max said. Helmut watched his son twist the unfamiliar silver ring on his left index finger and wondered why he was nervous.

At that moment Hudsucker's personal assistant walked in with a bottle of champagne and three flutes. 'Ah,' Hudsucker said, with some relief. The young woman was attractive, with dark hair and long legs, and as she placed the tray on the table Hudsucker put his hand on her rear. 'Thanks, Ellie,' he said.

Helmut kept his face blank as he watched the woman leave. Hudsucker was a hypocrite. He'd got into the Senate on a family-values ticket, but he was screwing his personal assistant while his wife and kids were in the US.

'Enough business talk,' Hudsucker said. 'Tell you what, I promise not to decide anything until after your wedding, okay?'

It was obvious that the man had decided to move his account but Helmut consoled himself with what lay in store for the senator. He remembered when Trapani had tried to blackmail him and the pleasure he had taken in slitting the Sicilian's throat. Hudsucker's fate would be slower but no less devastating. He returned the senator's easy smile. Revenge would be sweet.

Hudsucker stretched towards the newspaper rack on the wall beside him and took down a copy of the *International Herald Tribune*. He opened it on the table to reveal two pictures: one of Helmut and Phoebe, and one of the four bridesmaids. 'Let's drink to you, Helmut,' Hudsucker said, raising a glass. 'I don't know how you managed it. Phoebe Davenport, for Christ's sake.' He reached across and touched Helmut's waistcoat in an over-familiar gesture. Helmut resisted the impulse to react. 'Fancy waistcoat. What's going on? With the new haircut and natty threads, you're becoming a real ladies' man.' Then Hudsucker leered at Max. 'How did he pull it off? I like the ladies too, but Phoebe Davenport's in a class of her own. Not only is she young and beautiful, she's rich and famous, too.' He turned back to Helmut. 'What on earth did you offer her to get her to *marry* you? Whatever your secret is, I want to know it.'

Helmut clinked his glass against Hudsucker's. 'When you come to the wedding, Warren, perhaps I'll sell it to you.'

Hudsucker chortled. 'You know what? I'd buy it.'

Helmut tried to catch Max's eye as he drank, but his son was staring at the senator. Max had seemed preoccupied throughout much of the meeting and, for a second, Helmut wondered if Joachim was right about an attachment to Isabella posing a conflict. But Max was family, Helmut reasoned, his elder son. He might have his mother's blood but Helmut had raised him to be pure Kappel. Once Ilium was out of the way and he had married Delphine Chevalier, Max would be fine. By then Project Venus would be in place and it wouldn't matter anyway. Nothing would matter.

Max was aware of his father's searching eyes as he listened silently to the two men's conversation, but couldn't trust himself to meet his gaze. He felt so on edge he had to will himself not to toy with the hollow ring on his index finger in case he activated the tiny blood-extracting needle prematurely, or fired the drug secreted within.

What was happening to him? He never used to feel anxious. He had never felt anything except when he dived. Now, however hard he tried to control his emotions, they kept spilling out. Over the last few weeks Max had met the first three targeted clients – Lysenko, Corbasson and Nadolny – on his own, using the modified ring to inject the drug and extract a blood sample. But with Hudsucker – the client matched with Isabella – his father had insisted on attending. Max suspected that he wanted to find out whether Joachim's taunts had any basis in the truth.

What angered him most was that Joachim might be right. He only had to imagine Hudsucker with Isabella and his anxiety increased. He had to control himself. When the cellphone pulsed in his pocket, he welcomed the distraction. He checked the caller's number on the display. Why was Bacci calling him on his wedding night? 'Excuse me.' He rose and walked to the far end of the yacht, out of earshot. 'Carlo, congratulations. How was the wedding?'

'What have you done, Max?' Bacci hissed down the phone. He didn't sound like a man who had just got married: he sounded betrayed. Max could hear music in the background.

'What are you talking about?'

'Isabella told me about Phoebe and your father getting married and how they met. He used the drug, didn't he?'

Max's mind raced through possible responses. 'Calm down, Carlo. You're talking in riddles.'

'Max, I gave you a pair of nature-identical love drugs for your father and his wife. But he didn't use them to save his marriage, did he? He used the one with his facial imprint to snare Phoebe. This isn't what I created the drug for – to allow old men to abuse beautiful young women. The deal's off. I want out.'

'Carlo, calm down. Let's talk this through. I'll come and see you. If my father's done anything wrong, I'll be as shocked as you are. Where are you?'

'At my wedding reception, but we're going home now.'

Max checked his watch. 'I can be at your house

in Turin within two hours. Don't do anything until we've talked. If after our conversation you still think my father has abused your drug, I'll want it stopped as much as you do.'

There was a pause, and Max could almost hear Bacci's indecision. 'Two hours,' Bacci said, and hung up.

Max checked his watch and strode back to the table where Hudsucker and his father were still talking. All his indecision had gone. His mind was clear and cold, already running through the arguments he would use to keep Bacci on side. 'Excuse me, Senator, but I must go. Another client needs me urgently.' He reached out, squeezed the ring between his fingers, then shook Hudsucker's hand so tightly that the Senator didn't feel thirty milligrams of the NiL drug, coded with Isabella's facial imprint, explode through his skin, or the needle extract a minute blood sample.

Helmut frowned. 'Who is it, Max?'

'Professor Bacci. I can handle it.'

33

Two hours later

It was raining by the time Max reached Turin. He found Bacci sitting in the front room of his house, a crumpled piece of paper and a half-empty bottle of *grappa* on the coffee-table in front of him. The room was filled with flowers.

'Where's Maria?'

'I sent her to bed.' His eyes were bloodshot and he held his head in his hands. 'This isn't how I planned my wedding night. I want out of my deal with Kappel Privatbank, Max.'

Max thrust his hands into the pockets of his wet raincoat. 'Carlo, you don't *know* my father's done anything wrong.'

'I want out.'

'It's not that easy, Carlo. You've signed a contract.'

Bacci picked up the crumpled sheet of paper. 'Don't talk to me about signed pieces of paper. You said your father and his wife signed this request for treatment – but she knew nothing about it, did she?

I won't let you abuse what I've discovered. If you won't let me out of the deal, then I'll go public with what's happened.'

'Think about what you're saying, Carlo. Even if my father has abused the drug, consider who you'll hurt by going public. Your daughter for a start. Don't forget you used it on her.'

'Only to prove to you that it worked.'

'We didn't force you to do anything. You could have walked away. And what about your wife? You used the drug on Maria to make her love you.'

'But that was different. I took the drug first. We *both* fell in love. And when I tested it on Isabella, you took it too. It was equal. Fair.'

'Have you told Maria what you did? Did she willingly take the drug? And how will Isabella feel about you using her as an unwitting guinea pig? You gave your daughter to a stranger.'

'That was different. My intentions were good. I did it for love. Your father has *abused* the drug, Max. He used it to gain control. He's gone against everything I believe in.'

'You've no proof of that. And even if he did, why is it any different from what you did with Maria? Why should only you use the drug to find happiness? Phoebe may be younger than my father but she still believes she's in love with him. Where's the harm in that?'

Bacci looked confused. Then he shook his head. 'This is different. I never intended to abuse Maria, only to love her. I took the drug first. I want out of our deal.'

'You can't get out now.' Max looked Bacci in the eye, willing him to understand. 'It's too late for that.'

'Then I'll go public. And damn the consequences.'

'You're not listening to me, Carlo. You *can't* go public. For your own safety, you can't tell anybody anything, especially my father. Let me talk to him and sort this out.'

'You can't threaten me.'

'I'm not threatening you. Trust me. I'm warning you. Remember what happened to Trapani? You told him about the drug, didn't you?'

Bacci paled. 'The Corsicans killed him.' A pause. 'Didn't they?'

Max kept his face impassive. Finally the man understood. 'Go to bed and be with your wife. Tomorrow, go on honeymoon. By the time you come back, I'll have worked something out. But say nothing to anyone. If you do, then no one will be able to protect you, not me, not the police. If my father even suspects you want to go public he'll—'

'He'll do what?'

Max whirled round and saw Helmut Kappel standing in the doorway. Stein and two ex-Stasi stood behind him. His left hand gripped Maria's elbow. She was still dressed in her wedding gown and jewellery. Tears smudged her mascara and her eyes were wide with fear. 'Look who we found listening outside the door – and I don't think she liked what she heard, Professor.'

Bacci leaped foward and pulled her close to him. He glared at Stein and the two hard-faced men with him. 'Who are these men? What are you doing?' he shouted at Helmut.

'What are *you* doing, Professor?' Helmut said. He turned to Max and his eyes narrowed. 'I thought I'd come to find out if anything significant had happened. Has it, Max?'

Max stood motionless, his hands in his pockets. 'It's under control,' he said. 'I'll deal with it.'

'I know you will,' his father said. He turned back to Bacci. 'So, what's the problem, Professor? You think I've used your drug to make a woman fall in love with me? What if I have? It's no different from what you've done.'

'Of course it is.' Bacci embraced Maria. 'I love you, Maria,' he said. 'The love we feel for each other is real.'

'Your love is no more or less real than the love Phoebe has for me,' said Helmut. 'Do you honestly think that your nature-identical love should be used as emotional Viagra for unhappy couples? How naïve are you? Don't you realize what you've created? Apart from eternal life, the one thing money has never been able to buy is true love. But you've changed that. You've turned the world on its head.

'Your drug goes beyond morality. Who can

honestly say that, given the chance to possess their heart's desire, they wouldn't use it? A saint would be tempted. What politician or world leader wouldn't want to buy the worshipful adoration of his people? According to Joachim, there are countless variations on NiL in your samples cupboard. Variations that, if tapped, could do virtually anything. All that's required is the courage and imagination to do it. How can you be so stupid, Professor? You presented us with the emotional equivalent of an atom bomb and expected us not to exploit it?'

Max raised his hands. 'We can still talk this through, but first we must all calm down.'

Helmut reached into his coat and extracted a Glock pistol, complete with silencer. He aimed it at Bacci. 'I am perfectly calm.'

Acid seared the lining of Carlo Bacci's gut. His dream had become a nightmare. He had expressly avoided the big banks and pharmaceutical companies because their profit-obsessed philosophies would corrupt his vision of the drug. But the Kappels were now proving far worse than the most impersonal corporation. Unwittingly he had made a deal with the devil. And what made his stomach turn with shame was that he had involved his daughter and Maria.

'What's the gun for?' he asked. 'What are you going to do?'

Helmut Kappel lowered it. 'Me? Nothing.' His

rasping whisper was even quieter than usual. He turned to Max. 'You know what has to be done. Use your silencer.' Bacci stared at Max in disbelief, but when he saw the coldness in his eyes, his shoulders slumped in resignation. 'You don't know it yet,' he said, 'but you aren't like your father, Max. However well you try to hide it from yourself, you're a good man. Isabella told me how you saved her and how gentle you were with her. I can see the passion bubbling beneath the surface – the good in you trying to get out.'

'Finish it, Max,' Helmut said, in his cold, metallic whisper. 'Now.'

Max blocked his father's line of fire. 'Let me handle it my way.'

A flash of anger flared in Helmut's pale eyes. 'You've no option, Max,' he said.

'There must be another way,' Max said softly. 'It's not in the professor's interests to say anything and he could still be useful to us. Give me until the morning to work something out.'

'I'll think about it.'

Max nodded, then glanced back at Bacci. Daring to hope that Max had won them a reprieve Bacci hugged Maria and kissed her tear-stained face. 'It's going to be okay,' he whispered.

As Max turned, Helmut stepped past him, raised his gun and fired twice. The first bullet entered Maria's forehead, but even as Bacci registered what was happening the second pierced his temple. The newlyweds were dead before they hit the floor.

'There,' Helmut said, eyes bright, relishing the shock on Max's face. 'I thought about it.'

In that instant, a long-forgotten rage surged within Max, so strong it made him tremble. He had to restrain himself from lunging at his father. Stein and one of the Stasis also had their guns out, levelled at Max. They only lowered them when he regained control.

The second Stasi walked over to the two bodies, ripped the jewellery from Maria's ears and throat, and pulled the rings from the couple's fingers.

'Max,' his father rasped, 'help Stein and his men make this look like a burglary.'

Max was calm now, ice cold. He met his father's gaze. 'It's your mess. You fucking clear it up.' Then he walked out into the dark, wet night.

34

The next morning: 23 November

By the time Isabella arrived at her father's house to pick up the wedding flowers and take them back to Milan, it was a crisp morning and the sky was blue. She parked the car and walked to her father's rambling villa.

She smelt the flowers before she entered the house, but it wasn't the fresh scent she remembered from last night. This morning it seemed almost cloying, like the fragrance in the funeral parlour after her mother had died. A sudden irrational dread darkened her mood. She quickened her step. The scent was coming from a broken window by the front door.

The lock had been forced. She pushed, and the door opened without resistance. The smell of flowers was almost overpowering as she stepped into the hall. 'Papa? Maria?' Her voice sounded strange in the silence. All she could hear was the buzz of flies.

When she turned into the front room and saw

the mass of flowers, her first thought was that they wouldn't fit into her small car. Then she noticed that most were strewn over the floor. The whole place had been ransacked. Her mouth dried.

Then she saw the bodies. And the blood.

Her father and Maria lay beneath the long table at the end of the room, partially covered with white orchids and stephanotis. Still in their wedding finery they were locked together in a final embrace. His body lay over hers as though he was trying to protect her. Maria's jewellery had gone, and her father's wedding ring.

Unable to process what she was seeing, she stepped closer and saw the neat single bullet holes in their heads. She struggled to summon a professional detachment, but the sight of their bodies and the smell of flowers overwhelmed her. She collapsed to her knees and vomited on the petal-strewn floor.

Struggling for control, she moved to her father's body and checked his pulse, but his cold skin told her everything. She wanted to hold him then, but Maria's embrace had already claimed him. She slumped down and leaned against the table leg. Who could have done this?

Eventually she roused herself, rang the *carabinieri* and waited, desperate for comfort. Acutely aware that she was in a foreign country with no real family left alive, she rang the only person she knew she could turn to.

35

By the time Phoebe arrived from Schloss Kappel the police and the press were bombarding Isabella with questions. Phoebe's presence fanned the flames but within minutes she had spirited Isabella away to Milan.

The next two days passed in a daze. At night Isabella couldn't sleep but by day she didn't feel awake. As the news spread, everyone tried to contact her: people at work, old friends, her father's acquaintances and colleagues in the States. The calls came in to her mobile or to Phoebe's apartment, and they were relentless and exhausting. Many wanted to express shock and sorrow. Some probed for details. Others called to unburden their grief with little acknowledgement of hers.

Phoebe banned Isabella from answering her mobile. 'But what about my patients?' Isabella said numbly.

'Right now, you're *my* patient and you'll do as you're told.'

He came to see her on the afternoon of the second day while Isabella sat in the lounge looking out vacantly across the city. She barely registered the sound of the doorbell so Phoebe walked over to the intercom and let in the visitor. She only noticed Max when he was standing beside her.

'I'm so very sorry,' he said.

She looked at him, surprised. He was the last person she had expected to see. 'Thank you for all your help, Max. I've been a bit out of it, but Phoebe says you've been wonderful in helping to deal with the authorities.' She braced herself for a hollow spiel about her tragic loss, but he said no more, just smiled and sat opposite her.

'Can I get you a drink, Max?' Phoebe asked.

'No, thanks.' Max placed his briefcase beside him. 'Isabella, I'm here to offer you my services.'

'Thank you, Max, but why?'

'It's my job.' He raised his hand. 'Let me explain. Kappel Privatbank was your father's bank. We looked after his commercial interests. I worked for him. Now I work for you.'

Isabella willed her sluggish mind to process what he was saying. She remembered Trapani recommending a bank to her father. 'You're the bank my father approached to sort out his finances?'

'Yes, and our subsidiary Comvec consulted with him on his technological projects. After what happened to your father we want to take as much of the burden away from you as possible. Let us help. We'll even organize the funeral. Tell me what

254

you want – who you want to invite, how you want the service to be conducted – and I'll arrange everything. Likewise, if you need my assistance with his will or the police, I'm at your disposal. There are some outstanding business matters you need to be aware of with your father's estate, but I can discuss those with you later. If you need anything – anything at all – just ask.'

Isabella examined his face, and saw only compassion. 'Thank you, Max. I appreciate that. Why didn't you tell me you worked for my father?'

'We never divulge who our clients are and your father liked to keep his cards close to his chest.'

'What are the outstanding business matters of which I need to be aware?'

'Like I said, they can wait.'

'I'd prefer to get them over with.'

He reached into his briefcase and pulled out a folder. 'In here is a contract your father signed. He was working on a project for which we agreed to advance funding and provide consultancy – both commercial and technological. In effect, we were investing in him, and our only collateral was the equipment in his rented lab and the intellectual property in any technology he developed. He structured the deal to make sure you were provided for should anything happen to him. You also get his house and any savings. Kappel Privatbank, however, gets the contents of his lab and all his computer records. It's pretty transparent, but you should show this to a lawyer.'

She glanced at the document. It seemed so meaningless now. 'I trust you,' she said.

'Don't trust me. Show it to a lawyer.'

'What was my father working on? He never told me.'

He grimaced. 'I'm sorry, I can't tell you that. Not yet, anyway. To have any chance of recouping our losses we need to find another commercial partner and they'll demand total confidentiality.'

'I understand.' Her father's work no longer seemed important. Now that he was gone, nothing seemed important any more.

36

5 December

As Max stood beside Isabella in Turin's Santa Croce cemetery and watched earth shovelled into the graves, the words of her eulogy echoed in his mind.

'My father was everything to me. For the last sixteen years of my life he was my only family. When my mother died he told me that love was all that mattered and that our ability to love was what made us human. He explained that grief wasn't just the price of love but also its measure. I was young when Mama died but his words reassured me that my grief was good, because it proved how much I loved her. And as I stand here now, feeling equally wretched, his words console me. I must have loved him, too, very much.'

Isabella's words echoed what Max's mother had told him before she died. Brave words about love and loss that he had denounced years ago as foolish and dangerous, because his father had taught him that love made you weak. But now, as he looked at Isabella, pale but unbroken, it was hard to see this passionate, emotional person as weak.

Max wondered what he would feel when his father died. Nothing, probably. His father had trained him too well. And if grief was the measure of love, how much would anyone grieve at his own passing? He looked around at the pale mourners, many of whom had so recently witnessed the now deceased couple's marriage and, irrationally, envied them – and Isabella. Loss was hard to bear, but was it worse than having nothing to lose?

After Max had arranged the smooth transition of her father's laboratory and technology to the bank, his father had ordered him to distance himself from Isabella. But Max couldn't let her suffer alone. He felt responsible for her father's murder. His father might have pulled the trigger, but he had failed to stop him. When he had been arranging the funeral he had been surprised by how much he cared that the ceremony was carried out properly. It wasn't just guilt, he realized now. When he had dealt with the church, the undertakers and the cemetery, ensuring that Isabella's father had a plot next to his beloved Maria, it had felt as if he was completing something in his own life, organizing not only the interment of Isabella's father but of his mother, whom he had also failed to save from his father. When he thought of his mother's passion and courage he was reminded again of Isabella.

Throughout the last few days he had helped Isabella deal with the police and lawyers, but he had never seen her break down. And although she had accepted his assistance, she hadn't depended on him. When the police had again questioned her to try to ascertain who might have broken into her father's house, she had been calm and helpful. When one of the officers had offered her a tissue, she had said, 'Please don't be kind. I can handle anything but that.'

Max took his cue from her. He became her shadow, but never intruded. He answered her questions and made practical suggestions, but never offered emotional support. After all, what did he know about handling emotion? He might be able to suppress it, but he couldn't harness it as she did.

As the priest concluded the service and the mourners moved to their cars, he sensed Isabella's shoulders stiffen. When Phoebe came up and hugged her, he saw her eyes mist. After his father had escorted Phoebe back to his limousine, a line of well-wishers passed her – Maria's family, the Trapanis, other relatives and friends. All hugged and kissed Isabella. He understood from the way she bit her lip and didn't speak that this was hard to bear.

When the last mourners had moved to their cars and they were alone by the graves, Isabella glanced at him, lower lip trembling. She looked lost, and closed her eyes, as if to seal in her grief. A single tear escaped. Max stepped closer and instinctively laid a hand on her shoulder. She fell against his chest and held him. He put his arms round her, and felt her body shake.

When he looked towards the cars, he saw his father frowning at him. He didn't know how long they glared at each other, antlers locked, but it was his father who blinked first.

37

18 December

Schloss Kappel and its grounds were covered with thick snow. Helmut's crystal mausoleum pointed up at the sky like an icy thorn. Helmut paced inside the cone, gesturing to the central plinth. 'This is where my body will be displayed, on this revolving plinth, to look down across the lawns.'

Professor Gerhard Heyne removed his fedora, scratched his bald head and stared up at the panes of glass that formed the mausoleum's crystal shell. 'But it's mirrored, photosensitive glass, Herr Kappel. You can't look out.'

Helmut walked over to it and grinned at his reflection. 'I'm not going to need a view when I'm dead. I'm going to *be* the view. The glass was designed to meet your specifications for protecting my plastinated body from ultraviolet light and extreme temperatures, but it won't stop people seeing *into* the mausoleum, which is all I care about. Once inside they'll be able to walk round the plinth. And if they want a better view of me, they can walk round the spiral gantry.' He pointed to a metal double spiral staircase that followed the conical glass up fifteen feet then wound down. He imagined a never-ending queue of worshippers waiting to feast their eyes upon him. 'So I'll need to look my best.'

Heyne reached into the large Gladstone bag by his feet and retrieved a disembodied human head. 'When I replace your bodily fluids with my resin compound you will be preserved as you appear in death, but I can match a photographic reference, erase signs of age and disease and make you look younger. How old do you want to appear?' The anatomist raised the head and presented it to him. It belonged to a young male. He was smiling and the eyes radiated life. 'This man was over forty-five when he died, but I smoothed his flesh and reversed the effects of gravity so that he looks in his late twenties. His face is now frozen at that age. For ever.'

'May I touch it?'

'Of course.'

'I thought it would feel waxen, but it doesn't.'

'It's not wax.'

Helmut looked Heyne in the eye. 'However and whenever I die I want to look as I do *now*. This is important. I don't care if you use artistic licence on other parts of my body, but my face must look *exactly* as it does now. No cosmetic touches. Nothing.'

'I understand. My laser scanner can measure

the contours of your face to within a millionth of a millimetre. What pose do you want your body to adopt?' He reached into his bag again and brought out a digital camera, a laptop and a small pen device on a stand. He powered up the laptop, opened a file and turned the screen to Helmut. It showed a selection of poses: one figure stood erect, arm outstretched, finger pointing purposefully into the distance, as though to the future.

'That one,' he said.

'An excellent choice.' Heyne handed Helmut a sheaf of papers and a pen. 'Before I record your facial measurements, please sign this. It provides authorization and confirms the agreed fee.'

Helmut glanced at the document, checking the text was as his lawyers had agreed, then signed the three copies and handed them back to Heyne.

The anatomist placed his laptop on the plinth and the pen laser next to it. He plugged it into the laptop's firewire slot, and asked Helmut to be still. 'This won't take long.'

He took photographs of Helmut's head from every angle, while the pen laser emitted a harmless blue beam that traced and recorded the contours of his face. The process took less than ten minutes. As Heyne packed up his equipment, the mausoleum door opened. The anatomist did a double-take when he saw Joachim. He wore a heavy overcoat and his shoes were caked with snow.

'My second son,' Helmut said.

'I see the likeness. It's uncanny.'

'Joachim is a true Kappel.'

Joachim beamed with pride as Heyne shook Helmut's hand and left.

'So, Joachim, is everything ready for the wedding?'

Joachim patted the small aluminium case in his right hand. 'With the blood samples Max took from the four clients I've made up all the nature-identical love drugs for the bridesmaids, one temporary and one permanent version for each.'

Helmut's eyes narrowed. 'You've modified the permanent version as we discussed.'

'Yes, Vati.'

'Excellent.' Helmut pulled out his gold cigarette case, flipped it open and offered Joachim a cigarette. He noted with satisfaction that his son's fingers trembled as he took one; he saw it as the rare reward Helmut intended it to be. When he reached across with his lighter and lit his son's cigarette, Joachim's eyes sparkled with almost fanatical adoration. His younger son had always been biddable and hungry for approval, but since Helmut had injected him with the drug, he had been devoted to him, carrying out whatever task he required with unquestioning loyalty and discretion. 'And Venus?' Helmut asked. 'Will you have everything ready for the wedding?' Joachim reached into his aluminium case and brought out a vial of clear liquid. 'It's not powder,' Helmut said.

'No, the vector you requested I use for Venus means it has to be a liquid.' He shook the vial. 'This isn't quite the finished article but it'll be ready for our final review meeting before we fly out.'

'Will it do everything we discussed?'

Joachim nodded. 'I'm combining two tested elements – a vector I developed at Comvec, and Bacci's NiL Forty-two – so I know Venus will work. The process takes time to perfect but don't worry, Vati, it'll do exactly what you want it to.'

'What we *both* want it to, Joachim.' Helmut put his hand on his son's cheek and turned his head to the mirrored glass so that both their faces were reflected in it. In the dark glass the subtleties of age were removed and they looked almost identical, like twins. 'Look into the future, Joachim. If you get this right, you could well become my heir. Max might be the older but that doesn't mean he has to take over. And think of what this means for the longer term. You could have the whole world at your feet. Remember, Joachim, you're creating Venus for *us*, not just for me.'

Joachim was silent for a moment. 'Why did you inject me with NiL Forty-two, Vati?'

Helmut had been wondering when his son would realize. He considered denying it, then shrugged. 'Venus is too important. I need your help, Joachim, and I had to be sure of your loyalty.'

Joachim's voice broke, as though he couldn't

contain his emotion. 'But you had my loyalty, Vati. You didn't need to inject me. I'm your son. I'd do anything for you.'

'I know.' He patted Joachim's back. 'I'm sorry. I should have trusted you. After all, you were always my favourite.'

'Really?'

'Really. I'm sorry. Are we as one on this?'

Joachim nodded. 'Whatever I prepare for the wedding will meet our objectives.'

'Excellent.' Helmut laid a hand on his shoulder. 'No one must know of Venus. Don't mention it even to Max and Klaus at our review meeting. They might not understand what we're trying to achieve. This is *our* project.' He paused. Since Bacci's death and the funeral, Max had not only become more distant, he had defied Helmut's orders to stay away from Bacci's daughter. He remembered Isabella watching him having sex with Phoebe. Her shocked face had inflamed him to a level he hadn't known since he was a teenager. 'Speaking of Max, I'm sure your brother knows where his loyalties lie. The Kappel ethos has been ingrained in him. However, he does seem to be spending more time with Isabella Bacci than with Delphine Chevalier.'

'I agree.'

'I'll talk to him, but we should have an insurance policy. For his own good. Do you understand what I'm saying?'

The skin above Joachim's upper lip glistened with

perspiration. 'You want me to help Max regain his focus?'

'Yes. We need to show him, once and for all, how fickle and worthless love is.' Helmut pulled his son closer to him. 'Let me explain how I want to do this.'

38

Christmas Eve

Dr Roberto Zuccatto, Head of Neurology at Milan University Hospital, was a tall Roman in his fifties with a long nose, pince-nez and doleful eyes. He stopped Isabella in the corridor outside her office. 'I've got good news. The ethics committee have given full approval for the use of Amigo extract in your prosopagnosia trials. As long as your volunteers are fully briefed on the drug's effects, you can start recruiting in the New Year. You should receive the committee's written authorization in the next few days.' He removed his glasses and smiled at her. 'Now, why don't you go home? It's Christmas, and after all you've been through you need rest. You're no use to us exhausted.'

'I'm just going to finish off a few things and then I'll go.'

'Promise?'

'Promise.'

'Good. Happy Christmas.'

After her father's funeral, the hospital had told

Isabella to take some time off and come back when she was ready. She had needed the distraction of work, though, and since she had returned she had thrown herself into it. Concentrating on her research and focusing on her patients' problems took her mind off her own. She was pleased about the ethics committee. She had already received new stocks of the Amigo extract tablets, and begun approaching volunteers, including Sofia's father, for trials in the new year.

However, she couldn't hide in activity for ever. It was Christmas Eve and she would eventually have to go home and be alone with her thoughts. She dreaded Christmas: it was an occasion when families got together and everyone was supposed to be happy. Kathryn and others had invited her for the holiday but she couldn't bear to be in the midst of someone else's family. She would never forget that first Christmas alone with her father after her mother had died. At least this Christmas she had to contend only with her own grief. Phoebe had begged her to stay with her and Helmut, but the bleak Schloss Kappel hadn't appealed, and Phoebe was so preoccupied with her wedding in just over a week's time that Isabella didn't want to impose. In the end she had accepted a Christmas-lunch invitation from Maria's brother and his family. At least she would be with people who understood how she was feeling.

On her final rounds, she looked in on the children's wards, which were decorated with balloons and baubles. As she turned out the lights and said goodnight to the excited children, she told herself it would be good to have Phoebe's apartment to herself. She needed time alone. She had to decide what to do with her father's house.

Eventually Isabella put on her coat and walked to the reception area. There, doctors and nurses wished her a Merry Christmas, and some hugged her. The night looked cold through the glass doors, but Phoebe's apartment would be warm and she had stocked up the fridge. She pulled her coat tight and stepped outside.

She felt fine until she saw her car: the little Fiat was surrounded by empty spaces. Tears welled in her eyes and she realized how lonely she was. She took a deep breath and told herself the moment would pass.

As she resumed walking, a sleek Aston Martin stopped in front of her. She began to move round it but the driver's door opened and Max Kappel jumped out. 'Leave your car,' he said. 'I'm giving you a lift home.'

'But I've—'

He opened the passenger door. There was a coolbox and a hamper on the seat. 'It's Christmas Eve, Isabella. Get in.'

'Thank you, Max, but this isn't necessary. You've been very kind since my father's death and I appreciate all your help, but I'm fine. Anyway, surely you've got your own plans tonight – with Delphine?'

'I'm not seeing her any more and my plans are to have dinner with you at your apartment. Don't misunderstand me, Isabella, this isn't kindness. It's the act of a selfish man.'

'So I've no say in the matter?'

'Finally the good doctor's getting the idea.' He grinned. 'Now, get into the car.'

When they reached Phoebe's apartment he unpacked the hamper and laid out the contents in the kitchen. They started with caviar and ice-cold Stolichnaya vodka, then moved on to steamed lobster and asparagus tips with a chilled white Meursault, and ended with the most delicious chocolate torte Isabella had ever tasted. Max prepared and served each course with such self-deprecating humour that she caught herself laughing for the first time in weeks.

Just before midnight they wrapped up warmly and walked out on to the roof terrace to greet Christmas morning. They sat down together, he poured more vodka and together they watched the stars. She was a little drunk, which felt good. She would probably pay for it tomorrow when she drove over to Maria's brother, but for now all the pain of the last few weeks had blurred into the distance.

'What happened with Delphine? I thought you were getting engaged?'

'My family might want me to marry her, but *I* never agreed to anything.'

She smiled and sipped her vodka. 'Of course.

I forgot. You don't do love. It's against your religion.'

'Exactly,' he said. 'You understand me, Isabella, and I like you for that.'

'I like you too, Max.'

Sitting next to him, huddled in her coat, she felt secure and at peace. Since her father's death she had barely slept, but now she could feel sleep returning like an old friend. At first she tried to fight it but the sensation was too strong. Her last conscious act as she drifted off was to mumble, 'Thank you, Max.'

She didn't hear his reply or feel him carry her inside and put her to bed. She didn't see him pin a Christmas card above her pillow, on the corkboard of thank-you cards from her patients, or turn to leave, then change his mind. But as he lay down beside her she sensed his warmth, smiled in her sleep and rested her head on his chest.

39

'*Vous êtes fou, monsieur.* You're mad,' the man on the boat shouted. '*C'est trop dangereux.*'

Max knew the man was right. He shouldn't be doing this in winter. But he carried on. Careful to keep his balance, he raised his right hand and extended a finger into the air. '*Encore une fois,*' he shouted. Once more.

The man on the boat exchanged a look with his two colleagues. They and the safety scuba divers waiting for him under water had been paid generously, but they were right to try to stop him. He balanced in the black neoprene wetsuit on a forty-kilogram wedge-shaped bucket, called a sledge, attached to a cable suspended above the sea. The conditions were calm, but it was foolish to ballast-dive in winter when the water was cold. Yet it was the only way Max knew to gain momentary peace from the battle raging in his head.

To Max, diving was a personal communion with the deep, but he couldn't ballast-dive alone, and sometimes, like now, normal diving wasn't enough to resolve the conflicts in his mind. He exhaled quickly, expelling the carbon dioxide from his bloodstream, and took one final breath. Gripping the cable above the sledge, he looked up at the boat and signalled the men to release the pin.

The heavy sledge fell through the water like a runaway elevator at over four metres per second. The cold hit him but he ignored it, and concentrated on equalizing the pressure on his eardrums as he descended. He barely saw the safety divers in their scuba gear as he fell past them. Within one minute and thirteen seconds he was over four hundred feet below the surface of the water. The pressure on his body was thirteen times that on dry land but his mind felt lighter than it had in days. The indecision raging in his head cooled and when he released the sledge and kicked for the surface he willed the tension to leave him.

On land he was his father's son. But down here, for a few fleeting moments, his mother reclaimed his soul. Descending to the deep was almost a spiritual experience, but today the peace he yearned for wouldn't come. When hypoxia had claimed him and his mother appeared, she didn't soothe or reassure him. Today, as he rose to the surface, she didn't bathe him in love and forgive him for aligning himself with his father. Instead she was an avenging angel, fierce and uncompromising. She understood what he had done to save his sanity and didn't judge him for the men he had killed without pity or remorse. But now it was time, she seemed to say, to decide between his father's world and hers.

In his hypoxic epiphany Max saw Isabella as his mother's envoy, sent into his world to make him question his blind allegiance to his father. Whatever he felt for her had made it impossible for him to kill her father, and when his own father had killed Bacci he had felt the same impotent rage as he had when his mother died. A panicky voice in his mind told him to put Isabella out of his mind. But even as the watery sunlight above heralded his return to the air, he knew he would never regain the numb, unfeeling state that, over the years, had kept him safe. He could no longer deny his feelings for Isabella, which had melted the ice in his heart.

As he breached the surface, he gasped for air and opened his eyes . . .

At first he didn't know where he was. He put his hands over his face and his palms were damp. He was fully dressed, lying in Isabella's bed, drenched with sweat. He sat up and checked his watch. It was almost dawn. He would have to leave soon to get back to Schloss Kappel in time for Christmas lunch. He looked down at Isabella's sleeping form and, for a second, the face beside him wasn't Isabella's but his mothers. He rubbed his eyes and stared into the gloom. He would wait for her to wake, but then he must leave for Schloss Kappel.

'I'm concerned about how much time you're spending with Isabella Bacci,' Helmut said. 'I know what it's like to hear love's siren call, Max, but you must ignore it.'

Max looked back at the snow-covered Schloss Kappel, where the other Kappels were sleeping off Christmas lunch. Then he turned back to the frozen lake and thrust his hands deep into his coat pockets. 'I'm not in love,' he said evenly.

'I once believed I loved your mother. When she took you away and threatened to expose the Kappels if I came after you, I almost let her go. But *my* father explained that nothing must stand in the way of the family's destiny, not even love. I had to do my duty.' He tapped Max's arm. 'You were and are the Kappel's future, Max. I came for you out of duty. And it was duty and loyalty to the family that made me silence your mother – even though I thought I loved her. It was hard, but once I had accepted my responsibility everything became clearer. Bacci's drug must have taught you how disabling love is. It has no place in the modern, civilized world. It complicates everything. Duty and loyalty, however, are pure. They simplify everything.' He turned his hard face to Max.

'Put aside whatever you feel, or think you feel, for Isabella Bacci and do your duty. Senator Hudsucker's already been given the NiL drug, imprinted with her facial code. *You* injected him.

And Joachim's already made up the matching drug for Isabella, using the sample of Hudsucker's blood you supplied. You've already arranged for each target to receive a photograph of the bridesmaids with their wedding invitation. Hudsucker is probably obsessing over Isabella's picture as we speak. They've been paired off. It's all in place. She's destined to play her part in Ilium. Forget about her. Marry Delphine Chevalier.'

Max stared at the lake, imagining he could dive into its frozen depths and never return. He considered challenging his father about the murders of his mother and Professor Bacci, about all the other evils the Kappels had perpetrated in the name of duty and loyalty to the family, but he knew it would be futile. He could have made a stand once, after his mother died, but he was now too corrupted and embroiled in the Kappel way. 'I'm not going to marry Delphine Chevalier,' he said quietly.

'What do you mean?'

'We no longer need the Banque Chevalier merger. With the NiL drug and Project Ilium, Kappel Privatbank will get all the funding it needs. We'll have total control over our biggest clients.'

His father frowned.

'One other thing,' Max said. 'I don't want Isabella to be part of Ilium. We don't need her either. The bank will still bring in over three billion with the other bridesmaids. I'll support you with Ilium, as I've always supported you – I'll even support your ridiculous circus of a wedding – but you must keep Isabella out of it.'

'You can't be serious.'

'I am.'

'But we're committed. Hudsucker's primed.'

'Well, then, let a broken heart be his punishment for betraying our support and threatening to move his account. Now we have control of the NiL drug we can find another target for his love and take his money later.' He turned to his father and met his gaze. 'Vater, I'm not asking you this. I'm telling you.'

Helmut studied him for a long time. 'Max,' he said, 'I chose you to be best man at my wedding because you're my elder son and heir. You're my future. I can count on you, Max, can't I?'

Max turned back to the lake. When he spoke, his voice was devoid of emotion. 'Did I defy, fail or betray you after you murdered my mother in front of me?'

Kappel paused before he replied. 'No, Max. You didn't.'

'Then don't question my loyalty now.'

40

28 December

The door to the attic was hidden in an unused bedroom at the back of her father's Turin villa. It had been painted to match the ceiling and Isabella wouldn't have noticed it if the *carabinieri* had not told her about it when they were checking the house for evidence.

She dreaded going back to the villa, but having survived Christmas she felt braver. She wanted to salvage any personal items before the place was sold in the new year. She had considered asking Phoebe to accompany her, but her wedding was imminent. Everyone was flying out to the secret venue in two days' time. She had thought of asking Max Kappel to come with her for moral support, but sifting through her father's belongings was too personal.

The police tape had been removed from the doors and she used her father's key to enter the house. Although the flowers had been cleared from the front room, she imagined she could still smell them. She was relieved that there was no sign of where the bodies had lain. The flowers had screened the rugs and wooden floors from the blood. According to the *carabinieri*, her father and Maria had been 'soft targets'. Their murderers had probably known they were getting married, and would be laden with jewellery and gifts when they returned home. The police were confident they knew how the burglary and murders had been carried out. They were less confident of catching the perpetrators.

As Isabella looked around the house she was surprised that there was little trace of her mother among her father's paraphernalia. He was a hoarder, but there was barely a photograph in any of his drawers. He had collected empty biscuit tins, wine bottles and piles of outdated scientific journals but no mementoes of his adored first wife. That was why she braved her father's rickety old stepladder and climbed up to the attic.

The roof space ran from the front of the house to the back. The floor was boarded and Isabella could stand up straight in the centre where the roof was highest. There were boxes everywhere, except in an area at the far end with a small rug and an old armchair. She reached for the light switch before she registered that the late-afternoon sun was filtering through two small round windows in the roof. The armchair had been placed between them. Beside it were a table, two blankets and a brass lamp with a green shade. A bottle of red wine and a glass stood nearby. As she sat down and imagined her father coming up here to read, she felt close to him.

To her right, she saw a trunk with her father's name stamped on the lid. She recognized it from when she was a child. He had kept it crammed with books in his study in the United States. It was locked. She reached for her father's keys, picked one that looked as if it might fit and put it into the padlock. It turned smoothly. When she released the catch and opened the trunk, the fusty smell was achingly familiar. But it was no longer filled with books.

One side was stacked with photograph albums and sheafs of letters tied with faded blue ribbon. She flicked through the photos of her mother and father when they were a complete family, and a rush of emotion overwhelmed her. She was an obvious blend of both parents.

The letters were from her mother to her father. Most had been written while he was away on lecture tours, but the older ones dated back to their courting years. All were love letters. As she glanced through them she felt joy that her parents had shared such a love – the love that had produced her – but also a crushing sadness that they were both gone.

An old black folder, held together with an elastic binder, nestled in the other half of the trunk. It felt thick and heavy when she placed it on her lap. Inside she found paper covered with her father's handwriting. The leaves were dated and went back many years. Each entry began 'My dearest Lauren'. They were letters to Isabella's mother – written after her death. It was touching to think of her father coming up here with a glass of wine to write to his dead wife, as though she was simply in another country.

They were candid letters, which recorded her father's uncensored thoughts. As she flicked through them she saw her own name and read of her father's concern when 'that fool, Leo, broke Isabella's heart' – 'I try to comfort her but I was never any good at that sort of thing. I wish you were here to help her, Lauren, as you always helped me.'

Fascinated by this unique glimpse into her father's view of the world, she picked out pages randomly, careful to replace each one. Some saddened her because they expressed his disappointment with his work, and bitterness against the pharmaceutical companies, long diatribes, complaining of how he was undervalued and unappreciated. Isabella had always known that her father hungered for recognition but not of his desperation to make his mark on the world before the years slipped away from him. The tone of one entry, however, was different, triumphant. It caught her eye because it was underlined. 'I've done it. I've taken the NiL drug and tomorrow I'll know the effects.' A later entry read: 'Tonight I injected Maria with NiL #072. I'm sure I've done the right thing. How can love be bad?'

She began to search out references to NiL, going back to the earliest pages, where her father had summarized his discovery, using diagrams and fragments of formulae. She read each scribbled page with growing unease and disbelief. Her father was a brilliant man, and as she read his detailed notes, her own knowledge of neurology and genetics told her that his nature-identical love project was far from the ranting of a madman. But surely it was too bizarre to be genuine.

She flicked forward and threaded together the history of his project from the drug's conception in the research laboratories at MIT in the States to its development in his own laboratory in Turin. After a near disastrous trial with the forty-second version, which had almost made him scrap the venture, he had developed two stable variants, temporary version sixty-nine and lifelong version seventy-two. When he had successfully tested the temporary version on himself, falling madly in love with a variety of women, he had used seventy-two to fall permanently in love with Maria. He had then injected it into Maria – without her knowledge – to make her love him.

Isabella put down the letters. This was un-believable. Her father believed he had chemically induced his love for Maria and hers for him. He was so convinced that he had created a world-changing drug that he had approached the Kappels to finance his vision.

She went back to the letters and saw something

that made her catch her breath. The letter, dated five months ago, explained, 'Lauren, I have to believe that Max Kappel is an honourable man. Otherwise I can't justify what I've done. If Isabella ever learns of it I pray she understands my intentions were good. I harbour the hope that the Antibes test with NiL #069 will not only prove to the Kappels that the technology works, but also teach Isabella to love again. After losing you and then being betrayed by Leo, she deserves happiness in her life. Like the happiness I found with Maria.'

Isabella had to read the words three times to digest their meaning. Whatever his justifications, she couldn't believe her father had used her as an unwitting pawn to prove the effectiveness of his technology and gain funding. She found it harder to deny that NiL was real, though. She had indeed fallen for Max in Antibes. Something cold slithered in her stomach. She could no longer be certain now of her feelings for Max, or his for her. Which tainted even her father's love.

Her father, whom she had loved so much, had not only kept his momentous discovery from her, he had used it to abuse her love. Even Max had known about the experiment in Antibes. He, too, might have been a pawn, but at least he had been aware of what was going on. Whom could she trust? *What* could she trust? She felt dizzy and nauseous.

Willing herself to focus, she went back to the letters and sought out all references to nature-identical love. She lost track of how long she pored over the pages, switching on the lamp as the light faded. The notes were too general to explain the science in detail, but she found one heartening aspect of the drug, which her father referred to as the 'Zero Substitution Effect'. But even that raised as many questions as it answered.

When she could read no more she slumped back in the chair and looked up at the stars through the porthole windows. She felt emotionally spent, and when she checked her watch it was nearly morning. The only way to get to the bottom of this was to search her father's computer files, but the laboratory and his work now belonged to the Kappels and were off limits. She checked one of the last entries she had read: along the bottom her father had scrawled six digits and beside it a sequence of alphanumeric characters. Below the six digits he had written '*lab*' and below the alphanumeric sequence '*password*'.

She had the password and the key codes. It was dark. Who would know if she slipped into her father's laboratory?

41

29 December

Isabella sat in the gloom of her father's laboratory at the computer keyboard and entered her father's password. As the screen changed and his files appeared before her, she checked her watch. It was almost dawn. She had ridden his mountain bike through the woods at the back of the business park, climbed over the fence and crept across the back lawns to the laboratory. She had almost had a heart attack when one of the security guards passed two feet from where she had shimmied over the fence. After he had disappeared she had easily entered the laboratory with her father's code.

Leaving the lights off, she scanned the expensive equipment and recognized enough from her own research to realize it was consistent with her father's claims. She wanted to explore the rest of the laboratory, but there wasn't time. She decided to focus on the computer.

The database was standard, like the one she used at the hospital, and when she tapped NiL into the search box a list of files appeared. Rather than read them now, she inserted a blank data disk, dragged the files into it and pressed Burn Disk at the top of the screen. As she waited for the files to be copied, she typed her own name in the search box.

A single file appeared: 'NiL Trial Sample Schedule'.

She double-clicked and opened the schedule, which itemized and dated all the samples her father had made and all the trials he had conducted. There were records of earlier versions trialled back in the States, but the first recorded samples of NiL #069 and 072 were those he had tested on himself and Maria. Apart from the early trials, the samples were most listed in pairs for testing on couples.

She and Max had been the first couple tested after her father and Maria. In his files her father had labelled their samples 'Romeo' and 'Juliet'. The dates tallied with her holiday to Antibes and when she met Max. She had been under the drug's influence for only two days but it now undermined her confidence in everything she felt. Her father's drug had been designed to promote love, but it had made her distrust it.

A small box appeared on the screen informing her that the data burn on her blank disk was complete. She ejected the disk and put it into her pocket. She was about to click on the mouse and switch off the computer when she glanced at the bottom of the screen. Her finger froze on the mouse: the next pairing on the NiL Trial Sample

Schedule had been designed for Helmut Kappel and his last wife and both samples were permanent NiL #072 serums. One sample contained her facial imprint, the other his. The date indicated that her father had made them months ago, and a note in the comments column indicated that they had been handed to Helmut almost immediately. Yet since then Helmut Kappel had divorced his wife and become engaged to Phoebe Davenport.

A cold shiver ran down Isabella's back. But before she could develop the thought she heard a sound: tyres on gravel, cars parking outside. She checked her watch: 7:18 a.m. It was still dark. The slam of the first car door galvanized her to shut down the computer and rush for the laboratory exit. She closed it behind her and made for the outer door. Heart pumping, she ran outside and rushed into the trees just before three men appeared from the car park. She recognized them from Phoebe's surprise engagement dinner: Helmut, Joachim and Klaus Kappel.

'Why did we have to meet so early?' she heard Klaus mutter in the cold morning air.

'We've got a lot to cover,' Helmut rasped. 'I'll explain inside.'

Head spinning, she watched them enter the laboratory and close the door. Part of her wanted to go back and eavesdrop, but the greater part was desperate to get away. She patted her pocket, feeling for the disk, then turned into the woods where she had left her father's bike. She ignored the thorns tearing at her ankles, and concentrated on the nagging thoughts in her head.

Her father had given Helmut Kappel the nature-identical love drug to be used by him and his wife. Presumably Helmut had asked for them. Why had he and his wife not used them? Why had they got divorced instead? And why had Helmut become engaged to Phoebe Davenport?

That was the wrong question, she realized, as the disk pressed against her thigh. It was obvious why a diseased old man wanted to marry one of the world's most beautiful and desirable young women.

The real question was: how had Helmut Kappel persuaded Phoebe Davenport that she wanted to marry him?

42

Half an hour later

The final review meeting before they flew off for the wedding was scheduled for nine thirty in the morning, but the *autoroute* from the French riviera had been clear and Max had arrived over an hour early. He left his car in the main car park by the gatehouse so he could walk across the business park towards Bacci's laboratory. When he reached it he was surprised to see two limousines. He had expected Joachim to be there early but not his father. An alarm sounded in the back of his mind.

He punched the security code into the main door, careful to open it quietly, then crept into the main hallway and along the corridor to the laboratory. The door was open and he heard voices. His father and Joachim were talking. Then he heard Klaus. The meeting wasn't scheduled to start for over an hour, yet all three were there, clearly in the middle of something. When he heard Joachim say his name he paused outside the door.

'What about Max? You sure he's okay?'

'What do you mean?' Klaus said.

Max stepped closer and peered through the crack in the door. He saw Joachim shrug. 'Given his weakness for Isabella Bacci, are we sure he knows where his loyalties lie?'

'Be careful what you say, Joachim,' Klaus warned. 'Max has taken far greater risks than you ever have. He injected all four target clients, including Hudsucker, and he retrieved all the blood samples so you could make your drugs for the bridesmaids, including the Bacci girl. Why would Max do that if he was compromised?'

'Because he wants her out of Ilium,' Helmut rasped, 'and he doesn't yet know the true fate of the bridesmaids.'

Klaus frowned. 'What fate?'

Helmut sighed. 'Did you think I was just going to take our treacherous clients' money and let them live out their lives in uxorious bliss? They've betrayed us, Klaus. They've threatened the welfare of the bank and the family. And, as its head, they've threatened *me*. I don't just want to bleed them dry of their money. I want to punish them. And I want them to suffer for a long, long time.'

Klaus shrugged. 'How?'

'Joachim has made a modification to the permanent NiL Seventy-two version of the drug. He's spliced it with the genetic poison vector he created at Comvec to amplify and bring forward any inherited weaknesses in the bridesmaids' genomes.' Helmut rose from his chair and paced.

'It doesn't change the plan. We still inject them with the standard temporary version when they arrive at the wedding venue, ensuring they fall in love with their paired target client – who, of course, will already be smitten with them. Towards the end of the two-day trial – on the eve of my wedding – we will explain to the lovesick clients that if they wish to ensure their love's permanent devotion they must pay. The only difference now is that after we have extracted the payments we will inject the bridesmaids with the *modified* version of the permanent Seventy-two. This means that, although each client still leaves with his prize, she will die in six months' time of whatever weakness rides within her genome.'

Joachim checked the computer screen beside him. 'Two, including Isabella Bacci, will die of accelerated cancers, the other two of heart-related diseases.'

'You'll leave the treacherous bastards heart-broken and alone for the rest of their lives,' Klaus observed.

'And bankrupt,' said Helmut.

'But what about Isabella? You said Max wants her out.'

'That's not going to happen,' Helmut said. 'Isabella Bacci's face is our fortune. Not only is she worth over a billion dollars to us, she's also an unsettling influence on Max and a loose end that needs to be tied up. If she ever found out about her father's drug, or our role in his death, she might be a threat. By using her in Ilium we not only extract our payment from Hudsucker but eradicate any potential problems with her. It's neater this way.'

'But what about Max?' Klaus said.

Helmut glanced at Joachim. 'We'll handle him.'

Max stood still and silent, channelling all his energy into slowing his heartbeat. He had to stay calm and clear his mind. But as he stared at his father he could feel years of suppressed rage bubbling to the surface. Despite immense provocation he had never betrayed his father, and he had always subjugated his needs to those of the family. Yet now his father was not only questioning his loyalty, he was betraying *him*.

While he was studying for his MBA at Insead, a Canadian tutor had shown Max a psychological checklist used to identify psychopaths. It had itemized forty indicative traits, including social glibness, constant need for stimulation, lack of empathy and remorse. Anyone with twenty-six or more of these traits was diagnosed clinically psychopathic. A surprising number of business and political leaders scored in the high twenties and low thirties. Now Max had no doubt that Helmut Kappel was that rare creature who would score forty out of forty: a perfect psychopath who felt nothing, not even loyalty to his own kin.

Max wanted to demand that he spare Isabella, but he realized it would only reinforce his father's conviction that he was in her thrall and couldn't be trusted. Max saw then that he owed his family no bond of duty or loyalty. His only allegiance was to himself.

He took three silent steps back to the main door of the laboratory, noisily opened and closed it, then cleared his throat, walked to the laboratory door and threw it open.

All three looked up. 'You're early, Max,' Helmut said.

'Not as early as you. Have you started without me?'

His father laughed. 'Of course not. Come in – we've a lot to discuss.'

43

That night

Back in Phoebe's Milan apartment, the more Isabella explored the disk she had copied from her father's computer, the more its contents horrified her. His work was undeniably brilliant: she could see that. And it was obvious from his notes that he had believed he was creating a power for good in the world. But his assumption that nature-identical love – triggered by a superficial fixation with the human face – was the same as true love appalled her.

Even in purely scientific terms it was understood that, although synthesized nature-identical flavours and perfumes were indistinguishable from those found in nature, their creation was unnatural. Nature-identicals were chemical clones grown in a laboratory and were never as highly valued as the real thing. Nature-identical vanilla cost a fraction of the price that natural vanilla commanded.

Love, as she understood it, couldn't be chemically broken down into its component parts and synthesized. True love was as much about chance as it was about chemistry. The serendipity of that first meeting was what made it precious; the knowledge that if one had taken a different path one would never have found one's soulmate. But love was also about taking risks and investing something of oneself in a soulmate.

More fundamentally, the NiL drug gave the user absolute power and, as someone once said, absolute power corrupts absolutely. She believed that if she had the drug she wouldn't use it to possess the person she loved – but she would be sorely tempted. The more she discovered about how her father's NiL drug worked, the more she saw it as a licence for abuse. It didn't promote love as giving and selfless, but as superficial and controlling. As she dug deeper into the formulae and the symptoms she became convinced that Phoebe had fallen victim to its malign influence.

From her father's shocked reaction to the news of Phoebe and Helmut Kappel's engagement, Isabella was satisfied that he hadn't been involved. Which meant that Helmut had taken the drug her father had provided for him to repair his marriage and injected it into Phoebe. But she had no proof.

The disk proved that her father had created a brilliant but dangerous control drug dressed up in the language of love. It also showed that he had used the drug on his second wife and Isabella. But it provided no evidence of foul play by the

Kappels. If she went to the authorities or the press with it, she would only destroy her father's reputation.

And there was always the chance that Phoebe's love was genuine and Helmut had done nothing wrong. But when she recalled him abusing Phoebe on the night of the engagement party, she thought that the chance of that was slim.

She flicked through the folders until she came to one labelled 'Prosopagnosia'. She opened it, saw the contents, and almost cried. In the midst of her father's madness he had thought of her. He had itemized every area of his research that might be beneficial to her research into face-blindness. But even that didn't justify what he had done.

She stood up and paced around Phoebe's apartment. Everywhere she looked she saw photographs and mementoes of their friendship that made her determined to unearth the truth. But what could she do?

If she told Phoebe her suspicions, her friend would laugh at her. Or worse. Phoebe was about to marry the man she loved and would hardly thank Isabella for wrecking her big day by suggesting her love *might* have been drug-induced.

She could challenge Helmut Kappel direct, but what would that achieve? He was hardly likely to admit any wrongdoing.

Apart from the Zero Substitution Effect she had read about, there were no safeguards and certainly no antidotes. Her father had apparently decided that since most versions of his drug lasted only two days, there was no need to develop anything to reverse the DNA changes in the subject's target cells. Even when he had created the permanent version, he still hadn't deemed it necessary. After all, who needed an antidote for love?

She walked out on to the terrace and breathed in the cold evening air. A plane flew overhead, lights blinking in the dusk. Her own flight left tomorrow for the wedding. She knew only that she had to be at the airport by six o'clock tomorrow morning and would return almost four days later. She paced around the terrace. Her only option was to go to the wedding as planned and, while she was there, try to find proof that Helmut Kappel had used the drug.

What if he had? And what if he had used the permanent version? How could she rescue Phoebe without an antidote?

She retreated to the apartment. Her head ached and she went into her bedroom for aspirins. As she took the analgesics box from a cupboard by the bed, her eye strayed to the corkboard on the wall. She focused on a card that featured a childish drawing of a woman in a white coat.

'Christ,' she said, and dropped the unopened analgesics box. She rushed back to the laptop, checked the formula of her father's drug, and scrolled through his folders until she found the one she was looking for. 'Thanks, Papa,' she muttered. It was worth a try. She glanced at the clock on the wall, grabbed her coat and car keys, then dashed out of the apartment.

44

Moments earlier

Max Kappel paced the darkening pavement and looked up at the lights in the top-floor apartment. The glow from the street doors beckoned, but the road between him and her apartment represented the Rubicon, a river that divided his current life from a separate, unknowable future. Once he crossed it and entered the building, he could never go back.

As he stared up at the penthouse windows, he imagined Isabella padding around the apartment, making coffee, switching on the television, getting on with her life. The more he thought about her, the more he admired her. She was alone in the world, yet she had handled her father's murder without shutting down her feelings.

Ever since his mother's murder, he had buried his emotions in ice. And over the years, encouraged by his father, he had allowed its numbing, protective shield to freeze his heart. When he had first seen Isabella in Antibes, though, the ice had started to crack. He knew now that she had touched him even *before* he had taken the drug.

He had always depended on the ice to protect him, but watching Isabella deal with her loss had made him see that the ice had become a prison. He understood now that every dive he had made had been a bid for freedom, a desperate attempt to resurrect his childhood self.

As he acknowledged the thaw, he knew it would bring pain. By allowing himself to become his mother's son again, he had to accept the things he had done in his father's name. He had to face again the tormentors he thought he had banished for ever: guilt, grief and self-disgust.

He also had to face the family's vengeance when they discovered he had betrayed them. He knew better than anyone how ruthless his father could be. He looked up at the apartment and took a deep breath. 'So be it,' he whispered into the chilly air. He owed the Kappels nothing. He had spent his life following his father's code, yet Helmut Kappel still distrusted and betrayed him. And now he had sanctioned the murder of the only other person Max had ever cared about.

He thought of his last night in Antibes with Isabella, when they had watched *Wings of Desire*. He remembered the scene when the angel had fallen to earth, surrendering his unfeeling invulnerability to experience all the vivid sensations, painful and pleasurable, of being human. He himself might be more demon than angel, Max thought, but he could still surrender his emotional invulnerability to feel again the pain and joy of being human. He had been given a second chance. He had been unable to rescue his mother from his father, but he could warn Isabella and save her.

A weight lifted from him and new resolve flooded through him, filling him with something he hadn't felt in years. Hope.

He squared his shoulders and stepped into the road. If anyone could protect Isabella from his father, he could. His father had trained him well. When Max had let his mother die he had been a boy. Now he was a man. He wouldn't fail this time. Even if his own father tried to kill him for what he was about to do.

The speeding stretch limousine missed him by inches and halted just in front of him. Before he could register what was happening, two men had climbed out. One pressed a gun into his ribs while the other bundled him into the rear seat. The heavily tinted windows were closed and the black leather interior smelt of his father's cigarettes. The car pulled into a space beyond the apartment and stopped.

'Max, I apologize for being so heavy-handed, but it's for your own good. A precaution to stop you doing anything foolish.'

Helmut Kappel and Stein sat opposite him. Two Stasi agents flanked him. One pressed a gun into his ribs. His father wore an expression of disappointment. 'What were you about to do, Max? Warn her?'

'Why should I? I assumed you'd exclude Isabella from Ilium after what I'd said.' He wanted to lash out, but he knew the Stasi would pull the trigger if he moved.

'You heard us this morning, didn't you, Max? You heard what I'd planned for your friend.' He didn't sound angry. 'If you tell her anything I'll have to kill her anyway. I know it's hard but we're here to help.' Helmut reached across and embraced him, holding him closer than Max could remember his father holding him. He didn't respond.

'I forgive you for betraying me, Max,' Helmut whispered in his ear, with the intimacy of a lover. 'You're still my elder son, best man at my wedding. This will make it easier to remember your duty.'

Max felt a breath of air below his left ear and heard a hiss. He recoiled, but it was too late. When his father leaned back in his seat, Max saw the vaccine gun in his open hand. The vial was spent. Panic seized him. He was prepared for physical pain, even death, but not this. 'What have you done?'

His father nodded at Stein, who stuck a syringe into his arm.

'All I've done,' his father said, 'is inject you with a permanent version of the NiL drug containing Delphine Chevalier's facial imprint. Then Stein gave you a sedative. When you wake your confusion will pass and your priorities will be clear. You will be consumed with love for Delphine

Chevalier and think nothing of Isabella Bacci. It'll be easier for you to make the right decisions. It's for your own good, Max.'

'No, it's not,' he said. 'It's for *your* good. Like everything always has been.' Max tried to struggle but his arms were too heavy. He had to stay awake.

'Ssh, Max,' his father said. 'You'll feel better when you wake.'

'Look,' Stein said, pointing to the door of Isabella's apartment block.

Fighting torpor, Max turned his head. Isabella stepped out of the apartment block and walked briskly to her car, three spaces from the limousine. Max wanted to hammer on the window and shout, but he knew his father would immediately have her killed. His heart was beating so hard in his chest that he thought it would burst. He could hardly breathe. He stared through the tinted glass, straining to see her face, committing every feature to memory, knowing that when he woke her beautiful eyes would no longer move him. It was then, watching her climb into her car and drive off, that he realized he loved her.

But it was too late. However hard he fought to stay awake, his consciousness slipped away. He was back in the waters off Hawaii, and again his body was betraying him. He would sleep soon and when he woke he would forget his love for Isabella and love only the woman his father had chosen. Then Helmut would use his love for Delphine Chevalier to control him. As he lost consciousness his father said, 'Sleep, my son.'

Max tried to scream, but no sound came from his mouth. He was under water, drowning. There was no redemption. No second chance. His father had won.

PART 3

VALHALLA

45

30 December

When Isabella stepped off the plane in Norway and saw the sign, 'Welcome to Bergen – The Gateway to the Fjords', she guessed the secret venue for Phoebe's wedding. A member of SAS Airlines fast-tracked her through Customs and Passport Control, then took her to the VIP lounge to meet up with the other bridesmaids.

At first it was awkward to see Gisele, Kathryn and Phoebe's sister Claire. They wanted to express their shock and sympathy at her father's murder, which made her feel her loss more acutely. After a few minutes, however, the conversation turned to the secret venue, and it was clear they had reached the same conclusion as she. Despite Isabella's exhaustion, the prospect of visiting Odin's isolated crystal palace excited her.

'It makes sense for it to be Valhalla,' Gisele said, leaning back in the soft leather divan. 'Odin's a client of the Kappels and Phoebe is his favourite model. Also, once the wedding's over and the official photographs are sold to the press, he'll get so much free publicity.'

Kathryn reached into her Louis Vuitton cabin bag and fished out a lipstick. 'Why would Odin want any more publicity? I thought the whole point of building Valhalla in such a remote place was to get away from it all.'

Gisele brushed back her dark hair and laughed. 'Anyone can tell you're old money, Kathryn. If you were a tramp like me, who needs the media to sell her movies, you'd know that publicity is like oxygen to Odin. The best way to get the press to crawl all over you is to build a mad, beautiful palace in the middle of nowhere and shout, "Leave me alone." I bet you that after this wedding's over he turns the place into an exclusive hotel. When the official photos are released, Odin will be even more famous than he is now simply for hosting the world's glitziest, weirdest wedding.'

'My sister's wedding's weird, is it?' said Claire Davenport quietly.

'I didn't mean it like that,' Gisele said. But everyone knew exactly what she had meant and, for an instant, Isabella was tempted to tell them of her suspicions.

'It's okay,' said Claire. 'It *is* weird. Even our mother thinks so. That's why she's not coming. She says it's because she hates flying but it's really because she doesn't approve.'

'Ladies, I'm sorry I'm late, but I've been

checking on the Lear jet. It's now waiting to take us on the penultimate leg of our journey.'

Joachim Kappel seemed excited and nervous as he welcomed them to Norway. With him was a quiet man with grey-streaked black hair tied into a ponytail and an eyepatch. Isabella recognized him from Phoebe's engagement party at Schloss Kappel. She was surprised that Joachim and not Max had been selected to escort them. Max had told her once that Joachim was brilliant but weak, and hung on their father's every word. His bow-tie, thin pale face and round designer glasses didn't contradict Max's evaluation. He carried a reinforced insulated aluminium case under his right arm, and when the porters came to transport their bags to the private plane, he clutched it protectively to his chest.

The flight north lasted about ninety minutes before the jet made its descent on to an isolated airstrip, a lone black stripe in the snow-covered landscape of fields and mountains.

'Are we over the Arctic Circle?' asked Claire, as they stepped down from the cabin and hurried across the runway to the terminal building.

'No, we're just south of it,' Joachim said, still clutching his case. 'We're in the lower third of Norway, near the west coast, just above Trondheim. Norway's surprisingly long and thin. If you stuck a pin in Oslo in the south and rotated the country a hundred and eighty degrees its northern tip would reach Rome.' He pointed to the distant mountains, which looked metallic white against the clear blue sky. 'The Arctic Circle starts two or three hundred miles north of here, near the city of Bodø.'

Joachim ushered them into the warmth of the small wooden building. Inside, a fire was burning in a grate and six piles of furs were laid out on trestle tables. 'Apparently this part of Norway gets five or six hours of daylight in December and January. If you went up to Hammerfest in the far north it would be dark by now, and it wouldn't get light again for a month or two.' He gestured to the furs. 'While the men transfer your luggage to the sleighs you should put those on. You've probably guessed where we're going, so I can tell you that Odin designed them. They're reindeer, which I understand is the most insulating pelt.'

'Are the sleighs taking us to Valhalla?'

Joachim smiled. 'We're only a few miles away but it's important the furs are fastened correctly. You'll be out in the cold for over an hour so when you've put them on let Stein check them.'

Like excited schoolgirls, Isabella and the others donned the furs. They were lined with quilted silk, and when Isabella zipped the inner lining and buttoned the outer fur, she felt as if she was wearing a sleeping-bag. The lower hem could be folded out and buttoned over her feet. The hood covered her head and the cuffs contained glove linings. It was an exquisite sensation, rather like being embraced by a huge teddy bear.

'I wonder, if we asked nicely, whether Odin

would let us take these home with us,' said Gisele, stroking hers. When she smiled her teeth looked almost unnaturally white against her dark skin. 'They'd go down great in Aspen.'

Isabella was so wound up in the general excitement of putting on the coats that, for a moment, she forgot her suspicions about Helmut and Phoebe. Then she noticed Joachim stoop over his aluminium case. From the corner of her eye she watched him tap a code into the small alphanumeric keypad: three, forward slash, back slash, zero, one. He opened the case, turned it towards Stein, then closed it again. It happened so fast that she couldn't see much of what was in the case, but she glimpsed a laptop. She committed the code to memory as Stein asked to check her fastenings. He focused on the hood area behind the neck and Isabella felt his hand go inside her coat and touch her skin. He was quick and businesslike, then gave a tight smile. '*Alles in Ordnung.*' Then he moved on to Kathryn.

As Joachim put on his coat, Isabella glanced at his case again. The laptop she had glimpsed looked like one of the new Toshiba Tecras with face-recognition security. It was a powerful system, which her hospital was considering for its consultants. Did the computer in Joachim's case contain proof of Helmut Kappel's abuse of the drug?

She was so focused on the case and its contents that she didn't see Stein reach behind Kathryn's

313

neck to check her hood fastening, then slip a spent PowerDermic vaccine gun into his pocket and move on to Claire.

As Isabella followed the others outside, planning how to access Joachim's laptop, she was oblivious to the fact that she and her friends had just been injected with NiL #069.

SOME HOURS EARLIER

Max Kappel was woken by his Uncle Klaus and two Stasi. It was four in the morning and his head was thick. A shower helped, but he was still confused. In the car from Schloss Kappel to Zurich airport, Klaus explained that his father and Phoebe had already left and that Max was booked on the six o'clock flight to Norway with him and his wife.

Max was still trying to gather his thoughts as he stood at the Swissair first-class check-in desk in the airport terminal. Something bad had happened to him, he knew that much, but what?

Klaus jogged his elbow and pointed to three people entering the terminal building. 'Your father thought you might appreciate the company.'

As the trio approached, he tried to reconfigure his mind and place them in context. When they came into focus, he felt as though ice-cold water had been splashed into his face, and remembered what his father had done to him. He considered closing his eyes, but that was pointless: he couldn't closing his eyes, but that was pointless: he couldn't fight it.

The man reached him first and shook his hand. 'Good morning, Max. Is the best man all ready for the wedding?'

Max smiled, but his stomach was churning. 'I hope so.'

The man's wife was next and she kissed him on both cheeks.

But it was their daughter who made him want to avert his eyes. 'Max! Isn't it great that we're on the same flight?'

'Yes,' Max said, with a heavy heart, as he looked at her beautiful face and surrendered to the inevitable. 'Yes, it is, Delphine.'

46

For almost an hour, accompanied by the yelp of dogs and the crunch of steel runners on fresh snow, the three sleighs slid through a silent landscape of majestic mountains, glacial valleys and dense, snow-frosted forests. Eventually they reached a gentle rise and Isabella looked down on their final destination.

It was a breathtaking scene. To her right, in the shimmering distance, she could see the Atlantic Ocean, and to her left, towering peaks huddled together. Between them, a river flowed into a large round bowl, surrounded by closer white-capped mountains, whose sheer sides dropped straight into the water.

Except that it was no longer water. The lake had frozen, and in the centre she saw a small island upon which stood the crystal palace. She had read that Valhalla was made of insulated glass, frosted resin blocks and hardwood, but from this distance, sparkling in the dying sunlight, it fused with the island, which in turn melded into the icy lake, so the palace appeared to sprout out of the frozen plane like a huge inverted icicle, its central spire a vast translucent stalagmite reaching to the heavens.

As the sleighs wound their way down to the lakeside and crossed on to the ice, Joachim pointed to a smaller dome beside the island. In the sunlight it glistened like a diamond dewdrop. 'That's the wedding chapel. It's made of ice.'

Now that they were on the lake, Isabella was struck by how large it was. She glanced back at the sleigh's tracks and heard water rushing beneath the surface of the ice. She shivered. 'Joachim, the water underneath us sounds so fierce.'

'It is.' He pointed to the east, where the river entered the lake, then to the west, where a fjord formed a channel to the sea. 'The current's strong because the river and the sea meet in this bowl.'

'Is the ice safe?'

'It's been an unusually mild winter, and the contractors had to wait for it to thicken before they could build the chapel, but it's safe now. The Gulf Stream stops the coast freezing, but this inland bowl always ices over in winter.' He pointed to the narrow fjord. 'Over there it's pretty thin, but it's fine here and in the centre.'

As the sleighs neared the island, Valhalla loomed tall. Kathryn was right, Isabella thought, it looked more like a hotel than a house and was designed in tiers like a wedding cake. Arched windows lined the lower level, which was modelled on a vast, inverted Viking longship. The upper structures, supported by crystal flying buttresses and crowned by the translucent Gothic spire, were angular, with pointed lancet windows. The shimmering walls gave the illusion of transparency while reflecting the light like mirrors, revealing nothing.

A roaring *whup, whup, whup* broke the brittle silence. Then a helicopter appeared and landed on the ice beside the chapel. Isabella saw it disgorge six people and their luggage, then take off again, heading south. She wondered if Max was waiting in Valhalla.

The dogs yelped and the sleighs halted. As Isabella stepped gingerly on to the icy ground, Gisele caught her eye and whispered, 'I'll say this for Helmut Kappel. The old guy may be weird but he chose a pretty cool place for his wedding.'

47

'They'll be here soon, Phoebe.'

'I know, Helmut. I just wish more of *my* friends and family were coming.'

Helmut Kappel looked down from the mezzanine level at the guests entering the reception hall of Valhalla. Odin greeted them individually, while his staff, resplendent in furs and gleaming Viking breastplates of his own design, conducted the formalities. The receptionist photographed each guest's face with a digital camera linked wirelessly to the main computer. Then porters took the guests' luggage and showed them to their rooms. 'We've already discussed this. I chose Valhalla to give you a spectacular wedding, but space is limited. Your mother refused to come. There are guests I had to invite, and you agreed to let me handle everything.'

'Yes, but you're either with your family or your clients. I hardly ever see you, darling.'

'I can't be with you all the time. I've other responsibilities.' He lowered his voice and looked into her eyes, speaking as a parent to a child. 'If you don't like it, Phoebe, we can still call it off. No one's forcing you to marry me. We don't *have* to be together.'

'But we do,' she said quickly. He enjoyed the panic that crossed her face. He would tire of it soon, but it still pleased him to have total control of this exquisite creature. He looked down on the atrium and saw Odin greet a target client: Warren Hudsucker. The senator was alone. Excellent. Helmut smiled. 'Relax, Phoebe. The wedding will be magnificent, and after it's over, we'll see much more of each other.'

'Promise, darling? I love you so much.'

'I know. Now, why don't you wait for your friends in your room while I greet some of my guests? I promise to come to you when the bridesmaids arrive.'

'Don't be long.'

'I won't,' he said, and walked away from her down the huge glass staircase to the hall. As he passed a sheer translucent pillar he checked his reflection in the resin surface. Adrenaline surged through him when he considered the carefully selected guest list. Although there would be fewer than a hundred guests, they had flown in from Tokyo, Los Angeles, New York, London, Paris, Moscow, Delhi, Cape Town, Buenos Aires and Sydney. No corner of the world had been overlooked.

One of the three professional photographers

hired to record the event snapped him. A Japanese client with links to the Yakuza Mafia stopped to congratulate him and compliment him on the choice of venue.

'I owe it all to Odin's generosity,' he replied, as he reached Hudsucker and the Norwegian designer.

Odin flicked back his mane of strawberry-blond hair and smiled modestly. 'It's a pleasure.' In fact, Kappel Privatbank had paid Odin a significant fee to hire Valhalla. The proceeds from the photographs would also be split with the designer, and he would benefit from the publicity when eventually Valhalla opened as a boutique hotel.

Helmut turned to Hudsucker and shook the senator's hand. 'Warren, so glad you could make it. Has the receptionist taken your picture yet? Good, in that case let me show you to your room. Someone will bring your bags for you.'

Hudsucker followed him. His usual confidence had deserted him, his face looked pale beneath the tan. He seemed tired and nervy. Helmut led him to a room on the first tier. 'You're in room eight. It has one of the best views.' He pointed to the sensor pad and monitor by the door. The model, InterFace 3000, was printed beneath the pad. 'Odin's a stickler for security. Place your hand over that sensor pad and the computer will compare the genetic facial profile in your DNA with the photograph the receptionist took when you registered.' Hudsucker did as he was told and his face

321

appeared on the monitor. Then the door clicked open. 'Only you can enter the room.'

Hudsucker stepped inside and stared out of the large picture window at the darkening mountains. 'You're right. It *is* a fantastic view.'

'If we're lucky we might see the Northern Lights. You have to be above the Arctic Circle to guarantee a sighting, but Odin says that they're occasionally visible here at this time of year.'

Hudsucker took off his jacket and threw it on to the bed. His wallet and a creased photograph slid out of the inside pocket. He replaced them, but not before Helmut had seen the picture. Well thumbed, it had obviously been unfolded and scrutinized countless times. It was the one Max had sent Hudsucker with his invitation, a picture of the bridesmaids, focusing on Isabella Bacci's face.

'Good trip?'

Hudsucker nodded.

'You decided against bringing your wife?'

'She wanted to come but it was difficult. Kids' school starts soon.'

'Sure, sure. Anyway, I invited *you*, Warren. I wanted you to share in my good fortune. This is a magical place.' Helmut gazed at the snow-covered terrace and the view beyond. 'May I speak frankly?'

Hudsucker sat on the bed and frowned. 'Sure.'

'I've a feeling something important is going to happen to you here. I feel this because something important has happened to me. I know the world doesn't understand how I managed to win Phoebe

– they think I must have some dark secret.' He patted Hudsucker's shoulder. 'If I did I certainly wouldn't share it with everybody. But if, for example, a client of mine found himself preoccupied with someone – as I was with Phoebe – someone they couldn't stop thinking about, someone whose face filled their waking hours and interfered with their work and sleep, I'd want to help them.'

Hudsucker was staring at him. His eyes narrowed. He was evidently uncertain as to where this was heading. 'How?'

'In any way I could,' Helmut said earnestly. 'For example, let's say *you* desired one of the bridesmaids at my wedding. I wouldn't stand in your way. In fact I'd help make it happen.'

The colour drained from Hudsucker's face. 'But I'm married and I've never even met any of the bridesmaids.'

'Come, come, Warren, I'm playing "what if". I'm certainly not trying to judge you. I just want to share with you the secret of my happiness. Play a game with me, Warren. How much would you give to meet the object of your love? Let's say . . .' he looked Hudsucker in the eye '. . . it's Isabella Bacci.' Her name hung in the air between them. 'How much would you give to meet her and have her return the love that has tormented you for the last few weeks?'

Hudsucker's jaw dropped, but he said nothing.

Helmut continued: 'If I said you could meet

Isabella Bacci tonight, have two days of bliss, then leave with her and live happily ever after together, how much would that lifelong happiness be worth to you? A million dollars? A billion? Everything you own? More?'

Hudsucker sat statue still, stunned.

'Apologies, Warren, you must be tired. I'll let you get some rest.' He had to prime the other three target clients before the cocktail party. 'Forgive me for talking nonsense. I'm just overexcited about marrying Phoebe. I still can't believe that someone like her, who could have had anyone in the world, chose me. See you tonight.'

48

'I'm so glad to see you guys,' Phoebe said. She waited for Joachim to leave the room then ushered Isabella and the others into a small antechamber by the reception hall. 'Isn't this place incredible?'

Gisele looked through the glass wall at the other guests. 'It's like a fairy-tale, Phoebe.'

'Helmut arranged everything.'

'It's stunning,' said Claire.

Phoebe hugged her sister. 'I only wish Mummy was coming.'

Isabella saw Claire lower her eyes. 'I know,' she said, 'but it's a long way and you know how she feels about flying.'

Isabella hugged her friend. 'You look fantastic, Phoebe.'

'So do you guys in your furs.'

As the others embraced Phoebe, Isabella looked up at the ceiling: the wooden beams were carved into spear shapes with crystal tips. To their right was a plaque, which explained that Valhalla was named after the great hall of Odin, the chief god in Norse mythology. The Valkyries, Odin's flaxen-haired warrior maidens, flew over battlefields and selected only the bravest slain warriors to take with them to Valhalla, where they would eat and drink at Odin's table as they waited for Ragnarok, the final conflict between good and evil. Isabella wondered if Odin was his real name. She doubted that even the most doting parent would christen their child after the chief of the gods.

Isabella turned back to Phoebe. 'How do you feel? Excited?'

'Of course. But a little nervous too.'

Isabella studied her friend for a sign that she had been given the drug, but there was nothing. The only clue was that Phoebe seemed totally in Helmut Kappel's thrall and appeared to have surrendered her fiery independence. The old Phoebe would never have allowed someone else to organize every aspect of her wedding, however much she loved him.

'Welcome.' The door to the lobby opened and Helmut Kappel entered with a tray of four glasses. Phoebe's face lit up. 'Joachim told me your journey was smooth.'

'It was great, thanks,' said Gisele.

'The sleigh ride was fantastic,' said Claire.

'Good. I thought you'd prefer that to a heli-copter. Phoebe, pass these to your bridesmaids, but be careful – the glasses are made of ice.'

Obediently Phoebe handed them round.

'It's one of Odin's concoctions,' Helmut said. 'A blend of the local aquavit and mead – a kind of vodka and honey liqueur.' He held Isabella's gaze briefly, then flashed a cool, knowing smile. 'Odin's christened it the Perfect Marriage in our honour. I'm told it's best to down it in one.'

Isabella drank the sweet, yet fiery cocktail as she observed the hall. She recognized Klaus Kappel when he arrived with yet more guests. Then Max entered with Delphine, their arms linked, and an older, distinguished-looking couple, who were clearly her parents. She felt an irrational stab of jealousy. After what she had discovered about her father's drug and his Antibes experiment, she no longer trusted Max. If his father had abused Phoebe then Max might have been involved. But however much she wanted to hate him, she missed his strength.

As she watched Max, she became aware that Helmut was staring at her, with a small, cruel smile. 'Phoebe,' he said, 'why don't you show the ladies to their rooms? I must greet our other guests.'

She didn't know whether it was down to Helmut Kappel's welcome drink or the journey, but Isabella felt suddenly fatigued as Phoebe showed her the bedroom plan by the main stairs. Isabella recognized some of the names: minor royalty, politicians, captains of industry. She estimated that around a hundred guests would occupy sixty rooms, located mainly on the outer perimeters of the three upper tiers. The two main rooms, high in the tower, had been allocated to Helmut Kappel and Phoebe. A separate section marked 'Private' was presumably Odin's quarters.

Isabella's room was on the second tier. She searched the plan and saw that Joachim's room was four doors away. Good. She hadn't forgotten about the contents of his aluminium case.

As she used the DNA face-recognition sensor to enter her room, she noted that her hospital used the same system – the InterFace 3000. In her room she found a printed social schedule on the table beside the bed and a mask hanging on the door. It had two eye slits and was designed to cover the top half of the face. It was painted gold and gilded feathers hung on each side like flaxen hair. The top of the mask resembled the front of a Viking helmet with two mother-of-pearl horns. According to its tag, it had been moulded in a stylized likeness of Freya, the wife of Odin, chief of the gods.

Fighting off sleep, Isabella collapsed on the bed and read the schedule, which was printed in eight languages and began with a champagne reception that evening. Tomorrow there would be sleigh rides and helicopter trips to the Arctic Circle, followed by a New Year's Eve masked ball in the great hall. The wedding ceremony was scheduled for New Year's Day in the ice chapel. She changed her watch to local time, just after three o'clock.

Suddenly she thought of her father. His betrayal made her miss him more, not less. When he had died, her one consolation was that everything between them had been resolved. They loved each other and that was all that mattered. But now that he had made her doubt his love, her anger stopped her grieving properly. If only he had spoken to her about his project, perhaps she could have helped and guided him.

She set the alarm clock to wake her in three hours' time, then checked her luggage, which stood neatly by the door to the adjoining bathroom. She opened her suitcase, reached for her sponge-bag and looked inside. There were the foil strips of sleeping tablets she had used occasionally since her father's death, and the canister she had taken from the hospital. She unscrewed the cap and looked inside. The contents were a last resort and might not work, but if her worst fears were justified they were all she had.

Then she lay on the bed and surrendered to sleep.

Elsewhere in Odin's crystal palace, the other bridesmaids also slept, dreaming of strangers. The subjects of their dreams sat alone in their rooms, obsessing over photographs of the women *they* had been dreaming of recently. In a matter of hours they would meet the objects of their desire.

49

Four hours later

The Great Hall at Valhalla had been modelled on an upturned Viking ship, but as Helmut Kappel looked up at the huge ribs that formed the sweeping arched vault that supported the roof's curved glass panes he felt as if he was standing in the belly of a vast crystal whale. Tables laden with glasses and salvers of food lined the hall while staff in full Viking livery served food and drink to the guests.

A corpulent figure approached him through the throng and Helmut opened his arms in greeting. 'Feliks, good to see you.' He embraced the Russian, then steered the man towards a far corner of the room. 'There's someone I want you to meet.'

Fifty-eight-year-old Feliks Lysenko's expensively cut dinner-suit couldn't disguise his obesity. He had thick eyebrows and a thin moustache, and his bald, tanned head gleamed under the crystal chandeliers. His haunted dark eyes searched the room and finally settled on Kathryn Walker's face. Immediately an ecstatic smile wreathed his features.

Helmut smiled to himself. Love's poison weakened even the most ruthless mind. Soon he would teach the world how dangerous it could be.

'May I introduce one of Phoebe's bridesmaids? Kathryn's one of the New York Walkers.'

'I know,' Lysenko said, barely able to contain himself.

'Kathryn, may I introduce a friend of mine? Feliks Lysenko.'

Helmut watched her step away from Isabella and Phoebe to greet the Russian. It was no surprise that Lysenko was delighted to meet her: even if he hadn't been under the influence of the drug Lysenko, the social pariah, would have drooled at the prospect of hobnobbing with a beautiful young socialite like Kathryn. But it was her reaction that made Helmut laugh inwardly. Normally, he was sure, she would have greeted the arms dealer politely, then moved back to people of her own age and class. But now she looked at the short, bald, obese Russian with the shocked wonder that Phoebe had displayed when she had first seen himself at Odin's fashion show in Milan.

Helmut stepped back and watched one of the official photographers take a picture of the couple, with himself in the background. He had briefed all the photographers to ensure that his face appeared in at least half of the pictures. He turned to see Giscard Corbasson, the French pornography baron, striding through the crowd towards Gisele Steele, who had joined Isabella and Phoebe. From the look on Corbasson's face and the startled expression on Gisele's, no introductions would be necessary.

Helmut lit a cigarette and inhaled. Earlier, after talking to Hudsucker, he had primed the other target clients. Now each one was walking headlong into his dream, unaware of the nightmare to come. Nadolny was deep in conversation with Claire and after Helmut had steered Hudsucker to Isabella, Project Ilium would be poised for the final act.

When the time came he was sure they would pay whatever he asked. The fear of losing the greatest happiness they had ever known would be too compelling to resist. He looked across at Max, who was talking animatedly with Delphine. It was reassuring to know that his prodigal son had returned to the fold. Everything was back under his control. He was the puppet master and his blood sang.

Two guests approached and offered their congratulations on his marriage. He smiled graciously, although he knew they had only come to see Phoebe. But that would change. After the wedding everything would change. Joachim and his wife Anna were talking with the Chevaliers. He beckoned to his son. 'Venus?'

'It's all prepared, but we must finalize some minor details.'

'Good. You can tell me about them tonorrow.' He saw Warren Hudsucker approaching. 'Thank you, Joachim. You can go now. I want to introduce someone to Isabella Bacci.'

As he watched Joachim walk away, Helmut's heart swelled with anticipation. Ilium had made him Cupid, but Venus would give him the world.

50

Something was very wrong. Isabella felt dislocated, as if she was in a disturbing dream. The ball had come straight out of a fairy-tale: all the men were resplendent in evening dress, and the women wore the most exclusive designer gowns with jewels that threatened to eclipse the vast chandeliers hanging from the glittering crystal roof. Phoebe outshone them all in a figure-hugging, ankle-length cream dress, a gold necklace and gold slippers. Isabella had been observing her friend, and as they talked, Phoebe had kept looking over her shoulder to make sure Helmut was near.

It wasn't Phoebe's behaviour, however, that had made the hairs stand up on the back of Isabella's neck. It was the way Kathryn was mooning over the short fat Russian, who, if he stood any closer, would soon smother her. It reminded Isabella of Phoebe's first meeting with Helmut. And Gisele seemed similarly captivated by a leering French-man, who stroked her arm with the familiarity of a lover. Even Claire was giggling like a schoolgirl with a man old enough to be her grandfather.

Her fears increased when she noticed Klaus Kappel turn away from his wife and look directly at her. His cold eyes narrowed. Did he suspect that she had discovered something?

Then Max appeared with Delphine on his arm. 'You remember Delphine?' he asked.

'Yes, of course.' Isabella extended her hand. She imagined she saw a triumphant smile hover on Delphine's lips.

'How was your flight, Isabella?' Delphine asked.

'Fine. Yours?'

Delphine looked up at Max and smiled. 'We came together.' Their apparent intimacy added to Isabella's sense of isolation. Suddenly she felt cold. Max must have been involved in his father's abuse of the drug. All his recent kindness had been motivated by the need to keep an eye on her so that she didn't interfere in the smooth passage of her father's technology to Kappel Privatbank. Everything, including his claimed break-up with Delphine, had been a lie.

As she processed this, Helmut appeared with a handsome man who seemed familiar. He was in his fifties, had a film star's tanned looks, thick silver hair, which was almost Kappel-white, and smiled at her as if she was the only person in the world.

Helmut turned to his son. 'Max, perhaps you'd like to make the introductions.'

'Certainly,' said Max. 'Isabella, let me introduce

you to Warren Hudsucker. He's a senator for Nevada.' As Max spoke, Isabella noticed that Helmut was watching his son intently with a satisfied smile.

She smiled at Hudsucker. 'I thought I recognized your face. How nice to meet you.'

'I definitely recognized *you*.' He took her hand and kissed it. He had a small birthmark in the shape of Australia on the back of his hand.

Helmut touched Phoebe's forearm. 'Come, Phoebe,' he said. 'I want to show you off to some of our other guests.'

Hudsucker was charming and attentive, but as Isabella talked to him she had the uncomfortable sensation that she was being watched. She glanced away from him and saw Max looking in her direction. Then she caught Klaus, Joachim and Helmut staring at her. As Helmut's eyes met hers, she felt suddenly alone in the crowded room, a vulnerable deer in the cross hairs of four hunters' rifles. Seconds later he shifted his focus in turn to Kathryn, to Gisele, Claire and finally Phoebe. It was then, as she followed his gaze and saw what he was seeing, that she almost dropped her glass. They hadn't only used the drug on Phoebe. They had used it on all of her bridesmaids. They had used it on herself.

She looked into Hudsucker's eyes, saw his hunger, and a rush of nausea threatened to overcome her.

'You okay?' he asked.

'I'm fine. I just need some food.' She walked over to where Joachim and his wife were standing. Joachim put his glass beside him on a table laden with silver salvers of food, kissed both her cheeks and shook Hudsucker's hand.

Isabella checked that there was no lipstick on her glass, placed it next to his, then greeted Joachim's wife.

'So, what do you think of Valhalla?' Joachim said.

'Fantastic,' said Hudsucker.

'I've never seen anything like it,' said Isabella, and picked up Joachim's glass. 'How did you convince Odin to give you the run of the place?'

'Well, he's a satisfied, loyal client,' Joachim said emphatically, and glanced meaningfully at Hudsucker.

Isabella waited a few minutes, then excused herself. 'No, no,' she protested, when Hudsucker tried to escort her. 'I must go to the ladies' and I've left something in my room. I'll be back soon.'

She wanted no witnesses to what she was about to do.

51

Holding Joachim's glass, Isabella hurried away from the hubbub of the great hall. She passed Stein and one of his hard-faced men on the mezzanine above the entrance hall, but otherwise the corridors were deserted. Through the windows, she saw fresh snow dancing in the powerful arc lights that ringed the island below Valhalla, and a few metres from the ice lake the windows of a smaller building glowing in the night. Only a little snow had settled on its roof and she guessed, from the stack of fuel drums, that it housed Valhalla's boiler. Beyond, on the frozen lake, the ice chapel glowed an eerie blue.

She climbed the sweeping stairs to her floor, reached into her clutch bag and extracted a cotton bud. When she reached her corridor, she walked past her room and stopped four doors down.

With trembling fingers she wiped the cotton bud round the inner rim of Joachim's glass, glanced up and down the corridor, then rubbed it on to the sensor by the door. She had remembered that Sofia's father had told her that that facial-recognition system had a major flaw: if the facial profile in the scanned DNA matched the digital facial image stored in the computer database it granted access – whether or not the DNA belonged to the person wishing to enter. The new InterFace 3500 scanner incorporated a digital camera to photograph the person's face, but the earlier system did not. Within seconds the computer had isolated the unique combination of five hundred and ninety-seven genes that specified Joachim Kappel's face, and his image appeared on the monitor. The door unlocked.

As she entered, the lights inside the room flickered on automatically. Unlike her room, where she had left clothes strewn on the bed, wardrobes opened and her case half packed, Joachim and Anna Kappel's was so neat and ordered it looked unoccupied. She closed the door and looked around the bed, the lounge area and the adjoining bathroom. There was no sign of Joachim's aluminium case.

She opened the wardrobe. Suits and dresses hung in a regimented row. Shoes stood beneath them in perfectly aligned pairs. Joachim's clothes occupied half of the space and Anna's the rest.

She looked on the top shelf, but apart from a spare pillow and blankets there was nothing. Then she spotted the case in the far corner of the wardrobe, beneath his suits. She retrieved it and laid it on the empty dressing-table before a large vanity mirror. Between the case latches a small red diode flashed on an otherwise black LCD monitor. Her breathing was shallow and she felt light-headed with nerves, but she had come this far and she wouldn't turn back now. She reached into her bag and got out the piece of paper on which she had scribbled the code Joachim had revealed when he had opened the case. She laid the paper flat on the table so she could read it and pressed the small keys on the alphanumeric pad beside the LCD: three, back slash, zero, one.

Nothing happened.

Panic rushed into her throat. She must have memorized one of the symbols incorrectly or omitted one. She had failed. She reached for the paper and was about to put it back into her bag when she spotted the code reversed in the mirror. Her already racing heart accelerated. The inverted code looked like IO\E: if she inserted a forward slash between the back slash and the three, it would spell LOVE.

She pressed the keys again, inserting the forward slash. When she entered the last digit a message flashed on the screen. Access Authorized. The lock clicked. She opened the case. It contained a black laptop. Beside it were three foam wells, designed to carry canisters. All were empty.

With trembling hands she opened the laptop. She had been right: it was one of the new Toshiba Tecras with face-recognition security, configured to work only with the owner. She pressed enter and the screen lit up. It asked her to place her finger on the penny-sized white pad by the keyboard, then enter a code. She took the cotton swab from Joachim's glass and placed it on the sensor.

Joachim's face appeared and a line of text: 'Welcome Herr Doktor Joachim Kappel.' Then the screen booted up in Windows. She glanced at her watch. It felt as if she'd been away from the party for hours, but only five minutes had passed.

She scanned through the computer files until she found a folder labelled 'NiL: Project Ilium/Venus'. She double-clicked and two more folders appeared: 'Ilium' and 'Venus'. She double-clicked on Ilium, and a list of files appeared. She opened the first. It had been written in German and her schoolgirl knowledge of the language wasn't up to translating it. But as she scrolled down the text she came to a table, Four women's names were recorded in the left-hand column, four men's in the middle, and a figure in US dollars on the right. The amounts were vast, but that wasn't what had made her mouth dry and her hands tremble. It was the name at the bottom of the left-hand column: Isabella Bacci. All four bridesmaids were listed and each was paired with the men to whom they had been introduced earlier. Warren Hudsucker was listed beside her name.

She sat back on the bed in shock, unconcerned now about time. Unconsciously she raked her fingers through her hair. She couldn't understand the language the document was written in but she had seen enough to guess the Kappels' plan. She reached into her bag, pulled out a portable hard drive and attached it to the firewire socket at the back of the laptop. Then she copied the entire Project Ilium/Venus folder.

As she waited for the data to transfer from the laptop's hard disk to her hard drive she considered what she had seen. She had come in here looking for possible proof that Helmut Kappel had abused her father's drug to win her friend's love. It was now clear that the Kappels' plans went way beyond that.

A beep signalled that the transfer was complete. As she reached for her hard drive she looked at the three empty wells in Joachim's case. Where were the canisters now? Had they already been administered? If so, why didn't she feel—

'Isabella? Isabella!'

The first muffled calls from the corridor outside didn't register with her.

'Isabella!'

But the third did. She jumped up, unplugged her hard drive, closed down the computer and shut the case. She put it back into the far corner of the wardrobe and listened at the door. Silence.

She took a deep breath to slow her racing heart, eased open the door, stepped into the corridor, and headed for her room. As she reached it she heard footfalls on the carpet and saw a man's shadow loom round the curve of the corridor.

She put her palm on to her door's DNA sensor but her hand shook so violently that nothing happened.

'Isabella! There you are!'

She whirled round – and gasped with relief when she saw it was Hudsucker.

'I was worried,' he said, with a broad grin. 'Thought you might be trying to escape my clutches.' He linked his arm with hers. 'Luckily for me, that's impossible here.' He pointed out at the billowing snow, shimmering like quicksilver. 'How would you escape? You can't even call for help. The mountains block mobile-phone signals, and apart from Odin's satellite phone, there are no outside lines. He says he likes the seclusion but I hate being cut off. Usually.' He squeezed her arm. 'In this case I'll make an exception.' Music wafted up from the great hall. 'May I have this dance?'

Isabella was struggling to control her shaking hands. She was also desperate to get back to her room and study the hard drive, but she didn't want to raise anyone's suspicions. 'I'd love to dance,' she lied, and let Hudsucker lead her back to the party.

52

Two hours later

Isabella had never been good at keeping her emotions in check and the rest of the champagne reception passed in a hellish daze of false smiles, small-talk and polite laughter. She was aware of the Kappels constantly glancing at her. She tried to speak to Phoebe and the other bridesmaids but they were preoccupied with their freakish new partners, and Hudsucker never left her side.

As soon as the party began to wind down, she excused herself, promising Hudsucker she would accompany him on a sleigh ride the next day. In her room she unpacked her laptop, attached the portable hard drive from her clutch bag and opened the Ilium file she had copied from Joachim's. It was clearly a management summary document but the German made it virtually incomprehensible. However, as she scrolled down to the end of the document she came to another table in bold type. As with the first, all four bridesmaids were listed in the left-hand column but now there were words in the middle column and dates in the third. '*Herzinfarkt*' appeared beside Claire's and Kathryn's names, '*Krebs*' beside Gisele's and her own. Isabella swallowed hard. She understood these words, which she had come across in medical journals and pharmaceutical literature. '*Herzinfarkt*' meant heart attack and '*Krebs*' meant cancer. The dates in the third column were six months away. It was headed '*Todestag*'. She swallowed again. She knew that '*tod*' meant dead and '*tag*' meant day. She was looking at the dates when she and her friends would die.

She told herself she must be mistaken, that she had jumped to the wrong conclusion – why would the Kappels want to kill them all? She clicked on the other folder, 'Venus', but as she scrolled through the German text all she could think about was the date when she was to die. Part of her knew she should stay calm, find a way to translate the German, then decide what to do. But there was no time, and she had never been patient. She had to act now, and there was only one thing she could do.

She went to her toilet bag and extracted the canister. She read the scribbled label on the side as though it might tell her what to do. Then she unscrewed the cap and tapped a pill on to her palm. It was smaller than an aspirin with '#135' stamped on to one side. She put it into her bag, replaced the canister then went downstairs to the bar by the great hall. The barman appeared to be closing up, but when she asked for a bottle of Amaretto and two glasses, he handed them over without comment.

As she walked upstairs, she saw only one couple. Everyone else must have retired for the night. On the top landing an arched window looked down over the lake, in all its shimmering glory. It had stopped snowing and the moon sat full and plump above the mountains that lined the fjord to the sea.

There was a door on each side of the landing. Room one was Helmut Kappel's suite and room two was Phoebe's. Hoping Phoebe was alone, Isabella knocked at her door. Seconds later her friend appeared. She wore a dressing-gown and her hair hung loose to her shoulders. She gestured to the Amaretto bottle and laughed. 'You must be joking, Izzy. Aren't you exhausted?'

'C'mon, just a little one for old times' sake. Tomorrow's a full day and then there's the ball. And the day after that you're getting married. One last drink as single friends.'

Phoebe sighed. 'Okay, you've convinced me. Come in.'

'No, let's go outside. It's stopped snowing and the moon's up. Put on your furs – go on, it's beautiful. You've got the rest of your life to be the sensible Mrs Kappel.'

Isabella led Phoebe downstairs and outside, past the boiler-house to the ice on the lake. The chapel was essentially a domed amphitheatre of ice. A semicircle of tiered seats fanned out around a dais, with an altar. The seats had been carved from ice and covered with fur. An aisle down the centre allowed the bridal procession to reach the altar from the single doorway at the back. 'Isn't it beautiful, Izzy?'

'Stunning.' Isabella opened the Amaretto and looked up at the domed ice vault. Moonlight filtered through the ice, turning it blue, adding to the glassy chill. Only the thick red rugs on the tiles and the furs on the seats gave any illusion of warmth. Isabella was frozen, but it had been important to get Phoebe away from the Kappels and any interruptions. 'Beautiful. But cold.'

Phoebe hugged herself and smiled. 'Almost as cold as when we went to Mickey Tork's party all those years ago. Remember?'

'How could I forget?' said Isabella. 'It was minus ten, but we wanted to look sophisticated so we wore our skimpiest dresses.'

Phoebe laughed. 'Only we didn't know the house had no heating and everyone else had turned up in ski gear.' She walked to the dais. 'It seems so long ago. And now I'm getting married.'

Phoebe's back was towards her, so Isabella dropped the pill into her friend's glass and poured in the Amaretto. It dissolved instantly. She felt guilty about spiking her friend's drink, but it was the only way she knew to break Helmut's hold over her.

'I don't care what my mother says,' Phoebe declared suddenly, with heat in her voice. 'I'm glad

I'm getting married.' She was pacing the chapel now. Isabella followed her with the glass but Phoebe was just getting into her stride, venting her anger. 'As for the press, I don't care how old Helmut is. To me he's perfect. I've never looked at anyone else and felt such love.' She twirled round to face Isabella. 'Only you've understood, Izzy.' As Phoebe turned, her arm knocked the glass out of Isabella's hand and sent it crashing to the floor.

Isabella watched the liquid seep into the red rug. She'd have to fetch another tablet from her room. 'I'll get another glass.'

'Don't bother,' Phoebe said, reached for the bottle and swigged. 'As you said, there's time enough for me to be the sensible Mrs Kappel.'

Isabella quelled her rising panic.

'Thanks for being so supportive, Izzy – you understand why I'm marrying Helmut, don't you?'

When Isabella hesitated, Phoebe's smile faded. 'You do approve, don't you?'

Isabella had a choice. She could lie and try to administer the drug later – although it might not work in time to make Phoebe see sense – or she could speak now and hope to get through to her. 'We're friends, aren't we, Phoebe?'

'Of course we are. Best friends. Always have been, always will be.'

'There's something I need to tell you, something you won't want to hear. It's not what I feel. It's a fact.'

Suddenly Phoebe's beautiful blue eyes were as hard and cold as glass. 'About my wedding?'

'About Helmut.'

Phoebe didn't move or say anything.

'Your love for Helmut isn't real, Phoebe. He's given you a drug, which makes you think you love him. I know this because my father created it. But that's not all—'

'Oh, yes, it is,' Phoebe said tightly. Her voice quivered as if she could barely control her anger. 'At any rate, that's all I'm going to listen to.'

'Phoebe, this is important. I'm trying to help you – help all of us!'

But Phoebe was running down the aisle to the door, leaving Isabella alone in the freezing chapel, her warm breath misting the icy air.

Helmut Kappel stood on the landing between his room and Phoebe's, studying his reflection in the window. The evening had been a resounding success, and everything was in place. Phoebe's face might have attracted everyone here, but soon the world would look for guidance to him.

He looked down at the lake, and in the arc lights he saw a figure running from the ice chapel to Valhalla. When Phoebe arrived at her door, she looked as if she had been crying.

'Are you all right, darling?'

'I'm fine,' she said, placing her hand on the scanner, then opening her door.

Helmut followed Phoebe into her room, then

glanced out of the window and saw Isabella hurrying out of the ice chapel. He took Phoebe into his arms. 'What's wrong?'

'I can't believe it. First my mother, now Izzy. I thought she of all people would be happy for us.'

He held her close. 'Is this about you being younger than me and able to marry someone far more suitable? Both of which are true, by the way.'

'But I want *you*.'

'I know. I'm sure Isabella's just being a good friend, looking out for you.'

'It's more than that. She said you drugged me to make me love you.'

Helmut allowed only the slightest beat before he laughed. 'Perhaps I did.'

'I'm being serious! She said her father created the drug. She's supposed to be my best friend!'

'Don't be too hard on her, darling. She's not herself at the moment. She's just lost her father and now she's about to lose her best friend.'

Knock, knock.

Joachim stood in the open doorway, holding his aluminium case. 'Excuse me, Vati, we need to talk.'

53

'It was my shoes, Vati.'

Helmut Kappel walked over to the table at the far end of his suite. He was still thinking about Phoebe's conversation with Isabella. 'What are you talking about, Joachim?'

'After the party Anna and I went back to our room, and she went to bed. When I hung up my suit I noticed my brogues had moved. The left shoe was no longer parallel with the right. Its toe pointed inwards.' Joachim raised the aluminium case in his right hand. 'This was next to the shoes at the back of the wardrobe.'

Helmut narrowed his eyes. 'And?'

Joachim put the case on the table and opened it. 'Someone got into the case and gained access to my laptop.'

'How do you know?'

He reached into the case and retrieved a glossy dark hair. 'When I looked inside I found this. And that's not all.' He took a small bottle from his pocket, squeezed a drop on to the hair follicle, then placed it on the penny-sized facial DNA reader by the laptop keyboard. Seconds later Isabella's face appeared on the screen followed by a message: 'Access Denied'.

Helmut took a cigar from the box on the table, reached down for the assassin's knife in his ankle sheath and cut off the tip. He lit it, thinking hard. 'You travelled with Isabella Bacci from Bergen. One of her hairs could have attached itself to you, then fallen into the case.'

'I thought of that. But I checked when the system was last accessed and it was at twenty fifty-six this evening. At that time I was nowhere near my room, let alone the laptop. And only I can access it – or someone using my DNA profile and password. Vati, Isabella Bacci somehow got into the computer. I don't know which files she saw, but we have to assume she's seen Ilium and Venus.'

Helmut thought of what Isabella had told Phoebe about the drug. 'Why would she be snooping around?'

'Perhaps she suspects we had something to do with her father's death. Perhaps Max said something.'

'He would have told us if he had. Especially after you gave him the drug.'

'All I'm saying is she must be dealt with.'

Helmut sighed. He would prefer to wait until after the wedding. There was the Hudsucker deal –

the senator was hardly likely to pay for the love of a corpse – and Phoebe wouldn't react well to the death of her best friend. He reached for the internal phone, but before he dialled he turned to Joachim. 'What about the serums?'

'The canisters are in the safe, seals intact.'

'Good.' Helmut made two internal calls.

Within minutes Klaus and Max had arrived. The former wore pyjamas and a dressing-gown and looked as if he'd just woken up. Max had clearly been nowhere near his bed. He was still dressed, although his bow-tie was undone.

'You sure it was Isabella Bacci?' Klaus asked.

'Yes.'

'And that she's seen your files?'

'We must assume she has.'

Helmut told them about Phoebe's conversation with Isabella.

'What was Phoebe's reaction?'

'She thinks Isabella's making it up out of jealousy and fear of losing her. We can use that to our advantage.'

'So she knows about Ilium,' said Klaus. 'What can she do about it until after the wedding?'

'She can warn the others,' said Joachim.

'Phoebe didn't believe her. Why should they? Anyway, perhaps Hudsucker will distract her. Disposing of her might cause more problems than it solves. I say we watch her closely, take the money from Hudsucker and dispose of her later, if necessary. Once we give her the modified permanent NiL Seventy-two she'll die in a few months anyway.'

'Klaus, we can't rely on Hudsucker distracting her,' Joachim told him. 'The drug didn't distract her from geting into my laptop or trying to warn Phoebe. And maybe she knows about our plan to give her and the others the *lethal* permanent version. She could jeopardize everything. We *must* get rid of her. We can tell Phoebe she was injured and had to fly home.'

'Or we'll say Isabella left because she felt so strongly against the wedding that she wanted no part in it,' Helmut suggested.

'Exactly,' said Joachim. 'If we lose the Hudsucker contract we at least get the other three – we can find another woman for Hudsucker and sting him later.'

Klaus scratched his beard. 'After the time when you say Isabella Bacci got into your laptop I didn't see her talking with the other bridesmaids. She had her hands full with Hudsucker, and the others were pretty preoccupied with their partners.'

Helmut nodded slowly. 'After her futile attempt to warn Phoebe, it's unlikely that Isabella will tell anyone else tonight, but I'll get Stein and some of his men to watch her room. The question is, what do we do tomorrow?' He looked at his elder son, who was standing silently in the corner. 'Max, you've been very quiet,' Helmut said. 'What do you think we should do about your friend?'

Joachim frowned. 'Why ask him? We know what he'll say.'

Helmut raised his hand to silence him. 'Max, what do you suggest? How do we handle this?'

Max looked up slowly. 'We have no choice. For once I agree with Joachim. We have to silence her.'

'Really?' Helmut could barely contain his surprise.

Max didn't hesitate. 'I'll do it tomorrow during the sleigh rides. Give me one man.'

Helmut smiled. His son had never killed a woman before. 'Take Stein with you.'

'How can we be sure you'll carry it out, Max?' said Joachim.

'That's enough, Joachim.' Helmut turned to his elder son, savouring the power he held over him. 'We can trust you, Max, can't we?'

Max's face was an expressionless mask. 'Yes,' he said. He looked at Joachim, then Klaus. Finally, he turned back to his father. 'I'll prove it to you.'

54

The next morning: 31 December

Whenever Isabella had had nightmares as a child her father would sit by her bed and stroke her cheek till she was calm again. In the morning she had always been unable to understand the fear that had kept her awake, shivering, in the dark. But this morning the nightmare didn't evaporate and her father could no longer comfort her.

After her disastrous meeting with Phoebe she had considered going to the other bridesmaids, but they, too, were under the spell of the drug and she had been too discouraged to approach them. Instead she had tried to rest. When sleep had come, though, it had been short and troubled. She had woken in a cold sweat. In her mind's eye she had seen the Kappels kill her father because of what he knew. Max, the man she had thought she loved, had raised a gun and shot him.

Isabella carried the portable hard drive with her when she went to breakfast in the dining room. She sat with the other guests and listened to them discuss the day's excursions. The weather promised to be crisp and clear, and most were going on helicopter trips to the Arctic Circle to see the Northern Lights if they were lucky. Others were happy to take sleigh rides round the eastern side of the lake.

After breakfast she put on her fur coat and walked outside. Her friends were cavorting with their partners from last night. They greeted her, but were preoccupied. She saw no sign of Phoebe.

She walked to one of the sleighs to take a ride in the head-clearing cold air. Then she would seek out a German dictionary and discover exactly what the Kappels had planned. As she neared the sleigh Hudsucker appeared on her left.

'You promised to ride with me,' he said, helping her up. Then, before the driver could galvanize the dogs into action, a voice called Hudsucker's name and a figure by the main door beckoned to him. He frowned, then patted Isabella's knee. 'Back soon.'

She watched him walk back to Valhalla, then Max was climbing on to the sleigh beside her. The driver stepped off and Stein took his place. Before she could react, he glanced at her, cracked the whip and the barking dogs set off.

Anxious suddenly, she tried to get off the sleigh.

Max took her hand. 'Please, Isabella, just a quick ride. I've been wanting to talk to you ever since you got here,' he gestured over his shoulder at Hudsucker and Delphine who were now waving frantically to attract their attention, 'but someone's been monopolizing you.'

Her palms felt clammy, but she remained calm. 'You haven't exactly been at a loose end yourself, Max.' She glanced back. 'Perhaps your fiancée would like to join us?'

He smiled. 'I'm sure she and Hudsucker will get along famously. I want some time alone with you.'

Fear rose in her. Then she reminded herself that the Kappels needed her alive: according to Joachim's document, she wasn't supposed to die for at least six months. She glanced back at Valhalla, gleaming in the early sunlight, and noticed that the other sleighs were heading in the opposite direction, inland towards the river. 'Where are we going?' She looked down at the water flowing beneath the ice. 'I thought we were supposed to stay on the other side of the lake. Joachim said the ice was thin by the fjord. Something about the river flowing into the sea and the Gulf Stream.'

'We know the safe areas – and I want to show you something.'

'What?'

'You'll see.'

As the dogs pulled the sleigh over the ice, she realized that the high sides of the vast lake were riddled with long, narrow inlets, and the scale of everything around her made her feel small and vulnerable.

As they neared the narrow fjord the ice became visibly thinner and more watery: she could see where the mantle of ice on the lake gave way to the river, which flowed to the sea.

'Max, the ice looks so thin.'

'Relax, it's fine.'

The sleigh turned into one of the narrow inlets.

The towering mountains on either side of the canyon were so close and high that sounds echoed in the cold air, as though they were in a cathedral. Apart from the dogs and the sleigh's runners on the ice there was silence. She saw a solitary majestic eagle flying high above, but not another living creature seemed to inhabit this frozen world.

She looked behind her but could no longer see Valhalla, or even the lake. The canyon was tall and narrow, but it twisted and turned so she was hemmed in on all sides by icy rock. The sun failed to reach the bottom of the deep inlet and it was colder than it had been on the lake.

'Max, what do you want to show me?'

He tapped Stein's shoulder and pointed to a beach of snow and rock beneath a high overhang. The dogs pulled the sleigh off the ice and on to the ground. The sleigh stopped and Isabella was glad to be back on *terra firma*.

Her relief evaporated when Stein turned from the dogs and stared at her. There was a sadistic gleam in his eye and he held a curved Kukri knife in his right hand. 'I'll do it, Max.'

A hard, cold lump formed in Isabella's belly. 'Max, what the hell's going on?'

'I'll do it,' Stein said again. 'It'll be like old times.

Remember Hawaii, Max?' He tapped his eyepatch and grinned. 'You were just a pup when you gave me this on the night I drowned your mother. If you haven't the stomach for it, it'll be my pleasure.'

'Put the knife away,' Max said, and pulled a pistol out of his coat. There was a silencer on the barrel. His eyes were as cold and hard as the surrounding rock.

'A bullet's too quick,' Stein said. 'Let me use the knife on her.'

Max kept his eyes locked on hers. 'I know you got into Joachim's computer, Isabella.'

Isabella's left knee was shaking as it had on that night in Antibes. Max had saved her then, but now he was going to kill her. 'Not you, Max,' she said, hating the quaver in her voice. She remembered last night's dream. 'Tell me one thing. Did you kill my father?'

'No. For what it's worth I tried to save him. My father killed him.' Max raised the pistol. 'I don't expect you to believe me, Isabella, but I'm truly sorry about this. I wish there was another way.'

She wanted to look into his face when he killed her, but she couldn't. She held her breath, squeezed her eyes shut and waited for the explosion. The gunshot, when it came, was little more than a metallic spit that barely bruised the frozen silence. Her knees buckled, and as she crumpled forward she opened her eyes to see Stein keel over with a neat red hole in his forehead. The bullet had severed the strap of his eyepatch, and the empty socket was revealed.

She turned back to Max, uncomprehending. He put the gun away. 'Give me your hand, Isabella,' he said. 'We've got a lot to do.'

55

As Max looked down at Isabella he marvelled at how much he could feel for another person. His chest felt tight and his heart ached, almost as if it had been crushed. The pain was so acute that part of him almost wished Joachim's drug had worked, and that he now loved Delphine Chevalier. If anything, his love for Isabella now burned even more fiercely. He couldn't understand why the drug hadn't worked on him.

He put away his gun and stepped towards Isabella, but she recoiled from his outstretched hand. He hated seeing the distrust in her eyes. He had killed for her and would gladly die for her, but he deserved her fear, even her hatred. His only consolation was that his darker side now protected her.

Isabella stared at Stein's body, watching the blood form a red halo in the icy snow around his head. 'I don't understand,' she muttered. 'What the hell's going on?'

'You're safe with me, Isabella, and I'll explain everything, but for now you've got to trust me.'

'*Trust you?* After all you've done? After Antibes? The lies? *My father?*' She lunged forward and pounded his chest with her fists. He stood unmoving while the blows rained down on him and wished she could beat away his guilt and self-disgust. When her fury subsided, he held her in his arms.

'I hate you. I hate you,' she hissed.

'I know – and I don't blame you. But I love you. I've loved you from the first time I saw you. From before I took the drug.' He looked down at her face and her eyes glared up at him. He had no chance of winning her love, he knew, but he could still put right what he had done. 'It doesn't matter what you feel about me, Isabella, all that matters is that we stop Project Ilium and save the others.'

'Why should I trust you now?'

'Because I haven't killed you. And because I'm all you've got.'

She paused. 'So what do we do?'

He picked up the Kukri knife from beside Stein's corpse and felt the curved blade. The edge was razor sharp. 'First of all, roll up your sleeve.'

The fear returned to her eyes. 'Why?'

'Because you've still got to die.'

As Helmut Kappel sat in the ice chapel alone with his younger son, Isabella was far from his thoughts.

'Administering the Venus serum is straight-forward, Vati,' Joachim said, holding a vial in one hand and tapping at his laptop with the other. 'By tomorrow morning the guests will be primed.'

Helmut leaned back on the fur-covered seat, watching the smoke from his cigar loop up into the rainbow shafts of refracted sunlight, which danced round the prism of the ice-chapel vault. 'I understand how it's to be administered. I just want to be sure it works.'

Joachim turned the screen so it faced his father. 'In simple terms I've combined two tried and tested elements. We know that Bacci's NiL Forty-two genes induce an obsessive devotion to whoever's facial blueprint is encoded within them when neutralizing all other feelings of love. And I know exactly how the Tag Vector will deliver them, because I developed it. It'll work. The only issue is timing.'

'Timing?'

'Because my vector has an airborne component based on a virulent influenza retrovirus, I had to build in certain safety features when seeking approval from the European and American authorities. If you remember, the Tag Vector was originally developed to *spread* cures – specifically for Aids. It works in two stages. It's initially given to the patient orally, and once in the bloodstream it targets specific cells. If it detects a certain chemical signal – in the case of Aids it's the presence of HIV – it mutates and its airborne influenza component becomes active, triggering a mild irritation in the patient's respiratory tract. The Tag Vector and its therapeutic contents cure the patient of Aids and spread, through coughing, to the next patient, where the process starts again. However, if it detects nothing within forty-eight hours the Tag Vector dies and leaves the host. This safety feature was designed to ensure that the virus only survives and spreads if it can do some good.'

'What does this mean for Venus?'

'Obviously the Tag Vector here is delivering the NiL Forty-two genes and not an Aids cure, but the principle still applies. In this case, however, instead of HIV acting as the trigger, it's facial recognition. Basically the guests take Venus imprinted with your facial genetic code and the next morning they awake primed. Then as long as they see your face within forty-eight hours – or a picure of your face – the second airborne stage of the Tag Vector will be triggered, and Venus's effect will not only be permanent, it will spread.'

'If they don't see me in that period?'

'The drug fades from their systems and their brains correct themselves. But that's not going to happen, Vati. You're getting married tomorrow. You'll be the centre of attention. Everyone's going to see your face and nothing will go wrong. Just as you asked me, Vati, I've ensured that Venus is essentially an airborne, nature-identical love virus, from which there is no escape and for which there is no cure.'

Despite the chill in the chapel Helmut felt warm with anticipation. 'Excellent, Joachim.'

His son beamed with pride. 'But that's not all, Vati. The best bit is—'

Helmut heard raised voices outside the main door of the chapel. The two guards had been instructed to allow no one entry. Not even Klaus or Max. 'Put everything away, Joachim.'

Joachim hid the vial and closed the laptop as the door opened and Max strode into the chapel with a leather bag. A guard followed him, protesting, but Helmut raised his hand.

'Max?'

Max waited for the guard to leave, then placed the bag on the floor before them. His face was pale and expressionless.

'What is it, Max?'

Max reached for Joachim's laptop and opened it. Joachim made to stop him, but Helmut shook his head. Max switched it on and waited for the access screen to appear. Then he returned to the bag and opened it. 'You feared I'd given my heart to Isabella and betrayed you. But that's impossible. I'm a Kappel and have no heart.' Max pulled out a sealed plastic freezer bag and opened it to reveal another plastic bag, which contained what looked like meat. Both bags were wet with blood. 'Isabella had a heart, though,' Max said, and let a drop of blood fall on to the laptop's DNA sensor. Within seconds Isabella's face appeared on the screen, along with the words: 'Access Denied'.

Max reached into the inner bag and presented the bloody mass to Helmut. 'I said I'd prove my loyalty, Vater.' His father recoiled and his brother retched. 'Isabella had a large heart,' Max said, and pushed the bag into Helmut's face. 'Go on! Touch it! Smell it! *Taste it!* You once told me that a pure Kappel feels no emotion, has no conscience and shows no pain. Is this enough proof that I'm a pure, loyal Kappel?'

Helmut was stunned. Years ago he had ruthlessly killed a woman he had thought he loved because she threatened the family. Now their son had outstripped even his brutality.

'Do you trust me now, Vater?' Max demanded. 'Are you proud of me?'

Beneath his shock Helmut felt a surge of satisfaction. He had purged all trace of his first wife's nature from their son and shaped Max in his own image. 'Yes,' he whispered. 'I'm proud of you.'

'Good,' Max said. He repacked the plastic bags, replaced the bundle in the leather tote and strode out.

56

Max was shaking as he left the chapel, but he didn't feel cold. He headed straight for the deserted boiler-house. Inside there were two rooms. One contained steel hawsers, flares, drums of oil and emergency winter supplies. The second housed a back-up generator and two cast-iron boilers – one was oil-powered, and the auxiliary burned solid fuel. Both were in operation. He went to the smaller boiler, opened the feeder door and threw in the leather bag.

Outside, he saw two of the five ex-Stasi guards his father had brought to Valhalla to handle security. He had always taken them for granted, but now he saw them as a threat. They hailed him: 'Herr Kappel, have you seen Herr Stein?'

He could have told an elaborate lie, but in his experience the truth was always more credible. 'Not since I got back.'

He avoided the main glass doors and crunched through the snow to the steps that led to the summer terrace on the second tier of the crystal palace. Apart from two sets of fresh footprints – one large, the other small – the snow-encrusted steps were unused. When he reached the terrace he walked to the first set of tinted sliding doors. The reflective glass made it impossible to see inside the suite. He took off his glove, blew on his hand, then placed his palm on the DNA sensor. There was a delay because of the cold, then his face appeared on the monitor and the doors slid open.

He stepped on to the mat and, as the doors closed behind him, glanced around the lounge area of his suite. He kicked off his snowy boots, walked into the bedroom and opened the bathroom door. He glimpsed Isabella leaning over the bath, dressing the cut on her left arm, before she jerked round, eyes huge with panic. The fright dimmed when she saw it was him. She still looked as pale as she had when he had forced himself to cut out Stein's heart. Every cell in his body had resisted performing the butchery, but it had been effective: no Kappel could doubt him now – and, more importantly, he had bought himself and Isabella some time.

'You're safe for now,' he said, as gently as he could. 'They think you're dead.'

He led her into the lounge, poured two glasses of malt whisky and gave her one. She drank it and coughed. He refilled her glass. This time she held it in both hands and sipped.

'What do you know about Ilium?' he asked.

She reached into her jacket pocket and pulled out a firewire portable hard drive. 'Not much. The files are in German.'

'In that case,' he said, 'I'll tell you all I know.'

For the next half-hour, Max told her everything, keeping nothing from her. He told her how his mother had taken him from Zurich as a boy, given him a US passport and a new identity. And how his father had found them in Hawaii and killed her. He explained the Kappel family business and that he was its heir. He told her how he had murdered to help clients and the business. He told her how Trapani had recommended Kappel Privatbank and its Comvec offshoot to her father. He recounted the night of Bacci's death. Finally he told her about Project Ilium, explaining that after the wedding, assuming the respective target clients had paid their dues, each bridesmaid would be given a permanent version of the NiL drug, modified to kill them in six months.

'So, we have all received the harmless temporary NiL drug?' Isabelle asked.

'Yes. The others won't get the permanent lethal version until they leave tomorrow.'

'But you're sure we *all* got the temporary version? Including me?'

'Joachim and Stein injected you all on the way here.' Then it dawned on him. 'It hasn't worked on you, has it? You feel nothing for Hudsucker.'

'No.'

'The permanent version didn't work on me. But the drug worked on both of us in Antibes. Why not this time?'

Something flashed in her eyes, but she shook her head as though to dismiss the thought.

'What?' he said.

She sipped her whisky. 'Nothing.'

She looked so vulnerable and alone that he wanted to reassure her. 'I won't stand by and let my family kill you. I tried to warn you the night before you flew out here, but my father injected me with the drug then sedated me. I watched you leave your apartment as I lost consciousness.' He relived the moment. 'I've only ever felt so helpless and desolate once before. I was sure that when I awoke I'd forget I loved you. But I didn't.' He waited for her to say something.

After a brief pause she stood up and held out the portable hard drive. 'Your laptop?'

He pointed to the desk in the corner. She walked over and attached the firewire cable. 'You're sure we've got until tomorrow to stop Ilium?'

Max checked his watch. 'Yes. My father and Klaus should be meeting with the target clients at any moment to extract their payment. The lethal permanent dose will be administered as the brides-maids leave. But, I won't let that happen.'

She powered up the computer and opened the folder. 'Okay, I understand Ilium, but not Project Venus.'

'What?'

She pointed at a folder on the screen labelled 'Ilium/Venus'. 'You've never heard of it?'

'No.'

She double-clicked on the folder, revealing two separate ones, then highlighted Venus. 'It shares the same folder as Ilium, so I guess it's some kind of sister project. Perhaps it's the antidote.' She double-clicked and a list of files appeared. She opened the first.

It was a German text document, evidently a management summary of the project. The introductory paragraph made him gasp. He reached for the mouse. Helmut Kappel's project could never be called an antidote – unless you had the darkest sense of humour. As he scrolled down the screen he was appalled by his father's arrogance. And yet it all made a kind of sense. 'Shit,' he muttered.

'What is it?' she said. 'Tell me.'

57

Two hours later

'You asked to see me.' Feliks Lysenko was the third to be called into the small conference room near the atrium. Now that Isabella was dead they would have to wait to extract payment from Hudsucker, but Helmut Kappel wasn't dissatisfied. Over the last couple of hours Giscard Corbasson and Christophe Nadolny had agreed terms, and there was no reason to suppose that the Russian would be any different. Venus hadn't even begun, but Helmut had never felt more powerful.

The masked ball wasn't due to start for a few hours but Lysenko wore immaculate evening dress and carried an elaborate mask. The Russian glanced at Klaus Kappel, who was sitting in the corner looking at a laptop. 'Where are your masks?' he asked, as excited as a child at Hallowe'en.

'We'll wear them when the party starts,' Helmut said.

Lysenko wagged a finger. 'Is this a business

meeting? Shame on you! It is the eve of your wedding. You should have fun.'

'Have a seat, Feliks. Have you been enjoying yourself?'

Lysenko sat and a broad grin creased his face. 'I have never had such fun. The company has been perfect.'

Helmut smiled. 'Kathryn Walker is indeed exquisite – and to be in love with a beautiful young woman who reciprocates your passion! Believe me, I know how that feels.'

Lysenko grinned, and Helmut had to turn away to conceal his contempt. He marvelled at how quickly love's alchemy had turned the Russian into a foolish boy.

'But, Feliks, you of all people understand that everything has a price. Since I invited you to my wedding, you haven't been able to stop thinking about Kathryn. Don't deny it, my friend – you've been in a kind of hell. Then you came here, met the object of your dreams and are now in heaven. Am I right?'

Lysenko said nothing.

'It would be unthinkable to return to hell now, Feliks, wouldn't it? I know I'd hate it if Phoebe no longer wanted me.'

Lysenko frowned.

'Let me be frank with you, Feliks. Although you're intending to move your accounts from Kappel Privatbank, we remain loyal to you. We still wish to serve you as our client. We want nothing more than to see you leave here with your new love, and live happily ever after.' He paused. 'But there's a problem.'

'What are you saying?'

'That Kathryn Walker's love for you will expire by the end of tomorrow. When you leave here, the two blissful days you spent with her will be only a memory that'll haunt you for the rest of your life. If you agree to certain conditions, however, we can guarantee that her love for you will last her lifetime.'

Lysenko's initial reaction was no different from that of the Frenchman and the Swiss. He was furious. 'Who the fuck do you think you are? You don't control my private life. How dare you? I will destroy you.' He strode to the door.

'Don't be foolish, Feliks. Look at the facts. Your passion for Kathryn began after we sent you an invitation to my wedding. When I introduced you to her, she immediately fell madly in love with you. Why? She doesn't need your money. You're her social inferior. And she certainly isn't after you for your youthful looks.'

Lysenko's head was a red beacon of rage. But he hovered by the door.

Helmut marvelled again at how love's power could turn even the most ruthless, hard-headed man into a malleable fool. 'Don't be offended, Feliks. Look at Phoebe and me. How do you think I snared her? I don't fool myself that she'd be marrying me without a little help. You must have known it was too good to be true. You went from desperation to having your dream come true. But dreams cost money. Fortunately you have plenty of that.'

Lysenko reached for the door handle. But his feet didn't move. 'How much?' he said eventually.

'Well, here is the problem. There are other interested parties. Kathryn Walker is a very desirable woman. But we want *you* to have her. You've been a client for a long time and I hope you'll stay one for even longer.'

'How much do you want?' Lysenko said.

'How much do you want her?'

'A million?'

Helmut laughed, and turned to Klaus. 'How much can our good friend afford?'

'At least a thousand times more than that.'

'This is the deal, Feliks. If you want us to guarantee you Kathryn Walker's love for the rest of her life, you'll transfer a billion euros into an escrow account. We'll ensure that the payments are staggered so they don't look too obvious.'

'A billion? That's ridiculous. It would virtually bankrupt me.'

'You have an hour to decide. After that the price increases by a hundred million euros an hour. Once you leave here tomorrow the deal is off. Of course, if you can live without her then what I'm suggesting is ludicrous. If, however, you truly love her, it's the bargain of a lifetime. Why *search* for true love when you can *buy* it? Happiness is the best investment you'll ever make.'

Helmut lit a cigarette and relished the hit. 'You have an hour,' he repeated. 'Once you decide what you want to do, contact Klaus and he'll arrange everything.' He stood up and extended his hand. 'Enjoy the party, Feliks, and cherish your time with Kathryn. Don't be angry with us. We're not forcing you to do anything. We're merely offering you the chance to secure true love, which until now your money has been unable to buy.'

After Lysenko had left, Joachim entered the room with a tray of four small shot glasses moulded in ice. Each bore embossed images of Helmut and Phoebe's faces.

'Ah, thank you, Joachim.'

'I like the glasses.' Klaus took one.

Helmut smiled. 'They were designed for tonight's toast. I thought we'd sample them to celebrate the success of Project Ilium.'

'Where's Max?' Klaus asked.

Helmut smiled. 'I haven't seen him or Stein since Max reported back from his trip with Isabella Bacci. Let him be. I suspect he's resting after his exertions.'

'She's no longer an issue?' Klaus added.

Helmut turned to Joachim, who had paled. 'I think we can safely say she's out of the equation.' He raised his glass. 'To the power of love.'

'To love,' the other men echoed, and drank.

58

Isabella sipped her Scotch as she looked at the computer screen and her scribbled notes. She had always hated whisky, but as she struggled to make sense of the madness of Venus, its fiery taste soothed her jangling nerves and calmed her. For the last two hours she and Max had sat at the laptop, translating Joachim's scientific notes. She tried to ignore the confused and intense emotions Max brought out in her. On the lake she had been convinced he was going to kill her. And the shock, when he had turned the gun on Stein and told her he loved her, had been almost too much to bear. She still couldn't decide whether he was her tormentor or saviour. She believed him when he said he had tried to save her father, but doubted she could ever forgive him for his part in deceiving her and her friends with Ilium – regardless of what he might do now to put it right.

What added to her confusion was that this time the drug hadn't worked on her or Max. Assuming it had been administered correctly, there was only one reason for this: the Zero Substitution Effect she had read about in her father's notes. But she didn't want to think about that. Not yet anyway.

Instead she focused on what she had learned about Venus and what she could do to stop it.

'Tell me what we've got so far,' Max said. He looked as tired as she felt.

She glanced down at her notes. 'Venus is an earlier version of the NiL drug inserted into one of Comvec's smart vectors. Your half-brother selected one of my father's prototypes and combined it with his Tag Vector.'

'Joachim could never get the authorities to approve his Tag Vector.'

'Probably for the same reasons that your father wanted to use it. It's virtually impossible to contain.'

'But why use one of the earlier NiL prototypes?'

'Because NiL Forty-two has no gender boundaries.'

'What?'

'No *sexual* chemistry. Let's say I imprinted my facial genetic code on Venus and injected it into a heterosexual woman or a homosexual man. They wouldn't want to have sex with me, but they'd still adore me. What's more, any love they felt for anyone else – children, friends, family – would be neutralized by their passion for me. It's far stronger than NiL Sixty-nine or Seventy-two. This was the version that made my father almost scrap the project. In his notes he called it an *anti*-love drug.'

She remembered sitting in her father's attic, reading his letters to her dead mother. 'Anyone I injected with the drug would worship me. They'd be compelled to gaze at my face, or a likeness of it. If they couldn't get their fix, they'd be beset by an almost intolerable anxiety. I'd become the centre of their existence – a kind of god.

'But that's not all. By using the Tag Vector Joachim has added a new dimension. Let's say the patient, the victim, is a woman. As with NiL Sixty-nine or Seventy-two, her brain is reprogrammed while she sleeps, and love is triggered when she next sees the genetic facial imprint encoded in the drug. But after that Venus is different from both NiL Sixty-nine and Seventy-two.'

'How?'

'First, it works across genders, as I said, and it's a liquid that has to be drunk rather than the powder that's injected. Second, as soon as the subject's love is triggered the airborne influenza component of the Tag Vector kicks in and she becomes an unwitting, infectious carrier, who can spread her devotion with just a cough, perpetuating the cycle.'

Max's head ached. 'And it's my father's facial genetic imprint on the drug.'

'Of course.'

His father had always been obsessed with duty and destiny, Max knew, and this fulfilled his ultimate fantasy. Venus would cure the world of every conflicting, confusing, weak aspect of love, and in its place leave just one pure strain: single-minded devotion to him. Helmut had probably convinced himself that he was doing the world a great service in purging it of love. He was helping it find a new sense of direction, unity and duty. He would become the ultimate patriarch, and the entire human species would become his devoted and obedient family.

He got up and paced the room. 'And, of course, this explains why he wanted this circus of a wedding. It fits perfectly with his plans. While the guests are here in a controlled environment he can watch them and choose his moment. He must be loving this.'

'According to Joachim's files, they plan to administer the drug some time today or tonight so it becomes live tomorrow.'

'Perfect,' groaned Max. 'Tomorrow the guests will be primed and all eyes will be on the happy couple in the ice chapel. As soon as they see my father their devotion will be triggered. When they return home they'll infect everyone they come into contact with. And because of the global media feeding frenzy that's going to follow this wedding, his face will be everywhere.' Max could barely get his mind round the enormity of his father's mad ambition.

'He'll be bigger than Christ,' she said. 'Within days, Joachim's Tag Vector will have spread the

NiL Forty-two genes around the world. Studies have shown that, with modern air travel, a flu-like virus can travel the globe in less than a week. In a matter of days most of the world will be obsessed with your father and feel no love for anyone else.'

Project Ilium had been intended to protect the financial future of his father's bank and punish a few disloyal key clients – but it was a sideshow, Max realized now, a distraction from the main event. 'Are Klaus and Joachim in on this too?' he asked aloud. 'Joachim must be.'

'After the wedding it won't matter who was in on it. Once you're infected, you'll worship him too. But why do you think your half-brother helped him?'

Max could guess what had happened. From the first meeting, when Bacci had told them about his disastrous NiL #042 experiment, the seed would have been planted in his father's mind. It wouldn't have taken him long to come up with the combination of Bacci's drug and Joachim's Tag Vector. He would have flattered Joachim by asking him to make up a permanent version of the NiL #042 drug, which contained his facial imprint. And delighted, Joachim would have obliged, having no idea that his father intended to use it on him. Once Joachim was in his father's thrall, Helmut would have told him to combine it with the Tag Vector. The irony was that Joachim had always worshipped their father and would probably have done whatever he wanted anyway. His younger brother hadn't stood a chance.

'There's one more thing, Max,' Isabella said. 'Joachim's Tag Vector gives Venus a brilliant final twist that I'm sure delights your father.'

'What?'

'First, you've got to remember that the key difference between the temporary Sixty-nine and the lifetime Seventy-two of the conventional NiL drug lies in the *type* of cells they target. Sixty-nine uses a vector that targets the somatic or body cells, which have a finite life. Once these cells die, the drug and its effects die with it. In the case of NiL Sixty-nine that takes about forty-eight hours.

'The Seventy-two vector not only targets the somatic cells but also the stem cells, which are constant throughout a person's life. Seventy-two and its effects stay with the subject until they die.' She sipped her drink. 'Venus, however, takes it to a whole new level.'

Max groaned. He knew what was coming. 'Go on.'

'Venus uses the Tag Vector, which doesn't only target the somatic cells or the stem cells but the sex cells responsible for reproduction. The Tag Vector was designed not only to pass gene-therapy cures from patient to patient, but from generation to generation. Once the second stage is triggered, the Tag Vector worms its DNA into either the man's testes or the woman's ovaries. Venus goes beyond permanent – it's eternal. Your father got Joachim to use his vector to make humanity adore him *for ever*. Even after he's dead people will still adore him, their descendants too.'

Max thought of the planned mausoleum, complete with preserved corpse, and he paled at the enormity of his father's effrontery. 'I've got to stop him,' he said. 'I've got to stop them all.'

'What if they've already released Venus? They might have put it in the milk at breakfast.' She reached for the bottle of mineral water on the sideboard. 'The staff put one of these in the rooms every day. Only a few of the guests need to be affected for Venus to spread.'

'In that case I've got to find out if they've administered it yet. If they haven't, I'll do what's necessary to stop it. If they have . . .' his eyes were dark with dread '. . . I can't let anyone leave this island.'

Isabella felt some sympathy for Max. He appeared to be taking full responsibility for what Helmut Kappel had done, as though his father's sins were his own. She thought then that she understood Max. He saw his mother as being all that was good in him and his father as all that was bad. After her death, for which he had blamed himself, he had allowed his father's values to dominate his life. Now, for whatever reason, he was committed to defying his family and everything that until now had defined him – by destroying them if necessary. Like her, he was alone.

'Even killing your father won't stop its effects. The world will still worship his image. The drug makes him immortal. We've got to stop the drug.'

'But how do we stop it? Is there an antidote to Venus?'

'No.' She checked through her notes. Even the Zero Substitution Effect only applied to later versions of her father's drug. Then an idea came to her. 'There is one approach that might work,' she said. 'According to the files, Joachim's Tag Vector has an Achilles heel.' She told him about the tablets she had brought from Milan and unsuccessfully tried to give Phoebe. As she explained her plan, his eyes lit with fresh resolve.

'The problem,' she said, 'is how to administer the tablets secretly to *everyone*.'

'That's easy,' he said. 'We won't do it secretly. We'll do it openly. I'll *tell* everyone to drink whatever you give them.'

'I don't understand.'

'I'm the best man. If I propose a toast to the bride and groom everyone has to drink it.' His eyes flashed her a challenge. 'The real problem is getting the tablets into the toast.'

She saw the light in his eyes and a glimmer of hope sparked within her. At last there was something she could do. 'I think I know a way,' she said, 'but I can't do it alone.'

'Isabella, we're in this together,' he said, 'so you're not alone. Not any more.'

59

That evening

Tradition stipulates that on the eve of their wedding the bride and groom should not see each other, and although Helmut sat beside Phoebe during the New Year's Eve dinner, the rule was not breached. Everyone wore a mask. The women's represented Freya's face and the men's the god Odin's. No one was recognizable. Even the waitresses, attired in their breastplates, leather skirts, boots and helmets, wore gilded face visors.

As the hundred guests took their seats around the long trestle tables in the great hall, Helmut relished the irony that although tonight no one could recognize him soon everyone would. Tomorrow he would stand in the ice chapel beside the most beautiful woman in the world, and every pair of eyes, including Phoebe's, would be fixed on *him*. In a matter of days the world would look to him for leadership and direction.

He had once read that the most ubiquitous profile in the world was that of the Queen of

England. Her image appeared on stamps and currency in Britain and many Commonwealth nations around the globe. But he would eclipse all royalty, presidents and film stars. Religious messiahs and prophets would fade from view. The Beatles had once joked that they were bigger than Jesus. He *would* be bigger than Jesus. Everyone, however exalted or powerful, would seek his counsel. He would bring order and strength to a weak, chaotic world.

He sat back in his chair and basked in the promise of the future. Everything was in place. Ilium had met its objectives: an hour ago Lysenko had gone the way of the others and authorized the movement of a billion euros to an escrow account. But Venus would bring far more.

Phoebe tapped his arm. 'I still can't believe Isabella left. What did she say?'

'Forget about her,' he said. 'You've got three other bridesmaids.'

'But what did she say?'

'I told you. She was so ashamed of lying to you last night that she couldn't face you. She still doesn't agree with our marriage, and couldn't watch you make a huge mistake in marrying me.'

'She said that?'

'She's entitled to her opinion and I respect her candour. I'm sure that when she's had time to get used to the idea you'll be friends again. Now, concentrate on enjoying the evening.'

Explaining away Isabella's disappearance had

been less of a problem with Phoebe than it had been with Hudsucker. When Helmut had explained to him that Isabella had returned home, the senator had been inconsolable.

The exquisite food and drink were served on silver plates and in crystal glasses that sparkled like diamonds in the lights. The toast would be drunk after the main course, venison, and Helmut watched Joachim reach into his jacket and extract a small key, ready to pass round the drinks he had so painstakingly prepared. But before he could move, Max stood up.

'Where are you going?' Joachim asked.

'To prepare the toast.'

'But I've already arranged the moulded-ice glasses.'

'Leave it to me.'

'But—'

'I'm the best man. I should do it.'

Joachim glanced at his father and Helmut nodded. Max's change of attitude and renewed loyalty should be encouraged. Joachim frowned, but he handed Max the key. 'They're in the first freezer room next to the kitchens. The drinks are poured and laid out on trays. Just unlock the room, and tell the waitresses to serve them.'

Helmut watched Max walk through the great hall to the swing door that led to the kitchens. Then he saw two of Stein's Stasi enter from the reception hall. Both wore full Arctic gear with thick boots. They came into the room, walked over to him and one bent down to whisper, 'Herr Kappel, the dogs have found something you should see.'

When Helmut saw what the man held, his euphoria was replaced with anger. 'Come with me.'

Max strode casually through the great hall, smiling at the guests as he passed them. He wanted desperately to hurry because there wasn't much time, but he knew either Joachim or his father might be watching. He walked into the kitchens and asked the way to the freezers. He followed the directions, passing numerous waitresses.

There was a tap on his shoulder. 'Can I help you, sir?'

He turned and hesitated for only a second. 'Yes. It's time to serve the drinks for the toast,' he told the waitress.

'Where are they?'

'This way.'

He led her to the freezer room, unlocked the door and stepped inside. There were two rooms: an outer cold room, which the temperature gauge told Max was kept at four degrees Celsius, and an inner freezer kept at minus twenty-three. In the cold room, carcasses hung from hooks and large salmon lay in stainless-steel trays. He opened the inner door to the smaller freezer, which contained joints of meat hanging on hooks. A stainless-steel table stood in the middle with four square transparent trays set on it. Each held five rows of five ice glasses, moulded with the embossed faces of Helmut and Phoebe. Each had been filled with a shot of clear liquid.

'Are these for the toast?' the woman said.

He nodded and turned to close the door.

But a man was standing there. Even before he pulled off his mask Max knew it was his father. 'Please step outside, Max.'

Max frowned behind his mask. 'Why?'

Two of the ex-Stasi, in full Arctic gear, appeared behind Helmut. 'Just do it, Max.'

Max stepped out, leaving the waitress alone in the freezer room with the drinks. 'What's wrong?'

'These men have just returned from an excursion to find Stein. Their dogs followed a trail across the ice to an inlet on the fjord side of the lake.' His father extended a hand and opened it. Stein's torn eyepatch lay on the palm. 'I assume his body's in the lake. And I'm guessing that Isabella Bacci is alive.'

Max's first instinct was to fight, but when he considered his main objective, he decided against it. His father stared at him. 'I'm disappointed in you, Max,' he said eventually. 'Where's Isabella?'

'She's gone. I helped her escape. She told me all about Venus and she's got all the evidence on disk. She's taking it to the authorities.'

Helmut's jaw muscles clenched. 'Even if she reached civilization, it won't matter after tomorrow – because everyone here will have drunk that toast.' His eyes hardened. 'What concerns me is that you betrayed me again. Why?'

390

'Because you're insane and someone has to stop you.'

Helmut glared at him, apparently incredulous that anyone, especially his heir, could speak to him in such a way. 'You're like your mother. I could never reason with her. When you betrayed me in Milan, I forgave you, Max. I thought you were misguided. I see now that I was the one who was misguided.'

Another man appeared in a mask. 'Is the toast okay?'

'It's fine, Joachim. He could not have known we were going to deliver the drug in the toast, but please check.'

Joachim removed his mask and smiled malevolently at his brother. He disappeared into the freezer room. 'Wait outside,' Max heard him order the waitress.

She stepped out and stood a discreet distance away.

'So, you're using the toast to deliver Venus,' Max said. 'You won't get away with it.'

Helmut ignored him. Joachim reappeared less than a minute later and replaced his mask. 'You can serve them now,' he said to the waitress. 'I'll help you.'

Max's father waited until the woman and Joachim had left with the first two of the trays, then turned to the guards. 'I must get back for the toast. You know where to take him – somewhere we won't be disturbed when I talk to him later. He killed your boss, so I'll understand if you're not too gentle with him.'

60

'Follow me,' Joachim ordered. 'Take your tray to that table and make sure everyone has a glass. Serve the next tray when you've finished. I'll pass round the last one.'

Isabella tried to stop her hands trembling as she followed Joachim into the great hall. She had to force herself not to look back at Max, or to think about the fact that she was the sole dark-haired waitress among Odin's flaxen-haired Valkyries. She only hoped the mask and helmet proved adequate disguise.

The plan had been relatively simple. Since the Kappels had the run of Valhalla, Max had easily procured the mask and staff uniform from Housekeeping. In her disguise Isabella had to hang around in the kitchen until the toast was due and Max came out to her. Once they had located the glasses she was to drop one of her tablets into each drink before she rushed back to the security of his room.

Even if the plan had gone smoothly, the chances of stopping Venus were fifty-fifty at best. But now the odds of success had dramatically decreased. It had been a shock when Max was taken, but she had just had time to drop the tablets into the glasses while she was alone in the freezer. But when Max had said, 'So you're using the toast to deliver Venus,' her heart had sunk. It hadn't occurred to her that the guests would have to take the drugs together. She had no idea what the effect would be.

Then anger overcame fear. She or Max should have guessed that Helmut Kappel would use the toast to deliver Venus. Now, her plan was in jeopardy – and she was actually helping to *serve* his drug. She had no choice, though. She passed round the first tray without incident, although she felt a surge of anxiety when she recognized the Australia-shaped birthmark on the masked Warren Hudsucker's hand. He barely noticed her. Waitresses were ignored at the best of times. Masked waitresses were invisible.

She collected the second tray, and Joachim told her to serve the top table. She looked down to avoid even the possibility of eye-contact. First she served Klaus Kappel and his wife. As she placed a drink by Max Kappel's unoccupied chair, she heard Delphine Chevalier ask where Max had gone.

Serving Gisele, Claire and Kathryn was surreal. She wanted desperately to tell them what was happening, but they were so engrossed in their partners that she doubted they would have registered her presence even without the mask.

Helmut Kappel sat erect, and when she placed the ice glass in front of him, she could feel the rage radiating from him. Unconsciously he pushed it away. When she put a glass before Phoebe, she inadvertently brushed her friend's shoulder. Phoebe turned, and for a second their eyes locked. In that instant Isabella felt compelled to pull off her mask and tell Phoebe what her future husband planned. Then Phoebe turned away and the moment passed.

She forced herself to walk slowly past the diners to the kitchen until she reached the swing doors. As she pushed them open a sigh of relief escaped her lips.

Then Joachim called to her: 'You, the one who served the toast.'

She fought the impulse to run, then faced him.

He barely glanced at her as he gave her his empty tray. 'Take this to the kitchen.'

She took it, walked through the swing doors and out of the kitchen.

As Helmut listened to Joachim make the speech in Max's place, he couldn't stop thinking of his elder son's betrayal. Max was a Kappel. He had invested so much in his development. When Max had wavered with Isabella he had given him a second chance, stiffened his resolve by injecting him with the NiL drug. By now Max should have been besotted with Delphine Chevalier – he shouldn't have given a second thought to Isabella. Yet he had openly defied him and tried to thwart his destiny.

But this was still a moment of triumph. Lysenko, Corbasson and Nadolny were engrossed with the bridesmaids, having submitted to his demands. In six months their prizes would be dead. And, after tomorrow, the world would be Helmut's to control.

Yet he had been unable to control his own flesh and blood. Didn't Max appreciate his privileged position as one of the Kappel dynasty? He would punish him as he had punished Max's mother. His son's transgression was her fault. Her genes had diluted the Kappel stock. He had done all in his power to turn Max into a thoroughbred, but deep down he had always been a mongrel.

'What's wrong, darling?' Phoebe whispered. 'You seem tense and you should be happy.'

'I am happy,' Helmut rasped. As he heard Joachim thank Odin for the use of Valhalla and propose a toast to 'the happy couple', he calmed himself. Soon Max's betrayal wouldn't matter. Soon the entire world would be his family, his dynasty, and every future generation would recognize him as their head.

Joachim held his glass high and turned to Helmut. 'To tomorrow's ceremony and a glorious future. To destiny.'

'To destiny,' the room echoed. As the guests drained their ice glasses a murmur rustled round the great hall and everyone looked up at the crystal roof. Someone turned out the lights and the night sky was ablaze with shimmering colours. Spectral arcs and cones of red and green glowed against the night.

At that moment, a sense of power rushed through Helmut, purging his anger. He passed Phoebe her glass and watched her drink. As he gazed up at the shimmering ribbons of colour, he realized that Max was unimportant. No one mattered any more, not even Dieter Kappel. It was as though the gods of Valhalla were heralding his ascension to their elevated ranks.

61

As she left the kitchens and strode down the deserted corridors Isabella felt sick with anxiety and her head ached. When she heard the roar of the toast from the great hall she realized the die had been cast. She stared out the window and gasped. The sky was alight with ghostly flames. Red and green wraiths shimmered in the night, lighting up the darkness. She had never seen the Northern Lights before and they were far more impressive than she had imagined. But that they should appear on the eve of Helmut Kappel's Project Venus seemed like an omen, heralding a dark new dawn.

She looked down at the ice chapel and in the arc lights saw two armed guards escorting a third, taller man to the boiler-house. She immediately recognized Max as their prisoner. Two more guards met them by the boiler-house. One struck Max over the head with his rifle. When he fell to the snowy ground the others kicked him then dragged him inside. Max had killed one of their comrades to protect her, and now they were exacting their revenge. She remembered what Helmut had done to Max's mother, and doubted Max would survive the night.

Yet for all Max's evil deeds, he had twice saved her life. But how could she help him? She was alone. Phoebe and her other friends were spellbound by the NiL drug, and besotted with the ageing men who had bought them.

Then it came to her. It was a gamble, but there was no other way. After the risks Max had taken to save her and defy his family, she owed him something. And, as he had said, he was all she had.

She hurried to her room and opened the door. Max had already retrieved most of the items she needed, but in her suitcase she found the tranquillizers she had been prescribed after her father's death. She pulled out a foil strip, then thought better of it, and took all three. This was no time for half measures.

She checked her mask and walked back towards the great hall. Some of the diners were now dancing, but her target was still in his seat. She went to him and whispered that he was wanted in the reception hall. He stood up as obediently as a schoolboy and followed her out of the bustling great hall.

He looked around, then turned to her. 'Who wants to see me?'

She took off her mask. 'I do.'

Warren Hudsucker took off his own and stared

at her as if she was a ghost – or an angel. His face was radiant. 'You're here,' he said. 'They told me you'd gone. But why are you dressed as a waitress?'

'There's no time to explain, Warren. Will you do something for me?'

'Anything.'

TWO HOURS LATER

'Happy New Year, Max.'

Max got up from the concrete floor of the boiler-house storeroom and faced his father. He checked his watch: 12:35 a.m. The new year had begun.

'Happy New Year, Vater.'

His father pulled a cigar from his pocket, retrieved the assassin's knife from its sheath and sliced off the tip. He lit the cigar, sucked on it and sighed with satisfaction. 'It'll be an excellent new year, Max.' He turned to the guards. 'Give me a gun and leave us.'

Max's suit was crusted with blood and his ribs hurt from where the guards had beaten him, but he could cope with the pain – even with the prospect of death. At least Isabella hadn't been discovered. There was still a chance, he told himself.

'You can't stand in the way of destiny, Max,' Helmut said. 'The Venus drug is already working. Everyone will be feeling drowsy, and within an hour Valhalla will be silent. Tomorrow morning they'll wake to start not only a new year but a new era.

'The world's a mess, Max. No one can agree on anything. Everyone loves different things – different people, different gods, different countries, even different soccer teams. And they fight over them. They kill each other for what they love. Love doesn't bring the world together, it rips it apart. Patriotism isn't love of country, it's hatred of other countries. If you love one god, you must necessarily damn everyone else who loves another. Love excludes, separates and divides. But Venus will cure that. The world will be left with a single purpose, a single focus, a single love. Me. Humanity will be a single family and I will be its father.'

He paused. 'And you could have been part of it, Max. You could have been my right-hand man. But you have failed me.' He laughed bitterly. 'You let Isabella cloud your judgement. She made you weak. And for what?' He fingered the blood on Max's collar. 'Nothing.'

Max shook his head. 'You're wrong. My judgement has never been sounder. I've never seen more clearly who I am, and who you are.'

'Really? Tell me who you think I am.'

'I *know* who you are. You're a hypocrite and a coward. You speak of loyalty and family, then murder your wife and abuse your sons. You speak of dynasty and the duty of passing on a greater legacy than you inherited, then you conceive of a plan where you become immortal and all future generations become your slaves. You care nothing for family, dynasty or duty. You care only for yourself. You've killed my love for you and abused Joachim's by making him create a drug that *forces* everyone to love you.

'That's your worst hypocrisy: you ridicule love and yet you fear it. It terrifies you. You hate love, but haven't the courage to die unloved. Isabella didn't make me weak. She showed me how to be strong again. You made me forget what my mother taught me, but Isabella helped me remember. You're the weak one. Vater. You're the coward who hasn't the guts either to earn love, or to live and die without it.'

For several seconds Helmut stared at him. He appeared calm, but Max sensed his fury. 'As a son you've been a grave disappointment.'

Max laughed. 'As a father you've been a graver one.'

Helmut raised the pistol. 'I should have drowned you when I drowned your mother.'

'I often wish you had.'

A cruel smile illuminated Helmut's features. 'You'll learn, Max. I'm not going to kill you yet. I'm not even going to give you the Venus drug. I'll leave you here to think things through and greet the dawn. I want you to witness what Venus brings, and then, when you've seen my vision realized, I'll watch you catch the virus and love me too. That's when I'll punish you, Max. While you look into my eyes – the eyes of the father you'll adore – I'll drive a knife through your heart and watch you die.'

He turned to leave, then stopped.

'Your love for Isabella is meaningless. Whether you want to or not, you'll die loving me. And *only* me.'

62

Isabella waited until Helmut Kappel had returned to his suite in Valhalla before she knocked on the door of the boiler-house. She heard voices inside, then one of the guards she recognized from Schloss Kappel stepped out and closed the door behind him.

'What do you want?' he asked.

She proffered a tray of drinks. 'Herr Helmut Kappel asked me to bring you these to celebrate the new year and his wedding tomorrow.'

'We're on duty,' the guard said.

Despite the cold, her face was hot behind the mask. 'He insisted,' she said, trying to keep her voice light. 'Shall I go back to Herr Kappel and tell him you won't drink to his happiness?'

The guard smiled, but his eyes were hard. 'If Herr Kappel insists, it would be rude not to.'

'How many of you are in there?'

'Two.' He opened the door, passed one of the glasses inside and took one for himself. He pointed to the lake. 'The other two are by the helicopters. *Dankeschön*, Fräulein. Happy New Year.'

HALF AN HOUR LATER

Max didn't sleep. It wasn't the pain of his battered face and bruised body: he couldn't stop thinking of what tomorrow would bring. He hated his powerlessness, and not knowing what had happened.

He heard a door open and close, then the scrape of bolts being pulled on the storeroom's steel door. He looked around the room, picked up a cable with a padlock attached and held it over his head like a mace. If the guards wanted another go at him, he'd make them pay for the privilege. He moved to the door, muscles taut, and waited for it to open.

'Isabella! What the hell are you doing here?' He dropped his weapon.

'Getting you out.'

'Where are the guards?'

She pointed behind her. Over her shoulder, he saw them sprawled on the ground fast asleep. 'I gave them enough tranquillizers to down a horse. They won't wake in a hurry. The pair by the helicopters are sleeping like babies, too.'

He wanted to hug her, but he didn't. Instead he asked what had happened after he had been captured. When she had finished, he indicated the equipment in the storeroom. 'Come on. Until we know what happens tomorrow, we've got to make sure that no one leaves the island in a hurry.'

It took them almost an hour to harness the runners of both helicopters with steel hawsers, and tie up the sleighs with the spare cabling. 'I doubt if anyone's going to leave till after the wedding, but if things go to hell this should delay them.' He checked his watch. It was almost three o'clock. He felt suddenly exhausted. 'There's nothing more we can do now but wait.'

'Let's get some rest.'

'Great idea. But where?'

She smiled and led him back to Valhalla. 'Come with me.'

The crystal palace was deserted and Max was surprised when she led him to a guest room on the second tier. The door was ajar, held open by a shoe. He pushed it and saw Hudsucker lying on the bed, fully dressed, mouth open and snoring. On the table beside him was a glass.

Max smiled. 'More tranquillizers? Have you doctors no shame?'

'It's harmless. Anyway, he said I could use his room. Positively begged me to have it. I think he's got a bit of a crush on me.' She went into the bathroom, returned with a small bag and proceeded to make up Hudsucker's face so it looked as if he had a black eye and other bruises. Then she reached up to Max with a moist tissue, wiped the dried blood off his battered face, and smeared it on

405

Hudsucker's nose, forehead and cheeks until the senator was unrecognizable. Finally she put Max's mask on him. 'Come on, let's do a switch while everyone's asleep. It might buy us some time in the morning.'

Twenty minutes later, they were back in Hudsucker's room and Hudsucker was asleep in the boiler-house storeroom, wearing a mask. Isabella went to the fridge in the lounge and took out a bottle of Scotch. She poured two glasses. Her hands shook. 'I don't get it,' she said, handing a glass to Max. 'I was okay serving the toast under your father's nose, drugging the guards and dealing with Hudsucker – I was fine through all that – but now I can't even hold my glass.'

'It's because your body knows you can relax.' Max propelled her to the bed. 'You did well. Now come and rest.'

She followed him and sat on the edge, drank her whisky and coughed. 'I still don't like this stuff.'

'I know, but, like everything else, you get used to it.'

'What if it doesn't work tomorrow, Max?'

'It will.'

She was struggling to comprehend the enormity of what lay ahead. 'Tonight could be the last night before . . . before everything changes.'

'It'll work,' he insisted, although she was better qualified to judge than he was. 'It's got to.' He touched her cheek, then kissed her forehead, not daring to kiss her mouth. He didn't deserve to hope that she might still feel something for him.

'Tonight could be our last night,' she said again. And then, before he knew what was happening, her lips were on his, soft and urgent.

Part of Isabella hated Max and wanted to keep him at a distance. A larger part, however, needed his strength, especially tonight when even the incandescent sky seemed to signal that the world teetered on the brink of madness. She couldn't stop wondering why, this time, the drug hadn't worked on either Max or herself.

She pushed the thought from her mind. Now was not a time to think of the past or the future. As she pulled Max to her, she decided that this must be how people felt on the eve of war. As they undressed each other, she remembered their night in Antibes. Then their passion had been driven by the drug, but tonight it was real. She blanked from her mind everything that had happened since Antibes, and all that might happen in the morning. She concentrated only on the here and now: the feel of his skin against hers, the smell of his hair. For a few precious minutes, nothing else existed. And at the last moment, she could no longer keep the truth from herself or him: 'Max. I love you.'

Max felt tears under his eyelids for the first time since he was a child. Afterwards, when he lay beside her in the dark, he whispered, 'You must believe me, Isabella – whatever I've done, I love you too.'

'I know. And that's why the drug didn't work on us this time. According to my father's notes, after his experience with NiL Forty-two he built in a safeguard, which he called the Zero Substitution Effect. It uses the principle of vaccination, where people with cowpox can't get smallpox. With all versions after NiL Forty-two, including Sixty-nine and Seventy-two, if someone's brain shows signs that they are already in love the drug has no effect. He ensured that nature-identical love couldn't substitute for the real thing.'

Max thought of his past and the uncertain future. 'Can you really love me, even after what I've done?'

'Yes.'

'And can you forgive me?'

She didn't answer that, just stared into the dark. He understood her silence, though. He wasn't sure if he could ever forgive himself.

PART 4

VENUS

63

The next morning:
New Year's Day

The alarm woke Helmut with a start. He opened
his eyes, sweating, heart racing. He had been
dreaming of the future, of a world that revolved
around him.

There was a knock at the door.

He checked his watch, threw on a dressing-gown
and opened it. He took the breakfast tray from
the waiter and placed it on the table by his bed.
He had chosen not to eat in the great hall, because
he wanted no guest to see his face until he
made his grand entrance into the ice chapel. He
had even arranged for Phoebe to be there before
him.

He reached for the phone by his bed.

Joachim picked up on the third ring. 'Hello.' The
phone crackled with static.

'Joachim, you sound strange.'

'The Northern Lights interfere with the electricity

and the phone lines. Is everything all right with you?'

'Of course, but I want you to check on Max.'

'As you wish, Vati.'

64

Max and Isabella woke early and stole out of Hudsucker's room to select clothes from their own. When they met up again neither spoke of the night before or the day ahead. Max treasured their night together, and had decided he would settle for that: he didn't deserve her love. And whatever had happened between them paled into insignificance when he compared it with what might happen today.

The wedding was scheduled for mid-morning. Max and Isabella waited till the last guests were finishing breakfast, then put on concealing hats and furs and joined the procession to the chapel. Despite all the precautions they had taken, as Max stepped out of Hudsucker's room he found himself facing Feliks Lysenko. The Russian strode down the corridor towards him, wearing a frown that expressed fury and confusion in equal measure. He was alone. There was no sign of Kathryn, who had been by his side since the welcoming party. For a moment their eyes locked, but Lysenko blanked him and walked on.

Max watched him checking the room numbers until he stopped five doors down. He pounded on the door. 'Klaus! The deal is off! I keep my money!' He pounded on the door again and when he realized no one was coming out, he reached into his pocket, took out a piece of paper and a pen. He scribbled a note and slid it under the door.

Max and Isabella exchanged a glance. Keeping their heads down, they descended the stairs and went to the main doors. Half-way across, Isabella bumped into a figure backing out of the great hall.

The man turned, fingered his white beard nervously, and stared at her. He looked confused and anxious until she smiled at him. 'I apologize,' he said.

Max turned away quickly but not before the man had caught his eye. 'It's a strange morning,' the man said, to no one in particular. 'A very strange morning.' Then he walked away.

Max and Isabella almost smiled as they watched him ascend the stairs.

'It might just work,' he heard Isabella say, voice quivering with relief.

'It might,' he agreed, as he watched his uncle Klaus return to his room. Then Joachim appeared on the other side of the lobby. Max took Isabella's arm and walked briskly to the chapel.

*   *   *

Joachim felt disoriented. His only consolation as he watched the guests, in their furs, make their way to the chapel was that they looked equally fragile. As he passed the main doors he spotted his reflection in the glass and rubbed his eyes. He had drunk too much wine after the toast last night. Or perhaps it was the effect of the Northern Lights. The visual pyrotechnics might have disappeared with the rising sun but the air was still electric.

Outside, he walked across fresh snow to the boiler-house. He knocked on the door four times and one of the guards opened it groggily. 'Have you been sleeping?' Joachim demanded.

'No,' the guard said, but he clearly had.

'Where's my brother?' The guard ushered him inside. Joachim barely glanced at the other Stasi unbolting the storeroom: his head had begun to ache. The door opened to reveal a man sprawled on the ground, fast asleep. A mask covered his face. Joachim stepped closer. 'Max?'

Silence.

He leaned down and gingerly pulled up the mask, revealing the lower part of the man's face. He stared hard at the bruised features, covered with blood, and rubbed his eyes again. He had heard that electrical surges caused by the Northern Lights could play tricks on the mind. His head was pounding now. How much had he drunk last night? He looked back at the guard, who shrugged. Joachim replaced the mask and locked the storeroom door behind him.

When he returned to his room, his wife was still at breakfast. He felt feverish and confused. He took two painkillers from his first-aid bag, then checked the safe. Inside there were two locked canisters. He ignored the first, marked Ilium, which contained the four vials of the lethally modified, permanent NiL #072 drug.

He focused on the second canister, which contained a spare sample of Venus. He opened it and held the vial up to the light, then placed it in his aluminium case. It shouldn't be needed – he had watched the guests drinking the toast – but nothing could be left to chance. Today had to succeed or his father would never forgive him. He placed the case by the door, so that he would remember to take it with him to the chapel.

The phone rang.

'Joachim, it's Klaus. They want to call it off. Should we tell Helmut?'

'What are you talking about?'

'Project Ilium. Corbasson and Nadolny have just rung me. And Lysenko left a note. They all say they won't pay for the bridesmaids.'

The phone fizzed with static. What was going on? Joachim wondered.

'They believe we're lying. They've talked among themselves and decided to call our bluff,' Klaus said. 'Do we tell Helmut now?'

'There's no point in worrying him until after the wedding.' Joachim told himself that once Venus was activated everything would fall into place. After the wedding no one would defy his father's will. 'Don't worry about it, Klaus. Once they realize we're not bluffing, Lysenko and the others will fall into line.'

Joachim broke the connection, then dialled his father. 'Max is secure in the boiler-house, Vati.'

'Excellent,' his father rasped. 'I'll deal with him after the service. Call me when everyone's in the chapel.'

Helmut Kappel ate a full breakfast of cereal, cheese and *wurst*. Everything tasted fresher and more intense than usual. After breakfast he showered, took his wedding outfit from the wardrobe and laid it on the bed. Designed by Odin, it was a classic morning suit, except that the whole ensemble was white. A fur cape lay beside it. As he ran his hand over the soft pelt, he imagined Phoebe changing into her Odin creation. Undoubtedly his Snow Queen would look beautiful, but all eyes would be on him.

He wandered over to the window to watch the guests making their way from Valhalla to the ice chapel. Fresh snow had fallen overnight and everywhere was white, except for the red ribbon of carpet on the lake, linking the island to the chapel. Was it his imagination or did the shambling guests seem confused and subdued?

He dressed methodically. First he put on his underwear and socks. Next he strapped the assassin's knife to his ankle. Then he slipped on his trousers and shirt. After he had tied his cravat, he put on the white silk waistcoat, the ermine jacket, and completed the ensemble with a pair of black shoes. Then he combed his hair, lit a cigarette, and smiled at the effect in the mirror. Except for his pale blue eyes, the glowing black cigarette in his pallid lips, and his shoes, he was white from head to toe.

The phone rang.

'Everyone is in the chapel, Vati,' Joachim said. 'Are you ready to come down?'

'I'm ready.'

65

There was no wind as Helmut Kappel walked across the red carpet from Valhalla to the chapel, and it felt surprisingly mild. The pale sky merged with the mountains and the weak sunlight flattened the virgin snow into a featureless white plain. He felt as if he was walking through a void that contained only three solid objects: the crystal palace behind him, the ice chapel ahead and the red carpet beneath his feet. Even his own white form seemed invisible in the surrounding snowscape.

He paused before the gleaming dome, savouring the moment. In a few seconds he would be far from invisible. His face would become the most visible that the world had ever known. Today wasn't just the first day of a new year. It was the first day of a new era in human history. The two Stasi guards by the chapel door stared at him and his white hair and seemed about to speak. Then they thought better of it, opened the door and stood aside.

He entered the chapel, listening to the organ music, and watched every head in the amphitheatre turn towards him. Beyond the congregation, the aisle led to the dais where the bridesmaids and Joachim, his new best man, waited. A veiled Phoebe stood alongside the priest.

With slow, deliberate steps he walked down the aisle. He felt all eyes focus on him, scrutinizing him. He heard the congregation rustling in their seats and whispering to each other. He remembered what Joachim had told him: as each person recognized his face, the Venus drug would trigger their adoration and the influenza-based component of the Tag Vector, which would spread round the globe. Last night's dream would soon be reality.

As Helmut came towards him Joachim frowned briefly, then Helmut greeted him and he smiled. Helmut almost patted his son's shoulder for having made this possible, but restrained himself: his destiny was no more than he deserved. As he climbed the steps to the dais and saw Joachim and the bridesmaids staring at him, he felt as though he was ascending to a higher spiritual plane. This was no longer just a wedding but an assumption of deity.

He stood opposite Phoebe. Odin had fashioned her dress from white silk and ermine. Its simple, classic cut accentuated her tall, slender figure. She looked stunning, and Helmut looked forward to seeing the adoration in her eyes. The priest smiled at him and Helmut smiled back, then looked down on the congregation. He could barely contain his excitement. The sense of power running through him was like electricity.

Helmut signalled to the priest that he should start the ceremony and a hush descended on the chapel.

Isabella felt Max place a restraining hand on her thigh – perhaps he had sensed her restlessness. Wrapped in furs on the far left of the second row, she craned forward in her seat, willing her friend not to go through with the marriage. She wanted to stand up and shout: 'Don't do it, Phoebe. It's your last chance.'

But everything had to run its course, if she and Max were to be certain that their efforts to stop Venus had succeeded – and Phoebe was the acid test: she had received the permanent version of both Ilium and Venus. If Phoebe came to her senses, it would prove that their plan to thwart Helmut Kappel had been successful. If she went through with the marriage his brave new world had dawned.

The priest cleared his throat to start the service, and Isabella feared the worst. But before he could utter a word, Phoebe raised her veil.

Helmut smiled when Phoebe raised her veil prematurely. It had probably obstructed her view of his face. 'Hello, Phoebe,' he whispered.

She stared at him. Then she frowned and shook

her head. 'I'm sorry, Helmut, I don't want to hurt you, but I can't go through with this. I don't love you.'

An audible gasp rose from the congregation.

Helmut didn't understand what she had said. It wasn't possible. 'What do you mean, you don't love me?' he said.

Phoebe spoke in a low, intimate whisper: 'I'm sorry, Helmut, but I don't even know who you are.'

He grabbed her arm and thrust his face inches from hers. 'Of course you know who I am. Look at my face, Phoebe. You love me. You adore me.'

'No, she doesn't, Helmut.'

Helmut turned – and saw Isabella Bacci stand up and walk to the dais, with Max beside her. This couldn't be happening. 'What are you doing here?'

'Izzy, is that you?' Phoebe said. 'Helmut told me you'd left.'

The congregation was now buzzing.

'He told you a lot of things that weren't true, Phoebe. Look at Helmut again. Do you recognize him as the man you love?'

Phoebe shook her head, but Helmut ignored her. 'Of course she does. She adores me.' As Isabella and Max approached the dais, white-hot rage pulsed through him. 'You can't stop Venus,' he hissed, in his low, rasping whisper. 'You're too late. It's already started.' He indicated the restless congregation, who were now openly talking among themselves. 'They already adore me.'

When Max spoke, his voice was as quiet as his

father's. 'They're confused but they don't adore you. Venus has been neutralized.'

'What are you talking about?'

Joachim stepped on to the dais. 'They're bluffing, Vati,' he murmured. 'There's no cure.'

'But why is Max here? You said he was secure in the boiler-house.'

Joachim frowned hard at Max. 'I thought he was.'

'What do you mean, you *thought* he was? Can't you recognize your own brother?'

'No, he can't,' Max said, keeping his voice low. 'Apart from you, Isabella and me, no one here can recognize anyone's face – not even yours, Vater.'

66

As she faced Helmut Kappel, Isabella felt relief rather than triumph. Behind her, the congregation was muttering so loudly that even those straining to listen heard little.

'Joachim wasn't the only one to drug the toast last night,' she said. 'Everyone who toasted you last night not only drank Venus but also a test drug that causes temporary prosopagnosia. It's called Amigo Extract and I gave it to the guards as well.'

'Prosopagnosia? What are you talking about?'

'Even though they don't understand what's happening to them, everyone who drank the toast last night woke up this morning with temporary face-blindness.' As she watched the realization dawn on Helmut Kappel's face, she thought back to her last night in Phoebe's apartment. The thank-you card from little Sofia pinned to the board above her bed had made her wonder if Amigo Extract might undo the NiL drug's effects: the prosopagnosia folder her father had created for her had stressed the links between his face-obsessive love drug and her face-blindness research. Temporary prosopagnosia might break the spell. She had rushed to the hospital and raided her samples cupboard for a canister of the Amigo Extract tablets intended for the prosopagnosia trials. Phoebe had spilt the first dose she had prepared, but last night, while Helmut questioned Max, Isabella had spiked each toast with it, then helped Joachim deliver the glasses to the guests.

It had been a desperate gamble and she hadn't dared hope the tablets would succeed, especially as the Amigo Extract and Venus had been mixed in the same drink. It was only when she and Max had made their way to the chapel unrecognized, even though they had bumped into Klaus, that she had believed it might work. Phoebe's rejection of Helmut had confirmed their success.

'Helmut, your younger son designed his Tag Vector to meet safety regulations, and that was its Achilles heel,' Isabella said. 'If no one recognizes your face in the next forty-eight hours the infectious stage isn't triggered and Venus is neutralized. It will be flushed out of everyone's system and everything will return to normal. And, trust me, the Amigo Extract will keep these people face-blind long enough to neutralize Venus.'

Helmut scowled at her with disbelief, hatred and fury in his pale eyes.

'It's over,' Max said.

Helmut turned to Joachim. 'Tell me they're lying.'

Joachim was looking around in panic, as though searching for something.

'Speak to me, Joachim – could they have done this?'

'Trust me, Vati. It's not over yet. I won't let you down,' Joachim backed away and picked up an aluminium case from beside his seat. 'I'll show you, Vati. All is not lost.' He rushed out of the chapel shouting to the guards, 'Which one of you is Gustav? Who can fly the helicopter?'

Max felt no triumph or satisfaction as he witnessed his father's fury and his half-brother running from the chapel. He had known his father would never roll over and accept defeat. He pulled out his Glock and ran after Joachim. Whatever was in the case, he couldn't let Joachim leave with it.

He brushed past the Stasi guards on the door and chased his half-brother across the ice towards the helicopters. 'Don't do it, Joachim!' he yelled, as one of the guards by the Chinooks pulled the tarpaulin off the first helicopter and Joachim climbed aboard. 'You can't leave.'

The engine started and Joachim stood at the door, pointing a gun at Max. 'You don't tell me what to do, Max. You've ruined everything.'

Max stopped twenty yards from the helicopter and lowered his gun. 'It's not too late to end this madness. We can't let Vater get away with it. He drugged you, for Christ's sake. He doesn't love you, Joachim. He doesn't love me. He doesn't care about anybody except himself.'

Joachim smiled sadly. 'But I love *him*, Max. And I share his vision, whatever it is.' He held up the aluminium case. 'I've got more Venus in here. I'll give it to others. I'll wait till the prosopagnosia passes and drink more myself. I can still make Vati's vision come to pass. He can rely on me. And when it's done I'll sit at his right hand.'

'But you *can't* leave,' Max shouted, as the rotors roared into life, churning up the snow and drowning his words. He ran towards the helicopter but stopped when his foot hit one of the steel hawsers, frozen to the ground beneath the snow. 'The choppers aren't going anywhere,' he bellowed. 'Last night Isabella and I chained the landing runners.'

Oblivious to his cries the helicopter rose into the watery sky. It flew higher and higher and Max briefly thought it would escape. Then he saw the two hawsers unravel. When the first snapped taut the helicopter shuddered and jerked in mid-flight. As the second exerted its pull there was a tearing, grinding sound. For a moment it hung, suspended in the air, perfectly still apart from the whirring rotors. Then it fell in a flailing, helter-skelter spiral. It clipped the chapel's crystal dome, then crashed on to the lake, cracking the thick ice. One of the oil tanks exploded, and the aircraft burst into flames. Fissures appeared on the lake, running past the chapel and beneath it. As Max watched the helicopter grind through the ice and sink beneath the lake's freezing waters he felt a rush of sadness for his brother.

Panicked guests were streaming out of the chapel, down the red ribbon of carpet to the island. Fighting against the human tide, Max ran in the opposite direction, across the shifting ice. By the chapel doorway he saw Klaus and Odin, but no sign of his father or Isabella.

Inside, the chapel floor had been riven in two. An ever-widening crack cut across the ice, separating the front rows and the dais from the rest of the seats and the exit. Max could see water rushing beneath the fissure. In their desperate scramble for the exit, the bridesmaids and others in the wedding party leaped from the dais across the gap and streamed past him. Claire slipped on her high heels and slid back towards the water. Max grasped her hand, pulled her to her feet and shoved her towards the exit with the others.

His father was still standing on the dais like the captain of a doomed ship, with Phoebe and Isabella below him, poised to leap across the divide. Max locked eyes with him, but Helmut glared at him with such hatred and fury that Max almost didn't recognize him. 'Kill him!' his father yelled. 'Kill my son. The big man with the white hair. Shoot him.'

Max turned and saw one of the ex-Stasi fighting through the crowds, trying to reach his master. The

428

guard raised his gun and fired at Max. The bullet missed by inches, and Max didn't hesitate: he shot the man twice in the chest. When he turned back to his father, Helmut had his knife in his hand and was reaching for Phoebe.

67

Seconds earlier

What was happening was so far removed from what Helmut Kappel had imagined that he still couldn't accept it. He looked down on the fleeing masses and felt contempt, disgust, and rage. Venus might have been postponed but it wasn't over. Dreams only ended when they came true.

And who had betrayed him? His own son. The boy he had raised to be the perfect Kappel. Just the sight of Max made the bile rise in his throat. He should have drowned him with his mother. As Max turned to shoot the Stasi, Helmut drew the assassin's knife from his ankle sheath, stepped down to the next tier and grabbed Phoebe's arm.

'It's finished, Vater,' Max shouted, jumping the divide. 'Joachim's dead and he took Venus with him. Face it, you've lost! It's over.'

Helmut ignored him. His destiny might have been postponed — but Phoebe had adored him before Venus. 'Where are you going, Phoebe?'

She tried to shake him off. 'Leave me alone. We've got to get out.'

'You can't leave me. You're mine. You love me.'

'Get off me, Helmut. Please.' He saw fear in her eyes. And disgust.

He slapped her face. 'You adore me.'

A blow on his shoulder made him release her. He swivelled round to see that Isabella was about to hit him again. 'Leave her alone,' Isabella said. 'Come on, Phoebe, let's get out of here.'

'Out of the way, Isabella,' Max shouted, from the bottom of the steps, and levelled his gun at his father.

When he saw the look in Max's eyes, Helmut knew what he had to do. He pushed Phoebe down the steps, and pulled Isabella to him, pressing the knife blade to her throat.

Phoebe clambered to her feet and moved to help her friend, but Max restrained her. 'Phoebe, the ice is breaking up. Get out while you can. I'll handle this.'

'But—'

He pushed her across the widening crack in the ice. 'Go. Now.'

Max didn't look back as he walked, gun in hand, across the dais, towards his father.

'Shoot him, Max,' Isabella shouted. 'He murdered your mother. He murdered my father. Shoot him. Don't worry about me.'

'But that's the whole point,' Helmut whispered in her ear. 'Max does worry about you. Love has

431

made him weak, Isabella. *You* have made him weak. I can control him through you.'

Helmut smiled, as he gazed at the love in his son's eyes. Today hadn't been a complete disaster. He still had the technology and Joachim's files. He would pay a scientist to make up the serum and keep it simple this time. He would simply inject the first people he came into contact with and let Venus spread from there. That had been his mistake: he had been too theatrical. But his dream could still become reality. And when it did, no one would care about what happened today.

First, though, he must punish Max and the interfering bitch who had spoilt his plans. He would make Max pay for his treachery by forcing him to watch his love die. Then he would kill him too.

'Put the gun down, Max, or I'll slit her throat.'

68

'Don't you dare drop your gun!' Isabella screamed at Max. She knew that Helmut Kappel would kill her as soon as Max dropped his weapon, but she saw indecision in Max's eyes. Max really did love her, she saw now, and his love for her outweighed his hatred of his father. That didn't help her, though. 'For Christ's sake, shoot him.'

'Quiet,' Helmut rasped, pressing the flat side of the cold blade so hard against her throat she could barely swallow. 'The steel is millimetres from your jugular. You're a doctor – you must know that if I turn the blade you'll bleed to death in seconds. I've done this before. I know what I'm talking about.'

She stared at Max, willing him to be the killer he had been and not the man he was trying to become. For some seconds, father and son faced each other, saying and doing nothing. Then there was a sharp crack behind her and she felt the ice dais shift beneath her feet. Momentarily un- balanced, Helmut slackened his grip and the blade lifted from her skin. In that instant, she was centimetres rather than millimetres from death. With all her strength, she thrust backwards and pushed Helmut away from her.

He was too quick, though, and as she rolled out of his grip and fell to the ice he swung the knife in a downward arc, slicing her left cheek, the reindeer coat and her shoulder. She registered no pain in her face as the blade cut through the soft flesh but white-hot agony shot down her arm as she fell on to the ice. Instinctively she reached for her shoulder with her right hand and tried to staunch the blood. When her fingers pushed through the incision in the tough reindeer pelt and disappeared into the deep, sticky wound, she knew the tendons had been severed. Her arm hung useless by her side. Blood blurred her left eye as she saw Helmut Kappel move nearer. Time seemed to slow and she noticed that the knife blade in his hand was still gleaming. All she could think of was how sharp the curved steel must be: it had sliced through her face and arm so cleanly and quickly that there was no blood on it. She tried to get up. She had to get away from that blade.

Max squeezed his finger on the trigger but as the ice shifted beneath his feet he steadied himself instinctively before he fired. While his father raised his knife above Isabella's squirming form, preparing to deliver the *coup de grâce*, Max aimed at his chest. There was another sharp, cracking sound and the ice dome began to collapse. As he pulled the trigger a sheer block hit the floor beside him, upending the ice plate he stood on, throwing him to the ground. He fired skywards through the gaping hole in the fractured dome, as more blocks of ice crashed on to the dais, collapsing it beneath Isabella and his father.

Max heard Isabella cry out as he hit the shifting ice. The crunching impact knocked the gun from his hand. It skittered away from him and fell into the widening schism of dark water, eight feet across, that separated him from his father and Isabella. Helmut had also lost his knife, but it lay only a few yards to his right, across another narrow fissure. To Helmut's left, Isabella lay in a pool of blood, perilously close to the rushing water that prevented Max reaching her.

His father glanced at the knife, then at Isabella and Max, and finally at the exit. Helmut's only way out was by walking round the schism but Max could head him off. There was another break in the ice by the exit behind Max, but it was narrow and the ice was continually shifting. Max considered diving into the water or running round the schism but Helmut would reach either the knife or Isabella before he got close enough to do anything.

'I won't let you leave without Isabella,' Max shouted to his father. 'If she dies, you die.'

For the longest moment his father wavered between the knife and Isabella, then he moved towards her. As Max stood helplessly on his half of

435

the divide, watching his father bend over Isabella, he dared to think he might help her. Then Helmut slid Isabella towards the water. 'Get off me!' she screamed. She tried to kick him and roll away, but with her wounds she was defenceless.

Helmut looked at Max. 'I understand the current is particularly treacherous here. It'll pull her under the ice and out to sea.' His father smiled. 'Max, the question you have to answer is this: do you stop me or save her, as you tried to save your mother?' The smile broadened. 'I think I know your answer.' He rolled Isabella into the swirling, freezing water, then headed for the knife and the exit.

69

The shock of the icy water expelled the air from Isabella's lungs. Immediately she felt the pull of the current and tried to swim against it. With two good arms it would have been difficult, but with only one it was impossible. She kicked and clawed her way to the surface, gulping for air as the current dragged her to Max's side of the divide. It didn't take her directly to him: it pulled her diagonally across the schism, away from him.

As he ran to intercept her, she twisted herself towards the approaching ice shelf to where one of the tiers of seating extended over the swirling water. As her wounded shoulder hit it she braced herself for the pain, but in the cold she felt little. With all her remaining strength, she reached up and hooked her good arm over the extended seat, anchoring herself against the whirling current. Then the pain struck again, and she saw the icy water turn pink with her blood. The rational part of her hoped the cold would slow the flow, but the pain was intense. Just hanging on with one arm was excruciating, and the saturated reindeer coat was so heavy.

Max stretched his arm along the seat and tried to reach her. His lips were moving but she couldn't hear anything. She stared at his mouth: 'Hang on, Isabella. I've got you.'

She tried to call to him, but she had no more breath. Even as his hand edged towards her, she felt her arm slipping off the seat. She tried to regain her hold, but her body wouldn't obey her. She felt – or imagined she felt – his fingers brush her arm. Then she slipped off the seat and the water reclaimed her.

This time she couldn't even struggle as it sucked her down and swept her under the ice. She searched for an opening in the frozen ceiling, but all she could see was her own reflection and a shimmering white light beyond. The gash in her cheek was so deep and red. She watched herself smile at the absurdity of worrying about her appearance when she was about to die.

The pain faded. She was slipping away, her lifeblood leaking into the cold relentless water.

Then the pain returned with a hot, searing surge. Strong arms ripped her from the current's numbing embrace. She blinked and felt herself steered towards a bright light, an opening in the ice. Her first instinct was to struggle against the force that was wrenching her back to life and pain, but she was too weak. She felt an additional push and suddenly she broke through the surface of the water and her lungs filled with air. There was a final surge beneath her and she found herself gasping on the hard, cold ice. Fighting for breath she looked up – and tried to scream. She had surfaced in the gap beside the exit and Helmut Kappel stood over her. In his hand he held the curved, razor-sharp blade.

70

As Max had prepared to push Isabella out of the water he had seen the dark shape looming overhead, and known it was his father, but he had had no choice: Isabella had to surface now or drown.

There was only one way to end this.

He summoned all his strength, pushed her out of the water and on to the ice ledge, then took a deep breath and fell back into the water. Before the current could take hold, he pulled with his arms and kicked hard, projecting his body out of the water as far as he could. As he broke the surface he blinked against the light and saw his father looming over Isabella, knife in hand. Time seemed to slow. Max landed heavily on the frozen surface, slid past Isabella and yanked at his father's ankle, upending him like a skittle. Helmut's smile of triumph turned to shock as he fell to the ice, dropping the blade. Still gripping his father's leg, Max slid back into the water, pulling his father with him, taking rapid shallow breaths, expelling the nitrogen from his bloodstream. When the water closed in, he held the struggling Helmut as close as a lover, pinioning his arms to his sides. Then the relentless current dragged father and son beneath the ice.

Isabella watched Max pass directly beneath her, gripping his father. She forced herself to her knees and crawled after him until the water had carried him beneath the wall of the chapel. Then she clambered to her feet and staggered out of the exit. She looked in the direction of the current, to where the lake joined the distant channel to the sea, but all she could see was an unbroken expanse of ice.

The current seemed to be accelerating but she followed Max as far and fast as she could, watching him glide beneath her. Eventually she fell exhausted to the ice and saw him look up over his father's shoulder. He was smiling at her – a serene, peaceful smile. At that moment, when everything trivial had been stripped away, she *knew*, with a certainty she had never experienced before, that she not only loved but forgave him. True love was forgiveness.

But it was too late now. As she watched him slip away from her, she cried out, with all her remaining strength: 'Max! I love you, Max! I love you!'

Phoebe, the bridesmaids and some of the braver guests ran to her across the treacherous ice, but she was oblivious of them. Even as Phoebe wrapped her in a dry coat, Isabella stared out across the vast frozen lake and screamed her love for Max, hoping he would hear her before he died.

Under the ice, Helmut Kappel stared into his son's implacable eyes and realized it was futile to struggle any more. Even if he escaped Max's steel grip there was nowhere to go. As Isabella's muted cries of love reached his ears, an expression of peace came over Max's features and Helmut knew he was looking into the face of a man unafraid of death.

The bitter pill of contempt burst on his tongue. The man he had raised as his heir had become his nemesis. However hard he had tried to deafen Max to love's siren call, his son had still succumbed to it. Even at the point of death, Max believed that love gave his life meaning. The fool probably thought he would live on in Isabella's heart. But she, too, would eventually die and then what? Max still didn't understand that love was just an ingenious trick of nature – a sick delusion to ensure that humans reproduced.

But as his lungs ballooned in his chest and the impulse to breathe became impossible to resist, Helmut felt his certainties slip away. Suddenly he realized that for all his dreams of immortality, he was going to die alone and forgotten, with no one to grieve his passing. He would vanish from the face of the earth as though he had never existed.

As extinction approached, cold and dark, over-whelming panic welled within him. Suddenly he coveted Max's certainty and peace. He gripped his son, staring into his face, desperate to feed off his serenity and courage.

The first reflexive gulp of icy water made Helmut gag and convulse, but Max's hold was firm. As he choked on the water, Helmut saw a spark of compassion in his son's eyes, but that provided him with little consolation. In his heart, he felt only black despair as the water enveloped him in its dark, cold embrace.

Then there was nothing.

71

As his father's body floated away, Max became acutely aware of the water flowing past and under him. He felt lighter, almost buoyant, as if the icy current was washing him clean of his past sins. He had the bizarre sense that he was reborn, and the irony that this should come at the point of death made him smile.

He thought of Isabella's final declaration of love and sadness penetrated his meditative calm. He didn't deserve it, but he wanted her forgiveness, even though there wasn't time now to earn it. All he could do was forgive himself.

He consoled himself with the sudden insight that her feelings for him weren't what mattered. True love was about loving unconditionally, not just *being* loved. It was about giving, not receiving. His love for Isabella had made him strong, and proved that love wasn't something to be feared or controlled with a drug, and giving it endowed life with meaning. His mother had understood that, and now he did too. He was grateful that Isabella had reminded him of it before it was too late.

He wondered how long he had been submerged. He had slowed his heartbeat and wondered if the cold had done the same with his metabolism, further reducing his need for oxygen. Or perhaps it was just hypothermia – or even that he had entered the early stages of oxygen starvation and was experiencing hypoxic euphoria. Either way, he felt calm. The ice appeared to clear for a moment, revealing the bright sky above. When he looked up he thought he saw the distorted silhouette of an eagle following him. Then the image disappeared.

He looked around him and realized the ice was thicker here, the water darker. Ahead there were three channels. He wondered which led to the canyon-like inlets at the side of the lake, dead ends where his body would lie frozen and undiscovered for months, if not years – and which led through the narrow fjord to the sea, where the ice gave way to the river that flowed into the Gulf Stream.

As he pondered this, not really caring which route he took, a white figure rose from the depths beneath him. He recognized his mother and knew that hypoxia had taken hold. She smiled and held her arms wide – so different from the avenging presence she had been when he had last seen her. He was glad she'd come for him, and wanted to reassure her that he understood now what she had tried to tell him all those years ago in the boat off Hawaii: without love we are nothing.

As though she could hear his thoughts, her smile broadened and she placed a finger over her lips. Then she took his hand and led him down the left channel beneath the ice. The light ahead told Max he was approaching death, but he still wouldn't relinquish control of his body and surrender to the impulse to breathe. I did that once before and I'll never do it again, he thought. He felt relaxed, at peace, ready to die. He closed his eyes and let his mother's presence guide him. The numbing cold seemed to grow marginally warmer, and he imagined he was returning to the womb. Then his mind folded in on itself and he felt no more.

72

Odin used Valhalla's single satellite phone to call for help, but because it was New Year's Day there was a delay in the rescue services reaching them. Confused guests wandered around the palace. A dazed, bloodstained Warren Hudsucker was seen hovering around the boiler-house, asking where the chapel had gone. Some just stared out silently to where the helicopter had crashed into the lake. Others sat in huddles, asking each other what had happened. Klaus Kappel and the Kappel Privatbank clients retired to their rooms to pack. They wanted nothing to do with the police and the other authorities when they arrived. Even as they waited to evacuate the palace, the gaps in the ice were closing and refreezing, healing the lake's wounds.

Isabella's wounds would take longer to knit. A doctor stitched her face and temporarily sutured the gash on her shoulder, but she didn't care about the pain in her body. All she could think of was Max's once warm flesh cooling under that sheet of ice. A solitary eagle soared above the lake, heading for the fjord and the sea beyond. She wondered if it was the same eagle she had seen the day she thought Max was going to shoot her. Perhaps it could see Max under the ice, had witnessed his death, as she had once thought it would witness hers. An almost unbearable sadness weighed down on her. She felt as empty, flat and desolate as the lake itself. She only hoped that Max had died knowing she loved him.

Phoebe sat down beside her and held her hand. 'You okay?'

She nodded, feeling anything but.

'What the hell happened, Isabella?' Phoebe whispered. 'Why can't I recognize anyone's face? What do we tell the police or whoever comes to get us?'

Isabella was too tired to explain anything, and she wasn't sure she wanted the police to know about Venus or Ilium, or that she had drugged everyone last night. The fewer people who knew of the drugs' existence the better – it was too easy to abuse them and had caused enough heartache. What was the point in telling people anyway? Helmut was dead, and she would only drag her father's name through the mud. In time she would decide what to do. But not now.

She looked up at her best friend. She was sure that once the temporary prosopagnosia passed, the obsessive cycle would have been broken, leaving Phoebe and the others who had been dosed with the NiL drug free of their fixations. 'Shock does strange things, Phoebe. But, trust me, the face-blindness will pass. I'll explain it later, but for now be glad you had a lucky escape.' It was best if everyone believed they were simply in shock. And it wasn't too far off the mark, considering what had happened: people had been drunk last night; the Northern Lights had upset everyone's brain chemistry; and Phoebe's wedding had ended with a traumatic bang. She tried to smile but she felt like crying.

Phoebe squeezed her good hand. 'Thank you, Izzy. Thank you for rescuing me from Helmut.'

'It was Max. He rescued all of us.' Isabella looked out across the frozen lake and felt a pain more acute than any inflicted by Helmut Kappel's knife. 'He wasn't like his father.'

Phoebe put an arm round her. 'I'm so sorry, Izzy.'

As she listened to the *whup, whup, whup* of approaching helicopters, Isabella felt the tears come. 'So am I,' she said quietly.

EPILOGUE

Four months later

'It's remarkable, Dr Bacci, quite remarkable.' Roberto Zuccatto, head of neurology at Milan University Hospital, adjusted his pince-nez and pointed to the illuminated region of the subject's brain on the PET scan monitor. 'Look at how the whole area of her inferotemporal cortex lights up when she recognizes a face. I've never seen this before with a prosopagnosic.'

Through the glass partition Isabella kept her eyes on Sofia. All traces of the little girl's accident were gone. Her hair had grown back and there was no visible scarring. But that wasn't what made today so remarkable. The child wore a headset and sat in front of a large television screen as a series of human faces flashed before her. Her friends, family and herself were interspersed with strangers. And each time someone connected to her appeared, the area of her brain dedicated to face recognition lit up on the monitor. Sofia, who had been face-blind since her accident, was again recognizing the faces of those she knew and loved.

'I still don't understand how you managed to make so much progress in just a few months,' Zuccatto said.

'My father helped me,' Isabella said. 'He was working on a related area before he died, focusing on stimulating the facial-recognition area of the brain.'

'You should be proud of him.'

'I am.'

She was glad that something good had come of her father's misconceived love drug. It helped her forgive him for his betrayal and understand that although he had done wrong it had been for the right reason: to bring happiness. The prosopagnosia folder he had created for her had revolutionized her treatment of face-blindness, saving her decades of research. The treatment she had developed from his notes was still in the trial phase and the effects were only temporary, but in due course she was sure it would cure Sofia's and other sufferers' prosopagnosia. That was her father's true legacy – the real love drug.

When she returned to her apartment that night she took pleasure in the fact that it was hers. She had enjoyed sharing with Phoebe, but it felt good to have her own place and move on with her life. Her left arm twinged as she poured herself a neat Scotch on the rocks – an acquired taste that reminded her of Max. The severed tendons had healed but it would be some time before the pain and stiffness left her. She saw her reflection in the glass cabinet by the fridge and paused to study the thin silver scar that ran from her cheekbone to her jaw. The sharpness of Helmut Kappel's blade had meant that the scarring was minimal, but she was still conscious of it.

The evening was unseasonably cold and she lit the fire in the lounge. As she sat down, Phoebe's face stared out at her from one of the magazines on the coffee table. Like the others, Phoebe had recovered from her prosopagnosia with no trace of the NiL drug effects. If anything, her career had benefited from the mystery surrounding her aborted wedding and Helmut Kappel's death. Isabella reached for the red corner of the magazine beneath Phoebe's *Vogue* cover. *Time* showed a picture of Helmut Kappel captioned: 'Was this the face of the Swiss Mafia?' She turned to the cover feature. On its second page there was a blurred photograph of Max. As she read the article, she struggled to reconcile Max the killer with the man she had loved.

The article focused on the now famous sea-green folders, which had begun to arrive at Interpol's Paris headquarters shortly after the aborted wedding in Valhalla. Each folder contained incriminating evidence on Kappel Privatbank and its Comvec offshoot, itemizing laundered money, secret accounts and other nefarious activities. One by one, the folders had incriminated each family member – Helmut, Max, Joachim and Klaus – in the most damning terms. To save himself, the last surviving Kappel, Klaus, had made a deal with the prosecutors and handed over all information relating to their clients. According to *Time*, almost eighty per cent of the bank's client base was engaged in criminal activities. Warren Hudsucker was thrown out of the Senate and jailed. Others, including Lysenko, were in hiding. For a time she had worried that Klaus might send someone after her to punish her for wrecking Ilium and the Kappels' plans, but it seemed he had more important things to worry about. Last month he had been sentenced to life imprisonment for a litany of crimes, including murder.

Isabella's lawyers had also received a folder, but there was no mention of this in the press. It contained a letter, advising her that Kappel Privatbank and Comvec had signed over all the rights in her father's work to her. She had closed down the Turin laboratory, sold off all the equipment and – apart from research relevant to her prosopagnosia work – destroyed his samples and records.

The *Time* article made no mention of her father or his drug. There was also no mention of Ilium or Venus. However, it highlighted two outstanding mysteries.

The first concerned what had actually happened at Valhalla. Unsurprisingly, once the guests' prosopagnosia had faded, none had wanted to tell the police much or, indeed, had had much to tell. It wasn't the kind of publicity Odin wanted and the Kappels' clients had their own dark secrets to hide. Phoebe, Claire, Kathryn and Gisele were more than happy to forget the episode and get on with their lives, and Isabella was no different. She had no intention of saying anything that might expose the existence of her father's nature-identical love drug. The latest theory, which the *Time* article explored, was that Joachim and Max Kappel had been engaged in a long-term power struggle over who should succeed Helmut. This rivalry had exploded into violence when their father had changed his mind over who should be his best man and heir.

The second mystery interested Isabella more, because it was also a mystery to her: who had sent the folders? A disgruntled employee or ex-employee? A rival bank? Or even a vengeful client? Numerous candidates had been put forward but the truth was still unknown.

For a time Isabella had toyed with the notion that Max had somehow survived and sent them. She recalled watching him dive in Antibes and fantasized that he had been able to hold his breath under the ice until he reached the warmer outlet to the sea. His body had not been found. But that meant nothing – his father's body was missing too.

She placed the magazine on the coffee table, lay back on the couch and looked into the fire. Gradually her eyelids lowered, and as she dozed the dream returned. It had visited her countless times since she had returned from Valhalla. But this time it seemed even more vivid and complete.

She is an eagle soaring high above a frozen lake, looking down on a man trapped beneath the ice, moving where the current takes him. He is Max Kappel. As she descends to take a closer look, he opens his eyes and she sees his pain, reads his thoughts.

He has held his breath for minutes and is now blacking out. His first involuntary breath fills his mouth with water, choking him, shocking him back to consciousness. It is as though his body won't allow him to be absent from his own death and forces him to fight for survival – whether he wants it or not. He retches and convulses as he swallows more water, then gags and, in a final bid for life, inhales one last time.

Bracing himself, he waits for his chest to fill with water and his lungs to collapse. But it doesn't happen. Instead, he vomits the water he has swallowed. Coughing and spluttering, he breathes in, gasping. He opens his eyes. He is on his back, surrounded by light. Suddenly he feels cold – not the numbing chill of before but a dry, stabbing cold. And pain. His body is consumed with it.

Suddenly, mercifully, everything goes black. Then the pain returns and he is again retching water. He loses track of how long he lies there, passing in and out of consciousness. Eventually he looks up and sees that the light has faded. He raises his head and a rushing sound fills his ears. He extends his arms downwards, through the racing current, and his fingers scrape the river. Then his shoulder jars against something hard. The current accelerates around him

– and he realizes its speed hasn't changed. Instead his body has stopped moving.

He blinks and tries to sit up. His entire frame aches and his skin burns with cold, but no bones seem broken and his tortured muscles obey him. He finds himself sitting in an eddy of water, bounded by rocks, in the shallows of a river. High mountains loom to his left, and on the right bank a broad area of snow-covered open ground leads to a dark forest of dense firs. When he looks downriver, he sees only a flat plain in the far distance. The sea. He turns his head. Behind him there are more mountains, bisected by a narrow fjord where the river cuts through from the lake.

He glances at his watch. He has no idea how long he has been in the river, but he must have taken a breath after he passed under the ice or he would have drowned. He has to have been under water for seven or eight minutes. Certainly for longer than he has held his breath in the past.

Only now, as he stands on shaky legs, does he believe that he has survived. He thinks of her, and experiences a rush of joy. He is alive. Immediately he is shivering uncontrollably. He looks down at his waterlogged, blue-white palms and realizes that although the water did not kill him hypothermia soon will.

A distant whup, whup, whup intrudes on his consciousness, but instead of rushing into the open to hail the helicopters, he finds himself searching for cover. Stumbling over slick rocks on to the snow-covered open ground on the bank, he heads for the forest beyond. But when he tries to run, his legs tremble so violently he can barely move.

Something glints in the weak light. A few hundred yards away, a man with a sleigh and a team of dogs holds binoculars to the sky. He puts them away and cracks his whip, urging the dogs to pull the sleigh into the trees. He wears furs, carries a large rifle over his shoulder and his sleigh is laden with pelts and animal carcases. He must be a poacher or an illegal hunter.

As Max watches him head for cover, the man spies him. He seems to hesitate, weighing him up. But when Max collapses to his knees, the poacher cracks his whip and steers his sleigh towards him. Before Max knows what is happening, the man has bundled him on to the pile of carcases, some still warm, and taken him under the cover of the trees.

Max tries to speak but his jaw locks. The poacher's ageless, wind-burned face creases with concern. He draws a long knife from his thick belt and cuts off Max's saturated, frozen clothes, then wraps him in two large, still-bloody pelts. He takes a bottle from the sleigh and puts it to Max's lips. 'Drikke, drikke,' he orders. As the fiery spirit burns Max's mouth and courses through his body, the man rubs Max's arms and legs, forcing blood to the extremities.

Gradually, painfully, the circulation returns to his limbs, and as the poacher's strong fingers continue to work he maintains an insistent babble of unintelligible words. Lying there, staring up at the man's face, Max feels like an infant. Eventually, the man studies Max's hands and feet, gives a loud exclamation of delight and slaps his shoulder.

Max sits up and the poacher passes him a fur hat and a strip of leather to tie some pelts round himself. Then he moves to the front of the sleigh and cracks his whip, galvanizing the dogs into action. As Max lies back, *watching the dogs pull the sleigh into the darkening forest, an overwhelming sense of peace descends on him. He looks up and sees an eagle flying overhead.*

Suddenly Isabella is the eagle again, but now she is looking down on a city. She is flying over her apartment in Milan and can see herself sleeping by the fire.

A knock on the apartment door wakes her. She rises from the couch and opens the door. 'Can I help you?'

The man is lean. His long hair almost reaches his shoulders, and his skin is tanned dark from the sun. He wears a crumpled hat, sunglasses, faded jeans, a creased linen jacket and a red shirt. He has stubble on his chin and holds a battered leather briefcase. He takes off his sunglasses and removes his hat. 'You don't recognize me?'

He looks so different.

'Sorry I startled you,' *he says.* 'The door to the block was open so I came up. I thought you might not agree to see me if I rang.'

For some seconds she can't speak.

'Can I come in?'

She steps back, dazed. He enters the apartment and closes the door. 'I thought you were dead,' *she says.*

'Max Kappel is dead.' *He reaches into his jacket, pulls out a green US passport and opens it. Beside a picture of his changed face is a name she doesn't recognize. She remembers his telling her how his mother had got him a US passport a long time ago, when she'd tried to take Max away from the Kappels and give him a different life.*

She can't resist the impulse to reach out and touch him, to check he is real. Then, before she can step back, he touches her cheek. Instinctively she tries to turn away, but he holds

459

her and strokes her scar. 'It's so slight,' he says. 'It doesn't match the courage you showed getting it.'

'It's ugly,' she says.

'It's beautiful to me. It wasn't your face I fell in love with, anyway. It was your eyes, and the way you looked out at the world. I love you, Isabella. You've taught me that life lived without love isn't life at all.'

She stares at him, not sure what to think, feel or say. 'What have you been doing over the last few months? Where have you been?'

'Teaching diving around Europe, the States, Australia.'

She clenches her fists, anger rising. 'Why didn't you contact me?'

'I was busy.'

'What was so important that you couldn't contact me?'

He reaches into his briefcase and extracts a sea-green folder. 'MAX KAPPEL' is typed across the front. 'I had to put things right.'

She bends down to the coffee table and picks up her drink. Then she pours Scotch into another glass and hands it to Max. He sits down, looks at the tumbler and smiles. 'I thought you didn't like this stuff.'

She sits down beside him. 'I didn't. I changed.'

'I've changed too.' He takes a slug, then puts down the glass and picks up the folder. 'I've no intention of disrupting your life but I had to see you one last time. I'm going to hand myself in.'

'Why?'

He flicks through the folder. 'This is a copy of the dossier I sent to Interpol listing all my crimes. It's pretty thick, but I guess you know most of the contents by now. The point is,

I've done all I can to put things right. Kappel Privatbank is finished, Klaus is in prison and your father's work has been returned to you without anyone, including the authorities, learning of it. I'm now ready to hand myself in to the police, but before I do that I want to ask you something.'

'What?'

'I came to ask your forgiveness. Frankly, I don't care what the courts think about what I've done. But I do care about you.'

She takes a slug of whisky. When she speaks, her voice is thick with anger. 'Forgive you? How the hell can I?'

He looks sad. 'I understand.' He stands to leave.

She blocks the doorway. 'No, you don't understand. How can I forgive a dead man? The man who needed my forgiveness was Max Kappel. And I forgave him in Valhalla as he slid beneath the icy lake because I loved him. Max Kappel paid for his crimes and he's dead. Everyone says so. The police, the media, even you. So I can't forgive you, because forgiveness is about the past and that doesn't interest me any more. Right now, I care only about the future.'

'I've got to give myself up, Izzy. I've got to pay for what Max Kappel did.'

'But why should I pay for what he did? Like you said, life lived without love isn't life at all. Well, I want life and I want it with you. If I can forgive Max Kappel and put him behind me, so can you.'

She puts down her drink. 'Give me the folder.'

He passes it to her, and she throws it on to the fire. 'Max Kappel is dead,' she says. 'He's paid for his crimes. No more talk about giving yourself up.'

* * *

The noise penetrated her dreams and Isabella's sleeping smile turned to a frown. She was so lost in her reverie that she didn't register the first three knocks on her apartment door. The next ones were louder. She opened her eyes. As always when she woke from the dream she felt sad – particularly this time as the dream had gone on for longer than it had previously. It usually ended in Norway, with Max safe but far away.

More knocking.

Suddenly the sound inspired a sudden, irrational hope. She knew it wasn't possible, but she rose from the couch and, as she walked to the hall, her heart beat faster.

'Coming,' she said, suddenly breathless. She almost closed her eyes as she opened the door. But it wasn't the person she was hoping or dreaming it might be. It was the woman in the next apartment who was always coming round to borrow stuff. Usually stuff she didn't bring back. 'Signora Pitti – how can I help you?'

Signora Pitti wore a bright green coat. 'I'm going to the late-night store. Can I get you anything?'

Suddenly Isabella felt foolish, not only for thinking it might have been someone else but also for prejudging her neighbour. 'No, I'm fine. But thank you.' Isabella closed the door and went back to her drink. She picked up the copy of *Time* and threw it on to the fire. As she watched Max's face burn she told herself that it was good to dream, but it was better to move on with her life. She turned away from the fire, walked to the window and closed the blinds.

Pacing the pavement in the dusk, the man looked up at the apartment. As he watched her close the blinds he realized he had to act. He was lean, his hair was cut short and he had a beard. His skin was tanned dark from the sun. He wore shades and a Burberry overcoat, and held a brown leather attaché case.

He squared his shoulders as he listened to the traffic flowing through the city. It had been easy to get her address – he'd followed her from the hospital, but now that he stood outside her apartment he felt suddenly uncertain. He had been over this moment so many times, but he still couldn't decide what to say to her. And he couldn't even begin to guess at how she might react to his sudden appearance.

Then he remembered another life, a time when he had stood outside another apartment, willing himself to act, only to be thwarted at the last minute. This time he couldn't let anything stop him. He had done all he could to redeem his past life, and now he had to face her and ask her forgiveness.

The main door to the apartment block opened.

A woman stepped out. She was wearing a bright green coat. The man who had once been Max Kappel saw the colour as a signal. He took a deep breath, ran across the road, and reached the door just before it closed.

THE END